THE CHESTER MYSTERY CYCLE

THE CHESTER MYSTERY CYCLE

A New Edition with Modernised Spelling

by

DAVID MILLS

EAST LANSING

COLLEAGUES PRESS

Medieval Texts and Studies: No. 9

ISBN 0-937191-29-9
ISBN 0-937191-27-2 paper
Library of Congress Catalog Card Number 91–77547
British Library Cataloguing-in-Publication Data available
Copyright © 1992 David Mills

Published by Colleagues Press Inc.
Post Office Box 4007
East Lansing, Michigan 48826

Distribution outside North America
Boydell and Brewer Ltd.
Post Office Box 9
Woodbridge, Suffolk IP12 3DF
United Kingdom

CONTENTS

In memory of R. M. Lumiansky, who edited these plays with me and who suggested this edition.

PREFACE

IN 1965 R.M. LUMIANSKY and I began our collaboration on an edition of the Chester Mystery Cycle to replace the then standard edition, begun by Hermann Deimling and, after his death, completed by an otherwise unknown "Dr. Matthews," which had been published in two volumes by the Early English Text Society in 1892 and 1913.

Our original plan was to produce an edition in three volumes—the text with full variants; notes and glossaries; and essays on textual and production matters. Our first volume, *Text*, was published by the Early English Text Society in 1974. The second volume, *Commentary*, followed in 1986. But the Society was unable for economic reasons to produce the third volume, and we therefore published our essays as an independent volume with the University of North Carolina Press in 1983. These three books constitute a full edition with scholarly apparatus.

From the outset, however, we recognised that our edition was too elaborate for the general, non-specialist reader and determined that when it was complete we would prepare a modern-spelling edition on different principles which would make the cycle more readily accessible to teachers and students. The present edition attempts to fulfill that purpose. It builds directly upon the scholarly edition, and readers seeking fuller information about textual matters should consult that work. Sadly, Bob Lumiansky died before this edition was complete, but his researches have contributed immeasurably to it, and it was an enterprise which had his wholehearted support.

I gratefully acknowledge the release of copyright on our edited text of the cycle by the Early English Text Society and on our edition of the Post-Reformation Banns by the University of North Carolina Press.

David Mills
University of Liverpool

ABBREVIATED REFERENCES

Clopper 1974 | "The Rogers' Description of the Chester Plays," *LSE* 7 (1974): 63–94

EETS | Early English Text Society

e.s. | extra series

Hart and Knapp | Steven E. Hart and Margaret M. Knapp, *"The Aunchant and Famous Cittie": David Rogers and the Chester Mystery Plays* (New York, 1988)

Kolve | V. A. Kolve, *The Play Called Corpus Christi* (Stanford, 1966)

Lumiansky-Mills 1974 | R. M. Lumiansky and David Mills (eds.), *The Chester Mystery Cycle: Vol. 1, Text* (London, EETS supp. ser. 3, 1974)

Lumiansky-Mills 1983 | R. M. Lumiansky and David Mills, *The Chester Mystery Cycle; Essays and Documents. With an essay, "Music in the Cycle," by Richard Rastall* (Chapel Hill, 1983)

MED | *Middle English Dictionary*

Mills 1983 | David Mills (ed.), *Staging the Chester Cycle* (Leeds Texts and Monographs n.s. 9, Leeds, 1983)

n.s. | new series

OED | *Oxford English Dictionary*

o.s. | original series

REED | L. M. Clopper (ed.), *Records of Early English Drama: Chester* (Toronto, 1979)

Salter 1955 | F. M. Salter, *Medieval Drama in Chester* (Toronto, 1955)

SD | stage direction(s)

SH | speech-heading

s.s.   supplementary series
Stevens   Martin Stevens, *Four Middle English Mystery Cycles: Textual, Contextual, and Critical Interpretations* (Princeton, 1987)

INTRODUCTION

1. What is a "Mystery Cycle"?

The term "mystery cycle" or "mystery play" suggests to many a particular image of medieval entertainment—a series of somewhat simplistic biblical plays performed by ordinary working-people on carts in the streets of a town on a feast or fair-day. But this image, like the term itself, is a construct of recent centuries. The *Oxford English Dictionary* (OED) first records *mystery* as a name for a kind of play in 1744 and sees it as an extension of its theological reference to the "mysteries" or hidden truths of religion (from Latin *mysterium*). Although the term was extended to drama because of the subject and function of this kind of play, it was invested with a different etymology by nineteenth-century scholars who wished to discover in the culture of the Middle Ages evidence of a "popular" or "folk" movement and who therefore connected *mystery* with a different word of the same form meaning "service, occupation." This etymology directed attention towards the manufacturing and trading companies of the towns, the guilds, whose members were charged with the responsibility of producing the plays and which were often erroneously compared by later scholars to modern trades unions. Although this etymology is firmly denounced as "erroneous" by the OED, it has proved persistent and continues to colour our preconceptions about the plays and the appropriate means of producing them.

The Middle Ages most frequently referred to this kind of drama as a "Corpus Christi Play," after the occasion on which the plays were usually performed—the Feast of Corpus Christi, on the Thursday after Trinity Sunday—which, since it relates to the movable feast of Easter, fell within a range of dates from 23 May to 24 June (Kolve, 33–56). "Corpus Christi" means "body of Christ" and the Feast was instituted to honour the Blessed Sacrament in the form of the consecrated bread or Host which, since the Lateran Council of 1215, had been officially decreed to be essentially changed into the body and blood of Christ when consecrated by an ordained priest. In response to requests, Pope Urban IV created the Feast in 1264, but in that year he died, and the Feast was not instituted until the Council of Vienne under Pope Clement V in 1311. A feature of its celebration was a procession bearing the Host through the streets of the town, escorted by the clergy and by the hierarchy of incorporated guilds in the town in their due order. It was to this occasion, by a process still not fully understood, that the religious plays that we call "mysteries" became attached.

Corpus Christi Day was an act of mutual affirmation. The Church affirmed the God on whom all existence and all hope of salvation depended, leading Him like a king on a royal entrance. In so doing, it also affirmed the authority of the Church rooted in the priestly power to effect transubstantiation. The Town affirmed its acceptance of this belief and its support for the Church, while at the same time displaying the ordered hierarchy and splendour of the civic authority. In so doing, the Town was extending into a major religious feast the genre of civic pageantry which was a feature of medieval urban life. This mutuality was continued in the Corpus Christi Play, where the text provided a context for the religious celebration by playing God's major interventions into human history from Creation to Doomsday, while the production was a civic responsibility to which each guild was required to contribute and which continued the display of order and wealth. This mutuality is affirmed in Chester in the preamble to a Proclamation for the plays written in 1531–32 by the Town Clerk, William Newhall (REED, 27–28):

> not only for the Augmentacion *and* incres <of the holy *and* Catholick> faith o<f our S>auiour Jesu Crist *and* to exort the myndes of the common people <to good deuotion *and* holsome> doctryne th<ero>f but also for the commenwelth and prosperitie of this Citie.

The earliest reference to a play on Corpus Christi Day in England comes from York in 1376, although York's play must have been established before then. Such plays continue in English towns even after the abolition of the Feast in 1548 and evidently retained their popularity. But their association with the Roman Catholic Church, and specifically with its doctrine of transubstantiation, made the genre unacceptable to many sixteenth-century Protestants and, in an age when matters of religious doctrine had major political implications, the plays came under the censorship of the state and were gradually suppressed. By then also new kinds of play and new styles of acting and production had evidently reduced a once living art-form to the level of a civic custom. The tradition of such plays lived on only through their influence on the new drama, particularly on the history-play.

Because of the opposition to the plays, and the low regard in which they came to be held, very few texts have been preserved. No one has described a production of a play as a contemporary eye-witness or provided clear illustrations of a performance. Apart from what we can infer from the few textual remains and later antiquarian statements, our main evidence for production lies in cryptic allusions in civic and guild records whose main concern is with settling legal disputes or recording income and expenditure. Such records, moreover, are randomly preserved and often haphazard.

2. CHESTER'S "MYSTERY CYCLE": A BRIEF HISTORY

Chester's guild and civic records are particularly sparse before the sixteenth century and our picture of the city's play is correspondingly patchy. The first reference to it is in 1422, where, as with the York reference of 1376, we find a play already well established; the document records a dispute about responsibility of guilds for particular plays (REED, 6–7). We have no way of knowing when productions might have begun. The play is, however, referred to as "the Play of Corpus Christi" and was clearly part of the annual religious celebrations of that occasion. References such as that in an agreement (in Latin) of 1429–30 between the Weavers, Walkers, Chaloners and Shearmen to obligations to pay for the

> light of our Lady St. Mary and of Corpus Christi, and for the
> Play of Corpus Christi, both for the one and for the other, and
> for each and every time that it will happen that the said light
> is carried or the said Play is performed

make the association clear (REED, 6–7, translated in Lumiansky-Mills 1983, 205–6). We know that the procession went from the church of St. Mary on the Hill, past the town hall, to the church of St. John outside the city walls, and it seems likely that the play was not performed in the streets of the town but at St. John's when the procession ended. In other words, it was perhaps a fixed-set production rather than a processional production such as occurred at York. It is possible that this early play was on a smaller scale than the version that has survived.

Sporadically throughout the fifteenth century we have "sightings" of the Corpus Christi Play in Chester, the last definite one being in a charter of 1472 (REED, 13–15). Our next "sighting" is fifty years later, in an agreement between the Founders-Pewterers and Smiths in which all parties "byn fully condecendent *and* agreid to berre *and* drawe to whitson playe *and* Corpus *christi* light." The play has now moved to Whitsun, the festival on the seventh Sunday after Easter which commemorates the coming of the Holy Spirit at Pentecost. A verse-announcement of the Whitsun Play, written some time before 1539, indicates that, with the transfer of the guild play to Whitsun, the responsibility for putting on a

play at St. John's on Corpus Christi Day "in honor of the fest" now fell
to the clergy. The verses, or "Banns," make clear the spectacular nature
of the Corpus Christi procession (edited text in Lumiansky-Mills 1983,
278–84):

> Many torches there may you see,
> marchaunty and craftys of this citie   *merchants*
> by order passing in their degree—   *due rank*
> a goodly sight that day.
>
> (164–67)

We have no evidence to explain why the guild-play was separated
from the Feast. It may have something to do with the great extension of
the city's privileges by the royal charter granted to it in 1506. It may
reflect an organisational problem, such as certainly occurred at York, in
accommodating both play and procession in a single day. It may even
suggest a desire to give the play more prominence and expand its scope.
Some support is given to this last possibility by a development, attested
in a revision of the pre-1539 Banns—the expansion of the play from a
one-day to a three-day production, on the Monday, Tuesday and Wed-
nesday of Whitsun week. Henceforth, Chester's cycle is called "the
Whitsun Plays," a phrase first found in the proclamation for the plays by
the Town Clerk, William Newhall, in 1531–32 (REED 27–28), though it is
not clear if the phrase there implies a three-day production.

These Whitsun plays were certainly produced processionally,
placing each play on a movable stage and taking it round to various
playing-places or "stations" in the city. A Chester antiquarian, Archdeacon Robert Rogers, who died in 1595, left notes about the performance-route which were edited in a memorial volume on several occasions,
beginning in 1609, by his son David, on each occasion with some variations (Hart and Knapp). The general picture is, however, clear enough.
The plays began outside the gate of St. Werburgh's Abbey, later the
cathedral, the ecclesiastical centre of the city, in Chester's Northgate
Street. Each play in turn moved on to the High Cross in front of St.
Peter's Church, at the junction of Chester's four Roman streets, where the
mayor and aldermen watched the play from the "Pentice" or Town Hall,
an arcaded annex to the church. Each play then moved on down Chester's Watergate Street to an unspecified playing place, and then cut
through the side lanes to join the Bridge Street where the final station
was located. The last two stations were perhaps felt to be for the populace, for discontent was reported at the last performance in 1575 because
it was in only one part of the city (REED, 110). The performance-route
was thus different from that of the Corpus Christi procession and had a
different symbolic resonance.

Organisation for such an event was complex. Processional production involves large numbers of people because a different actor is re-

quired for the same character in each separate play in which he or she appears. So Chester requires eleven different actors for Christ in the plays 12–24 in processional production whereas only one would be needed in fixed-set production. This in turn increases expenses on costumes. Sets are duplicated, twenty-four or twenty-five different stages must be built, and men paid to push them through the streets. Hundreds of people were involved in some way in the production. Though economically inefficient, processional production had the advantage of involving the whole community. It also created a unique consciousness of the disparity between actor and role; clearly, if eleven men acted the part of Christ, no one person could be identified with the historical Christ who remained, as it were, a reality beyond the reach of any play.

A further problem for the authorities was the control of the complex operation of staging the cycle. Chester's play was not—at least in the troubled times of the sixteenth century—an automatic annual event (Lumiansky-Mills 1983, 184 and 188). The civic authorities had to authorise a production, to approve the text (which was subject to constant revision) and to agree the allocation of its plays to the individual guilds (the subject of the dispute in 1422 which gives us our first record). Then the Banns would be read in the city on St. George's Day by a herald accompanied by representatives of the guilds costumed as characters from the plays. In advance of the production, what Rogers calls "scaffolds and stayes" were put up in the streets, presumably to restrain the considerable crowds who are said to have attended, although some scholars have suggested that they were supplementary stages. And, when the performance was in progress, the movement of waggons between the stations was co-ordinated by a system of messengers running between the locations giving news of the progress of each play—necessary since plays over- or under-running could cause considerable problems at other stations along the route.

Chester's problems were not as acute as those of York, however, because of the three-day production. Whereas York had to move about forty-eight plays around twelve stations in a single day, Chester had to move only nine plays (numbers 1–9) around its four stations on the first day, eight (10–17) on the second, and seven (18–24) on the third. Moreover, the fact that plays were spread across three days meant that the same waggon could be used for more than one play if a group of guilds agreed to share the waggon and its expenses. The first such agreement, of 1531–32, is between the Vintners, who produced *The Three Kings* (day one, play 8); the Dyers, who produced *Antichrist* (day three, play 23); and the Goldsmiths and Masons, who produced *The Massacre of the Innocents* (day two, play 10) (REED, 26–27). The three plays require "king-figures"—Herod or Antichrist—and it is probable that major features of the same set would serve for all three.

Chester's Whitsun play continued into the reign of Elizabeth. In

1572, in the mayoralty of the Protestant John Hanky, the authorities approved a production which went ahead despite the known opposition of the national authorities and of factions within the city. Various records tell us that the plays were "againste ye willes of ye Bishops of Canterbury Yorke *and* Chester" (REED, 96); that "manye of the Cittie were sore against the settinge forthe therof" (REED, 97); and that "an Inhibition was sent from the Archbishop to stay them but it Came too late" (REED, 97). These events should have given the authorities reason to proceed cautiously. Nevertheless, in 1575, under the mayoralty of an eminently respectable Protestant dignitary, Sir John Savage, the aldermen again approved a production, by 33 votes to 12. This time, however, they made two provisos: first, Sir John was to take expert advice on how the plays might most appropriately be emended—presumably to meet the doctrinal and legal requirements of the time; and second, that they should be performed not at Whitsun but over four days at midsummer (REED, 103–4).

Chester already had a celebration at midsummer. Reputedly begun in 1497–98, the midsummer show was a sort of carnival associated with the midsummer fair (REED, lii-liii). Rogers states that, when the plays were performed, the show did not take place (REED, 252). Certainly, its date could coincide with Corpus Christi, and we also know that both "popular" figures from the cycle, such as the shepherds on stilts, or the devil in his feathers, or the ale-wife of play 17, and also religious figures, such as Isaac from play 4 (REED, 469), went in the show. There was, evidently, a connection between the plays and the civic secular carnival. The change of date in 1575 may therefore represent an attempt to stress the secular and traditional aspect of the cycle as opposed to its religious function.

But the production led to swift action by the national authorities, for Sir John Savage at the end of his mayoralty was summoned before the Privy Council to explain his action in promoting the production and had to write back to Chester to obtain a letter affirming that he was only carrying out the collective will of the aldermen and council. A similar statement was required also for John Hanky (REED, 111–17). This clear warning seems to have been enough. There were no more cycle-productions at Chester until 1951, though in 1577 the *Shepherds' Play* was performed at the High Cross for the entertainment of Lord Derby and his son, both men with a keen interest in the theatre (REED, 124–25).

3. THE TEXT OF THE CYCLE

Today the text of Chester's cycle is attested by eight manuscripts—three containing individual plays in complete or fragmentary form, and five containing versions of the complete cycle (Lumiansky-Mills 1974, ix-xxvii). None is an acting text. In fact, the five cyclic manuscripts date from 1591–1607, long after the last performance in 1575. All the cyclic manuscripts are, however, copies of the same base text—perhaps the "Regynall" ("original" in the sense of "official text") mentioned in the records, which was kept at the Pentice and from which the individual guilds took copies for their particular plays (Lumiansky-Mills 1983, 186; *contra*, Stevens, 263–65). That base text had itself been subject to repeated revisions over the years and incorporated alternatives and alterations which caused the scribes of our extant manuscripts considerable difficulties at times. "The Chester Mystery Cycle" is not therefore a definitive label but a generic term embracing a whole series of different authorised versions (Lumiansky-Mills 1983, chap. 1).

The Regynall was obviously preserved long after there was any prospect of further productions and was sufficiently regarded by Cestrians to warrant repeated copying. This interest is in contrast to the situation in other English towns, where the text has been lost or survives only by happy accident. The reason that Chester's cycle is better attested than any other seems to lie in the strong traditions about its authorship and origins which were disseminated in the sixteenth century.

Interest in the origins of the plays in Chester seems to develop with the introduction of the three-day Whitsun performance. William Newhall offers one version in his Proclamation: the play, he says "was devised *and* m<ade by one Sir> henry ffraun*ses*, 'somtyme' moonck" of St. Werburgh's (REED, 28), and was

> d<euised> to the hono*ur* of god by Iohn arneway, then mair
> of this Citie of chester, *and* his brethren *and* holl co*minal*<ty>
> therof to be bro<ught> forthe declared *and* plaid at the Cost*es*
> *and* chargez of the craft*es* men *and* occupacons of <the> said
> Citi<e>. (REED 28)

Newhall seems to say that the text originated with a monk called Henry Frances, of whom nothing more is known than a name on three lists of monks of 1377, 1379 and 1382; and that the production by the guilds was instigated by John Arneway, who was up to 1594 erroneously believed to have been Chester's first mayor. His mayoralties were in consecutive terms, from 1268 to 1276, a century before Frances.

After the Reformation, while the part played by Arneway continues to be acknowledged, a new candidate is advanced as author and features strongly in a later version of the Banns which was kept with the "Regynall." This candidate was a famous scholar-monk of St. Werburgh's called Ranulf Higden who entered the monastery in 1299 and died in 1364. His dates, also, do not correspond to those of Arneway. Higden's most famous work was a universal history, written in Latin, called *Polychronicon*, which was translated into English later in the fourteenth century and was among the books printed by William Caxton in the later fifteenth century. The Post-Reformation Banns present Higden as a proto-Protestant who defied the Church of his day by inventing cycle-drama in order to bring the Bible to the people in their native tongue. Since not all Chester's material has scriptural warrant, the Banns seek to excuse those sections—such as the midwives at the *Nativity*—as comic relief; or to justify them—as with the *Harrowing of Hell*—as depending upon accepted theology.

Such interest in a cycle's origins is unique to Chester and, although the candidates proposed are implausible (Salter 1955, 32–42; Lumiansky-Mills 1983, 166–68), the ascription to Higden seems to represent a defensive move on the part of the civic authorities. Higden was famous. His work was known and respected. To argue that the cycle was an offshoot of the same scholarly interest, and hence Higden's only vernacular work, was to give it a status well above that of the normal urban religious play. To present Chester's play as inspired by a Protestant evangelising zeal rather than a Catholic sacramental concern was an ingenious attempt to separate the cycle from the proscribed genre of Corpus Christi play and allow it to continue. In this process, the alleged author is reconstructed as a Protestant in defence of the text. And it seems likely that this oft-repeated ascription assisted the preservation and copying of "Higden's" text.

The later copyists were men of scholarly inclination and ecclesiastical affiliation. Edward Gregory, copyist of 1591, calls himself a scholar of Bunbury, a village near Cheshire; probably identifiable as the son of a yeoman from Beeston, a village in the parish, he was from time to time warden at the Bunbury church, a Puritan centre. George Bellin, copyist in 1592 and 1600 (he also copied *The Trial and Flagellation of Christ* in 1599, which is still owned by the Coopers' guild, one of the companies responsible for the play's production), was scribe to a number of Chester guilds, clerk to Holy Trinity church in Chester, and an antiquarian. William Bedford, scrawling a copy in 1604, was clerk to St. Peter's church, Chester, and clerk to the Brewers' Company. And in 1607 James Miller, rector of St. Michael's church in Chester and precentor at the cathedral, oversaw a further copy with the help of two other scribes, intelligently editing and reconstructing the battered text. Miller had a library of books, including English histories and chronicles, and was evidently a devout and learned man. To these, and to other antiquarians (such as Rogers), the cycle-text had scholarly worth as a record from the past.

The attitude to the plays in the Later Banns indicates that they were already considered more of a tradition than a meaningful art form. Attention is drawn to the curious waggon-staging, the archaic language which may not carry meaning for contemporary audiences, and the dramatic crudity of allowing God to be impersonated on stage by an actor with a gilded face. The plays are compared disadvantageously to the sophistication of the modern theatre, its actors and audiences. We are asked to make allowances for the time in which the plays were written and the circumstances of their performance:

> By craftsmen and mean men these pageants are played,
> and to commons and country men accustomably before.
>
> (204–5)

Yet these disclaimers should not be taken too seriously. The Later Banns are an attempt to defend the plays publicly against criticisms of them as theologically unsound and dramatically blasphemous. To present them as something once revolutionary which has now lost its purpose is a clever way of urging their continuation as a worthwhile but harmless local custom.

The idea that Chester's cycle was the work of a single author seems strikingly at odds with what we know of the creation of cycle-texts. As working documents, subject to constant revision, we know that they changed according to circumstances—the demands of playing-time and organisation, changes in the economic fortunes of the performing guilds, shifts in theology, and perhaps the dramatic effectiveness of the plays. Chester's cycle was certainly subject to such revisions. A fragment of the episode of Peter's Denial was used as divider in the base text between the two parts of play 16 and was mechanically transcribed in its incomplete state and misplaced position by three of our scribes. The scribes were also confused about the distinction between the episodes of Christ's *Trial and Flagellation* and his *Crucifixion* which make up play 16, since at some time they were obviously treated as two separate plays while at another time they were combined as a single continuous play; four manuscripts opt for the former arrangement, one for the latter, and the "part" division in this edition is an attempt to signal that confusion. The meeting of the resurrected Christ with Mary Magdalen and with the other Maries at the end of *The Resurrection* (play 18, 433+SD-End) seems to have been cancelled at some time; three manuscripts omit it and two retain it (Lumiansky-Mills 1974, Appendix 1D). Play 5, *Balaam and Balak*, appears in two quite distinct versions in our manuscripts—one ending with the account of the punishment inflicted by Moses and his supporters on God's enemies (the version given here) and the other (found only in the 1607 manuscript) including a sequence of prophets who look towards the New Testament plays to come (Lumiansky-Mills 1974, Appendix 1B). Perhaps significantly, the majority version indicates that it was to conclude the first day's performance, whereas no such reference occurs in the 1607 version, and we may perhaps assume that it was followed immediately by the play of *The Nativity* (play 5, 404–15). And in the Smiths' accounts for 1575 we find the entry: "Spent at Tyes (an innkeeper) to heare 2 plays before the Aldermen to take the best xviiid" (REED, 105), suggesting that choices were available. The manuscripts indicate revisions at all levels, from individual words, through speeches and episodes, to entire plays.

Yet Chester's text conceals this underlying diversity beneath a structural and formal uniformity that contrasts markedly with the diversity found within texts of other cycles such as York or Towneley. An obvious indicator of this uniformity is the "Chester stanza," which is found in all the plays except the first and which is the dominant form in all the plays except play 7 (*The Shepherds*) and play 11 (*The Purification: Christ Before the Doctors*) (Lumiansky-Mills 1983, 311–18). The stanza consists of eight lines rhyming aaabcccb or aaabaaab; the b-lines contain three stresses, the a- and c-lines four stresses. Variations on this stanza include aaaaaaaa rhyme-schemes, quatrain forms, and "short-line" forms (such as are used by the Torturers in play 16) with fewer stresses. Well over 80 percent of the cycle is written in this stanza, giving it an insistent rhythm and movement and contributing considerably to the impression of consistent tonality. Though the rhymes are often sustained by formulae and tags such as *in good manner* ("fittingly") and *in fere* ("together")— recurring phrases to which the Late Banns draw attention as strikingly archaic—the stanza in performance gives the actor ample opportunity to resist its end-stopped potential and its air of finality in the b-lines. Nevertheless, it is not a form adaptable to naturalistic dialogue, and its use typifies the more formal concerns of the Chester text.

These concerns can be seen in the structure of the cycle. Like all mystery cycles, Chester's cycle deals with God's interventions in human history, focusing on the Incarnation and Passion of Christ. Its action is, however, "framed" by the speech of God which opens the first play and by the speeches of the four evangelists which end the last play. Both are speeches "outside time" addressed directly to the audience. In the first lines of the cycle, God explains, in somewhat abstruse language, the relationship between the source of Being (*essentia*) and the material forms that it takes through the creative power of God in the Trinity. God alone has this power and stands outside time, and all that occurs within time moves to the rhythm of God's will:

> It is my will it should be so,
> it is, it was, it shall be thus.
>
> (3–4)

Hence, what we see is the progressive revelation of God's power and purpose throughout history until time ends. Then, at the end of the cycle, the evangelists come forward to confirm the truth of what has been witnessed, assuring the audience that what began as the hidden will of God has now been revealed and can be read in their writings. In so doing, they invite a retrospect of the whole cycle from the standpoint of the fully informed present. There can be no excuse of ignorance for neglecting one's Christian duties.

The action of the cycle is thus, from one point of view, a progressive revelation of God's purpose at significant moments in history. Even before the creation of Man, Lucifer knows what God intends. Even before the Fall Adam knows what God has planned to follow it. Alongside the continuing consequences of sin in Cain's fratricide and the evils that bring about the Flood, there develops an upward movement of optimism as through Noah God preserves his creatures, and Abraham, by his faithful obedience, gains the covenant with God which results in the chosen race of the Jews and the special authority given to Moses. Even there, however, a wider purpose is envisaged. The strange figure of Melchysedeck, priest and king, suggests a priestly order outside that of the Jews, enacting a ritual foreshadowing the Christian Eucharist. Abraham's obedience in sacrificing Isaac also looks on to God's sacrifice of his own Son for all Mankind, while the Gentile soothsayer Balaam is, with comic reluctance, compelled to foretell the passing of privilege from the Jews and to deliver a prophecy which is taken up by the Gentile Magi who journey to Christ's birth. Hereafter, the cycle pursues the extension of Christ's mission against the vested opposition of the Jewish leaders who wilfully resist his truth. Against them are set not only the ordinary believers, but also the pagan Roman emperor Octavian and the thoughtful but helpless Roman ruler Pilate. As befits a Whitsun play, moreover, Chester's action continues beyond the life of Christ to show the coming of the Holy Spirit at Pentecost and the creation of the Apostles' Creed under its influence. The mission of the Church, thus started, ends (as foretold by the prophets) in the coming of Antichrist, who blasphemously parodies the miracles of Christ to convince the rulers of the nations (on Antichrist as actor, see further, Mills 1983, 10–13; Stevens, 303–7). This, too, is seen as part of God's purpose, for it brings down the final witnesses of Christ, Enoch and Elijah, and effects the conversion of the Jews to faith in Christ. With that achieved, the cycle moves directly to the Last Judgement.

Chester suggests that history has a purposive shape which can be recognised in retrospect and which reflects the controlling will of God. But it also suggests that history is a kind of code by which God communicates with Man. Abraham's willingness to sacrifice his son has not only the literal pathos of a father caught between his natural emotions and his religious obligation, and is not only an example to the audience of outstanding obedience and faith; it also has a figural significance which is explained to the audience. Abraham represents God the Father; Isaac, God the Son. While there is nothing original about this interpretation, it is significant that this meaning is available to the audience through a contemporary Expositor but is concealed from both Abraham and Isaac, who rest solely upon the immediate rewards of their obedience. Similarly, when Christ is tempted by the Devil, his action is not simply the literal outwitting of the Devil or the exemplary resistance to temptation required of the Christian; the temptations themselves reflect the temptations to which Adam succumbed, and hence the triumph of Christ in debate marks the reversal of the Fall which he has come to effect.

Chester's plays do not simply dramatise historical events or draw morals from them. They focus upon significant actions which bear a wider meaning and which must be carefully explained (Lumiansky-Mills 1983, 99–110). Many of Chester's plays are "multiple action" plays in which ostensibly disparate actions are brought together under a common theme. Thus, the healing of the blind man and the raising of Lazarus come together in play 13 as miraculous demonstrations of Christ's power, as emblems of spiritual enlightenment and as foreshadowings of the liberation of Man from the consequences of the Fall through Christ's Passion. Hence, although Chester—like the other cycles—plays the miraculous interventions of God, miracles and wonders are in themselves worthless, little more than divine conjuring tricks, unless they serve a wider purpose. Simeon in play 11 is rightly cautious about the significance of the textual changes he witnesses, while the kings of play 23 are too ready to believe the replicated marvels that Antichrist performs:

> They were no miracles but marvellous things
> that thou showed unto these kings
>
> (410–11)

claims Elijah, and answers the tricks with the doctrines of the Church and the recurring miracle of the Eucharist, all that is necessary in the contemporary world.

To reach this level of understanding, the audience is taken to a contemplative distance from the emotional immediacy of the action by speeches of commentary, often by figures who step outside or stand outside the action. The obvious vehicle of this commenting voice is the Expositor who offers interpretations in plays 4, 5, 6, 12 and 22. At other points, Christ himself offers an appropriate comment upon his own acts. I have suggested elsewhere that this concern with commentary reflects an unease about the immediacy and openness of drama itself and a desire that audiences should be led to contemplate the action as a whole rather than identify with individuals within it closely (Mills 1983, 10–13). The Post-Reformation Banns' invitation to "All that with quiet mind / can be content to tarry" (211–12), while ostensibly referring to critics of the plays, does suggest the kind of response which the plays demand.

Two further aspects of this approach may be noted. The first is the extent to which the audience is encouraged to respond to actions figuratively rather than literally by implication. The Fall of Lucifer, for example, relates the separation of the rebellious angels from the loyal angels and their respective locations in hell and heaven to the separation of darkness and light by God at the end of the play, thereby giving a symbolic implication to an event which is realised on a literal level at the start of the second play. And the shepherds of play 7, who begin as comic Welsh rustics in search of their sheep, conclude by exchanging literal pastoralism for an anachronistic spiritual pastoralism. Both plays build upon traditional readings of their actions but do not lead the audience explicit-ly to them by way of commentary.

The second aspect is the way that the cycle reaches out constantly to external authorities to validate its actions. The most obvious form that this takes is the use of quotations from the Vulgate Bible, which are usually translated into English immediately afterwards by the speaker; the readings from the Jewish prophets by Herod's Counsellor in play 8 provide a sustained example of this approach. Because of the translation, the Latin is not strictly necessary, but it provides an authentic "Church" voice which merges with the liturgical allusions both in the Creed and in the numerous liturgical pieces which are either integrated into the text (as with the *Magnificat* in play 6) or accompany triumphal actions (as with the singing of the *Te Deum* by the redeemed souls in play 17 (see Rastall, in Lumiansky-Mills 1983, chap. 3). Authorities are also expressly cited by the Expositor (using, for example, St. Jerome and St. Augustine to validate his interpretations of the Temptation and the Woman taken in Adultery in play 12), and there are repeated passing allusions to biblical authorities scattered throughout the cycle. These references seem to confirm the evangelising purpose of the cycle attributed to Higden in the Banns, and the use of the Vulgate text would also reinforce that picture of him as a translator and would give support to the continuation of productions in the Reformation period. The citing of the Bible might also serve to reassure Protestant observers, while the inclusion of the Creed would guarantee orthodoxy. This concern extends on occasion even to the stage-directions. If possible, in play 24 Christ is to descend in clouds to judge mankind because that is the opinion of scholars about the Judgement.

A consequence of this approach is that the cycle acquires a unity of method and purpose, demanding a sustained response from its audienc-es. It becomes tonally unified. It also manifests a considerable self-aware-ness in its use of cross-references. Some of these take the forms of pro-phetic utterances or figures, as with Adam's dream or the sacrifice of Isaac. Others represent prophecies recalled after their fulfilment, as with the prophecies recited to Herod or the prophecy of Virgin Birth initially disbelieved by Simeon. Christ, of course, fulfills the prophecies he makes of himself in his Passion and Resurrection and the coming of the Holy Spirit, while the Creed picks up many of the actions already dramatised. More subtle cross-links include the stage-direction requiring John to sleep on Christ's bosom at the Last Supper in play 15 and the revelation in his statement in play 22 (lines 173–80) that it was then that he had his vision of the Apocalypse; and the echo of God's opening words of the cycle and of play 2 at the start of the final play: "Ego sum alpha et omega, primus et novissimus." This network of cross-references suggests that the cycle was consciously conceived at some time as a whole rather than as a loose amalgamation of discrete episodes and has been carefully shaped.

This structural awareness is the more surprising given the fragment-
ed nature of production. Inevitably the system of processional production, involving the coming and going of waggons and companies, intensifies the sense of each separate play. At Chester, however, the overall
coherence is further obscured by the three-day division of the performance. To some extent it seems that there was an attempt to give each day
its particular triumphal shape, since each ends on an appropriate dramatic "high." The formal ritual of presenting gifts to the Christ-child in play
9 ends the first day and has been carefully separated from the preceding
visit to Herod, with the comic raging of the tyrant king, to permit full
explanations of the symbolic appropriateness of the gifts. The second day
ends with the *Harrowing of Hell* (play 17); here it is tempting to suggest
that the 1607 version, omitting the "damned ale-wife" episode, reflects
the recorded arrangement, making the triumphal exit of the redeemed a
climax, whereas the other manuscripts may envisage a different distribution of plays, much as they do at the end of play 5. Play 24 is, of course,
the necessary and spectacular end of the whole cycle.

The textual cohesion of the cycle, however, works across these
divisions, picking up and reiterating points made earlier and continuing
the emphasis upon prophecy and sign from one day to the next. These
features account for the recurring sense of progression, retrospection and
reiteration in the cycle and sustain the feeling that we are looking at
something that is as much a work of literature as a piece of drama.

The known sources of Chester, apart from the biblical accounts, are
few but nonetheless significant (Lumiansky-Mills 1983, 87–89). At some
point the whole cycle was revised to incorporate material from a vernacular poem believed to have been written in Chester called *A Stanzaic Life
of Christ*. The poem draws partly upon Higden's *Polychronicon*—a fact
which may serve to support the claims of Higden's authorship—but
primarily upon *Legenda Aurea* ("The Golden Legend"), itself a compila-
tion of largely miraculous material made before 1267 as an inspiration to
devotional living by a Dominican friar called Jacobus da Varagine. Like
the *Polychronicon* it was printed in translation by Caxton and was a
familiar work into the sixteenth century. It is impossible to date the
composition of *Stanzaic Life* accurately, but it survives in fifteenth-century
manuscripts and was the major source of the miraculous material, such
as the midwives of the Nativity or Simeon's book-miracle, that occurs in
the plays. Additionally, the sacrifice of Isaac in Chester is a reworking of
another play on the same subject now preserved in the Book of Brome;
a comparison of the two plays reveals that Chester has skilfully reduced
the pathetic role of the boy Isaac in order to enhance the figural significance of the action and avoid the obvious criticism of God's purpose that
might be implicit in the realisation of paternal cruelty We know that the
episode of "Christ before the Doctors" derives from another version of
the play which underlies the same play in York, Coventry and Towneley;

the source explains the suspension of the Chester stanza at this point.)No doubt there are other immediate sources which the final reviser of our text used, but they remain unknown. What is significant is the way in which a diversity of material has been integrated into a unified whole.

4. THE STAGING OF THE CYCLE

The only account of the Chester pageant-waggons surviving comes from Archdeacon Rogers, who describes them as "a highe place made like a howse with 2 rowmes beinge open on the tope the lower rowme theie. apparrelled and dressed them selues. and the higher rowme, theie played" (REED, 239). Modern critics doubt the necessity for a lower dressing-room, debate the variation between six and four wheels on each waggon which occurs in David Rogers' different versions, and speculate whether, though open at the top, the waggon would not have had some sort of cover or canopy to protect the set (Salter 1955, 68–69; Clopper 1974; Hart and Knapp, chap. 3). Rogers gives no clear indication of size, but a recent estimate based on carriage-house sites, street-sizes and logistics suggests that a waggon may have measured twelve feet in length, five feet six inches in width, and stood up to twelve feet in height (Marshall, in Mills 1983, 34).

It seems, however, unlikely that there ever was a "standard" waggon design. A play such as *The Flood* required a waggon built as an ark, on which pictures of animals could be hung and a mast and sail raised. *The Ascension* and *The Judgement* require lifting gear which must have necessitated not only special apparatus but also adequate counter-weights. Double and triple acting levels are relatively frequent. *The Fall of the Angels*, *The Ascension*, *Pentecost*, and *The Judgement* are among the plays which require the levels of heaven, earth and/or hell, while any play involving God or his messengers suggests a high place from which the Deity can speak or his servants descend, such as is demanded at the opening of play 3. The 1550 Shoemakers' accounts include a payment "for ssetteng op of oure stepoll (steeple)" (REED 50) for the "Purification" and "Doctors" play—evidently the temple to the top of which Christ is taken. And the Early Banns make much of the spectacular appearance of the waggons; for example:

> The Hewsters that be men full sage   *dyers*
> they bring forth a worthy carriage;
> that is a thing of great costage—   *expense*
> "Antichrist" it hight.   *is called*
>
> (140–43)

The waggons seem to have carried the main sets for the historical action of the Bible stories, but the reality of a trading and manufacturing community is never far from these plays. The Mercers are said by the

Early Banns to decorate their waggon for the *Magi's Presentation* with a range of their splendid cloths, and the Goldsmiths and Masons clearly used the same waggon next day for the *Slaughter of the Innocents* "their craft to magnify" (Early Banns 73) in the splendour of Herod's court. The Bakers, playing *The Last Supper*, are urged in the Later Banns to "cast God's loaves abroad with accustomed cheerful heart," as free samples. Joseph the Carpenter in *The Nativity*, played by a carpenter, seems to voice the complaint of all carpenters against the punitive taxation of the king (play 6, 368–91), while the ale-wife of the *Harrowing of Hell*, played by a member of the Cooks and Inn-keepers, solemnly warns of the importance of maintaining the quality of Chester's ale (play 17, 301–24). It is not hard to see an appropriateness in having the Waterleaders and Drawers in Dee perform *The Flood* or the Ironmongers nail Christ to the cross, and one may surmise that the Drapers staged *Creation* with a series of painted cloths and the Cappers provided the elaborate horned head-dress for Moses and the animal mask for Balaam's ass in play 5.

These plays thus have a double focus. At one extreme, in the historical time represented by the waggon, lies the biblical action of the past. At the other, in the occupational allusions, lies the contemporary force of the plays. Much of the action took place away from the waggon. Characters such as the three kings of play 8 ride up separately to meet, and similarly disperse at the end of play 9, and must surely have done so through the spectators in the street. Mary and Joseph resolve to journey to Jerusalem in play 11, 119+SD, from a position a little way from the temple. Play 6 involves journeys between Elizabeth's house, Joseph's house and Jerusalem, and then cuts between Jerusalem and Rome; we do not know how much of the action took place on the waggon and whether subsidiary sets were established at a distance from it, but it seems probable that at least some of the play may have been acted at street level. The shepherds in play 7 have come into the streets of Chester from nearby Wales. It is unlikely that Christ's journey to Calvary in part 2 of play 16 could have taken place entirely upon the waggon.

The audience are drawn into the action not only by this proximity but also by the use of direct address from the actors, for they become a crowd to be swayed and moved—the Israelites addressed by Moses in play 5, the subjects of Herod's opening harangue in play 10, the onlook-ers at Lazarus's rising or the crowd clamouring for Christ's death. Fittingly, the cycle ends with direct address to its audience.

We have, unfortunately, no detailed information about sets and costumes. Waggon-sharing agreements might be made on the basis of compatible sets, and it seems possible that the diverse events of the "Purification" and "Presentation" are juxtaposed in play 11 because they both require a temple as set. Certain features, such as God's throne in play 2 or the hill of play 4, may additionally assume symbolic value. It seems likely that the guilds renewed costumes and properties only when necessary, limiting expense and preserving some sort of visual continuity. While it is unlikely that many (if any) of the actors appeared in contemporary dress, some degree of improvisation was probably always involved and costuming was probably always a mixture of styles (see Twycross, in Mills 1983, 100–23); in 1575 the Smiths borrowed a Doctor's gown and hood for their eldest Doctor (REED 106).

The actors were paid for their work. Typical are the Smiths' accounts of 1572 (REED 91):

> Symion. Dame Anne. 2 Angells xij d Ioseph. Mary xviij d
> Deus xvj d primus docter xvj d 2 docter 3 docter
> for the clergy for the songes 4s 2d.

The parts of women-characters are assumed to have been taken by boys. We know little of acting style, but modern experiments suggest that large gestures and a very strong delivery are necessary for open-air performance before a crowd, and a forceful personality and confident movement are required to clear a space and gain silence at the start of an action. The opening speeches of many of the plays are accordingly strong and direct, designed to restore order after the confusion of breaking the previous set and moving the next waggon into place. The beginning and end of play 4 (1–8 and 485–92) incorporate this process into the action of the play.

Particular mention must be made of the importance of music in the plays (see Rastall, in Lumiansky-Mills 1983, chap. 3). References to "minstrels" in play 2 indicate instrumental accompaniment which may occur unmarked elsewhere. Liturgical music occurs throughout, taking the Latin form. The reference to payment to the clergy by the Smiths above indicates what we know from other sources—that choristers from the cathedral were hired by the companies to perform the liturgical pieces. A chorister Mary would thus sing the Magnificat in play 6, while the Gloria in play 7 was performed by an angelic chorus of choristers who subsequently seem to have been incorporated into the action as the shepherds' boys. It is important to remember that our text contains only the beginnings of these liturgical pieces, serving as cues for the singing of the whole item, and that therefore there is more singing in the text than the brief references might at first seem to suggest.

All these factors point to an experience very different from that of modern audiences sitting through "revivals" of the plays and suggest that the modern reader must be prepared always to visualise the action concretely, consider the importance of appearance, movement and sound, and recognise that the presence of a character, even when silent, can have a powerful impact. The puzzled reactions of the kings to Herod's tirade (play 8, 161–212) or the extended ritual action of the washing of the feet at the Last Supper (play 15, 141–68+SD) cannot be scripted but are both important. The resurrections of both Lazarus and Christ need to be slow, deliberate, preceded by a moment of stillness and suspense to create a dramatic miracle appropriate to the divine miracle enacted. Timing and staging are essential to draw out the full power of the text.

5. THE PLAYS AND THE MODERN RESPONSE

The greatest divide separating the modern audience or reader from the cycle is the loss of the theocentric view of history on which the cycle is structured, together with the weakening of the general Christian consensus which informs the cycle. Modern audiences can no longer be assumed to recognise the biblical narratives from which the plays are drawn or to distinguish scriptural from non-scriptural material, still less to accept that history is an artifact shaped purposefully by God. The divide is nevertheless not so great as might at first appear. While apologists of the later sixteenth century regarded the plays as at best an inadequate substitute for the Bible, which was by then officially available in English, they also assume a period when the general populace were ignorant of the Scriptures, as many are today. Surprisingly, in what has been called a post-Christian era, audiences are perhaps closer to the fifteenth century in their lack of prior assumptions and can see the plays the more readily as drama. Nevertheless, knowledge of the biblical narratives on which the plays draw will increase appreciation of the achievement of the dramatists.

The theocentric view of history, while central to the cycle, is also less of an obstacle to modern understanding than might appear because the cycle itself seems slightly sceptical of the viewpoint it propounds. God communicated with his creation in the past through signs, miracles, prophecies, revelations; but since Pentecost man has had full understanding and access to the Word and the Eucharist. In the penultimate play, marvels are the instruments of Antichrist and the methods used to expose his evil are those available to all. The past is another world, and its occupants are frequently bemused by the wonders that God works, dutifully accepting (like Abraham), comically doubting (like the midwife of play 6) or wilfully resisting (like the High Priests). Disbelief is accommodated within the action as a perfectly intelligible initial response to the suspension of natural law.

The dramatists cannot, however, escape two consequences of their Christian narrative that may trouble the modern audience. First, in a narrative initiated by Eve's foolish yielding to the Devil's temptation, women play a subordinate role and are at times subject to anti-feminist ridicule, as by the Devil (185–204) and later by Adam (353–60) in play 2, and by Noah in play 3 (105–12). Eve, however, achieves a degree of pathos in her self-accusations in play 2 (689–96), taking upon herself the responsibility for Abel's death, while Mrs. Noah proves a robust match for her husband and stoutly defends her practical values. Elsewhere, women are accorded much higher status as the followers of Christ who

[margin note: Can medieval ones?]

accompany him to Calvary and are the first witnesses of his Resurrection. Far less gender-orientated comedy is found in Chester than in some other plays.

Equally, the cycle inevitably is critical of the Jews as Christ's enemies, leaving us with an uncomfortable consciousness of anti-semitism. Again, however, Chester avoids easy solutions. The cycle traces the fortunes of the Jews from the covenant with Abraham to the rise of a great and powerful nation, blessed with the revelation of God. Paradoxi- yes cally, it is the reverence for their God that makes their leaders incapable of recognising him incarnate in Christ. Consequently the cycle presents Christ's mission as primarily to the poor, to the ordinary Jews who have no love for their leaders—as the Blind Man's parents say in play 13, 161–69. The Crucifixion thus becomes a pragmatic political act instigated by the High Priests, and its effects are reversed by the conversion of the Jews in play 23, one of the signs of the impending Judgement. While one can hardly imagine a cycle which would give a fair hearing to the Jewish case, Chester does offer a dramatic explanation for the events, indicating both the Jewish legacy to Christianity and the accommodation of the understandable antagonism of the Jewish leaders within the unfolding purpose of God. The Jews are accordingly shown not as evil but as misguided, the victims of their own privileged position.

6. EDITORIAL PRACTICE

This edition supplements and presupposes earlier work on the cycle. Its text is based on the Early English Text Society edition of 1974 in which R. M. Lumiansky and I took the 1591 manuscript as base. Since that edition gives all significant variants and, in the *Commentary* of 1986, evaluates them, I have in the main incorporated the preferred readings from it without explanation. Major deviations from the 1974 base text are itemised in an Appendix; in particular, since some passages have been omitted, rearranged or added from later mansucripts, the line-numbers in this edition do not always correspond to those of the 1974 edition, and the reader is referred to the Appendix where the correlations can be established. I have not attempted to give full details of music, since that specialist aspect is authoritatively discussed by Richard Rastall in our 1983 volume, *Essays on the Chester Cycle*.

My main purpose here has been to provide a modern spelling text of the cycle with accompanying guidance about the meanings of obsolete words or difficult passages and a minimum of "background annotation." Fortunately, because the final versions of our text belong to the sixteenth or early seventeenth century and contain few dialect words, many words are still in current use and the language-barrier is not as great as in other medieval play-cycles. Where they are not current, readers should remember that the Post-Reformation Banns warn contemporary audiences that there are words that they will find strange. The same word may be glossed differently according to context, to a sense of stylistic felicity, and to restrictions of space.

I have tried to be as conservative as possible, holding to the view that a manuscript-version must in principle be assumed to have an authority greater than any reconstructed form. I have, however, tended to "emend" in order to preserve rhyme and stanza-forms, since Chester's insistent verse-form is important. While the metre is flexible, there are a few occasions on which it seems important to pronounce a syllable where today we do not; in such cases the word is hyphenated to guide the reader. Spellings have been "normalised," but sometimes to forms which resemble modern equivalents (e.g., *lieve* rather than *leve* for "believe") to assist comprehension. Punctuation is modern, but sometimes differs from that in the EETS edition. Stage-directions, when in Latin, have been translated, but quotations in Latin have been kept in the text with footnote translation and reference because the Latin would have been spoken or sung in performance. I have not supplied additional staging directions within the text itself since these represent an editorial intrusion and frequently acquire a spurious authority of their own in the mind of the reader.

Each play is prefaced by a short head-note giving the biblical (or other) source and briefly indicating matters of staging and interpretation which may be explored further. The titles of the plays are editorial. I have supplied a list of speaking parts at the start of each play, though many plays also require a number of non-speaking characters.

FURTHER READING

Space does not permit full footnoting in the introduction or the inclusion of a comprehensive bibliography, but the following suggestions for further reading will be helpful for readers wishing to pursue any aspect of the cycle.

REFERENCE

Bibliographies

The standard bibliography of medieval drama is the two-volume *Bibliography of Medieval Drama*, edited by Carl J. Stratman (2d rev. ed., New York, 1972), whose references cover the period to c. 1970. Sidney E. Berger's *Medieval English Drama: An Annotated Bibliography of Recent Criticism* (Garland Medieval Bibliographies, vol. 2, New York, 1990) both extends the listing to c. 1989 and also includes references for the pre-1970 period not included by Stratman. For a bibliography of major modern editions and criticisms of medieval European drama together with a series of critical reviews of research progress and needs, see *The Theatre of Medieval Europe: New Research in Early Drama*, edited by Eckehard Simon (Cambridge, 1990).

Editions

The history of editions of the Chester Cycle begins in 1818, when J. H. Markland edited the plays of "The Flood" and "The Massacre of the Innocents" for the Roxburghe Club. The first edition of the full cycle, by Thomas Wright for the New Shakespeare Society in 1843 and 1847, was based primarily on the 1592 manuscript and attempted no full collation. The second, begun by Hermann Deimling and completed by a Dr. Matthews for the Early English Text Society (e.s. 62, 1892, and e.s. 115,

1916) did not take the 1591 manuscript into account in selecting as base the 1607 manuscript. Both are superseded by the modern standard edition of the cycle, *The Chester Mystery Cycle*, edited by R. M. Lumiansky and David Mills for the Early English Text Society. The first volume, *Text* (EETS s.s. 3, London, 1974), contains the text based on the 1591 Huntington manuscript, together with all significant variants from the other manuscripts. The second volume, *Commentary* (EETS s.s. 9, London, 1986), includes English glossary, and textual notes which give in full reasons for preferring the "non-Huntington" readings used here.

This edition is the basis for *A Complete Concordance to "The Chester Mystery Plays,"* compiled by Jean D. Pfleiderer and Michael J. Preston (New York, 1981). It is also the subject of essays on the textual and performance-histories of the plays, on the music and the sources, in R. M. Lumiansky and David Mills, *The Chester Mystery Cycle: Essays and Documents, with an Essay, "Music in the Cycle," by Richard Rastall* (Chapel Hill, 1983), which includes a breakdown of the variety of stanza-forms and a collection of edited documents relating to the cycle, together with both sets of Banns. Facsimile editions of the 1604 Bodley and 1591 Huntington manuscripts have been produced for the Leeds Medieval Drama Facsimile series by R. M. Lumiansky and David Mills, and a reduced facsimile of the 1607 Harley 2124 manuscript for the same series by David Mills (Leeds, 1973, 1980, and 1984 respectively).

Records

A topographical guide to records of drama in England to the accession of Elizabeth I is provided by Ian Lancashire's *Dramatic Texts and Records of Britain: A Chronological Topography to 1558* (Toronto, 1984). Records relating to the full range of dramatic activity in Chester up to 1642 are described and transcribed by L. M. Clopper in *Records of Early English Drama: Chester* (Toronto, 1979). *The Breviary of Chester History* by Robert and David Rogers, which provides a much-quoted description of the plays and their production, is analysed in the context of medieval and Tudor historiography by Steven E. Hart and Margaret M. Knapp in *"The Aunchant and Famous Cittie": David Rogers and the Chester Mystery Plays* (University Studies in Medieval and Renaissance Literature, vol. 3, New York, 1988). Sally-Beth MacLean offers a descriptive list of extant and lost art in Chester, including items relevant to early drama, in *Chester Art* (Early Drama, Art, and Music, Reference Series 3, Kalamazoo, 1982).

SOURCES

Chester's immediate vernacular sources are *A Stanzaic Life of Christ*, edited by Frances A. Foster (EETS o.s. 15, London 1926), and, for play 4, the Brome play, in *Non-Cycle Plays and Fragments*, edited by Norman Davis (EETS s.s. 1, London, 1970), Text V. The relationships between the

different cycle-versions of "Christ Before the Doctors" are analysed in
"'Christ and the Doctors' and the York Play" in *The Trial and Flagellation
with Other Studies in the Chester Cycle*, edited by W. W. Greg (Malone
Society, London, 1935), 101–20. Sources are also discussed by A. C.
Baugh, "The Chester Plays and French Influence," in *Schelling Anniversa-
ry Papers*, edited by A. H. Quinn (New York, 1923), 35–63; and Robert H.
Wilson, "The *Stanzaic Life of Christ* and the Chester Plays," *Studies in
Philology* 28 (1931): 413–32.

BACKGROUND AND CRITICISM

Medieval drama was for long valued as "pre-Shakespearean,"
largely due to the pervasive influence of E. K. Chambers' two-volume
study of 1903, *The Mediaeval Stage*. The evolutionary view of drama there
propounded has largely been abandoned by modern critics, who prefer
to concentrate on the evaluation of the plays as works of art in their own
right, as practical theatre for the medieval or the modern stage, and as
functional activities within their original urban contexts. Among the
many studies of medieval drama in general, and of the play-cycles in
particular, which include part or all of Chester's cycle, special mention
should be made of V. A. Kolve's *The Play Called Corpus Christi* (Stanford,
1966), with its emphases upon the artifact of historical time and upon the
figural principles underlying cycle-structure, since this book gave major
impetus to new lines of critical thought. Rosemary Woolf examines *The
English Mystery Plays* (London, 1972) in the light of iconographic and
theological traditions. Stanley J. Kahrl's *Traditions of Medieval English
Drama* (London, 1974) evaluates medieval plays in relation to the theatres
for which they may have been intended. Lois Potter's *Medieval Drama*
(London, 1983), the first volume of *The Revels History of Drama in English*,
deals with all aspects of medieval drama, including staging, and provides
a chronological table and bibliographies. In *Four Middle English Mystery
Cycles* (Princeton, 1987), Martin Stevens extends the work of Travis (see
below), emphasising the unity of Chester's cycle, its significant depend-
ence—unique among the English cycles—upon St. John's Gospel, and its
movement toward logical closure. A new collection of essays is forthcom-
ing in the *Cambridge Companion to Medieval English Theatre* (Cambridge),
edited by Richard Beadle.

Work on the records and performance-history of Chester's cycle was
pioneered by F. M. Salter, whose *Medieval Drama in Chester* (Toronto,
1955) is a scholarly and readable account of prolonged research, exposing
the myths of authorship and revealing the lavish scale of production. L.
M. Clopper's work on the documents and the cycle forms the basis of his
important article, "The History and Development of the Chester Cycle,"
Modern Philology 75 (1978): 219–46, and his more recent study of the social
and cultural contexts of cycle-drama, "Lay and Clerical Impact on Civic
Religious Drama and Ceremony," in *Contexts for Early English Drama*,

edited by Marianne G. Briscoe and John C. Coldeway (Bloomington, 1989), 102–36, which focuses upon Chester. In "The Rogers' Description of the Chester Plays," *Leeds Studies in English* 7 (1974): 63–94, he defends the *Breviary* descriptions against objections by other scholars, including Salter.

The most significant study of the cycle as a cohesive and unified whole is Peter Travis's book-length study, *Dramatic Design in the Chester Cycle* (Chicago, 1982), which analyses the interrelated dramatic and theological concerns from which the cycle has been constructed. Its organising themes are the cycle's structural unity, its strategy of affective relationship with the audience, and the theoretical models which determine its shape; these themes are pursued by means of a serial commentary upon the cycle which incorporates sensitive and perceptive critical comments.

There is space to mention only a few of many useful shorter studies. In "Divine Power in the Chester Cycle and Late Medieval Thought" (*Journal of the History of Ideas* 39 [1978]: 387–404), Kathleen M. Ashley links the cycle to later medieval philosophical concerns with nominalist thought through its insistence on divine omnipotence. L. M. Clopper discusses "The Principle of Selection in the Chester Old Testament Plays" (*Chaucer Review* 13 [1979]: 272–83), and J. J. McGavin broaches the wide issue of sign as a recurring device in the cycle in "Sign and Transition: The *Purification* Play in Chester" (*Leeds Studies in English* n.s. 11 [1979]: 90–101). Essays by diverse hands, based on a series of public lectures given at the University of Leeds in 1973 in connection with a production of the cycle and covering the cycle's history, its pageant-waggons, players, music and costumes, have been brought together by David Mills in *Staging the Chester Cycle* (Leeds Texts and Monographs 6, Leeds, 1985).

Although discussions of medieval plays may be found in many different journals, the following may be mentioned as among those which most frequently carry such material: *Comparative Drama, EDAM Newsletter, Medieval English Theatre, REED Newsletter.*

THE CHESTER MYSTERY CYCLE

THE POST-REFORMATION BANNS

ON ST. GEORGE'S DAY in a year when the cycle was to be performed, a verse-announcement of the plays, describing their content, was proclaimed in the streets of Chester. Rogers, in the *Breviary* (1619), describes the crier as "war-like apparaled like Saint George." Each company supplied a horse and a representative in play-costume to ride with the crier through the city. The Banns were probably proclaimed at the city Bars at the Eastgate, where the crier would call up the companies, and the procession would go through the streets to the various city gates, passing the prisons at the North Gate and the Castle where monetary gifts were left for the prisoners.

Two versions of the verse-announcement still survive. One, in MS Harley 2150 (copied in 1540), preserves a version from the period before the Reformation. The composition of this version cannot be precisely dated—indeed, it probably incorporates a number of revisions made at different times from what was a working document—but in its final form it relates to a period when the guild-play had moved to Whitsun and the clergy had assumed responsibility for a play on Corpus Christi Day.

The second version, of which four copies are extant, was certainly written at some time after the Reformation. Two of our copies (in MS Harley 2013 of 1600, and MS Bodley 175 of 1604) preface copies of the cycle, and a reference in David Rogers' *Breviary of Chester History* (1619 version) to the "prologue before his booke of the Whitson Playes" seems to confirm that this version was kept with the official Register of the cycle at the Pentice. Rogers, in fact, provides us with the other two copies of these Post-Reformation Banns (1609). It is this version which is given here.

The Banns generally describe the cycle as we now have it, but there are a number of interesting discrepancies which may suggest that the

cycle continued to undergo modifications after these Banns had been
composed. They provide, however, important evidence not only about
the priorities and performance of the cycle but also about the attitude of
Cestrians towards the plays after the Reformation. They lay particular
emphasis upon the traditions of authorship and production which had
grown up around the cycle, claiming the plays as the innovatory product
of an allegedly Protestant-inclined monk, Ranulf Higden. And they
present the plays as a kind of dramatic fossil, strangely out of place in
the new drama of the modern world, and urge their audiences to make
due allowance for the circumstances of their original composition and
performance. Throughout the Banns there is a defensive tone which
suggests the awareness of potential opposition to the plays on theological
and theatrical grounds. Objectors are urged simply to walk away from
the production; those who stay to watch should do so with a "quiet
mind."

Reverend lords and ladies all
that at this time here assembled be,
by this message understand you shall
that some time there was mayor of this city   *at one time*
5   Sir John Arneway, knight, who most worthily*   *honourably*
contented himself to set out in play   *was pleased; as a play*
the device of one Randle, monk of Chester Abbey.*   *creation*

This monk (not monk-like in Scriptures, well seen!—
in stories travelled with the best sort)
10   in pageants set forth apparent to all een*   *plays*

---

5 Sir John Arneway appears in the early mayoral lists of Chester as the city's first
mayor, an error corrected only in 1594; in fact, the first mayor was Sir Walter
Lynett (1257–58, 1258–59, 1259–60). Historically, Arneway was mayor consecu-
tively from 1268–76.

7 *Randle*—i.e., Ranulf Higden, monk from 1299 to his death in 1364 at St. Werburgh's Abbey, Chester (from 1541, the Cathedral).

8–10 "This monk (who was not a bit like a monk when it came to knowledge of
the Scriptures, as is very evident—he moved among the best kind of narratives)
set out in plays visible to all eyes the Old and New Testament with life-giving joy."

entertainment evangelism ?

the Old and New Testament with lively comfort,
intermingling therewith, only to make sport,   *entertainment*
some things not warranted by any writ   *biblical text*
which glad the hearts—he would men to take it.

15   This matter he abbreviated into plays 24
and every play of the matter gave but a taste,   *subject*
leaving for better learn-ed the circumstance   *context*
   to accomplish,   *complete*
for all his proceedings may appear to be in haste.   *actions*
Yet altogether unprofitable his labour he   *worthlessly*
   did not waste
20   for at this day, and ever, he deserves the fame
that few monks deserve, professing the same.   *being monks*

These stories of the Testament at this time,   *from the Bible*
   you know,
in a common English tongue never read nor heard.   *(were)*
Yet thereof in these pageants to make open show,   *public display*
25   this monk—and no monk—was nothing afeared*
with fear of burning, hanging, or cutting off head,
to set out that all may discern and see,   *so that*
and part of good belief, believe ye me   *impart true faith*

As in this city diverse years they have been set out,
30   so at this time of Pentecost called Whitsuntide—*
although to all the city follow labour and cost—   *ensue*
yet, God giving leave, that time shall you in play
for three days together, begin on Monday,   *beginning*
see these pageants played to the best   *plays performed*
   of their skill,   *ability*
35   wherein to supply all want shall be   *make good; deficiency*
   no want of good will.   *lack*

As all that shall see them shall most welcome be,
so all that do hear them we most humbly pray
not to compare this matter or story   *subject-matter*

---

25 "This monk, who was by no means a typical monk."

30 Pentecost was the occasion when the Holy Spirit descended from God upon the disciples; see play 21. Whit Sunday is the contemporary liturgical celebration of that occasion.

with the age or time wherein we presently stay—   *now live*
40   but to the time of ignorance wherein we did stray.*
And then dare I compare that, this land   *make comparison*
        throughout,
none had the like, nor the like durst set out.

If the same be liking to the commons all,   *pleasing; populace*
then our desire is satisfied; for that is
        all our gain.   *our entire reward*
45   If no matter or show thereof, anything special,   *in particular*
do not please but mislike most of the train,   *displease; those attending*
go back again to the first time, I say.*
Then shall you find the fine wit, at this day
        abounding,   *in abundance*
at that day and that age had very small being.   *limited existence*

50   Condemn not our matter where gross words you hear
which import at this day small sense or understanding
as sometimes "posty," "lewty," "in good manner" or "in fere"—
with such-like will be uttered in their speeches speaking.
At that time those speeches carried good liking.
55   Tho if at this time you take them spoken at that time,
as well matter as words, then all is well fine!*

This worthy knight Arneway, then Mayor of this City,
this order took, as declare to you I shall:
that by twenty-four occupations—arts, crafts, or mystery—   *trade*
60   these pageants should be played after brief rehearsal;
for every pageant, a carriage to be provided withall.   *as well*
In which sort we purpose this Whitsuntide   *in this way*
our pageants into three parts to divide.

---

40 *the time of ignorance*—i.e., the period before the Reformation.

45–47 "If any subject-matter or performance in it, anything specific, does not please but displeases the majority of the people following, think back again to the first occasion of their performance, I say."

50–56 "Do not condemn our subject-matter wherever you hear uncouth words which impart at this day little sense or meaning, such as on occasion "posty" (power), "lewty" (loyalty, faith), "in good manner" (fittingly), or "in fere" (together)—utterances of that sort will be spoken in delivering their speeches. At that time those speeches were well received. Then if you at this present time take them as if they were being spoken at that former time, then all is well, subject-matter as well as words!"

Now, you worshipful Tanners, that of custom old
65   *The Fall of Lucifer* did truly set out!
Some writers a-warrant your matter; therefore be bold
lustily to play the same to all the rout.*
And if any therefore stand in any doubt
your author his author hath. Your show let be!   *authority*
70   Good speech, fine players, with apparel comely!   *fine costume*

Of the Drapers you, the wealthy company,
The Creation of the World! Adam and Eve
according to your wealth, set out wealthily,   *appropriately*
and how Cain his brother Abel his life did bereave.   *take away*

75   The good, simple Waterleaders and Drawers of Dee,
see that in all points your Ark be prepared.   *respects*
Of Noah and his Children the Whole Story:
and of the Universal Flood, by you shall be played.

The Sacrifice that Faithful Abraham of his Son should Make,
80   you Barbers and Wax-chandlers of ancient time
in the fourth pageant with pains ye did take.
In decent sort set out—the story is fine.   *proper manner*
The offering of Melchysedeck of bread and wine
and the preservation thereof set in your play.   *continuation*
85   Suffer you not in any point the story to decay.   *aspect*

Cappers and Linen-drapers, see that ye forth bring
in well-decked order *That Worthy Story*
of Balaam and his Ass and of Balaack the King.
Make the ass to speak, and set it out lively.   *vividly*

90   Of Octavian the Emperor, that could not well allow   *agree to*
the prophecy of ancient Sibyl the sage,*
ye Wrights and Slaters with good players in show
lustily bring forth your well-decked carriage.
The Birth of Christ shall all see in that stage.
95   If the Scriptures a-warrant not of the midwives' report

66–67 "Some writers provide authority for your subject-matter; therefore be confident to play the same enthusiastically to all the people."

90–91 Octavian does not, in our play, object to Sibyl's words.

the author telleth his author; then take it in sport.*

The appearing Angel and Star upon Christ's birth,
The Shepherds, poor, of base and low degree,
you Painters and Glaziers, deck out with all mirth   *joy*
100   and see that "Gloria in Excelsis" be sung merrily.*
Few words in the pageant make mirth truly,*
for all that the author had to stand upon
was "Glory to God on high, and peace on Earth to Man."

And you worthy Merchant-vintners, that now have plenty of wine,
105   amplify the story of those *Wise Kings Three*
that through Herod's land and realm, by the star that did shine,
sought the sight of the Saviour that then born should be.

And you worshipful Mercers, though costly and fine
you trim up your carriage as custom ever was,
110   yet in a stable was he born, that mighty King divine,
poorly in a stable betwixt an ox and an ass.   *between*

You Goldsmiths and Masons, make comely show,   *attractive*
how Herod at the return of those kings did rage,
and how he slew the tender male babes
115   being under two years of age.

You Smiths—honest men, yea, and of honest art—   *trade*
how *Christ Among the Doctors* in the temple did dispute,
to set out your play comely it shall be your part.   *attractively*
Get minstrels to that show—pipe, tabret, and flute.   *drum*

120   And next to this, you the Butchers of this City,   *after*
the story of *Satan that would Christ needs Tempt*

95–96 "If the Scriptures provide no authority for the account of the midwives, the
author is only repeating what his author says; consider it as light relief." On the
midwives, see further, play 6.

100 "Glory to God in the highest"—the song of the angels to the shepherds. See
play 7.

101 "Few words in the play make merriment authentically," i.e., on the authority
of the Scriptures. The Banns evidently seek to excuse the meeting of the shepherds and their feasting and wrestling which precede the appearance of the
angels and constitute a different kind of "comedy" from the angelic song.

set out as accustomably used have ye—   *customarily*
the Devil in his feathers, all ragged and rent.   *torn*

The Death of Lazarus and his Rising Again
125 you of the Glovers the whole occupation   *trade*
in pageant with players orderly—let it not be pain—   *distressful*
finely to advance after the best fashion.   *splendidly; proceed*

The story How to Jerusalem Our Saviour Took the Way
you Corvisors that in number full many be   *shoemakers*
130 with your Jerusalem Carriage shall set out in play.
A commendable true story, and worthy of memory!

And how Christ our Saviour at his *Last Supper*
gave his body and blood for redemption of us all
you Bakers see that with the same words you utter
135 as Christ himself spake them, to be a memorial
of that death and Passion which in play after ensue shall.
The worst of these stories doth not fall to your part;   *i.e. saddest*
therefore, cast God's loaves abroad with accustomed
     cheerful heart.*

You Fletchers, Bowers, Coopers, Stringers, and Ironmongers,*
140 see soberly ye make out *Christ's Doleful Death,**
his scourging, his whipping, his bloodshed and Passion,
and all the pains he suffered till the last of his breath.
Lordings, in this story consisteth our chief faith
the ignorance wherein hath us many years so blinded;
145 as though now all see the path plain,
yet the most part cannot find it.*

---

138 "Therefore distribute God's loaves around with your usual happy heart."
Evidently the Bakers tossed small loaves to the crowds during the performance.

139 *Fletchers, Bowers, Coopers, Stringers, and Ironmongers*—i.e., arrow-makers, bow-makers, barrel-makers, bow-string makers and ironmongers.

140 "Look that you perform *The Pitiful Death of Christ* in a serious manner."

143–46 The lines stress the abandonment of the "misguided" Roman Catholic teaching on the Eucharist in favour of the recently established doctrines of Protestantism founded upon the biblical text. 145–46 seem to imply that, though the theological truth is now available, it is still not widely understood.

As our belief is that Christ after his Passion
descended into Hell—but what he did in that place,
though our author set forth after his opinion,
150 yet credit you the best learned; those he doth not not disgrace.
We wish that of all sorts the best you embrace.[*]
You Cooks with your carriage see that you do well;   perform
in pageant set out *The Harrowing of Hell*.

The Skinners before you after shall play   in front of; next
155 the story of *The Resurrection*,
how Christ from death rose the third day—
not altered in many points from the old fashion.   respects

The Saddlers and Friezers should in their   frieze-makers
          pageant declare
the appearance of Christ, his *Travel to Emmaus*,
160 his often speech to the woman and his disciples dear,[*]   frequent
to make his Rising-again to all the world notorious.   known

Then see that you Tailors with carriage decent   fine
the story of *The Ascension* formally do frame,   correctly; devise
whereby that glorious body in clouds most ardent   shining
165 is taken up to the heavens with perpetual fame.

Thus of the Old and New Testament to end all the story
which our author meaneth at this time to have in play,[*]   intends
you Fishmongers to the pageant of *The Holy Ghost*
          well see   attend

147–51 "As it is our Creed that Christ went down into hell after his Passion—but
though our author sets out what he did in that place according to his own
opinion, nevertheless you may believe what the most learned men say; he does
not fail to do justice to them. We would like you to comprehend the best opinions from all kinds of sources." The credal article claiming that Christ descended
into hell rests upon uncertain scriptural foundation. The Banns accordingly
attempt to reassure performers and audience that what they will witness is
doctrinally sound.

160 *often speech*—an unusual construction. In our extant *Emmaus* play Christ does
not speak to a woman.

167 "The whole story that our author intends to dramatise at this time." The
implication seems to be that the Banns were at some time designed for a performance ending with *Pentecost*, though possibly there is an intention to separate the last
three plays from the rest as being less directly derivative from the biblical text.

that in good order it be done, as hath been alway.   *always*
170   And after those ended, yet doth not the author stay[*]
       but by *Prophets* showeth forth how Antichrist should rise—
       which you Shearmen see set out in most   *should ensure is*
            comely wise.   *attractive way*

       And then, you Dyers and Huesters, *Antichrist* bring out—   *dyers*
       first with his Doctor, that goodly may expound   *counsellor*
175   who be Antichrists the world round about—[*]
       and Enock and Hely, persons walking on ground,   *Elijah*
       in parts well set you out, the wicked to confound;   *roles*
       which, being well understanded Christ's word   *understood*
            for to be,
       confoundeth all Antichrists and sects of that degree.   *status*

180   The coming of Christ to give eternal judgement,
       you Weavers last of all your part is to play.
       Doomsday we call it, when the Omnipotent
       shall make an end of this world by sentence, I say.   *judgement*
       On his right hand to stand God grant us that day,
185   and to have that sweet word in melody:
       "Come hither, come hither." "Venite Benedicti."[*]

       To which rest of joys and celestial habitation   *in bliss*
       grant us free passage, that all together we,
       accompanied with angels and endless delectation,   *delight*
190   may continually laud God and praise that King of Glory.

                        CONCLUSION OF THE BANNS

       The sum of this story, lords and ladies all,
       I have briefly repeated, and how they must be played.
       Of one thing warn you now I shall:
       that not possible it is those matters to be contrived   *devised*

---

170 "And after those have ended, yet the author does not stop."

174–75 The Banns seem to promise a denunciation of contemporary Antichrists
and an attack upon heretical sects; but the Counsellor never makes this declaration in our play.

186 "Come, blessed ones"; see play 24, line 453. The words evidently served as
a cue for the singing at that point in the play of the *Benedictus* antiphon for the
first Sunday in Lent, but no direction exists in the play itself for this singing.

195   in such sort and cunning and by such players   *manner; skill*
         of price   *worth*
      as at this day good players and fine wits could devise.

      For then should all those persons that as Gods do play
      in clouds come down with voice, and not be seen,
      for no man can proportion that Godhead, I say,   *match*
200   to the shape of man—face, nose and een.   *eyes*
      But sithens the face-gilt doth disfigure the man, that deem
      a cloudy covering of the man—a voice only to hear,
      and not God in shape or person to appear.*

      By craftsmen and mean men these pageants are played,
205   and to commons and country men accustomably before.*
      If better men and finer heads now come, what can be said
      but, "Of common and country players take you the story"?   *from*

      And if any disdain, then open is the door
      that let him in to hear—pack away at his pleasure!*
210   Our playing is not to get fame or treasure.

      All that with quiet mind
      can be contented to tarry,   *remain*
      be here on Whitsun-Monday.
      Then beginneth the story!

                            THE END

201-3 "But since the gold paint on the face does conceal the human features,
understand that to be a covering of clouds for the man—understand that you
hear only a voice, and not God appearing in shape or person." The lines seek to
defend the players from the charge of blasphemous impersonation.

205 "And customarily in front of audiences of commoners and rustics."

208-10 "And if anyone scorns (the production), then the door that let him in to
hear it is wide open—let him pack away whenever he wants. Our acting is not
to win fame or material reward." Since the production was in the streets, the
reference to the door is presumably ironic, although L. M. Clopper has suggested
that the door may be that of the Pentice, Chester's Town Hall, and the reference
may be to an occasion on which the Banns were read to the mayor and aldermen
to deflect criticism of a proposed production (Clopper 1978, 238–40). Line 210
stresses that, unlike professional players, the actors have nothing to gain person-
ally and are not dependent upon the approval of their audience.

PLAY 1: THE FALL OF LUCIFER

Performed by the Tanners

THE FIRST PLAY describes the first day of creation and explains how sin—separation from God through disobedience of his laws—entered the universe. There is no biblical account of the creation of the angels and of the rebellion and expulsion from heaven of Lucifer, the brightest angel of all, but the story had authority from the interpretation of a number of scattered biblical texts. Here the separation of the good and bad angels is symbolically associated with the separation of light from darkness on the first day of creation (Genesis 1.4–5).

The play falls into three sections. First, God addresses the audience in a learned style which might well have been too abstruse to be intelligible to the audience in the Chester streets but which in its magniloquence is stylistically appropriate to the Deity. It explains the doctrine of the Trinity—a single Godhead comprising the Persons of Father, Son and Holy Spirit—and establishes God as the energising source of all created things. Then God begins his act of creation, calling on to the stage the nine groups of angels who move or sit in hierarchy about his throne, and creating earth and hell. Finally, the action proper begins as God retires to observe invisibly the conduct of his angels, and Lucifer ascends the throne and causes division in heaven. The rebellious angels are cast down into hell, changing their appearance and character, and God completes his first day of creation.

The waggon-set is described in the Pre-Reformation Banns as "the hevenly manshon" and obviously had below it a hell-mouth, probably in the form of a barred dungeon; possibly hell glows or smokes when God names it. The earth may simply have been represented by the street, but a painted cloth or a ball could have been used. At the centre of the set was God's throne, the focus of action, with other seats arranged in hierarchy about it. We know that God throughout the cycle had a gilded face, and face paint may have been used also for the angels, since Lucifer draws attention to his own radiance. The costumes, according to the Post-Reformation Banns, were splendid ("apparel comely"—the angels are described as "gayer than gold") and there is a marked change when the angels arrive in hell as "two fiends black." "The devil in his feathers all ragged and rent" (Banns) of *The Temptation* may give a clue to this costume and perhaps indicate that the angels' costumes were feathered.

The waggon offers a hierarchy of seats to be filled and while the first section of the play establishes the pre-eminence of God at the centre and as Creator of all, the second section consists of the filling of that space in a great spectacle of costume, light and music. This tableau of harmony moves into dynamic action as Lucifer, voicing rebellion, moves out of his appointed rank to occupy the position just vacated by God. God's return, to a hymn of praise (symbolising the restoration of harmony), and his anger leads to the dramatic exit of Lucifer and his supporter, perhaps through a floor-trap. The figures in hell could be different actors. In contrast to the harmony of heaven, hell is a place of darkness, stench and dispute. But as God proceeds with creation, Lucifer already knows God's will and is set to thwart it, preparing the way for the next play.

Cast   GOD, LUCIFER/FIRST DEVIL, ANGELS, ARCHANGELS, LIGHTBORNE/ SECOND DEVIL, VIRTUES, CHERUBIM, DOMINATIONS, SERAPHIM, PRINCIPALI- TIES, THRONES, POWERS.

GOD	Ego sum alpha et oo,
	primus at novissimus.*
	It is my will it should be so;
	it is, it was, it shall be thus.
5	I am great God gracious,
	which never had beginning.
	The whole food of parents is set
	in mea essentia.
	I am the trial of the Trinity

1–2 "I am alpha and omega, the first and the last." The same quotation, from Apocalypse 22.13, precedes plays 2 and 24 and links the beginning and end of the cycle to the beginning and end of time.

10   which never shall be twinning,
          Peerless patron imperial
            and Patris sapientia.
          My beams be all beatitude;
            all bliss is in my building.
15   All mirth lieth in mansuetude,   *humility*
            cum Dei potentia.
          Both visible and invisible,
            all lies in my wielding.
          As God greatest and glorious,
20   all is in mea licentia.*

          For all the mirth of the majesty
            is magnified in me,
          Prince principal, proved
            in my perpetual providence,
25   I was never but one
            and ever one in three,
          set in substantial soothness
            within celestial sapience.
          The three trials in a throne
30   and true Trinity
          be grounded in my godhead,
            exalted by my excellency.
          The might of my making
            is marked in me,
35   dissolved under a diadem
            by my divine experience.*
          Now sith I am so solemn

5–20 "I am the great and glorious God that had no beginning. The whole
progeny of your ancestors is founded in my essential nature ('essence'). I am the
tripartite Godhead that can never separate, the matchless royal Lord and the
wisdom of God the Father. My rays are all blessedness, all joy lies in my creation. All your happiness lies in humility, together with the power of God. All
things, both visible and invisible, lie under my rule. As gracious and glorious
God, all lies at my disposal." God, comprehending the three Persons of Father,
Son and Holy Spirit, defines his trinitarian nature and power which will be
manifest throughout the cycle.

21–36 "For all the delight that pertains to majesty is exalted in me, the greatest
of princes, proved so in my eternal providence. I was always One alone, and
always One in Three, grounded in manifest truth. The three Persons in one
Godhead and the true Trinity are established in my Divine Person, exalted by my
excellence. The might of my creative power is manifested in me, enlarged under
one crown by my divine condition."

and set in my solation,	
a bigly bliss here will I build,	
40 a Heaven without ending,	
and cast a comely compass	
by comely creation.*	
Nine orders of angels*	
be ever at once defending!	
45 Do your endeavour and doubt you not	*duty; fear*
under my domination	
to sit in celestial safety.	*secure in Heaven*
All solace to your sending!	*joy; mission*
For all the liking in this lordship	*desire; company*
50 be laud to my laudation.	*praise; glory*
Through might of my most majesty	*highest*
your mirth shall ever be mending.	*joy; increasing*

LUCIFER	Lord, through thy might thou hast us wrought,*	
	nine orders here that we may see:	*ranks*
55	Cherubim and Seraphin through thy thought;	
	Thrones and Dominations in bliss to be,	
	with Principates, that order bright,	*Principalities*
	and Potestates in blissful light;	*Powers*
	also Virtutes, through thy great might	*Virtues*
60	Angeli and also Archangeli.	*Angels; Archangels*
	Nine orders here been witterly	*certainly*
	that thou hast made here full right.	*most properly*
	In thy bliss full bright they be,	*radiant*
	and I the principal, Lord, here in thy sight.	

37–42 "Now since I am so dignified and established in my happiness, I shall build here a place of perfect joy, an everlasting heaven, and create a beautiful realm by a noble act of creation." Here the action of the play begins.

43 *nine orders* was traditionally the number of ranks in the heavenly hierarchy, although sometimes those that fell with Lucifer were regarded as an additional order. The orders—Seraphim, Cherubim, Thrones, Dominations, Virtues, Powers, Principalities. Archangels, Angels—all have biblical reference. They speak as the play continues.

51+SH *Lucifer* was construed as the name for the Devil by influential commentators from a reference in Isaiah 14.12. The etymological sense of "light-bearer" is the source of his heavenly function and the image used in the play.

GOD	Here have I you wrought with heavenly might,	
66	of angels nine orders of great beauty,	*ranks*
	each one with other, as it is right,	
	to walk about the Trinity.	*move*
	Now, Lucifer and Lightborne,	
70	look lowly you be attending.	*humbly*
	The blessing of my benignity	*grace*
	I give to my first operation.	*action*
	For craft nor for cunning,	
	cast never comprehension;*	
75	exalt you not too excellent	*splendidly*
	into high exaltation.	*highest position*
	Look that you tend righteously,	*apply yourselves*
	for hence I will be wending.	*going*
	The world, that is both void and vain,	*empty*
80	I form in the formation,	*creation*
	with a dungeon of darkness, !	*i.e. Hell*
	which never shall have ending.	
	This work is now well wrought	*made*
	by my divine formation.	*creation*
85	This work is well done,	
	that is so clean and clear.	*pure; bright*
	As I you made of nought,	
	my blessing I give you here.	
ANGELS	We thank thee, Lord, full sovereignly,	*most royally*
90	that us hath formed so clean and clear,	*pure; radiant*
	ever in this bliss to bide thee by.	*remain*
	Grant us thy grace ever to bide here.	*remain*
ARCH-	Here for to bide God grant us grace	*remain*
ANGELS	to please this prince withouten peer;	*without equal*
95	him for to thank with some solace,	*rejoicing*
	a song now let us sing here.	

*"Dignus Dei"**

73–74 "Do not try to understand what is happening out of a desire for power or knowledge."

96+Latin Probably the Benedictus anthem for the second Sunday after Easter:

GOD

100

Now seeing I have formed you so fair
and exalted you so excellent—   *raised up*
and here I set you next my chair,   *throne*
my love to you is so fervent—
look you fall not in no despair.
Touch not my throne by none assent.   *by no agreement*
All your beauty I shall appair,   *destroy*
and pride fall ought in your intent.   *if; at all; will*

LUCIFER
106

Nay, Lord, that will not we indeed,
for nothing trespass unto thee.   *sin towards*
Thy great Godhead we will ay dread,   *always*
and never exalt ourselves so high.   *raise up*
Thou hast us marked with great might and main, *strength*

110

in thy bliss evermore to bide and be,   *remain*
in lasting life our life to lead.   *everlasting*
And bearer of light thou hast made me.

LIGHT-
BORNE
115

And I am marked of that same mould,   *stamped from*
loving be to our Creator   *to be loving*
that has us made gayer than gold,   *more splendid*
under his diadem ever to endure.   *rule*

GOD

I have forbid that ye near should;   *approach*
but keep you well in that stature.   *position*
The same covenant I charge you hold,

120

in pain of Heaven your forfeiture.   *your forfeiture of*

For I will wend and take my trace   *go; way*
and see this bliss in every tower.
Each one of you keep well his place;
and, Lucifer, I make thee governor.   *regent*

125

Now I charge the ground of grace
that it be set with my order.*
Behold the beams of my bright face,
which ever was and shall endure.
This is your health in every case: *happiness*

"Thou, O Lord, art worthy to receive glory and honour and power because thou created all things," etc.

125–26 "Now I command heaven ('the ground of grace') to be established with my angelic order."

130   to behold your Creator.
Was never none like me, so full of grace,
nor never shall as my figure.   *person*
Here will I bide now in this place
to be angels' comforture.   *source of comfort*
135   To be revisible in short space   *visible again*
it is my will in this same hour.

Then they sing and God shall withdraw.

LUCIFER   Aha! That I am wondrous bright
amongst you all shining full clear!
Of all Heaven I bear the light
140   though God himself and he were here. *even if God*
All in this throne if that I were,   *might be*
then should I be as wise as he. ✳
What say ye, angels all than been here ? *are*
Some comfort soon now let me see. *consolation*

VIRTUES   We will not assent unto your pride
146   nor in our hearts take such a thought;
but that our Lord shall be our guide, *other than that*
and keep that he to us hath wrought. *made for us*

CHERUBIM Our Lord commanded all that been here *are*
150   to keep their seats, both more and less.
Therefore I warn thee, Lucifer,
this pride will turn to great distress.

LUCIFER   Distress? I command you for to cease
and see the beauty that I bear.
155   All Heaven shines through my brightness
for God himself shines not so clear.

DOMIN-   Of all angels yee bear the prize
ATIONS   and most beauty is you befall.
My counsel is that you be wise, *should be*
160   that you bring not yourselves in thrall. *bondage*

PRINCI-   If that ye in thrall you bring, *bondage*
PALITIES   then shall you have a wicked fall;
and also your offspring,
away with you they shall all. *flee away*

SERAPHIM	Our brothers' counsel is good to hear,	
166	to you I say, Lucifer and Lightborne.	
	Wherefore, beware you of this chair,	
	lest that you have a foul spurn.	*downfall*

LIGHT-	In faith, brother, yet you shall	
BORNE	sit in this throne—art clean and clear—	*you are*
171	that ye may be as wise withall	
	as God himself, if he were here.	
	Therefore you shall be set here,	
	that all Heaven may ye behold.	
175	The brightness of your body clear	
	is brighter than God a thousandfold.	

THRONES	Alas, that beauty will you spill	*destroy*
	if you keep it all in your thought; *morality*	
	then will pride have all his will.	*desire*
180	and bring your brightness all to nought.	
	Let it pass out of your thought	
	and cast away all wicked pride;	
	and keep your brightness to you is	*made for you*
	wrought,	
	and let our Lord be all our guide.	

POWERS	Alas! That pride is the wall of beauty *2*	*barrier*
186	that turns your thought to great offence.	
	The brightness of your fair body	
	will make ye to go hence.	

LUCIFER	Go hence? Behold, seigneurs on every side,	*lords*
190	and unto me you cast your een.	*eyes*
	I charge you, angels, in this tide,	*at this time*
	behold and see now what I mean.	
	Above great God I will me guide	*direct myself*
	and set myself here, as I ween.	*think*
195	I am peerless, and prince of pride,	*unequalled*
	for God himself shines not so sheen.	*brightly*
	Here will I sit now in his stead,	*place*
	to exalt myself in this same see.	*seat*
	Behold my body, hands and head—	
200	the might of God is marked in me.	*imprinted*
	All angels, turn to me, I read,	*advise*

and to your sovereign kneel on your knee.
I am your comfort, both lord and head,
the mirth and might of the majesty.

LIGHT-   And I am next of the same degree,
BORNE   replete by all experience.   *perfect as all can see*
207   Methinks if I might sit him by
all Heaven should do us reverence.
All orders may assent to thee and me;   *agree*
210   thou hast them turned by eloquence.
And here were now the Trinity,   *even if*
we should him pass by our fulgence.   *brightness*

DOMIN-   Alas, why make ye this great offence?
ATIONS   Both Lucifer and Lightborne, to you I say,
215   our sovereign Lord will have you hence
and he find you in this array.   *if; fashion*
Go to your seats and wend you hence.   *go*
You have begun a parlous play.   *perilous action*
Ye shall well witt the subsequence—   *know the sequel*
220   this dance will turn to teen and tray.   *sorrow and woe*

LUCIFER   I read you all do me reverence   *advise*
that am replete with heavenly grace.   *full of*
Though God come, I will not hence,

And he sits down

but sit right here before his face.

"Gloria tibi Trinitas"*

GOD   Say, what array do ye make here?   *show of force*
226   Who is your prince and principal?   *leader*

Then they shall shake and tremble.

I made thee, angel, and Lucifer,   *i.e. Lightborne*
and here thou would be lord over all?
Therefore I charge this order clear   *shining*
230   fast from this place look that ye fall.

224+Latin "Glory to thee, O Trinity," the Vespers antiphon for Trinity Sunday.

| | Full soon I shall change your cheer. | *mood* |
| | For your foul pride, to Hell you shall! | |

	Lucifer, who set thee here when I was go?	*gone*
	What have I offended unto thee?	*in what respect*
235	I made thee my friend; thou art my foe!	
	why hast thou trespassed thus to me?	*sinned against*
	Above all angels there were no moe	*more*
	that sat so nigh my majesty.	*near*
	I charge you to fall till I bid "Whoa!"	*stop*
240	into the deep pit of Hell ever to be.	

Now Lucifer and Lightborne fall.

1ST DEVIL	Alas! that ever we were wrought,	*made*
	that we should come into this place!	
	We were in joy; now we be nought.	
	Alas! We have forfeited our grace!	

2ND DEVIL	And even hither thou hast us brought	
246	into a dungeon to take our trace.	*way*
	All this sorrow thou hast us sought.	*sought out for us*
	The devil may speed thy stinking face.	*take*

1ST DEVIL	My face! False faitour! For thy fare	*cheat; doings*
250	thou hast us brought to teen and tray.	*sorrow and woe*
	I cumber, I conger, I kindle in care,[*]	
	I sink in sorrow; what shall I say?	

2ND DEVIL	Thou hast us brought this wicked way	
	through thy might and thy pride,	
255	out of the bliss that lasteth ay,	*for ever*
	in sorrow evermore to abide.	

1ST DEVIL	Thy wit it was as well as mine,	
	of that pride that we did show;	
	and now been here in Hell-fire	*we are*
260	till the day of doom that beams	*when trumpets*
	shall blow.	*shall sound*

| 2ND DEVIL | Then shall we never care for woe, | *move* |

---

251 "I am overwhelmed, I beg, I burn in misery."

but lie here like two fiends black.
Alas! that ever we did forget so,
that Lord's love to lose that did us make.

1ST DEVIL   And therefore I shall for his sake   *etiological*
266   show Mankind great envy.   *myth.*
                 As soon as ever he can him make,
                 I shall send, him to destroy,

                 one—of my order shall he be—
270   to make Mankind to do amiss.
         7.   Ruffin, my friend fair and free,   *noble*
                 look that thou keep Mankind from bliss.

                 That I and my fellows fell down for ay   *down from; ever*
                 he will ordain Mankind again,   *for mankind*
275   in bliss to be, in great array,   *splendour*
                 and we evermore in Hell-pain!

2ND DEVIL   Out, harrow! where is our might   *alas*
                 that we were wont to show,   *accustomed*
                 and in Heaven bore so great light,
280   and now we be in Hell full low?

1ST DEVIL   Out, alas! For woe and wickedness   *of The throne*
                 I am so fast bound in this chair
                 and never away hence shall pass,
                 but lie in Hell alway here.

GOD   Ah, wicked pride! Ah, woe worth thee, woe!   *befall*
286   My mirth thou hast made amiss.
                 I may well suffer; my will is not so,
                 that they should part thus from my bliss.
                 A, pride! Why might thou not brast in two?   *burst*
290   Why did they that? Why did they this?
                 Behold, my angels, pride is your foe.
                 All sorrow shall show wheresoever it is.   *appear*

                 And though they have broken my commandment,
                 me rues it sore full sufferently.*
295   Nevertheless, I will have mine intent—

---

294 "It grieves me deeply, because I am most noble."

that I first thought, yet so will I.*
I and two Persons be at one assent   *accord*
a solemn matter for to try.
A full fair image we have i-meant,   *intended*
that the same stead shall multiply.   *place*

     300

In my blessing here I begin
the first that shall be to my pay.*
Lightness and darkness, I bid you twin: *separate*
the dark to the night, the light to the day.
Keep your course, for more or min,   *less*
and suffer not, to you I say;   *stand still*
but save yourself, both out and in.
That is my will, and will alway.   *will be always*

     305

As I have made you all of nought   *from nothing*
at mine own wishing,   *my own desire*
my first day here have I wrought.   *made*
I give it here my blessing.

     310

THE END

296 "What I first thought, yet so will I do."

301-2 "Here, with my blessing, I begin the first of a series of acts which shall be to my pleasure."

PLAY 2: ADAM AND EVE: CAIN AND ABEL

Performed by the Drapers

PLAY 2 deals with the creation of man and with the beginnings of sin among mankind. Man's first and "original" sin is the wilful disobedience of God's known will, mythologised as the eating of the fruit of the Tree of the Knowledge of Good and Evil. For this man is denied eternal life and is expelled from Eden into a harsh world. Within this world in our play the consequences of that sin are enacted in Cain's fratricide of Abel, Man's sin against God being paralleled by his sin against his fellow-Man. The two are linked in Eve's self-recrimination when Cain returns to his parents before going into exile.

The material in the play derives from the book of Genesis. The continuation of creation, reverting to the first day, is in Genesis 1.1–2.2; the creation and fall of man in 2.4–3.4; and Cain's killing of Abel in 4.2–15. But into this bleak picture of human destiny the playwright inserts a promise of hope in Adam's account to his children of the vision of the future which he had in paradise during Eve's creation, a prophecy which was well established in the traditions of the Church.

The Post-Reformation Banns make it clear that this was a production of great cost and spectacle. The waggon for the play is called "Paradyce" in the Pre-Reformation Banns and seems to have represented the Garden of Eden. The Banns also speak of "the Mappa Mundi," perhaps a large cloth-map of the earth. Modern productions have successfully enacted creation using large painted cloths, which would be appropriate in a production by the Drapers, though emblematic stars, carried by angels have also been successfully employed. The Garden must have the Trees of Knowledge and of Life in the middle, the former with the traditional but unbiblical apple as its fruit. The waggon also has a trap-door through which the Serpent enters.

Though it would be possible to play Cain and Abel against the same "Garden of Eden" set, it would surely seem awkward. The passage of time in the text is covered by music from the minstrels and it would be possible at this point to make some changes to the set on the waggon. Possibly further backcloths were used to change the setting. No provision seems to be made for the removal of Abel's body, and the laments of Adam and Eve at the end may well be over it while Cain departs.

It is usually assumed that Adam and Eve (Eve, like all women in the cycle, being played by a boy) wore body-stockings in their pre-lap-sarian state. The Serpent, here given the traditional face of a woman, was obviously a spectacular figure; in modern productions the part is often taken by a woman wearing a close-fitting gown with a long train which represents the snake's tail when she is condemned to go on her belly. God and the cherubim who guard Eden with fiery swords are richly dressed and awe-inspiring, contrasting with Adam and Eve who, on their expulsion, are clad in skins. If indeed there is an interval after the expulsion, Adam and Eve may leave and re-enter wearing more contemporary costume and carrying the emblems of their labour, the spade and the distaff. Their children likewise seem to be contemporary country folk.

For the director this play offers occasions for scenically spectacular effects. For musicians instrumental music underlines key dramatic moments. And for actors there is the challenge of a wide range of emotions. The temptation in particular requires careful timing and finely modulated delivery.

Cast   GOD, ADAM, DEVIL/SERPENT, EVE, FIRST ANGEL, SECOND ANGEL, THIRD ANGEL, FOURTH ANGEL, CAIN, ABEL.

Minstrels play.

GOD   Ego sum alpha et omega,   *I am alpha and omega*
              primus et novissimus.   *the first and the last*

              I, God, most of majesty,   *greatest in royal power*
              in whom beginning none may be;
              endless also, most of posty,   *power*
              I am and have been ever.

5   Now Heaven and Earth is made through me.
the Earth is void only, I see;
therefore light for more lee   *greater happiness*
through my might I will kever.   *secure*

      At my bidding made be light.
10   Light is good, I see in sight.
Twinned shall be through my might   *separated*
the light from thesterness.   *darkness*
Light "day" I will be called ay,   *always*
and thesterness "night," as I say.   *darkness*
15   Thus morn and even, the first day,
is made full and express.   *complete and clear*

      Now will I make the firmament
in midst the waters to be lent,   *placed*
for to be a divident   *divider*
20   to twin the waters ay;   *separate; always*
above the welkin, beneath also,   *sky*
and "heaven" it shall be called tho.   *then*
Thus comen is morn and even also   *come; evening*
of the second day.

25   Now will I waters everychone   *desire; every one*
that under heaven been great wone,   *in abundance*
that they gather into one,
and dryness soon them show.   *at once reveal*
That dryness "earth" men shall call.
30   The gathering of the waters all
"seas" to name have they shall;   *for their name*
thereby men shall them know.

      I will on earth that herbs spring,   *plants*
each one in kind seed-giving;   *by nature*
35   trees diverse fruits forth bring
after their kind each one;   *according to their nature*
the seed of which ay shall be   *always*
within the fruit of each tree.
Thus morn and even of day three
40   is both comen and gone.   *come*

      Now will I make through my might
lightnings in the welkin bright,   *lights*
to twin the day from the night   *separate*

and lighten the Earth with lee.	*gladden;happiness*
45 Great lights I will two—	*desire*
the sun and eke the moon also—	*in addition*
the sun for day to serve for oo	*ever*
the moon for night to be.	

Stars also through mine intent	
50 I will make on the firmament,	
the Earth to lighten there they	*illuminate;where*
be lent	*placed*
and known may be thereby	
courses of planets, nothing amiss.	
Now see I this work good iwiss.	*indeed*
55 Thus morning and even both made is,	
the fourth day, fully.	

Now will I in waters fish forth bring,	
fowls in the firmament flying,	*birds*
great whales in the sea swimming;	
60 all make I with a thought—	
beasts, fowls, fruit, stone, and tree.	
These works are good, well I see.	
Therefore to bless all well liketh me,	*pleases me well*
this work that I have wrought.	*made*

65 All beasts, I bid you multiply	
in earth and water by and by,	
and fowls in the air to fly.	*birds*
the Earth to fulfill.	*populate*
Thus morn and even through my might	
70 of the fifth day and the night	
is made and ended well aright,	*most appropriately*
all at my own will.	

Now will I on earth bring forth anon	*at once*
all helply beasts, everychone	*helpful;every one*
75 that creepen, flyen, or gone,	*creep, fly or walk*
each one in his kind.	*species*
Now is this done at my bidding:	
beasts going, flying, and creeping;	*walking*
and all my work at my liking	*to my delight*
80 fully now I find.	

*Then, going from the place where he was, he cometh to the
place where he createth Adam.*

	Now Heaven and Earth is made express,	*evident*
	make we Man to our likeness.	
	Fish, fowl, beast—more and less—	*bird; great; small*
	to master he shall have might.	
85	To our shape now make I thee;	
	man and woman I will there be.	
	Grow and multiply shall ye,	
	and fulfill the earth on height.	*populate; completely*

To help thee thou shalt have here

90 herbs, trees, fruit, seed in fere.   *plants; together*

All shall be put in thy power,

and beasts eke also;   *in addition*

all that in Earth been living,   *are*

fowls in the air flying,   *birds*

95 and all that ghost hath and liking,   *spirit; desire*

to sustain you from woe.

Now this is done, I see, aright,   *correctly*

and all things made through my might.

The sixth day here in my sight

100 is made all of the best.

Heaven and Earth is wrought all within

and all that needs to be therein.*

Tomorrow, the seventh day, I will blin   *cease*

and of works take my rest.   *from*

105 But this man that I have made,

with ghost of life I will him glad.   *spirit; gladden*

Adam rising.

Rise up, Adam, rise up rade,   *quickly*

a man of soul and life,

and come with me to Paradise,

└ not made in Paradise !

101-2 "Heaven and earth and all that needs to be in them is completed within
the space of the sixth day." The reading *with win*, "with joy," found in three
manuscripts, is also possible.

110   a place of dainty and delice.   *pleasure; delight*
            But it is good that thou be wise;
            bring not thyself in strife.

            Then the Creator bringeth Adam into Paradise, before the Tree
            of Knowledge, and saith (Minstrels play):

            Here, Adam, I give thee this place,
            thee to comfort and solace,   *cheer*
115   to keep it well while thou it has,
            and done as I thee bid.   *do*
            Of all trees that been herein   *are*
            thou shalt eat, and nothing sin;   *in no way*
            but of this tree, for weal nor win,   *riches nor joy*
120   thou eat by no way.   *by no means*

            What time thou eatest of this tree,
            death thee behoves, leave thou me,   *believe*
            Therefore this fruit I will thee flee[*]
            and be thou not too bold.
125   Beasts and fowls that thou may see   *birds*
            to thee obedient shall they be.
            What name they be given by thee,
            that name they shall hold.

            Then God taketh Adam by the hand and causeth him to lie
            down and taketh a rib out of his side, and saith:

            It is not good man only to be;   *alone*
130   help to him now make we.   *for*
            But excite sleep behoves me   *induce*
            anon in this man here.

            He sleeps.

            On sleep thou art, well I see.
            Here a bone I take of thee,
135   and flesh also, with heart free,   *happy*
            to make thee a fere.   *mate*

---

123 "Therefore it is my will that you should shun this fruit."

Then God doth make the woman of the rib of Adam. Then Adam waking saith to God:

ADAM	A, Lord! Where have I long been?	
	For sithence I slept, much have I seen—	*since*
	wonder that withouten ween	*without doubt*
140	hereafter shall be wist.*	*known*

GOD	Rise up, Adam, and awake.	
	Here have I formed thee a make;	*for you; mate*
	her to thee thou shalt take	
	and name her as thee list.	*you please*

Adam, rising up, saith:

ADAM	I see well, Lord, through thy grace	
146	bone of my bones thou her mase;	*from; makes*
	and flesh of my flesh she has,	
	and my shape through thy saw.	*word*
	Therefore she shall be called, iwiss.	*indeed*
150	"virago," nothing amiss;*	
	for out of man taken she is,	
	and to man she shall draw.	

	Of earth thou madest first me,	
	both bone and flesh; now I see	
155	thou hast her given through thy posty	*power*
	of that I in me had.*	
	Therefore man kindly shall forsake	*by natural process*
	father and mother and to wife take;	*cleave to his wife*
	two in one flesh, as thou can make,	
160	either other for to glad.	*gladden*

137–40 Adam's ecstasy, in which his soul—as yet sinless—was ravished into heaven to receive intimations of divine intention, was a well-established tradition. His vision is described at 437–72.

150 " 'Virago', appropriately." *virago*, Latin "woman," is the term used in the Vulgate (Genesis 2.23) and its appropriateness is there explained by relating its etymology to *vir*, Latin "man."

156 "Some of what I had within me."

*Then Adam and Eve shall stand naked and shall not be
ashamed. Then the Serpent shall come up out of a hole, and
the Devil, walking, shall say:*

DEVIL	Out, Out! What sorrow is this,	
	that I have lost so much bliss?	
	For once I thought to do amiss,	
	out of Heaven I fell.	
165	The brightest angel I was or this,	*before*
	that ever was or yet is;	
	but pride cast me down, iwiss,	*truly*
	from Heaven right into Hell.	

moral lesson *

	Ghostly Paradise I was in,*	
170	but thence I fell through sin.	
	Of Earthly Paradise now, as I ween,	*understand*
	a man is given mastery.	
	By Beelzabub, I will never blin	*cease*
	till I may make him by some gin	*trick*
175	from that place for to twin	*part*
	and trespass as did I.	*sin*

	Should such a caitiff made of clay	*wretch*
	have such bliss? Nay, by my lay!	*law*
	For I shall teach his wife a play	
180	and I may have a while.	*if; space of time*
	For her to deceive I hope I may,	*believe*
	and through her bring them both away;	
	for she will do as I her say.	*because*
	Her hope I will beguile.	*expectation; deceive*

185	That woman is forbidden to do	*what*
	for anything they will thereto.	*go to it*
	Therefore, that tree she shall come to	
	and assay which it is.	*try what kind*
	Dight me I will anone tyte*	
190	and proffer her of that ilk fruit;	*some of that same*
	so shall they both for her delight	

---

169 The Devil distinguishes the Spiritual Paradise of heaven, occupied by the
angels, from the Earthly Paradise of Eden, created for Man.

189 "I will prepare myself at once quickly."

be banished from that bliss.

	A manner of an adder is in this place	*kind*
	that wings like a bird she has—	
195	feet as an adder, a maiden's face—*	
	her kind I will take.	*nature*
	And of the Tree of Paradise	*i.e., of Knowledge*
	she shall eat through my cointise,	*cunning*
	for women, they be full licorous.	*most greedy*
200	That will she not forsake.	*renounce*

	And eat she of it, full witterly	*if; most certainly*
	they shall fare both as did I—	
	be banished both of that valley	*from*
	and her offspring for ay.	*ever*
205	Therefore, as broke I my pon,	*sure as; my skull*
	the adder's coat I will take on;	*(my head*
	and into Paradise I will gone	*go*
	as fast as ever I may.	

*Upper part of the body with feather of a bird; serpent, by shape in the foot; in figure, a girl.**

SERPENT	Woman, why was God so nice	*foolish*
210	to bid you leave for your delice	*refrain; delight*
	and of each tree in Paradise	
	to forsake the meat?	*avoid; food*

EVE	Nay, of the fruit of each tree	
	for to eat good leave have we,	*full consent*
215	save the fruit of one we must flee;	*except that; shun*
	of it may we not eat.	

	This tree here that in the midst is—	*middle*
	eat we of this, we do amiss.	*if we eat*
	God said we should die iwiss	*certainly*
220	and if we touch that tree.	*if*

SERPENT	Woman, I say, lieve not this;	*believe*

---

195 and 208+SD The serpent was held to be erect before the Fall, and exegetes such as Bede considered it to have a woman's face, which enabled it to establish a rapport with Eve.

for it shall ye not lose this bliss
nor no joy that is his,
but be as wise as he.

225	God is subtle and wise of wit	*cunning*
	and wotteth well when ye eat it	*knows*
	that your een shall be unknit.	*eyes;opened*
	Like gods ye shall be	
	and know both good, and evil also.	
230	Therefore he warned you therefro.	*from it*
	Ye may well wot he was your foe;	*know*
	therefore, do after me.	*as I say*

	Take of this fruit and assay;	*try it*
	it is good meat, I dare lay.	*food;wager*
235	And, but thou find it to thy pay,	*unless;pleasure*
	say that I am false.	
	Take thou one apple, and noe moe,	*more*
	and ye shall know both weal and woe	*happiness*
	and be like gods both two,	
240	thou and thy husband als.	*also*

EVE	Ah, Lord, this tree is fair and bright,	
	green and seemly to my sight,	*beautiful*
	the fruit sweet and much of might,	*of great power*
	that gods it may us make.	
245	One apple of it I will eat	
	to assay which is the meat;*	
	and my husband I will get	
	one morsel for to take.	

Then Eve shall take some of the fruit from the Serpent, and shall eat thereof, and say to Adam:

EVE	Adam, husband lief and dear,	*beloved*
250	eat some of this apple here.	
	It is fair, my lief fere;	*beloved husband*
	it may thou not forsake.	*reject*

ADAM	That is sooth, Eve, withouten were,	*true;without doubt*
	the fruit is sweet and passing fair.	
255	Therefore I will do thy prayer—	*what you ask*

---

246 "To test what kind of food it is."

one morsel I will take.

Then Adam shall take the fruit and eat thereof, and in weeping manner shall say:

ADAM	Out, alas! What aileth me?	
	I am naked, well I see.	
	Woman, cursed mote thou be,	*may*
260	for we be both now shent.	*destroyed*
	I wot not for shame whither to flee,	*know*
	for this fruit was forbidden me.	
	Now have I broken, through read of thee,	*counsel*
	my Lord's commandment.	

EVE	Alas, this adder hath done me noy!	*harm*
266	Alas, her read why did I?	*counsel*
	Naked we been both forthy,	*therefore*
	and of our shape ashamed.	

ADAM	Yea, sooth said I in prophecy	*the truth*
270	when thou was taken of my body	*from*
	man's woe thou would be witterly;	*certainly*
	therefore thou was so named.*	

EVE	Adam, husband, I read we take	*suggest*
	these fig-leaves for shame's sake,	
275	and to our members an hilling make	*covering*
	of them for thee and me.	

ADAM	And therewith my members I will hide,	
	and under this tree I will abide;	
	for surely, come God us beside,	*if God should come*
280	out of this place shall we.	*we must go*

Then Adam and Eve shall cover their members with leaves, hiding themselves under the trees. Then God shall speak (Minstrels play).

GOD	**Adam**, Adam, where art thou?

ADAM	A, Lord! I heard thy voice now.	
	For I am naked, I make avow,	*confess*

---

272 I.e., man's woe = woe-man = woman.

therefore now I hid me.

GOD 286	Who told thee, Adam, thou naked was save only thine own trespass, that of the tree thou eaten has that I forbade thee.	*sin*

ADAM 290	Lord, this woman that is here— that thou gave me to my fere— gave me part, at her prayer, and of it I did eat.	*partner* *entreaty*

GOD	Woman, why hast thou done so?	

EVE 295	This adder, Lord, she was my foe and soothly me deceived tho, and made me to eat that meat.	*truly; then* *food*

GOD 300	Adder, for that thou hast done this annoy, amongst all beasts on Earth thee by cursed thou shalt be forthy, for this woman's sake. Upon thy breast thou shalt go, and eat the earth to and fro; and enmity between you two I ensure thee I shall make.	*committed* *grievance* *beside you* *therefore* *assure*

305 310	Between thy seed and hers also I shall excite thy sorrow and woe; to break thy head and be thy foe, she shall have mastery ay. No beast on Earth, I thee behet,[*] that Man so little shall of set; and trodden be full under feet for thy misdeed today.	*ever* *animal; promise* *esteem* *utterly*

Then the Serpent shall withdraw, making a noise like a snake.

GOD	And, woman, I warn thee witterly,	*certainly*

309–12 The construction is elliptical. "There shall be no animal on Earth, I promise you, that Man shall esteem so little, and you shall be trodden under foot utterly for your misdeed today."

(*to Eve*)	thy much pain I shall multiply—	*great*
315	with pains, sorrow, and great annoy	*anguish*
	thy children thou shall bear.	
	And for that thou hast done so today,	
	man shall master thee alway;	*dominate*
	and under his power thou shalt be ay,	*always*
320	thee for to drive and dere.	*direct; discipline*

GOD	And, man, also I say to thee—	
(*to Adam*)	for thou hast not done after me,	*as I said*
	thy wife's counsel for to flee,	
	but done so her bidding	
325	to eat the fruit of this tree,	
	in thy work warried the earth shall be;	*cursed*
	and with great travail behoves thee	*it behoves*
	on Earth to get thy living.	

	When thou on earth travailed has,	
330	fruit shall not grow in that place;	
	but thorns, briers for thy trespass	*sin*
	to thee on earth shall spring.	
	Herbs, roots thou shalt eat	*plants*
	and for thy sustenance sore sweat	
335	with great mischief to win thy meat,	*misfortune; food*
	nothing to thy liking.	*not at all*

	Thus shall thou live, sooth to sayen,	*truth to tell*
	for thou hast been to me unbain,	*disobedient*
	ever, till the time thou turn again	
340	to earth there thou came fro.	*where*
	For earth thou art, as well is seen;	
	and after this work, woe and teen,	*suffering*
	to earth there thou shalt, withouten ween,*	
	and all thy kind also.	

Adam shall speak mourningly.	*mournfully*

ADAM	Alas, now in languor am I lent!	*cast in despair*
346	Alas, now shamely am I shent!	*shamefully; destroyed*
	For I was unobedient,	*disobedient*
	of weal now am I waived.	*from joy; banished*

343–44 "You, and all your race as well, shall assuredly [return] to the earth there."

	Now all my kind by me is kent	*race; instructed*
350	to flee women's enticement.	
	Who trusteth them in any intent,	
	truly he is deceived.	

	My licorous wife hath been my foe;	*greedy*
	the Devil's envy shent me also.	*destroyed*
355	These two together well may go,	*accord*
	the sister and the brother!	
	His wrath hath done me much woe;	
	her gluttony grieved me also.	*harmed*
	God let never man trust you two,	
360	the one more than the other.	

GOD	Now we shall part from this lee.	*depart; joy*
	Hilled behoveth you to be.	*you must be covered*
	Dead beasts' skins, as thinketh me,	*it seems to me*
	is best you on you bear.	
365	For deadly now both been ye	*mortal*
	and death no way may you flee.	*shun*
	Such clothes are best for your degree	*condition*
	and such shall ye wear.	

Then God, putting garments of skins upon them:

GOD	Adam, now hast thou thy willing,	*desire*
370	for thou desired over all thing	
	of good and evil to have knowing;	
	now wrought is all thy will.	*accomplished; desire*
	Thou wouldest know both weal and woe;	*joy*
	now is it fallen to thee so.	
375	Therefore hence thou must go,	
	and thy desire fulfill.	

	Now, lest thou covetest more	
	and do as thou hast done before—	
	eat of this fruit—to live evermore	
380	here may thou not be.	
	To Earth thither thou must gone;	*go*
	with travail lead thy life thereon,	*labour*
	for sicker, there is no other won.	*certainly; dwelling*
	Go forth; take Eve with thee.	

> *Then God shall drive Adam and Eve out of Paradise, and saith
> to the Angel (Minstrels play):*

GOD	Now will I that there leng within	*remain*
386	the Angels' order Cherubim,	
	to keep this place of weal and win	*happiness;joy*
	that Adam lost thus hath,	
	with sharp swords on every side	
390	and flame of fire here to abide,	
	that never an earthly man in glide;	*mortal;go*
	for given they been that grace.*	

1ST ANGEL	Lord, that order that is right	
	is ready set here in thy sight,	
395	with flame of fire, ready to fight	
	against Mankind, thy foe,	
	to whom no grace is claimed by right.	*for;by justice*
	Shall none of them bide in thy sight	*stay*
	till Wisdom, Right, Mercy and Might	
400	shall buy them, and other moe.*	*redeem;others;more*

2ND ANGEL	I, Cherubim, must here be chise	*solicitous*
	to keep this place of great price.	*worth*
	Sithen man was so unwise,	*since*
	this wonning I must were—	*dwelling;defend*
405	that he by craft or cointise	*skill or cunning*
	shall not come in that was his,	*into what*
	but deprived be of Paradise,	
	no more for to come there.	

3RD ANGEL	And in this heritage I will be,	*inheritance*
410	freely for to ever see	*nobly*
	that no man come in this city	*mortal*
	as God hath me behight.	*commanded*
	Swords of fire have all we	

---

392 "For they (the Cherubim) are granted that special privilege, to keep that place."

398–400 An allusion to the debate of the Daughters of God; cf. Psalms 84 (AV 85).11: "Mercy and truth are met together; righteousness and peace have kissed each other," which provided the basis for an allegorical debate between these ostensibly conflicting attributes of God in medieval literature.

	to make Man from this place to flee,	
415	from this dwelling of great dainty	*pleasure*
	that to him first was dight.	*prepared*

4TH ANGEL	And of this order I am made one,	
	from Mankind to were this wone	*defend this dwelling*
	that through his guilt hath forgone	*forfeited*
420	this wonning full of grace.	*dwelling*
	Therefore depart they must each one.	
	Our swords of fire shall be there boun	*ready*
	and myself their very fone,	*foe*
	to flame them in the face.	*burn*

Minstrels play.

ADAM	High God and highest king	
426	that of nought made all thing—	
	beast, fowl, and grass growing—	*animal; bird*
	and me of earth made,	
	thou gave me grace to do thy willing.	*desire*
430	For after great sorrow and siking	*sighing*
	thou hast me lent great liking,	*given; joy*
	two sons my heart to glad—	*gladden*

	Cain and Abel, my children dear,	
	whom I gat within thirty year	*begat*
435	after the time we deprived were	
	of Paradise for our pride.	
	Therefore now them I will lere,	*teach*
	to make them know in good manner	*well*
	what I saw when Eve, my fere,	*partner*
440	was taken of my side.	*from*

	While that I slept in that place	
	my ghost to Heaven banished was;*	*spirit*
	for to see I there had grace	
	things that shall befall.	
445	To make you ware of cumberous case	
	and let your doing from trespass,*	

---

442 See above, 137–40.

445–46 "In order to make you aware of dangerous circumstances and to keep your deeds from sin."

some I will tell before your face,
but I will not tell all.

I wot by things that I there see   *know; saw*
450   that God will come from Heaven on high
to overcome the Devil so sly
and light into my kind;   *alight; race*
and my blood that he will win
that I so lost for my sin;
455   a New Law there shall begin˙ ✳
and so men shall it find.

Water or fire also witterly   *certainly*
all this world shall destroy,
for men shall sin so horribly
460   and do full much amiss.
Therefore, that ye may escape that noy,   *harm*
do well and be ware me by.   *warned*
I tell you here in prophecy
that this will fall, iwiss.   *indeed*

465   Also I see, as I shall say,   *saw*
that God will come the last day
to deem Mankind in flesh verray,   *judge; real*
and flame of fire burning—
the good to Heaven, the evil to Hell.
470   Your children this tale ye may tell.
This sight saw I in Paradise or I fell,   *before*
as I lay there sleeping.

Now will I tell how ye shall do
God's love to underfoe.   *receive*
475   Cain, husband's craft thou must   *husbandman's trade*
     go to;   *apply yourself*
and Abel, a shepherd be.
Therefore of corns fair and clean   *ears of corn*
that grows on ridges out of rain,   *furrows*
Cain, thou shalt offer, as I mean,   *intend*
480   to God in majesty.

And Abel, while thy life may last
thou shalt offer—and do my hest—   *obey my command*

---

455 *New Law*—i.e., as opposed to the Old Law of the Jews.

to God the first-born beast;   *animal*
thereto thou make thee boun.   *ready*
485   Thus shall ye please God almight
if ye do this well and right,
with good heart in his sight
and full devotion.   *total*

Now for to get you sustenance
490   I will you teach without distance.   *assuredly*
For sithen I feel that mischance   *since; misfortune*
of that fruit for to eat,
my lief children fair and free,   *dear; noble*
with this spade that ye may see
495   I have dolven. Learn this at me,   *dug; from*
how ye shall win your meat.   *get; food*

> *Then Adam shall till the earth and shall teach his sons, and*
> *Eve shall have a distaff.*

EVE   My sweet children, darlings dear,
ye shall see how I live here
because unbuxom so we were   *disobedient*
500   and did as God ne would.   *willed it not*
This pain thereas had been no need.   *otherwise*
I suffer on Earth for my misdeed.
and of this wool I will spin thread by thread,
to hill me from the cold.   *cover*

505   Another sorrow I suffer also:
my children must I bear with woe,   *suffering*
as I have done both you two;
and so shall women all.
This was the Devil, our bitter foe,
510   that made us out of joy to go.
To please God, sons, therefore be throw,   *eager*
in sin that ye ne fall.

CAIN   Mother, for sooth I tell it thee,   *truth*
a tillman I am, and so will be.   *farmer*
515   As my father hath taught it me,
I will fulfill his lore.   *carry out his teaching*

> *Here he brings in the plough.*

CAIN   Of corn I have great plenty;

	sacrifice to God—soon shall ye see—	
-------	--------------------------------------	
	I will make, to look if he	
520	will send me any more.	

ABEL And I will with devotion
to my sacrifice make me boun. *ready*
The comeliest beast, by my crown, *fairest animal*
to the Lord I will choose *for*
525 and offer it before thee here
meekly in good manner. *in an appropriate fashion*
No beast to thee may be dear *animal*
that may I not lose.

Here Adam and Eve go out till Cain have slain Abel.

CAIN I am the elder of us two;
530 therefore first I will go.
Such as the fruit is fallen fro *from*
is good enough for him.
This corn standing, as mote I thee, *growing; so may I thrive*
was eaten with beasts, men may see. *by animals*
535 God, thou gettest no other of me,
be thou never so grim. *however angry you may be*

It were pity, by my pen, *would be; head*
those fair ears for to bren, *burn*
Therefore the Devil hang me then
540 and thou of it get ought. *if*
This earless corn grew next the way; *next to*
of these offer I will today.
For clean corn, by my fay, *by my faith*
of me gettest thou nought. *from; not a bit*

545 Lo, God, here may thou see
such corn as grew to me.
Part of it I bring to thee
anon withouten let.*
I hope thou wilt quite me this *repay me for*
550 and send me more of worldly bliss;
else forsooth thou dost amiss *indeed*
and thou be in my debt. *should be*

---

548 "At once, without hesitation."

Then Abel will sacrifice his beasts.

ABEL   Now my brother, as I see,
      hath done sacrifice to thee.
555   Offer I will, as falleth for me,   *befits me*
      such as thou hast me sent.
      The best beast, as mote I thee,   *so may I thrive*
      of all my flock with heart free   *willing*
      to thee offered it shall be.
560   Receive, Lord, my present.

Then a flame of fire shall descend upon the sacrifice of Abel.

ABEL   Ah, high God, and king of bliss,
      now soothly know I well by this   *truly*
      my sacrifice accepted is
      before the Lord today.
565   A flame of fire thou sent has
      from Heaven on high into this place.
      I thank thee, Lord, of thy grace   *for*
      and so shall I do ay.   *ever*

CAIN   Out, out! How have I spent my good? *portion*
570   To see this sight I wax near wood. *grow almost mad*
      A flame of fire from Heaven stood
      on my brother's offering.
      His sacrifice I see God takes,
      and mine refuses and forsakes.
575   My semblant for shame shakes   *form*
      for envy of this thing.

GOD   Cain, why art thou wroth, why?   *angry*
(*to Cain*) Thy semblant changes wondrously. *countenance*
      If thou do well and truly,
580   thou may have meed of me.   *reward*
      Wots thou not well that for thy deed *know*
      if thou do well thou may have meed; *reward*
      if thou do foul, foul for to speed
      and sicker thereof to be?*

583–84 "If you act wickedly, you may fare badly, and may be certain of that."
The infinitives, "to speed" and "to be," require a modal verb such as "may" to
be understood.

585	But, Cain, thou shalt have all thy will,	*desire*
	thy talent if thou wilt fulfill.	*innate potential*
	Sin of it will thee spill	*against it; destroy*
	and make thee evil to speed.	*to fare badly*
	Thy brother buxom ay shall be	*obedient; ever*
590	and fully under thy posty;	*power*
	the lust thereof pertains to thee.*	
	Advise thee of thy deed.	*think about*

CAIN   Ah! Well, well! Is it so?
        Come forth with me. Thou must go
595   into the field a little fro;   *a little way away*
        I have an errand to say.   *message*

ABEL   Brother, to thee I am ready   *for you*
        to go with thee full meekly.
        For thou art elder than am I,
600   thy will I will do ay.   *ever*

CAIN   Say, thou caitif, thou congeon,   *wretch; imbecile*
        weenest thou to pass me of renown?   *think; surpass in*
        Thou shalt fail, by my crown,
        of mastery, if I may.   *in dominance; can (stop it)*
605   God hath challenged me now here
        for thee, and that in foul manner;   *because of you*
        and that shalt thou abide full dear   *pay for; dearly*
        or that thou wend away.   *before; go*

        Thy offering God accepted has.
610   I see by fire that on it was.
        Shalt thou never eft have such grace,   *again*
        for die thou shalt this night.
        Though God stood in this place
        for to help thee in this case,
615   thou should die before his face.
        Have this, and get thee right!

Then Cain killeth his brother Abel; and God, coming, saith (Minstrels play):

GOD   Cain, where is thy brother Abel?

589–91 "Your brother shall always be obedient and entirely under your authority; the enjoyment of that rests with you."

CAIN   I wot ne'er; I cannot tell   *know never*
           of my brother. Wots thou not well   *know*
620   that I of him had no keeping?   *control*

GOD   What hast thou done, thou wicked man?
           Thy brother's blood asks thee upon
           vengeance, as fast as it can,
           from earth to me crying.

625   Cain, cursed on Earth thou shalt be ay.   *ever*
           For thy deed thou hast done today,
           earth warried shall be in thy work ay   *cursed; always*
           that wickedly hast wrought.
           And for that thou hast done this mischief,   *evil*
630   to all men thou shalt be unlief,   *hateful*
           idle and wandering as a thief
           and overall set at nought.   *esteemed as nothing*

                Cain speaketh mournfully.

CAIN   Out, alas! Where may I be?
           Sorrow on each side I see.
635   For if I out of the land flee
           from men's company,
           beasts I wot will werry me.   *know; gnaw*
           And if I leng, by my lewty,   *stay; by my truth*
           I must be bond, and nothing free—   *a bondman*
640   and all for my folly!

           For my sin so horrible is,
           and I have done too much amiss,
           that unworthy I am, iwiss,   *indeed*
           forgiveness to attain.
645   Well I wot wherever I go   *know*
           whoso meets me will me slow,   *slay*
           and each man will be my foe.
           No grace to me may gain.   *be a help*

GOD   Nay, Cain, thou shalt not die soon,
650   horribly if thou have ay done.   *even if; always*
           That is not thy brother's boon,   *prayer*
           thy blood for to shed.
           But, forsooth, whosoever slayeth thee   *truly*
           sevenfold punished he shall be,

655	and great pain may thou not flee for thy wicked deed.	
	But for thou to this deed was boun, thou and thy children trust mon—	
660	into the seventh generation— punishment for the whole.*	
	For thou today has done so,	
	thy seed for thee shall suffer woe;	*descendents*
	and while thou on Earth may go	
	of vengeance have thy dole.	*you shall have; portion*
CAIN	Out, out! Alas, alas!	
666	I am damned without grace.	
	Therefore I will from place to place	*will (go)*
	and look where is the best.	
	Well I wot, and witterly,	*know; certainly*
670	into what place that come I,	
	each man will loathe my company;	
	so shall I never have rest.	
	Foul hap is me befall:	*evil fortune*
	whether I be in house or hall	
675	"Cursed Cain" men will me call.	
	From sorrow may none me save.	
	But yet will I, or I go,	*before*
	speak with my dame and sire also,	*mother and father*
	And their maleson both two	*curse*
680	I wot well I must have.*	*know*
	Dame and sire, rest you well,	
	for one foul tale I can you tell.	
	I have slain my brother Abel	
	as we fell in a strife.	
ADAM	Alas, alas! Is Abel dead?	
686	Alas, rueful is my read!	*sorrowful; destiny*

657–60 "But because you were prepared to do this deed, you and your children
may expect—into the seventh generation—punishment for all your sinful acts."

677–80 The meeting of Cain with his parents is unbiblical, but serves to link the
murder of Abel with the Fall of Man, as Eve recognises at 689–96.

| | No more joy to me is led, | *given* |
| | save only Eve my wife. | |

EVE | Alas! Now is my son slain? | |
690 | Alas, marred is all my main! | *destroyed;power* |
     | Alas, must I never be fain | *happy* |
     | but in woe and mourning? | |
     | Well I wot and know iwiss | *know;indeed* |
     | that verray vengeance it is. | *just* |
695 | For I to God so did amiss, | |
     | mon I never have liking. | *must;pleasure* |

CAIN | Yea, dame and sire, farewell ye! | |
     | For out of land I will flee. | |
     | A losel ay I must be, | *scoundrel ever* |
700 | for scaped I am of thrift.* | |
     | For so God hath told me, | |
     | that I shall never thrive ne thee. | *nor prosper* |
     | And now I flee, all ye may see. | |
     | I grant you all the same gift. | |

THE END

---

700 "For I am escaped from the means of earning my livelihood." Cain has, in fact, become a "scapethrift" or "waster."

PLAY 3: NOAH'S FLOOD

Performed by the Waterleaders and Drawers of Dee[*]

THE THEME OF MAN'S separation from God through sin continues in play 3 with the account of the destruction of all living things by a great flood sent from God in his anger against sinful mankind. Only Noah and his wife, and his three sons and their wives are spared, because of their righteousness, and are entrusted with the responsibility of building a boat, the ark, in which breeding specimens of all animal species will be preserved to re-stock the earth when the flood subsides. The grace shown to Noah is the first sign of God's mercy to his servants, and God's promise of greater forbearance in future is confirmed in the final vision of the rainbow.

The main events in the play derive from Genesis 6.1–9.17, but in common with other playwrights, the Chester dramatist transforms the universal flood into a more manageable episode of domestic relationships, focusing in a non-biblical fashion upon Noah's independently-minded wife (played by a man or boy). The play has as background the town and its society, and Noah should be imagined as a craftsman whose sons are following him into the trade, while his wife is a prosperous burgess's wife with a circle of drinking-companions whom she does not want to abandon to sail in an absurdly designed vessel.

It should perhaps be noted that the major episode of the sending out of the birds is found only in the manuscript of 1607. Its absence from the other four manuscripts may indicate some damage or loss in the

---

Guild-ascription The Waterleaders and Drawers of Dee had the responsibility of bearing water from the River Dee to the people of the city of Chester.

common exemplar, which the final scribes were able to rectify; but it has been noticed that the version of the play without that section is dramatically intelligible. In the version here, the despatch of the birds is included.

The Pre-Reformation Banns enjoin the Waterleaders and Drawers in Dee (an appropriate choice for the play) to "loke that Noyes shipp be sett on hie," and the ark-shaped waggon was clearly the major scenic feature. It has on its sides means to attach the pictures of the animals listed by the family as entering the ark, and Noah raises a mast upon it, perhaps with a sail, and certainly with a pulley-device along which the birds are sent out to see if the flood has abated sufficiently. The ark must have means of access from the ground, since the family is standing beside it at the start of the play, and it is big enough to accommodate the eight characters inside for the duration of the flood. Presumably the construction-work, the episode with the Wife and her Gossips, and the final sacrifice are performed on ground-level.

In addition, the opening stage-direction asks that God be located "in some high place," perhaps a stage separate from the waggon. Perhaps he oversees the whole action of the play, though he may enter only for his speeches and then depart; his presence or absence will, however, have a significant effect upon the audience's perception of the action. The rising waters of the flood have been effectively represented in modern productions by large sheets of blue cloth, moved by "angel" stage-hands, which can be raised to envelop the gossips. The rainbow in modern productions is usually raised up from inside the waggon so that it appears above the ark.

The drinking-song of the Gossips is a raucous affair, to be contrasted with the hymn which the 1607 manuscript requires the Noah family to sing within the ark.

Cast   GOD, NOAH, SHEM, HAM, JAPHET, NOAH'S WIFE, SHEM'S WIFE, HAM'S WIFE, JAPHET'S WIFE, THE GOOD GOSSIPS.

> *And first in some high place—or in the clouds, if it may be—*
> *God speaketh unto Noah standing without the ark with all his*
> *family.*

GOD   I, God, that all this world hath wrought,   *made*
           Heaven and Earth and all of nought,   *from nothing*
           I see my people in deed and thought

are set foul in sin.

5 My ghost shall not leng in mon   *spirit; dwell; man*
  that through flesh-liking is my fone   *fleshly lust; foe*
  —but till six score years   *but not until*
   be comen and gone   *come*
  to look if they will blin.   *cease*

  Man that I made I will destroy,
10 beast, worm, and fowl to fly;*
  for on Earth they do me noy,   *harm*
  the folk that are thereon.
  It harms me so hurtfully,
  the malice that doth now multiply,
15 that sore it grieves me inwardly
  that ever I made mon.   *man*

  Therefore, Noah, my servant free,   *noble*
  that righteous man art as I see,
  a ship soon thou shalt make thee
20 of trees dry and light.
  Little chambers therein thou make
  and binding slutch also thou take;   *sealing mud*
  within and without thou ne slake   *don't be idle*
  to anoint it through all thy might.

25 Three hundred cubits it shall be long
  and fifty broad to make it strong;
  of height sixty. The meet thou fong;*
  thus measure thou it about.
  One window work through thy wit;   *construct*
30 a cubit of length and breadth make it.
  Upon the side a door shall sit,   *be located*
  for to come in and out.   *for coming*

  Eating places thou make also
  three; ronet chambers one or two;   *round*
35 for with water I think to flow   *intend to drown*
  Man that I can mase.   *have made*

---

10 "Animal, reptile, and flying bird." Strictly, "to fly" depends upon "I made" in the preceding line.

27 "Of height sixty. You take the measurement."

	Destroyed all the world shall be—	
	save thou, thy wife, thy sons three,	*except*
	and their wives also with thee—	
40	shall fall before thy face.*	

NOAH	Ah, Lord, I thank thee loud and still	*aloud; and silently*
	that to me art in such will*	
	and spares me and my household	*refrains from*
	to spill,	*destroying*
	as I now soothly find.	*truly*
45	Thy bidding, Lord, I shall fulfill	
	and never more thee grieve ne grill,	*nor provoke*
	that such grace hath sent me till	*to me*
	amongst all Mankind.	

	Have done, you men and women all.	
50	Hie ye, lest this water fall,	*hurry up*
	to work this ship, chamber and hall,	*construct*
	as God hath bidden us do.	

SHEM	Father. I am already boun;	*prepared*
	an axe I have, by my crown,	
55	as sharp as any in all this town	
	for to go thereto.	*get to work on it*

HAM	I have an hatchet wonder keen	*marvellous sharp*
	to bite well, as may be seen;	
	a better ground, as I ween,	*believe*
60	is not in all this town.	

JAPHET	And I can well make a pin*	
	and with this hammer knock it in.	
	Go we work, without more din,	*let's go to work*
	and I am ready boun.	*prepared*
NOAH'S		
WIFE	And we shall bring timber to,	*to (the work)*

---

40 "(The world) shall be destroyed before your eyes."

42 "Who have such good intention towards me."

61 *a pin* - i.e., a wooden peg for securing the boards together. Nails are not used in the construction.

66	for we mon nothing else do,	*may*
	Women been weak to underfo	*undertake*
	any great travail.	*major work*

SHEM'S	Here is a good hackstock;	*chopping block*
WIFE	on this you may hew and knock.	*hammer*
71	Shall none be idle in this flock,	
	ne now may no man fail.	*nor*

HAM'S WIFE	And I will go gather slitch,	
	the ship for to clam and pitch.	
75	Anoint it must be, every stitch,	
	board, tree, and pin.*	

note here that women are 'helpmeets'

JAPHET'S	And I will gather chips here	
WIFE	to make a fire for you in fere,	*all*
	and for to dight your dinner	*prepare*
80	against you come in.	*for when*

Then Noah beginneth to build the ark.

NOAH	Now in the name of God I begin	
	to make the ship that we shall in,	*must board*
	that we may be ready for to swim	*sail*
	at the coming of the flood.	
85	These boards I pin here together	
	to bear us safe from the weather,	
	that we may row both hither and thither	
	and safe be from this flood.	

*Then Noah with all his family shall make a sign as though
they wrought upon the ship with diverse instruments.*

NOAH	Of this tree will I make the mast	
90	tied with cables that will last,	
	and with a sail-yard for each blast,*	

73–76 "And I will go gather mud to daub and smear the ship with pitch. Every
inch of it must be anointed—the planks, the ribs, the pins." The gaps between
the boards are made watertight with wet clay and sealed with a coat of pitch.

91 *a sail-yard*, i.e., the spar on which the sail is spread. The mast will later serve
as a means of launching the birds; see 276+SD.

and each thing in their kind.   *according to their function*
With topcastle and bowsprit,*
both cords and ropes I have all meet   *appropriate*
95   to sail forth at the next weet. ᵔ ᵂᵉᵗ   *rainstorm*
This ship is at an end.   *complete*

Wife, in this vessel we shall be kept,   *housed*
my children and thou. I would in ye leapt.

NOAH'S   In faith, Noah, I had as lief thou slept.
WIFE   For all thy Frenish fare,
101   I will not do after thy read.*

NOAH   Good wife, do now as I bid.

NOAH'S   By Christ, not or I see more need,   *before*
WIFE   though thou stand all day and stare.

NOAH   Lord, that women be crabbed ay,*
106   and none are meek, I dare well say.
                That is well seen by me today
                in witness of you each one.
                Good wife, let be all this bere   *din*
110   that thou makest in this place here,
                for all they ween that thou art master—   *believe*
                and so thou art, by St. John!

And after that God shall speak to Noah as followeth:

GOD   Noah, take thou thy meny   *household*
                and in the ship hie that ye be;   *hasten*
115   for none so righteous man to me
                is now on Earth living.

---

93 *topcastle and bowsprit,* i.e., a platform on the top of the mast and a spar jutting forward from the prow of the ship.

99–101 "Really, Noah, I'd rather you didn't bother ('slept'). In spite of all your Frenchified goings on, I won't do what you suggest." The Wife pretends that Noah has been elaborately courteous.

105 "Lord, how ill-tempered women always are!"

Of clean beasts with thee thou take*
seven and seven or then thou slake;   *before you stop*
he and she, make to make,   *mate for mate*
120   beleve in that thou bring.   *quickly;into that*

Of beasts unclean two and two,
male and female, bout mo;   *and no more*
of clean fowls seven also,   *birds*
the he and she together;
125   of fowls unclean twain, and no more,   *birds;two*
as I of beasts said before,   *animals*
that mon be saved through my lore,   *must;teaching*
against I send this weather.   *for the time when*

Of all meats that mon be eaten   *foods;may*
130   into the ship look they be getten,   *be got*
for that may be no way forgotten.   *forgotten*
And do this all bedene   *quickly*
to sustain Man and beasts therein   *animals*
ay till the water cease and blin.   *ever;stop*
135   This world is filled full of sin,
and that is now well seen.

Seven days been yet coming;   *are still to come*
you shall have space them in to bring.
After that, it is my liking   *pleasure*
140   Mankind for to annoy.   *grieve*
Forty days and forty nights
rain shall fall for their unrights.   *sins*
And that I have made through my mights   *what;powers*
now think I to destroy.

NOAH   Lord, at your bidding I am bain.   *obedient*
146   Sithen no other grace will gain,   ✲   *since:avail*
it will I fulfill fain,   *eagerly*
for gracious I thee find.
An hundreth winters and twenty   *years*
150   this ship-making tarried have I,
if through amendment thy mercy   *(to see) if*
would fall to Mankind.

---

117 *clean beasts*—the term relates to the Jewish dietary laws.

	Have done, ye men and women all;	*stop*
	hie you lest this water fall,	*hurry*
155	that each beast were in stall	*animal*
	and into the ship brought.	
	Of clean beasts seven shall be,	
	of unclean, two; thus God bade me.	
	The flood is nigh, you may well see;	*near*
160	therefore tarry you nought.	

Then Noah shall go into the ark with all his family, his wife excepted, and the ark must be boarded round about. And on the boards all the beasts and fowls hereafter rehearsed must be painted, so that their words may agree with the pictures.

SHEM	Sir, here are lions, leopards in;	*inside*
	horses, mares, oxen and swine,	
	goats, calves, sheep and kine	*cattle*
	here sitten, thou may see.	*sit*

HAM	Camels, asses, man may find,	
166	buck and doe, hart and hind.	
	And beasts of all manner kind	*all kinds of species*
	here been, as thinketh me.	*it seems to me*

JAPHET	Take here cats and dogs, too,	
170	otters and foxes, fulmarts also;	*polecats*
	hares hopping gaily can go—	
	here, have kale to eat!	*cabbage*

NOAH'S	And here are bears, wolves set;	*located*
WIFE	apes, owls, marmoset,	
175	weasels, squirrels and ferret,	
	here they eaten their meat.	*eat their food*

SHEM'S	Here are beasties in this house;	*animals*
WIFE	here cats maken it crouse;	*make it lively*
	here a ratten, here a mouse	*rat*
180	that standen nigh together.	*stand close*

HAM'S WIFE	And here are fowls less and more—	*birds*
	herons, cranes and bittore,	*bitterns*
	swans, peacocks—and them before	*in front of them*
	meat for this weather.	*food*

| JAPHET'S WIFE 187 | Here are cocks, kites, crows, rooks, ravens, many rows, ducks, curlews. Whoever knows each one in his kind? And here are doves, digggies, drakes, | *species* *ducks* |
| 190 | redshanks running through the lakes— and each fowl that ledden makes in this ship man may find. | *bird; sound* |

| NOAH | Wife, come in. Why stands thou there? Thou art ever froward, that dare I swear. | *impudent* |
| 195 | Come in—in God's half, time it were—* for fear lest that we drown. | |

| NOAH'S WIFE | Yea, sir, set up your sail and row forth with evil hail; for withouten any fail | *bad luck to you* *without a doubt* |
| 200 | I will not out of this town. | |

| | But I have my gossips everychone, one foot further I will not gone. They shall not drown, by Saint John, and I may save their life. | *all my friends* *go* *if* |
| 205 | They loved me full well, by Christ. But thou wilt let them into thy chest, else row thou forth, Noah, when thou list, amd get thee a new wife. | *ship* *wish* |

| NOAH 210 | Shem, son, lo! Thy mother is wrow; by God, such another I do not know. | *angry* |

| SHEM | Father, I shall fetch her in, I trow, withouten any fail. Mother, my father after thee send and bids thee into yonder ship wend. | *trust* *for certain* *sends* *go* |
| 215 | Look up and see the wind, for we been ready to sail. | *look* *are* |

| NOAH'S WIFE | Son, go again to him and say I will not come therein today. | |

---

195 "Come in—for God's sake, it's high time."

NOAH 220	Come in, wife, in twenty devils' way! —or else stand there without.	*outside*
HAM	Shall we all fetch her in?	
NOAH	Yea, sons, in Christ's blessing and mine! I would ye hied you betime for of this flood I stand in doubt.	*made haste; soon* *fear*
GOOD GOSSIPS* 227	The flood comes fleeting in full fast, on every side that spreadeth full far. For fear of drowning I am aghast; good gossip, let us draw near.	*flowing*
230	And let us drink or we depart, for oft-times we have done so. For at one draught thou drinks a quart, and so will I do or I go.	*before* *before*
235	Here is a pottle full of Malmsey* good and strong; it will rejoice both heart and tongue. Though Noah think us never so long,* yet we will drink atite.	*tankard* *gladden* *quickly*
JAPHET 240	Mother, we pray you all together— for we are here, your own childer— come into the ship for fear of the weather, for his love that you bought.	*children*
NOAH'S WIFE	That will I not for all your call, but I have my gossips all.	*shouting* *unless; friends*

224+SH The 1592 manuscript here reads "The Good Gossips' Song." It is not clear whether all or part of what follows constitutes a song, or if the reference is a cue for a song which is not specified but is sung by the Gossips as they approach. 227 indicates that, despite the plural heading, only one Gossip is speaking at the start, apparently to a second (228). Any song was surely a drinking song, and hence an effective contrast to the sacred song specified for Noah and his family in the 1607 manuscript at 260+SD (see note).

233 *Malmsey* A very sweet Madeira wine.

235 "Though Noah may think we're taking ever such a long time."

SHEM   In faith, mother, yet thou shall,
             whether thou will or nought.   *not*

             Then she shall go.

NOAH   Welcome, wife, into this boat.

NOAH'S   Have thou that for thy note!   *reward*
WIFE
             And she gives him a blow.

NOAH   Aha, marry, this is hot!   *violent*
             It is good to be still.
             Ah, children, methink my boat remeves,   *is moving off*
250   Our tarrying here me highly grieves.   *deeply*
             Over the land the water spreads.
             God do as he will.   *may God do*

             Then they sing, and Noah shall speak again.

NOAH   Ah, great God, that art so good,
             that worchis not thy will is wood.   *works; mad*
255   Now all this world is on a flood,
             as I see well in sight.
             This window I will shutt anon,   *at once*
             and into my chamber I will gone   *go*
             till this water, so great won,   *quantity*
260   be slacked through thy might.   *diminished*

             *Then shall Noah shut the window of the ark and for a little
             space within the boards they shall sing the psalm "Save me, O
             God"; and afterward opening the window and looking round
             about, saying:*

             Now forty days are fully gone.
             Send a raven I will anon,   *at once*

260+SD The direction here is supplied from the 1607 manuscript. That in the 1591
manuscript reads: "Then shall Noah shut the window of the ark and for a little
space within the boards he shall be silent; and afterwards opening the window
and looking round about saying:" Richard Rastall [Lumiansky-Mills 1983, 157–60]
suggests that "Save me, O God" cues a metrical version of Psalm 69—probably
that by John Hopkins in the psalter of Thomas Sternhold and John Hopkins,
popular in the later sixteenth century.

if ought-where earth, tree or stone   *anywhere*
be dry in any place.
265   And if this fowl come not again,   *bird*
it is a sign, sooth to sayn,   *truth to tell*
that dry it is on hill or plain,
and God hath done some grace.

Then he shall send a raven, and taking a dove in his hands,
shall say:

Ah, Lord, wherever this raven be?   *may....be*
270   Somewhere is dry, well I see!
But yet a dove, by my lewty,   *by my faith*
after I will send.
Thou wilt turn again to me,   *return*
for of all fowls that may fly   *birds*
275   thou art most meek and hend.   *noble*

Then he shall send forth a dove; and there shall be in the ship
another dove carrying an olive-branch in its beak, which
someone shall send from the mast by a rope into Noah's
hands; and then Noah shall say:

Ah, Lord, blessed be thou ay,   *always*
that me hast comfort thus today.   *comforted*
By this sight I may well say
this flood begins to cease.
280   My sweet dove to me brought has
a branch of olive from some place.
This betokeneth God has done us some grace,   *signifies*
and is a sign of peace.

Ah, Lord, honoured must thou be;
285   all Earth dries now I see.
But yet till thou command me,
hence will I not hie.   *hasten*
All this water is away.
Therefore, as soon as I may,
290   sacrifice I shall do in fay   *in faith*
to thee devoutly.

GOD   Noah, take thy wife anon,   *quickly*
and thy children every one;
out of the ship thou shalt gone,   *go*

295 and they all with thee.
Beasts and all that can fly, *animals*
out anon they shall hie, *at once;hasten*
on Earth to grow and multiply.
I will that it so be.

NOAH Lord, I thank thee through thy might;
301 thy bidding shall be done in hight. *immediately*
And, as fast as I may dight, *prepare*
I will do thee honour
and to thee offer sacrifice.
305 Therefore comes in all wise,*
for of these beasts that been his *animals*
offer I will this stour. *at this time*

*Then, leading forth from the ark with his whole family, he
shall take his animals and birds and offer them and slay them.*

NOAH Lord God in majesty
that such grace hast granted me
310 where all was lorn, safe to be! *lost*
Therefore now I am boun— *ready*
my wife, my children, and my meny— *household*
with sacrifice to honour thee
of beasts, fowls, as thou mayest see, *animals:birds*
315 and full devotion.

GOD Noah, to me thou art full able *most worthy*
and thy sacrifice acceptable;
for I have found thee true and stable,
on thee must I min. *have mind*
320 Warry Earth I will no more *afflict*
for Man's sins that grieves me sore;
for of youth Man full yore *for a very long time*
has been inclined to sin.

Ye shall now grow and multiply,
325 and Earth again to edify. *(must) establish*
Each beast, and fowl that may fly, *animal;bird*
shall be feared of you. *afraid*
And fish in sea, all that may flet, *swim*

---

305 "Therefore come, everyone."

	shall sustain you, I thee behet;	*promise*
330	to eat of them ye ne let	*do not refrain*
	that clean been, you mon know.	*may*

	Thereas ye have eaten before	*whereas*
	trees and roots since ye were bore,	*born*
	of clean beasts now, less and more,	
335	I give you leave to eat—	
	save blood and flesh both in fere	
	of wrong dead carrion that is here.*	
	Eat not of that in no manner,	*by no way*
	for that ay ye shall let.	*always; abandon*

	Manslaughter also ay ye shall flee,	*always; shun*
340	for that is not pleasant unto me.	
	They that shedden blood, he or she,	*shed*
	ought-where amongst mankin,	*anywhere; mankind*
	that blood foul shed shall be	*foully*
345	and vengeance have, men shall see.	
	Therefore beware now all ye,	
	you fall not into that sin.	

	And forward, Noah, with thee I make	*agreement*
	and all thy seed for thy sake,	*descendants*
350	of such vengeance for to slake,	*from; cease*
	for now I have my will.	*desire*
	Here I behet thee an hest,	*pledge; promise*
	that man, woman, fowl ne beast	*bird nor animal*
	with water while this world shall last	
355	I will no more spill.	*slay*

	My bow between you and me	
	in the firmament shall be,	
	by verray tokening that you may see	*true sign*
	that such vengeance shall cease,	
360	that man ne woman shall never more	*nor*
	be wasted by water as hath before;	*destroyed*
	but for sin that grieveth me sore	

336–37 "Except the flesh and blood both together of the corpses that are here, which have not been killed by the permitted means." The reference seems unlikely to be to the sacrificial beasts; possibly it refers to animals destroyed in the flood.

therefore this vengeance was.

Where clouds in the welkin been,	*sky*
that ilk bow shall be seen,	*same*
in tokening that my wrath and teen	*as sign; anger*
shall never thus wroken be.	*avenged*
The string is turned towards you	
and towards me is bent the bow,	
that such weather shall never show;	*appear*
and this behet I thee.	*promise*

My blessing now I give thee here,
to thee, Noah, my servant dear,
for vengeance shall no more appear.
And now farewell, my darling dear.   *dearly beloved*

THE END

PLAY 4: ABRAHAM, LOT, AND MELCHYSEDECK: ABRAHAM AND ISAAC

Performed by the Barbers

ABRAHAM, the central and unifying figure of play 4, continues the theme of grace begun with Noah. We see three episodes in his life in which he showed exemplary obedience to the will of God. In the first, from Genesis 14, Abraham acknowledges God's help in the rescue of his nephew Lot from four kings by offering a tenth part of his spoils to the strange Gentile figure of Melchysedeck, who responds by presenting Abraham with gifts of bread and wine. In the second, from Genesis 15.1–2 and 17.1–14, God promises Abraham that he will have a son, and Abraham promises to obey God's injunction to circumcise him, as henceforth all male children must be circumcised. Finally, the sacrifice of Isaac, in Genesis 22.1–13, commanded by God without explanation to Abraham, provides the climax to the play.

These three episodes, widely separated in time, are linked together thematically in Chester by a figural interpretation, which is offered to the audience by a contemporary teacher called the Expositor. The first episode prefigures the giving of tithes and the institution of the sacrament of the Eucharist; the second prefigures the sacrament of Baptism; the third prefigures the sacrifice of Christ the Son by God the Father, the event which marks the supersession of these Jewish practices by the Christian sacraments. This thematic structure is "framed" by the speeches of a messenger who at the start of the play draws the audience's attention away from the departing ark to the historical action about to begin, and who at the end of the play interrupts the Expositor's prayer to announce the arrival of the next waggon. The contemporary world bursts in upon the historical action.

Although the original source of the episodes is the Bible, the immediate source of the sacrifice of Isaac is another play on the same subject, known as "The Brome Play" after the manuscript in which it is found. Chester follows that play in making Isaac a young child threatened with unaccountable violence by his aged father, and the resulting tensions generate considerable pathos. The dialogue between the two is prolonged as Isaac slowly realises what is to happen, then seeks to understand it, and finally, through a series of ritualised actions, prepares to obey God's will. Abraham remains firm to his resolve but is correspondingly moved by his natural human love of his child. But Brome stresses this naturalism to a far greater extent than Chester, where Isaac's part is considerably reduced; we do not see, as in Brome, his relief, bewilderment and suspicion when set free. In consequence, questioning of God's ways is minimised and the figural meaning emphasised.

Little information about staging is given in the Banns, but the play obviously requires a small cast and limited resources. Melchysedeck apparently occupies the waggon while Abraham and Lot, with their laden horse, enter at ground-level; the exchange evidently occurs at ground-level. The waggon may then be occupied by God who addresses Abraham below. Abraham is joined by Isaac and, presumably, they ascend the waggon for the sacrifice. Thus the sacrifice would significantly take place on the same location at which Mechysedeck previously prepared the bread and wine. The interventions of the contemporary Expositor, standing between the audience and the action, emphasises the breaks in dramatic continuity, giving the effect of separate scenes, and distances the action from the audience, requiring them to contemplate its meaning rather than respond to it solely on an emotional level.

Cast   MESSENGER, ABRAHAM, LOT, MELCHYSEDECK, KNIGHT, EXPOSITOR, GOD, ISAAC, FIRST ANGEL, SECOND ANGEL.

MESSENGER	All peace, lordings that been present,	*gentlemen*
	and harken to me with good intent,	*carefully*
	how Noah away from us he went,	
	and all his company.	
5	And Abraham, through God's grace,	
	he is comen into this place,	*come*
	and ye will give him room and space	*if*
	to tell you this story.	

    This play, forsooth, begin shall he   *truly*
10   in worship of the Trinity
    that ye may all hear and see
    that shall be done today.
    My name is Gobbet-on-the-Green.
    With you I may no longer been.   *be*
15   Farewell, my lordings, all bedene *gentlemen; at once*
    for letting of your play.   *so as not to hinder*

    Abraham, having restored his brother Lot into his own place,
    doth first of all begin the play, and saith:

ABRAHAM Ah, thou high God, granter of grace,
    that ending ne beginning has,   *nor*
    I thank thee, Lord, that thou has
20   today given me the victory.
    Lot, my brother, that taken was,[*]
    I have restored him in this case *rescued; situation*
    and brought him home in this place
    through thy might and mastery.   *dominance*

25   To worship thee I will not wond,   *delay*
    that four kings of uncouth land   *foreign*
    today hath sent into my hand   *delivered*
    and riches with great array.   *abundance*
    Therefore, of all that I can win   *have won*
30   to give the tithe I will begin,   *tenth part*
    the city soon when I come in,
    and part with thee my prey.   *share; spoils*

    Melchysedeck, that here king is
    and God's priest also iwiss,   *indeed*
35   the tithe I will give him of this,   *tenth part*
    as skill is that I do.   *wisdom*
    God that has sent me the victory
    of four kings graciously,   *over*
    with him my prey part will I,   *spoils; share*
40   the city when I come to.

---

21 Lot was not Abraham's brother but rather the son of Abraham's brother
Haran; he had been taken from his home by four kings who had plundered
Sodom and Gomorrah. Abraham led a rescue mission which rescued Lot and
captured the plunder; cf. Genesis 14.1–16.

Here Lot, turning him to his brother Abraham, doth say:

LOT	Abraham, brother, I thank thee	
	that this day hast delivered me	
	of enemies' hands and their posty,	*from; power*
	and saved me from woe.	
45	Therefore I will give tithing	*offer a tenth part*
	of my good while I am living;	*goods*
	and now also of his sending*	
	the tithe I will give also.	*tenth part*

*Here the Knight doth come to Mechysedeck, King of Salem,
and rejoicing greatly doth say:*

KNIGHT	My lord the king, tidings on right	*true*
50	your heart to glad and to light!	*gladden and rejoice*
	Abraham hath slain in fight	
	four kings since he went.	
	Here he will be this ilk night,	*same*
	and riches enough with him dight.	*arrayed*
55	I heard him thank God Almight	
	of grace he had him sent.	*for*

*Here Mechysedeck, looking up to Heaven, doth thank God for
Abraham's victory, and doth prepare himself to go present
Abraham.*

MELCHYSE-	Ah, blessed be God, that is but one!	
DECK	Against Abraham will I gone	*towards; go*
	worshipfully, and that anon,	*in honour; at once*
60	mine office to fulfill,	
	and present him with bread and wine,	
	for grace of God is him within.	
	Speed, for love mine,	*make haste*
	for this is God's will.	

*Here the Knight, offering to Melchysedeck a standing-cup and
bread also, doth say:*

---

47 "And also from what he (i.e., God) has sent now."

64+SD *a standing-cup,* i.e., a goblet or similar vessel which has a large supporting
base and stem; a chalice would be appropriate.

KNIGHT (*with a goblet*)
65   Sir, here is wine, withouten were.   *certainly*
    and thereto bread both white and clear   *with it*
    to present him with good cheer,   *give; good will*
    that so us holpen has.   *helped*

    Here Melchysedeck answering saith:

MELCHYSE-
DECK   To God I wot he is full dear,   *know; most*
70   for of all things in his prayer
    he hath withouten danger,   *without opposition*
    and specially his grace.

    Melchysedeck, coming unto Abraham, doth offer to him a cup
    full of wine, and bread, and saith unto him:

    Abraham, welcome most thou be—   *may*
    God's grace is fully in thee.
75   Blessed ever must thou be
    that enemies so can meek.   *humiliate*
    Here is bread and wine
     for thy degree   *appropriate to your rank*
    I have brought, as thou may see.
    Receive this present now at me,   *from*
80   and that I thee beseek.   *beseech*

    Here Abraham, receiving the offering of Melchysedeck, doth
    say:

ABRAHAM   Sir king, welcome in good fay;   *truly*
    thy present is welcome to my pay.   *pleasure*
    God hath holpen me today,   *helped*
    unworthy though I were.
85   Ye shall have part of my prey   *spoils*
    that I won since I went away.
    Therefore to thee that take it may
    the tithe I offer here.   *tenth part*

    Here Abraham offereth to Melchysedeck an horse that is laden.

ABRAHAM   And your present, sir, take I
90   and honour it devoutly,
    for much good it may signify

in time that is coming.*

	Therefore horse, harness and perry,	*precious stones*
	as falls for your dignity,	*befits*
95	the tithe of it takes of me	*tenth part; from*
	and receive here my offering.	

> *Then shall Abraham receive the bread and wine, and Melchy-*
> *sedeck the laden horse by way of tithe. Here Lot doth offer to*
> *Melchysedeck a goodly cup, and saith:*

LOT	And I will offer with good intent	*will*
	of such goods as God hath me lent	*granted*
	to Melchysedeck here present,	
100	as God's will is to be.	
	Abraham my brother offered has,	
	and so will I through God's grace.	
	This royal cup before your face,	*in your sight*
	receive it now of me.	

> *Here Melchysedeck receiveth the cup of Lot.*

MELCHYSE-	Sir, your offering welcome is;	
DECK	and well I wot, forsooth iwiss,	*know; truly indeed*
107	that fully God's will it is	
	that is now done today.	
	Go we together to my city;	
110	and God now heartily thank we	
	that helps us ay through his posty,	*always; power*
	for so we full well may.	*very well should*

> *Here they do go together, and Abraham doth take the bread*
> *and wine, and Melchysedeck the laden horse.*

EXPOSITOR (*riding on horseback*)		
	Lordings, what this may signify	*sirs*
	I will expound it apertly,	*clearly*
115	that the unlearned standing hereby	*by here*
	may know what this may be.	
	This present, I say verament,	*truly*

91–92 The future figural meaning of the exchange is explained by the Expositor
at 113–44.

signifieth the New Testament
that now is used with good intent   *with good meaning*
120   throughout all Christianity.   *Christendom*

In the Old Law, without leasing,   *telling no lies*
when these two good men were living
of beasts were all their offering   *animals*
and eke their sacrament.   *also*
125   But since Christ died on rood-tree,   *cross*
in bread and wine his death remember we;
and at his last supper, our Maundy
was his commandment.*

But for this thing used should be   *practised*
130   afterwards, as now done we,   *do*
in signification—as lieve you me—*
Melchysedeck did so.
And tithings-making, as you seen here,   ✳   *tithe-offering*
of Abraham begunnen were.   *by; begun*
135   Therefore to God he was full dear,   *very*
and so were both two.

By Abraham understand I may
the Father of Heaven, in good fay;   *in good faith*
Melchysedeck, a priest to his pay   *at his pleasure*
140   to minister that sacrament
that Christ ordained the foresaid day—*
in bread and wine to honour him ay.   *always*
This signifieth, the sooth to say,   *truth*
Melchysedeck his present.   *Melchysedeck's*

Here God appeareth to Abraham, and saith:

GOD   Abraham my servant, I say to thee,

125–28 "But since Christ died on the cross, we remember his death in bread and
wine; and at his last supper, our own 'Last Supper' (i.e., the Eucharist) was
commanded by him."

131 "In signification—so believe you me," i.e., the deed existed not in its own
right but as a "figure" or sign ordained by God to intimate something that
would happen in the future.

141 "the foresaid day," i.e., Maundy Thursday at the Last Supper.

146	thy help and thy succour will I be.	
	For thy good deed much pleaseth me,	
	I tell thee witterly.	*truly*

Here Abraham, turning to God, saith:

ABRAHAM	Lord, one thing that thou wouldest see	*attend to*
150	that I pray after with heart full free!	*most sincere*
	Grant me, Lord, through thy posty	*power*
	some fruit of my body.	

	I have no child, foul ne fair,	*nor*
	save my nurry, to be my heir;	*foster-child*
155	that makes me greatly to apair.	*suffer shame*
	On me, Lord, have mercy.	

GOD	Nay, Abraham, friend, lieve thou me—	*believe*
	thy nurry thine heir shall not be;	*foster-child*
	but one son I shall send thee,	
160	begotten of thy body.	

	Abraham, do as I thee say—	
	look and tell, if thou may,	*count*
	stars standing on the stray;	
	that unpossible were.	*impossible*
165	No more shalt thou, for no need,	*any necessity*
	number of thy body the seed	*offspring*
	that thou shalt have, withouten dread;	*assuredly*
	thou art to me so dear.	

	Therefore, Abraham, servant free,	*noble*
170	look that thou be true to me;	
	and here a forward I make with thee	*agreement*
	thy seed to multiply.	
	To much folk father shalt thou be.	*a great people*
	Kings of this seed men shall see;	
175	and one child of great degree	*high rank*
	all Mankind shall forbuy.	*redeem*

---

154 The reference is apparently to Ishmael, Abraham's son by his wife's hand-
maiden, Hagar; the son of his steward Eliezer may also be indicated.

163 No satisfactory gloss has been found for "on the stray."

	I will hethen-forward alway	*henceforth*
	each man-child on the eighth day	
	be circumcised, as I thee say,	
180	and thou thyself full soon.	
	Whoso circumcised not is	
	forsaken shall be with me, iwiss,	*indeed*
	for unobedient that man is.	*disobedient*
	Look that this be done.	

ABRAHAM	Lord, all ready in good fay!	*truly*
186	Blessed be thou ever and ay,	*always*
	for thereby know thou may	
	thy folk from other men.	
	Circumcised they shall be all	
190	anon, for ought that may befall,	*at once; whatever*
	I thank thee, Lord, thine own thrall,	*servant*
	kneeling on my kneen.	*knees*

EXPOSITOR	Lordings all, take this intent	
	what betokens this commandment:*	
195	this was sometime a sacrament	
	in the Old Law, truly tane.	*truly understood*
	As followeth now verament,	*truly*
	so was this in the Old Testament.	
	But when Christ died, away it went,	
200	and then began bapteme.	*baptism*

	Also God a promise behet us here	*pledged*
	to Abraham, his servant dear:	
	so much seed, that in no manner	
	numbered it might be;	
205	and one seed Mankind for to buy.	
	That was Christ Jesus, witterly,	*indeed*
	for of his kind was Our Lady,	*nature*
	and so also was he.	

GOD	Abraham, my servant Abraham!

ABRAHAM	Lo, Lord, all ready here I am.

193–94 "Gentlemen all, accept this interpretation of what this command signifies." Again, *betokens* implies that the event functions as a sign, prefiguring a later injunction.

GOD   Take Isaac, thy son by name,
     that thou lovest the best of all,
     and in sacrifice offer him to me
     upon that hill there besides thee.   *beside*
215   Abraham, I will that it so be,
     for ought that may befall.   *whatever happens*

ABRAHAM My Lord, to thee is mine intent   *intention*
     ever to be obedient.
     That son that thou to me hast sent
220   offer I will to thee,
     and fulfill thy commandment
     with hearty will, as I am kent,   *heartfelt; taught*
     high God, Lord omnipotent.
     Thy bidding, Lord, done shall be.

225   My meny and my children each one   *household*
     lengs at home, both all and one, *remain; every one*
     save Isaac. My son with me shall gone *go*
     to an hill here beside.

    Here Abraham, turning him to his son Isaac, saith:

ABRAHAM Make thee ready, my dear darling,
230   for we must do a little thing.
     This wood do thou on thy back bring;
     we may no longer bide.   *stay*

     A sword and fire, that I will take,
     for sacrifice me behoves to make.   *I have to*
235   God's bidding will I not forsake,
     but ever obedient be.

    Abraham taketh a sword and fire.

    Here Isaac speaks to his father, taketh the bundle of sticks, and
    beareth after his father.

ISAAC   Father, I am all ready
     to do your bidding most meekly,
     and to bear this wood full bain am I, *obedient*
240   as ye command me.

ABRAHAM O Isaac, Isaac, my darling dear,

	my blessing now I give thee here.	
	Take up this faggot with good cheer	*happily*
	and on thy back it bring.	
245	And fire with us I will take.	

ISSAC	Your bidding I will not forsake;	*disobey*
	father, I will never slake	*cease*
	to fulfill your bidding.	

| ABRAHAM | Now Isaac, son, go we our way | |
| 245 | to yonder mount, if that we may. | |

Here they go both to the place to do sacrifice.

| ISAAC | My dear father, I will assay | *try* |
| | to follow you full fain. | *most gladly* |

Abraham, being minded to slay his son, lifts up his hands to Heaven and saith:

ABRAHAM	O, my heart will break in three!	
	To hear thy words I have pity.	*take pity on hearing*
255	As thou wilt, Lord, so must it be;	
	to thee will I be bain.	*obedient*

Lay down thy faggot, my own son dear.

Isaac layeth down the wood and goeth to his father and saith:

ISAAC	All ready, father—lo, it here!	*it is*
	But why make ye so heavy cheer?*	
260	Are you any thing adread?	*in any way afraid*
	Father, if it be your will,	*with your permission*
	where is the beast that we shall kill?	*animal*

| ABRAHAM | Thereof, son, is none upon the hill | *none such* |
| | that I see here in stead. | *in this place* |

Isaac, fearing lest his father will slay him, saith:

| ISAAC | Father, I am full sore aferd | *afraid* |

---

259 "But why do you have such a sad expression on your face?"

| 266 | to see you bear that drawn swerd.
I hope for all middleyerd   *middle earth*
you will not slay your child. | *sword*
all the world |

Abraham, comforting his son, saith:

| ABRAHAM
270 | Dread thee not, my child, I read.
Our Lord will send of his godhead
some manner of beast into this stead,*
either tame or wild. | *advise*
from |

| ISAAC | Father, tell me or I go
whether I shall have harm or no. | *before*
injury |

| ABRAHAM
276 | Ah, dear God, that me is woe!
Thou breakest my heart in sunder. | *how miserable I am* |

| ISAAC

280 | Father, tell me of this case:
why you your sword drawn has
and bear it naked in this place.
Thereof I have great wonder. | *about this situation*

at that |

| ABRAHAM | Isaac, son, peace, I pray thee!
Thou breakest my heart anon in three. | *at once* |

| ISAAC | I pray you, father, lain nothing from me,
but tell me what you think. | *conceal*
are thinking |

| ABRAHAM | Ah, Isaac, Isaac, I must thee kill. | |

| ISAAC | Alas, father, is that your will
Your own child for to spill
upon this hill's brink? | *destroy* |

| 290 | If I have trespassed in any degree,*
with a yard you may beat me.
Put up your sword, if your will be,
for I am but a child. | *stick*
it be your will |

---

271 "Some kind of animal into this place."

289 "If I have done wrong in any way."

ABRAHAM	Oh, my dear son, I am sorry	*sorrowful*
	to do to thee this great annoy.	*harm*
295	God's commandment do must I;	*command*
	his works are ay full mild.	*always most merciful*

ISAAC	Would God my mother were here with me!
	She would kneel down upon her knee,
	praying you, father, if it might be,
300	for to save my life.

ABRAHAM	Oh, comely creature, but I thee kill*	
	I grieve my God. and that full ill.	*most sorely*
	I may not work against his will	*act*
	but ever obedient be.	*must be*
305	O, Isaac, son, to thee I say	
	God has commanded me today	
	sacrifice—this is no nay—	*there's no denying*
	to make of thy body.	

ISAAC	Is it God's will I shall be slain?

ABRAHAM	Yea, son, it is not for to lain;	*not to be concealed*
311	to his bidding I will be bain,	*obedient*
	ever to him pleasing.	*be pleasing*
	But that I do this doleful deed,	*unless:sorrowful*
	my Lord will not quite me my meed.	*repay;reward*

ISAAC	Marry, father, God forbid	
316	but you do your offering.	*other than;make*
	Father, at home your sons you shall find	
	that you must love by course of kind.	*force of nature*
	Be I once out of your mind;	*let me be at once*
320	your sorrow may soon cease.	
	But yet you must do God's bidding.	
	Father, tell my mother for nothing.	*in no way*

Here Abraham, wringing his hands, saith:

ABRAHAM	For sorrow I may my hands wring;
	thy mother I cannot please.

---

301 "Ah, fair creation, unless I kill you."

325	O Isaac, Isaac, blessed most thou be!	*may*
	Almost my wit I lose for thee.	*sanity*
	The blood of thy body so free	*beautiful*
	I am full loath to shed.	

Here Isaac, asking his father's blessing on his knees, saith:

ISAAC	Father, since you must needs do so,	
330	let it pass lightly and over go.	*quickly; away*
	Kneeling upon my knees two,	*as I kneel*
	your blessing on me spread.	*lay*

ABRAHAM	My blessing, dear son, give I thee,	
	and thy mother's with heart so free.	*willing*
335	The blessing of the Trinity,	
	my dear son, on thee light.	*descend*

ISAAC	Father, I pray you, hide my een	*eyes*
	that I see not the sword so keen.	*sharp*
	Your stroke, father, would I not seen,	*see*
340	lest I against it gright.	*complain*

ABRAHAM	My dear son Isaac, speak no more;	
	thy words make my heart full sore.	

ISAAC	Oh, dear father, wherefore, wherefore,	
	sithen I must needs be dead?	*since; have to*
345	Of one thing I would you pray,	
	sithen I must die the death today:	*since*
	as few strokes as ye well may,	*you possibly can*
	when ye smite off my head!	

ABRAHAM	Thy meekness, child, makes me afray.	*afraid*
350	My song may be "Weal away."	*"alas"*

ISAAC	Oh, dear father, do away, do away	*stop*
	your making of so much moan.	*complaint*
	Now truly, father, this talking	
	doth but make long tarrying.	*delay*
355	I pray you, come off and make ending	*be quick*
	and let me hence be gone.	

ABRAHAM	Come hither, my child; thou art so sweet!	
	Thou must be bounden hand and feet.	

Here Isaac riseth and cometh to his father, and he taketh him
and bindeth him.

ISAAC	Father, we must no more meet	
360	by ought that I can see.	*as far as*
	But do with me then as thou will;	
	I must obey, and that is skill,	*right*
	God's commandment to fulfill,	*command*
	for needs so must it be.	*necessarily*
365	Upon the purpose that you have set you,	
	forsooth, father, I will not let you;	*truly;hinder*
	but evermore to you bow	*be obedient*
	while that ever I may.	*as long as*
	Father, greet well my brethren ying,	*young*
370	and pray my mother of her blessing;	*for*
	I come no more under her wing.	*may come*
	Farewell, for ever and ay.	*always*
	But father, I cry you mercy	
	for all that ever I have trespassed to thee,	*done wrong*
375	forgiven, father, that it may be	*so that*
	until Doomsday.	
ABRAHAM	My dear son, let be thy moans;	*complaints*
	my child, thou grieves me every once.*	
	Blessed be thou, body and bones,	
380	and I forgive thee here.	
	Now, my dear son, here shalt thou lie.	
	Unto my work now must I hie.	*hasten*
	I had as lief myself to die	*rather*
	as thou, my darling dear.	
ISAAC	Father, if ye be to me kind,	
386	about my head a kerchief bind;	*cloth*
	and let me lightly out of your mind;	*let me pass easily*
	and soon that I were sped!	*let it be soon;gone*
ABRAHAM	Farewell, my sweet son of grace.	

377–78 "My dear son, stop your laments; my child, you make me unhappy every
time (you utter them)."

Here kiss him, and bind the kerchief about his head; and let
him kneel down and speak.

ISAAC 391	I pray you, father, turn down my face a little while, while you have space, for I am full sore adread.	*time* *sorely afraid*
ABRAHAM	To do this deed I am sorry.	*sorrowful*
ISAAC 395	Yea, Lord, to thee I call and cry! Of my soul thou have mercy, heartily I thee pray.	*on* *with heartfelt prayer*
ABRAHAM	Lord, I would fain work thy will. This young innocent that lieth so still, full loath were me him to kill* by any manner of way.	*willingly do* *by any means*
ISAAC	My dear father, I thee pray, let me take my clothes away, for shedding blood on them today at my last ending.	*to avoid shedding*
ABRAHAM 406	Heart, if thou would break in three, thou shall never master me! I will no longer let for thee; my God I may not grieve.	*delay*
ISAAC 410	Ah, mercy, father! Why tarry ye so? Smite off my head, and let me go. I pray you rid me of my woe, for now I take my leave.	*delay*
ABRAHAM 415	My son, my heart will break in three to hear thee speak such words to me. Jesu, on me thou have pity, that I have most of mind.	*in*
ISAAC	Now, father, I see that I shall die. Almighty God in majesty, my soul I offer unto thee.	

---

399 "I would be most reluctant to kill him."

420   Lord, to it be kind.

Here let Abraham take and bind his son Isaac upon the altar,
and let him make a sign as though he would cut off his head
with the sword. Then let the Angel come, and take the sword
by the end, and stay it, saying:

1ST ANGEL	Abraham, my servant dear!	
ABRAHAM	Lo, Lord, I am all ready here.	
1ST ANGEL	Lay not thy sword in no manner	*in no way*
	on Isaac, thy dear darling,	
425	and do to him none annoy.	*no harm*
	For thou dreads God, well wot I,	*know*
	that of thy son has no mercy	*upon*
	to fulfill his bidding.	*in order to*
2ND ANGEL	And, for his bidding thou dost ay,	*always*
430	and sparest neither for fear nor fray	*dread*
	to do thy son to death today—	
	Isaac, to thee full dear—	
	therefore God hath sent by me, in fay,	*truly*
	a lamb that is both good and gay,	*splendid*
435	into this place, as thou see may.	
	Lo, have him right here.	*find*
ABRAHAM	Ah, Lord of Heaven and king of bliss,	
	thy bidding shall be done iwiss.	*indeed*
	Sacrifice here me sent is,	*a sacrifice*
440	and all, Lord, through thy grace.	
	An horned wether here I see.	
	Among the briers tied is he.	
	To thee offered now shall he be	
	anonright in this place.	*immediately*

Then let Abraham take the lamb and kill him; and let God say:

GOD	Abraham, by myself I swear:	
446	for thou hast been obedient e'er,	*ever*
	and spared not thy son to tear	
	to fulfill my bidding,	
	thou shall be blessed that pleased me.	
450	Thy seed I shall so multiply	

| | as stars and sand, so many het I, | *promised* |
| | of thy body coming. | *from* |

	Of enemies thou shalt have power,	
	and thy blood also in fere.*	
455	Thou hast been meek and bonere	*agreeable*
	to do as I thee bede.	*command*
	And of all nations, lieve thou me,	*believe*
	blessed evermore shall be	*you shall be*
	through fruit that shall come of thee,	*progeny;from*
460	and saved through thy seed.*	

Here the Expositor saith:

EXPOSITOR	Lordings, this signification	*sirs;significance*
	of this deed of devotion—	
	and ye will, ye wit mon—	*if you wish;may know*
	may turn you to much good.	*bring;for you*
465	This deed ye see done here in this place,	
	in example of Jesus done it was,	
	that for to win Mankind grace	
	was sacrificed on the rood.	*cross*

	By Abraham I may understond	*understand*
470	the Father of Heaven that can fond	*contrived*
	with his Son's blood to break that bond	
	the Devil had brought us to.	*to which*
	By Isaac understand I may	
	Jesus that was obedient ay,	*always*
475	his Father's will to work alway,	*always*
	and death to underfo.	*undertake*

Here let the Expositor kneel down and say:

EXPOSITOR	Such obedience grant us, O Lord,	
	ever to thy most holy word,	
	that in the same we may accord	*in the same way;agree*
480	as this Abraham was bain.	*obedient*

453–54 "You shall have power over your enemies and also over all your kins-men."

460 "And (all nations shall be) saved through your descendents."

And then all together shall we
that worthy king in Heaven see,
and dwell with him in great glory,
for ever and ever. Amen.

Here the Messenger maketh an end.

MESSENGER	Make room, lordings, and give us way,	*sirs*
486	and let Balaack come in and play,	*perform*
	and Balaam that well can say,	*spoke well*
	to tell you of prophecy.	
	That Lord that died on Good Friday,	
490	he save you all, both night and day.	
	Farewell, my lordings, I go my way;	*gentlemen*
	I may no longer abie.	*remain*

THE END

PLAY 5: MOSES AND THE LAW:
BALAACK AND BALAAM*

Performed by the Cappers

PLAY 5 continues the themes of obedience and disobedience through two contrasting examples. The Israelites have emerged as the nation promised to Abraham and, after a period of exile and enslavement in Egypt, are being led by Moses towards the land promised to them by God. The version of the play given here continues the themes of obedience and disobedience to God's will. It opens with the giving of the Ten Commandments by God to Moses as set out in Exodus 20.1–17 and 34.1–35.6 and in Deuteronomy 5, to which absolute obedience is enjoined. It then moves abruptly to the strange story of the Gentile soothsayer Balaam who, as described in Numbers 22.1–24.25, is hired by Balaack, king of the Moabites, to halt the Israelites' advance by cursing them. Balaam seeks to do so even though he knows that such action is against the will of God, but he is rebuked on his journey by his she-ass and warned by an angel, so that he is compelled to do as God wishes. Finally, however, he sees a means of arousing God's anger against the Israelites and earning reward from Balaack. He is held responsible for the seduction of the Israelites, described in Numbers 25.1–18 and 31.1–12; but the offenders are punished, the Moabites defeated, and Balaam killed.

The waggon-set for the play was apparently a hill on which Moses receives the Commandments and from which Balaam delivers his pro-

---

Title The 1607 manuscript contains a different version of play 5 which was evidently intended for a different distribution of plays among the three days. See Lumiansky-Mills 1974, Appendix 1B.

nouncements upon the Israelites. The true spectacle of the play was
certainly the talking ass—"Make the Ass to speak, and set it out lively,"
command the Post-Reformation Banns. The stage-direction after 183
makes it clear that someone was to be disguised as the ass. This effect
has been achieved in a modern production by having the front part
played by an actor and having Balaam tie the back of the ass about him
like a skirt to provide the back legs. The 1607 version of the play also
calls for Moses to return from the mountain with "horns" and a shining
face, and possibly we should assume similar head-dress here. The
Cappers and Pinners' Company would be well equipped to provide such
costuming. We may assume King Balaack was richly but bizarrely clad to
contrast with Moses.

The play draws the audience into its action as the chosen people
addressed by Moses and blessed by Balaam. Much of the central action
is played at their level. Balaack enters riding through them, and Balaam's
journey and his arrest by the angel seem also to be at crowd level. The
audience is also addressed by the Expositor who serves both to explain
and to abridge the action and to signal its structural divisions. Moses is
a God-like figure invested with divine authority, unlike Balaam—a rather
nasty, vain and mercenary man who is momentarily possessed by God
but resumes immediately his familiar role. Though Balaam in his final
prophecy signals possession by God through his stylised pose and
unexpected ringing voice, he is a comically reluctant servant of God,
rebuked by his own ass and nervously looking over his shoulder at
Balaack before he speaks in anticipation of the wrath to come. Balaack is
an irascible pagan king whose increasing exasperation and descent into
most unkingly language at Balaam's disobedience is part of the comedy
of the play's central action.

Balaam was not one of the Jewish prophets, and this play denies
him any permanent high status. But his prophecy is seen to remain with
the Gentiles, becoming the starting-point for the response of the three
kings to the star in play 8.

Cast   GOD, MOSES, EXPOSITOR, BALAACK, KNIGHT, BALAAM, ASS, ANGEL.

GOD	Moses, my servant lief and dear,	*true*
(to Moses)	and all my people that been here,	*are*
	ye wotten in Egypt when ye were	*know*
	out of thralldom I you brought.	*slavery*

5   I will you have no God but me;
               no false gods none make ye.
               My name in vain name not ye,
               for that liketh me nought.   *pleases*

               I will you hold your holy day
10   and worship it eke alway,   *honour; also; always*
               father and mother all that you may,*
               and slay no man nowhere.
               Fornication ye shall flee.   *shun*
               No men's goods steal ye,
15   nor in no place leng ne be   *stay*
               false witness for to bear.

               Your neighbour's wife desire you nought,
               servant, ne goods that he hath bought,   *nor*
               ox nor ass, in deed nor thought,
20   nor nothing that is his,
               nor wrongfully to have his thing*
               against his love and his liking.   *desire*
               In all these keep my bidding,   *these matters*
               that ye do not amiss.   *act; wrongly*

MOSES   Good Lord that art ever so good,
26   I will fulfill with mild mood   *humble heart*
               thy commandments, for I stood
               to hear thee now full still.
               Forty days now fasted have I,   Lent reference?
30   that I might be the more worthy
               to learn this token truly.*
               Now will I work thy will.

Then Moses on the mountain shall speak to the people:

MOSES   Good folk, dread ye nought.

---

11 "(And also honour) father and mother as much as possible"; *worship*, from the previous line, is to be understood.

21 "Nor wrongfully desire to have his possessions"; *desire*, from the first line of the stanza, is to be understood.

31 "To understand the true meaning of this sign"; *token* means here "an act serving to demonstrate divine power or authority."

	To prove you with God hath	*as a means of testing*
	this wrought.	
35	Take these words in your thought;	
	now knowen ye what is sin.	*know; constitutes*
	By this sight now ye may see	
	that he is peerless of posty.	*unrivalled in power*
	Therefore this token look do ye,	*act; perform*
40	thereof that ye ne blin.*	

EXPOSITOR	Lordings, this commandment ⁊	*sirs*
	was the first law that ever God sent; ⌐ '	
	ten points there been— that takes intent—	
	that most effect is in.*	
45	But all that story for to fong	*incorporate*
	to play this month it were too long!	*perform; would be*
	Therefore most fruitful	*profitable parts;*
	ever among	*from within it*
	shortly we shall min.	*briefly; recall*

	After, we readen of this story	
50	that in this Mount of Sinai	
	God gave the Law witterly	
	written with his hand	
	in stony tables, as read I,	
	before men honoured maumentry—	
55	Moses brake them hastily,	
	for that he would not wand.*	

	But after, played as ye shall see,	*later; performed*
	other tables out carved he,	
	which God bade written should be	*inscribed with*
60	the words he said before.	
	the which tables shrined were	*put in a shrine*
	after, as God can Moses lere;	*afterwards; instructed*

---

40 "Look that you do not cease from that."

43–44 "There are ten items—take heed of that—that have the greatest force."

49–56 "We read in this story that, after God gave the Law on this Mount of Sinai—written assuredly with his own hand on tablets of stone, as I read, before the Israelites ('men') turned to idolatry—Moses then broke the tablets in anger because he could not endure that idolatry." While Moses was on Mount Sinai, the Israelites turned to idolatry, worshipping the golden calf; see Exodus 31–32.

and that shrine to him was dear
thereafter evermore.*

Here God appeareth again to Moses.

GOD	Moses, my servant, go anon	*at once*
66	and carve out of the rock of stone	
	tables to write my bidding upon,	
	such as thou had before.	
	And in the morning look thou hie ~high~	*hasten*
70	into the Mount of Sinai.	
	Let no man wot but thou only,	*know*
	of company no more.	*with no other companions*

MOSES	Lord, thy bidding shall be done	
	and tables carved out full soon.	*immediately*
75	But tell me— I pray thee this boon—	*ask; favour*
	what words I shall write.	

GOD	Thou shalt write the same lore	*teaching*
	that in the tables was before.	
	It shall be kept for evermore,	
80	for that is my delight.	

*Then Moses shall make a sign as if he were carving out the
tables from the mountain and, writing upon them, shall say to
the people:*

MOSES	God's folk of Israel,	
	harkens you all to my spell.	*words*
	God bade ye should keep well	
	this that I shall say.	
85	Six days bodily work all;	
	the seventh "Sabbath" ye shall call.	
	That day, for ought that may befall,	*whatever happens*
	hallowed ay shall be.	*kept holy; always*

	Who doth not this, die shall he.	
90	In houses fire shall no man see.	
	First-fruits to God offer ye—	

55–64 The reference is to the special chest or ark for the Covenant, whose
construction is described in Deuteronomy 10.1–5.

for so himself bede—   *commands*
purpur and bise both two   *purple and silk*
to him that shall save you from woe
95   and help you in your need.

Then he shall come down from the mount, and King Balaack
shall come riding on horseback beside the mountain and shall
say:

BALAACK   I, Balaack, king of Moab lond,   *land*
all Israel and I had in hand,   *if; in my power*
I am so wroth I would not wond   *angry; hesitate*
to slay them, every wight.   *person*
100   For their God helps them so stoutly
of other lands to have mastery
that it is bootless witterly   *useless; truly*
against them for to fight.

What nation doth them annoy,   *harm to them*
105   Moses prayeth anon in hie,   *immediately*
then have they ever the victory
and their enemies the worse.
Therefore, how I will wroken be   *be avenged*
I am bethought, as mote I thee:*
110   Balaam shall come to me,
that people for to curse.

*Flourish.**

No knife nor sword may not avail
that ilk people to assail.   *same*
That founds to fight, he shall fail,   *attempts*
115   for sicker it is no boot.   *certainly; futile*

*Cast up.**

---

109 "I have considered, so may I thrive."

111+SD "Brandish a sword." These one-word stage-directions occur mainly in
the margins of the manuscripts and seem to have been actors' cues.

115+SD Perhaps "Wave the sword above your head."

All nations they do annoy,	*harm*
and my folk comen for to destroy,	*come*
as ox that gnaweth busily	
the grass right to the root.	

120 Whosoever Balaam blesseth, iwiss,   *indeed*
    blessed that man soothly is;   *truly*
    whosoever he curses fareth amiss,   *comes to grief*
    such name over all hath he.   *reputation*
    Therefore, go fetch him, batchelor,   *knight*
125 that he may curse these people here.
    For sicker, on them in no manner,   *certainly; in no way*
    may we not wroken be.   *avenged*

The knight speaks to king Balaack.

KNIGHT   Sir, on your errand will I gone,   *commission; go*
          that it shall be done anon.   *at once*
130   And he shall wreak you on your fone,   *avenge; foes*
          the people of Israel.

BALAACK   Yea, look thou het him gold great won,*
          and lands for to live upon
          to destroy them as he con,   *is able*
135   these frekes that been so fell.   *men; fierce*

*Then the knight of king Balaack shall go to Balaam and shall
say:*

KNIGHT   Balaam, my lord greets well thee
          and prayeth thee soon at him to be,   *with*
          to curse the people of Judee   *Judea*
          that done him great annoy.   *do; harm*

BALAAM   Abide a while there, bachelor,   *knight*
141   for I may have no power
          but if that God's will were;
          and that shall I wit in hie.   *know at once*

*Then Balaam shall go to consult the Lord in prayer. Seated,
God shall say:*

---

132 "Yes, see that you promise him a great quantity of gold."

GOD   Balaam, I command thee
145   King Balaack's bidding for to flee.   *reject*
            That people that blessed is of me   *by*
            curse thou by no way.   *by no means*

BALAAM   Lord, I must do thy bidding
            though it to me be unliking,   *unpleasant*
150   for thereby much winning
            I might have had today.

GOD   Yet, though Balaack be my foe,
            thou shalt have leave thither to go.
            But look that thou do right so
155   as I have thee taught.

BALAAM   Lord, it shall be done in height.   *at once*
            This ass shall bear me aright.   *fittingly*
            Go we together anon, sir knight,   *at once*
            for leave now have I caught.   *gained*

            Then Balaam and the Knight shall ride together, and Balaam
            shall say:

BALAAM   Knight, by the law that I live on,   *by which I live*
161   now have I leave for to gone,   *go*
            cursed they shall be everychone   *every one*
            and I ought win may.   *if; anything*
            Hold the king that he behight,*
165   God's hest I set at light.   *command; care little for*
            Warried they shall be this night,   *cursed*
            or that I wend away.   *before; go*

KNIGHT   Balaam, do my lord's will
            and of gold thou shalt have thy fill!
170   Spare thou nought that folk to spill,   *destroy*
            and spurn their God's speech.

BALAAM   Friend, I have gods wonder fell;   *wondrous fierce*
            both Ruffin and Ragnell*

---

164 "If the king will keep to what he has promised."

173 Ruffin and Ragnell both occur in the Middle Ages as the names of devils.

will work right as I them tell.   *act*
175   There is no will to seech.*

> *Then Balaam shall climb upon his ass and ride with the Knight; and an angel of the Lord shall meet them with drawn sword; and the ass— and not Balaam— shall see him, shall fall prostrate to the ground. And Balaam shall say:*

BALAAM   Go forth, Burnell! Go forth! Go!*
          What the Devil! My ass will not go!
          Served she me never so.
          What sorrow soever it is?*
180   What the Devil! Now she is fallen down!
          But thou rise and make thee boun   *unless; ready*
          and bear me soon out of this town,
          thou shalt abie iwiss.   *suffer indeed*

> *Then Balaam shall beat his ass. And here someone ought to be transformed into the guise of an ass; and when Balaam strikes, the ass shall say:*

ASS   Master, thou dost ill, sickerly,   *certainly*
185   so good an ass as me to noy.   *hurt*
          Now hast thou beaten me here thrie,   *three times*
          that bare thee thus about.

BALAAM   Burnell, why beguilest thou me   *deceive*
          when I have most need of thee?

ASS   That sight that before me I see
191   maketh me down to lout.   *bow*

          Am I not, master, thine own ass
          to bear thee whither thou wilt pass,
          and many winter ready was?
195   To smite me, it is shame.   *disgraceful*

---

175 "There is no deception to look for"; in other words, "I will not deceive you."

176 *Burnell* is the name of the ass. It was a popular name for an ass, established in literature (compare modern "Neddy"). Balaam was said to have ridden a she-ass, hence the feminine pronouns.

179 "Whatever misery is it (that causes this now)?"

	Thou wottest well, master, perdee,	*know; indeed*
	that thou haddest never none like to me,	
	ne never yet so served I thee.	*nor*
	Now am I not to blame.	

Then Balaam, seeing the angel bearing his drawn sword, shall fall suddenly down on his knees and speaketh to the angel.

BALAAM
201

A, lord, to thee I make avow,   *swear*
I had no sight of thee or now.   *before*
Little wist I that it was thou   *knew*
that feared my ass so.   *frightened*

ANGEL
205

Why hast thou beaten thy ass, why?
Now am I comen, thee to noy   *come; punish*
that changed thy purpose so falsely
and now wouldest be my foe.

If this ass had not down gone.
I would have slain thee here anon.   *at once*

BALAAM
211

Lord, have pity me upon,
for sinned I have sore.
Lord, is it thy will that I forth go?

ANGEL

215

Yea, but look thou do that folk no woe   *harm*
otherway than God bade thee do   *otherwise*
and said to thee before.

Then Balaam and the Knight shall ride together and king Balaack shall meet them; and the king shall say:

BALAACK

Ah, welcome, Balaam my friend,
for all my anger thou shalt end,
if that thy will be to wend   *go*
and wreak me on my foe.   *avenge*

BALAAM
221

Nought may I speak, as I have win,   *joy*
but as God putteth me within   *puts inside me*
to forbuy all the end of my kin.*
Therefore, sir, me is woe!   *I am sorry*

---

222 "To redeem the later generations of my race (the Gentiles)."

BALAACK	Come forth, Balaam, come with me,	
225	for on this hill, so mote I thee,	*so may I thrive*
	the folk of Israel shalt thou see—	
	and curse them, I thee pray!	
	Gold and silver and eke perry	*also precious stones*
	thou shalt have, great plenty,	*great abundance*
230	to curse them, that it soon may be—	*come to pass*
	all that thou sayest today.	

Then Balaack descends from his horse and Balaam from his ass, and they shall climb the mountain; and King Balaack shall say:

BALAACK	Lo, Balaam, now thou seest here	
	God's people all in fere.	*assembled*
	City, castle, and river—	
235	look now. How likes thee?	*do you like (the sight)*
	Curse them now at my prayer	*bidding*
	as thou wilt be to me full dear	*most*
	and in my realm most of power	
	and greatest under me.	

Then Balaam, facing east, shall say:

BALAAM	How may I curse here in this place	
241	the people that God blessed has?	
	In them is both might and grace,	
	and that is ever well seen.	
	Witness may I none bear	
245	against God, that them can were,	*has protected*
	his people that no man may dere	*harm*
	ne trouble with no teen.	*nor; suffering*
	I say this folk shall have their will,	*desire*
	that no nation shall them grill;	*harm*
250	the goodness that they shall fulfill	*benefit; gain*
	numbered may not be.	
	Their God shall them keep and save,	
	and other reproof shall they none have;	
	but such death as they shall have	
255	I pray God send to me.	
BALAACK	What the devil ails thee, thou popelart?	*fool*
	Thy speech is not worth a fart!	

	Doted I hope that thou art,	*stupid;believe*
	for madly thou hast wrought.	*acted*
260	I bade thee curse them everychone	*every one*
	and thou blessest them, blood and bone!	
	To this north side thou shall gone,	*go*
	for here thy deed is nought.	*worthless*

Then King Balaack shall take Balaam to the northern part of the mountain and Balaam shall say in a loud voice:

BALAAM	Ah, Lord, that here is fair wonning—*	
265	halls, chambers, great liking,	*much that is pleasant*
	vales, woods, grass growing,	
	fair yards, and eke river.	*gardens;also a river*
	I wot well that God made all this,	
	his folk to live in joy and bliss.*	
270	That curses them, cursed he is;	*who*
	who blesseth them is dear.	*whoever;beloved*

BALAACK	Thou preachest, popelard, as a pie;	*fool;magppie*
	the Devil of Hell thee destroy!	
	I bade thee curse my enemy—	
275	therefore thou come me to.	*are come*
	Now hast thou blessed them here twy,	*twice*
	for thou means me to annoy.	*harm*

| BALAAM | Sir king, I told thee ere so twy | *before;twice* |
| | I might none other do. | |

*Then Balaam turns to the east on the mountain side, and, looking to Heaven, says in a prophetic spirit: "Orietur stella ex Jacob et exurget homo de Israel et consurget omnes duces alienigenarum, et erit omnis terra possessio eius."**

| BALAAM | Now one thing I will tell you all, | |

---

264 "Ah, Lord, what a beautiful place to live."

268–69 "I know well that God made all this so that his people might live in joy and happiness."

279+SD "There shall come a star out of Jacob and a man shall arise out of Israel, and he shall raise up all the leaders of the Gentiles, and the whole Earth shall be his possession." The text quoted is a variation of that in Numbers 24.17.

281	hereafter what shall befall:	
	a star of Jacob spring shall,	
	a man of Israel,	
	that shall overcome and have in band	*bondage*
285	all kings and dukes of strange land;	*foreign*
	and all this world have in his hand	
	as lord to dight and deal.	*assign and dispose*

BALAACK	Go we hence; it is no boot	*avail*
	longer with this man to moot,	*debate*
290	for God is both crop and root	*all-powerful*
	and Lord of Heaven and Hell.	
	⟨Now see I well no man on live more! ?	*alive*
	against him is able to strive.⟧	
	Therefore here, as mote I thrive,	*so may I thrive*
295	I will no longer dwell.	

Here Balaam speaketh to Balaack: "Abide a while."

BALAAM	Oh, Balaack king, abide a while!	
	I have imagined a marvellous wile	*trick*
	thy enemies how thou shalt beguile,	
	my counsel if thou take.	

300	There may no pestilence them dismay,	*daunt*
	neither battle them affray.	*terrify*
	Plentiful they shall be ay	*always*
	of gold, cattle and corn.	*in*
	Their God of them takes the cure	*care*
305	from passions, that he makes them sure,	*sufferings; secure*
	them to preserve in great pleasure	
	as he before hath sworn.	

	Ye shall not them destroy for ay—	*for ever*
	but for a time vex them ye may!	
310	Mark well now what I shall say	
	and work after my lore.	*according to my teaching*
	Send forth women of thy country—	*from*
	namely, those that beautiful be—	*especially*
	and to thy enemies let them draw nigh,	
315	as stalls to stand them before.	*decoys*

	When the young men that lusty be
	have perceived their great beauty,

they shall desire their company,
love shall them so inflame.
320   Then, when they see they have them sure   *secure*
in their love withouten cure,   *heedlessly*
they shall deny them their pleasure
except they grant this same—

to love their great solemnity   *solemn ceremonies*
325   and worship the gods of thy country,
and all things commonly   *in common*
with other people to use.
So shall they their God displease
and turn themselves to great disease.   *misfortune*
330   Then may thou have thy heart's ease,
their law when they refuse.   *reject*

BALAACK   Balaam, thy counsel I will fulfill.   *carry out*
It shall be done right as thou will.   *just as you wish*
Come near, my knight that well can skill   *knows well how*
335   my message to convoy.   *convey*
Go thou forth, thou valiant knight;
look thou ne stop day ne night.   *do not stop; nor*
Bring those women to my sight
that shall my enemies destroy.

340   Spare thou neither rich ne poor,   *nor*
widow, maid ne ilk whore,   *nor any*
if she be fresh of colour.   *of beautiful complexion*
Bring her with thee, I say.

KNIGHT   My lord, I shall hie me fast   *hasten*
345   to do your will in goodly haste.
Trust ye well at the last
your enemies ye shall dismay.   *discomfort*

The Expositor speaketh:

EXPOSITOR   Lords and ladies that here been lent,   *are present*
this messenger that forth was sent

347+SD The Expositor gives a compressed account of Numbers 25.1–9 concerning
Moses' response to his people's disobedience, their potential rebellion, and its
suppression.

350	as ye have heard— to that intent—	*for that purpose*
	these women for to bring—	
	so craftily he hath wrought,	*contrived*
	the fairest women he hath out sought;	
	and to God's people he hath them brought—	
355	God knoweth, a perilous thing!	*full of danger*

For when they had of them a sight,
many of them against right   *wrongfully*
gave themself with all their might
those women for to please.
360 And then soon to them they went;
to have their love was their intent,
desiring those women of their consent   *for*
and so to live in peace.

But those women them denied
365 their love. They said it should be tried—
which they might not else abide*
for fear of great deceit.   *gross betrayal*
Those blind people sware many an oath   *swore*
that neither for lief nor for loath   *in no circumstances*
370 at any time they would have them wroth,   *anger for them*
nor never against them plete.   *plead*

So by these women full of illusion   *deception*
God's people were brought to great confusion
and his displeasure; in conclusion,
375 his law they set at nought.
God spake to Moses— lieve ye me—   *believe*
bade him set up a gallows-tree,
the princes of the tribes there hanged to be
for sins that they had wrought.   *committed*

380 With that Moses was sore grieved,   *deeply troubled*
and generally he them repreved.   *as a group:rebuked*
Therefore they would him have mischieved,   *harmed*
but God did him defend.
For the good people that tendered the law,   *administered*
385 when they that great mischief saw,   *misfortune*
wholly together they can them draw,   *drew together*

---

366 "Otherwise they could not allow it."

	those wretches to make an end.	*upon those wretches*
	Anon Phineas, a young man devout,*	*at once*
	captain he was of that whole rout—	*company*
390	and of these wretches, without doubt,	*certainly*
	twenty-four thousand they slew.	
	And then God was well content	
	with Phineas for his good intent,	*virtuous resolve*
	as the prophet writeth verament,	*truly*
395	and here we shall it shew:	*reveal*

*"Stetit Phineas, et placavit, et cessavit quassatio, et reputatum est ei ad justitiam in generatione sua," etc.**

	Soon after, by God's commandment,	*command*
	to the Midianites they went,	
	and there they slew, verament,	*truly*
	Balaam, with five giants more.	
400	Lordings, much more matter	*sirs; material*
	is in this story than ye have heard here.	
	But the substance, withouten were,	
	was played you before.*	

	And by this prophecy, lieve ye me,	*believe*
405	three kings, as ye shall played see,	
	honoured at his nativity	
	Christ when he was bore.	*born*
	Now, worthy sirs both great and small,	
	here have we showed	*shown*
	this story before,	*before whom*
410	and if it be pleasing to you all,	*if*
	tomorrow next ye shall have more.	

---

388 Phineas was, in fact, Chief Priest. He slew an Israelite and the Moabite woman whom the man had brought into the Israelite camp. He subsequently accompanied the expedition to punish the Midianites. The account here differs somewhat from that in Numbers, q.v.

395+Latin "Then stood up Phineas and executed judgement; and so the plague was stayed. And that was counted unto him for righteousness among his generation," etc.; Psalms 105 (AV 106).30–31.

402–3 "But the essential matter of the story, assuredly, was performed before you."

Praying you all, both east and west
where that ye go, to speak the best. *speak well of us*
The Birth of Christ, fair and honest,
415 here shall ye see; and fare ye well.

THE END

PLAY 6: THE ANNUNCIATION AND THE NATIVITY

Performed by the Wrights

PLAY 6, which begins the section of the cycle dealing with the life of Christ, is a surprisingly complex play. Its biblical material comprises the annunciation to the Virgin Mary and her visit to her cousin Elizabeth (Luke 1.28–56); the jealous suspicions of her husband Joseph (Matthew 1.20); the taxation of the world by order of the emperor, Augustus Caesar, which took Joseph and Mary from their home in Nazareth to Bethlehem (Luke 2.1–3); and the birth of Jesus Christ in a stable (Luke 2.6–7). These accounts have been amplified from apocryphal New Testament gospels—writings which were excluded from the recognised biblical canon in the fourth century AD but which had been used by the earlier Church Fathers and permeated legendaries and other authorised texts. From them derive the fuller account of Joseph's jealousy, Mary's vision of the two peoples, and the presence of two midwives at Christ's birth, one of whom is punished for her disbelief.

The dramatist has also incorporated the legend of the vision and conversion of the emperor Octavian, drawing particularly on material in guidebooks to the wonders of Rome. This story is intercut with the biblical material, providing a strong social and theological contrast between the poor Jewish family who are chosen as Christ's earthly parents and the powerful emperor who rules all the known world. Commentators frequently noted that the Prince of Peace was born during the *pax Romana*, the period of peace under Roman rule, and the play points the contrast in the misguided offer of deification to Octavian by the Senate because the earthly peace—effected through a diabolically contrived temple—is misread as a sign of supernatural power. Octavian is, however, a rational pagan who can understand the nature of Godhead, recognises his mortality, and consequently accepts the interpretation of the vision he receives.

The action requires considerable shifts of location—from Mary's house to Elizabeth's and back; Joseph's place of departure and return; the journey to the stable in Bethlehem; and the intercutting between Bethlehem and Rome. The "well-decked carriage" of the Post-Reformation Banns may have carried two sets in close juxtaposition—the stable and the court—since the Pre-Reformation Banns speak of "your cariage of Marie, myld quene, and of Octavian"; if so, they may have been curtained off, leaving a small "unspecified" acting area in front for the annunciation at one side and the meeting with Elizabeth on the other. Joseph could simply cross the stage on his departure. Alternatively, parts of those actions could have been acted at ground-level, as other parts of the play surely must have been. Octavian and his court seem to enter through the audience, since room is demanded for them; the messenger's dialogue with Joseph would gain contemporary force if conducted among the crowd; and the journey to Jerusalem with the vision of different people must in practical terms have required space at ground-level. The Expositor probably enters at ground-level, halting the action on stage and thus emphasising the structural transitions.

Mary, presumably dressed in traditional blue and wearing a crown, would be played by a boy-chorister who could sing the *Magnificat.* Joseph was traditionally played as an old man with a long beard. As the historical carpenter played by a contemporary Chester wright (i.e., a carpenter), it is appropriate that at lines 368–95 he should complain against excessive state taxation on behalf of Chester's craftsmen.

Cast   GABRIEL/ANGEL, MARY, ELIZABETH, JOSEPH, MESSENGER, OCTAVIAN, FIRST SENATOR, SECOND SENATOR, SIBYL, TEBEL, SALOME, EXPOSITOR.

GABRIEL   Hail be thou, Mary, mother free,[*]
               full of grace. God is with thee.
               Amongst all women blessed thou be,
               and the fruit of thy body.

---

1 "Good fortune to you, Mary, noble mother." The first four lines are an amalgamation of Gabriel's words in Luke 1.28 and Elizabeth's in Luke 1.42, known as the *Ave Maria.*

MARY	Ah, Lord that sits high in see,	*on the high throne*
6	that wondrously now marvels me!*	
	A simple maiden of my degree	*station*
	be greet thus graciously!	*should be greeted so*

GABRIEL	Mary, ne dread thee nought this case.*	
10	With great God found thou has	
	amongst all other special grace.	*other women*
	Therefore, Mary thou mon	*may*
	conceive and bear—I tell thee—	
	a child. Jesus his name shall be—	
15	so great shall never none be as he—	
	and call-ed God's Son.	*(he shall be) called*

	And our Lord God, lieve thou me,	*believe*
	shall give him David, his father's, see;	*throne*
	in Jacob's house reign shall he	
20	with full might evermore.	
	And he that shall be born of thee,	
	endless life in him shall be,	
	that such renown and royalty	*so that*
	had never none before.	

MARY	How may this be, thou beast so bright?	*being*
26	In sin know I no worldly wight.	*earthly person*

GABRIEL	The Holy Ghost shall in thee light	*Spirit; alight*
	from God in majesty	
	and shadow thee, seemly in sight.*	
30	Therefore that holy, as I have hight,	*promised*
	that thou shalt bear through God's might,	
	his Son shall called be.	

	Elizabeth, that barren was,	
	as thou may see, conceived has	
35	in age a son through God's grace,	

---

6 "How wondrously I marvel now!"

9 "Mary, have no fear at all about this situation."

29 "And enfold you, beautiful to behold"; *shadow,* in its senses of "cast a shadow" and "enfold," suggests the mystery of the immaculate conception of Jesus, born of a virgin and without taint of original sin.

= herald

	the beadle shall be of bliss.	*herald*
	The sixth month is gone now again	
	sith men called her barren;	*since*
	but nothing to God's might and main	
40	impossible is.	

MARY	Now sith that God will it so be	*since*
	and such grace hath sent to me,	
	blessed evermore be he;	
	to please him I am paid.	*contented*
45	Lo, God's chosen meekly here—	*chosen one*
	and, Lord God, prince of power,	
	leve that it fall in such manner,	*grant; come about*
	this word that thou hast said.	

Then the angel shall go, and Mary shall greet Elizabeth.

MARY	Elizabeth, niece, God thee see.	*cousin; God keep you*

ELIZABETH	Mary, blessed mot thou be,	*may*
51	and the fruit that comes of thee,	*from*
	among women all.	
	Wonderly now marvels me	*wondrously; I marvel*
	that Mary, God's mother free,	*noble*
55	greets me thus, of simple degree.	*of lowly status*
	Lord, how may this befall?	

	When thou me greetest, sweet Mary,	*greeted*
	the child stirred in my body	
	for great joy of thy company	
60	and the fruit that is in thee.	
	Blessed be thou ever forthy,	*therefore*
	that lived so well and steadfastly;	
	for that was said to thee, lady,	*what*
	fulfilled and done shall be.	

Mary, rejoicing, shall begin the canticle "Magnificat," etc.

MARY	Much has that Lord done for me,	
66	that most is in his majesty.	*greatest*

64+SD *Magnificat*—The first word of, and hence the name given to, the Vespers
canticle from Luke 1.46–55.

     All princes he passes of posty,   *surpasses in power*
     as showeth well by this.   *appears*
     Therefore with full heart and free   *open*
70   his name alway hallowed be;   *always; esteemed holy*
     and honoured evermore be he
     on high in Heaven-bliss.

     Elizabeth, therefore will I
     thank the Lord, king of mercy,
75   with joyful mirth and melody
     and laud to his liking.   *praise; pleasure*
     "Magnificat," while I have tome,
     "anima mea dominum"
     to Christ that in my kind is come,
80   devoutly I will sing.*

        "Et exultavit spiritus meus in Deo" etc.   / *paraphrases The Magnificat*

     And, for my ghost joyed has   *spirit; rejoiced*
     in God, my heal and all my grace—   *joy*
     for meekness he see in me was,   *because; saw*
     his fere of mean degree—*   *spouse*
85   therefore bless me well may
     all generations for ay.   *for ever*
     Much has God done for me today;
     his name ay hallowed be,   *always; esteemed holy*

     as he is boun to do mercy   *ready*
90   from progeny to progeny.
     And all that dreaden him verily
     his talent to fulfill,
     he through his might gave mastery.
     Disparcles proud dispitously
95   with might of his heart hastily
     at his own will.*

77–80 "While I have the opportunity, I shall reverently sing to Christ, who has come into my nature, 'My soul doth magnify the Lord.'"

72+Latin "And my spirit hath rejoiced in God," etc. The Latin is apparently a cue for the continuation of the canticle to its end.

84 "His spouse of low estate."

89–96 "As he is pledged to show mercy from generation to generation. And to all

Deposeth mighty out of place,
and meek also he hanced has;
hungry, needy, wanting grace
100   with good he hath fulfilled.*
That rich power he hath forsaken;   *mighty power*
to Israel his Son he has betaken.   *entrusted*
Weal to Man through him is waken,   *joy; awoken*
and mercy has of his guilt.*

105   As he spake to our fathers before,
Abraham and his seed full yore.   *very long ago*
Joy to the Father evermore,
the Son and the Holy Ghost.
As it was from the beginning
110   and never shall have ending,
from world to world ay wending.   *ever continuing*
Amen, God of might most.   *greatest in power*

ELIZABETH   Mary, now read I that we gone   *advise; go*
to Joseph thy husband anon,   *at once*
115   lest he to miss thee make moan;   *complain*
for now that is most need.

MARY   Elizabeth, niece, to do so good is,   *cousin*
lest he suppose on me amiss;   *falsely suspect*
but good Lord that hath ordained this   *the good Lord*
120   will witness of my deed.   *will bear witness to*

Then they shall go to Joseph.

ELIZABETH   Joseph, God thee save and see!   *watch over you*
Thy wife here I brought to thee.

---

who truly fear him he gave power through his might, to accomplish his will. He
scatters the proud fearlessly whenever he wishes, speedily with the resolve of his
heart." Compare the Gospel version: "And his mercy is on them that fear him
from generation to generation. He hath shewed strength with his arm; he hath
scattered the proud in the imagination of their hearts" (Luke 1.50–51).

97–100 "He puts the mighty out of their place, and he has also exalted the meek;
the hungry, the needy who lack favour he has filled with good things."

104 "And he has mercy on his (Man's) sin."

JOSEPH   Alas, alas, and woe is me!
            Who has made her with child?
125   Well I wist an old man and a may   *knew; maiden*
            might not accord by no way.   *be compatible*
            For many years might I not play   *make love*
            ne work no works wild.

            Three months she hath been from me.
130   Now has she gotten her, as I see,
            a great belly, like to thee,
            sith she went away.   *since*
            And mine it is not, be thou bold,   *sure*
            for I am both old and cold;
135   these thirty winters, though I would,   *might wish to*
            I might not play no play.   *have sexual intercourse*

            Alas! where might I leng or lend?   *stay or dwell*
            For loath is me my wife to shend,*
            therefore from her will I wend   *go*
140   into some other place.
            For to discrive her will I nought,   *betray*
            feebly though she have wrought.*
            To leave her privily is my thought,   *secretly; resolve*
            that no man know this case.   *may know; situation*

145   God, let never an old man
            take to wife a young woman
            ne set his heart her upon,   *nor*
            lest he beguiled be.   *deceived*
            For accord there may be none,   *compatibility*
150   ne they may never be at one;   *nor*
            and that is seen in many one
            as well as on me.

            Therefore, have I slept a while,   *when I have slept*
            my wife that me can thus beguile,   *deceive*
155   I will go from her; for her to file   *accuse*

---

138 "For I am unwilling to cause my wife's death." As indicated in play 12,
stoning to death was the legal punishment for adultery.

142 "Even though she may have acted foolishly"; *feebly* suggests "weakness of
will."

me is loath, in good fay.*
This case makes me so heavy   *situation; weary*
that needs sleep now must I.
Lord, on her thou have mercy
160   for her misdeed today!

Then he sleeps.   =foolish (?)

ANGEL   Joseph, let be thy feeble thought.   *put aside; evil*
Take Mary thy wife, and dread thee nought,
for wickedly she hath not wrought;   *acted*
but this is God's will.
165   The child that she shall bear, iwiss,   *truly*
of the Holy Ghost begotten it is,
to save Mankind that did amiss,   *sinned*
and prophecy to fulfill.

JOSEPH   Ah, now I wot, Lord, it is so,   *know*
170   I will no man be her foe;   *wish no man to be*
but while I may on Earth go,
with her I will be.
Now Christ is in our kind light, ✳   *human form; come down*
as the prophets before hight.   *promised*
175   Lord God, most of might,   *greatest in power*
with weal I worship thee.   *joy*

MESSENGER   Make room, lordings, and give us way,   *sirs*
and let Octavian come and play,   *perform*
and Sibyl the sage,
that well fair may,   *most beautiful maiden*
180   to tell you of prophecy.
That Lord that died on Good Friday,
he save you all both night and day!   *didactic?*
Farewell, lordings. I go my way;   *sirs*
I may no longer abide.   *stay*

OCTAVIAN*   Seigneurs tous ici assembles a mes probes estates!

---

156 "I am reluctant, truly."

184+SH *Octavian*, i.e., the first Roman Emperor, Augustus Caesar. Although there
was a pervasive tradition that he was evil—a picture found in the Towneley
Plays—Chester follows an alternative tradition in which his reign of peace

186   Je pousse faire lerment et lees, et met en longeur!*
        Vous tous prest ne sorts de faire entent a mes volents,
        car je suis souverain bien sage, et du monde l'empereur.
        Je suis person nul si able; je sais tant faire et leable.
190   En tresorice ne tresagile, me de toile plerunt.
        Discret et sage je suis en conseil—ami, ou dame, et ou
            pucelle.
        De claire et sancte mere fraile, un tel n'est pas vivant.*

King, coysel, clerk, or knight,	*emperor; cleric*
saudens, senators in sight,	*sultans; here*
195 princes, priests here now dight	*arrayed*
and present in this place,	
peace! Or here my truth I plight—	*pledge*
I am the manfullest man of might—	*most manly*
takes mind on my menace.	*heed of; threat*

200 All ledes in land be at my liking—	*men; will*
castle, conqueror, and king—	
bain to do my bidding;	*obedient*
it will none other be.	
Right as I think, so must all be;	*exactly as*
205 for all the world does my willing	*performs my wishes*
and bain been when I bid bring	*are obedient*
homage and fealty.*	

---

provided the appropriate context for the coming of Christ. The Post- Reformation Banns, however, seem to suggest the "bad" Octavian.

185–86 Octavian begins his speech in French, which the manuscripts present in a garbled and often unintelligible version. An attempt is here made to modernise it where possible, but it, and the translation offered in the note below, is *very* tentative. Though the lines were once meaningful, it is unlikely that the contemporary audience was expected to understand them.

185–92 "Lords, all assembled here at my noble council, I can make (people) miserable or happy, and cast (them) into despondency. None of you should leave here intending to perform evil deeds, for I am the sovereign full of wisdom, and the emperor of the world. I am a person, none so capable; I know how to do many praiseworthy deeds. [Next line totally obscure!] Discreet and wise I am in counsel, friend to lady and maiden. By the pure and holy mother—such another ruler does not live!"

207 *fealty*—i.e., the feudal obligation of fidelity from vassal to lord.

Sithen I was lord, withouten leas- lies
with my wit I can more increase
210   the empire here than ever it was,
as all this world it wiste.*   *knows*
Sith I was sovereign, war clear   *since; completely*
    can cease,   *has ceased*
and through this world now is peace,   *throughout*
for so dread a duke sat never on dais   *fearsome*
215   in Rome—that you may trust.   *believe*

Therefore, as lord now likes me   *I am pleased*
to preve my might and my posty,   *demonstrate; power*
for I will send about and see
how many heads I have.   *i.e., people I rule*
220   All the world shall written be,   *be registered*
great and small, in each degree,   *every class*
that dwell in shire or in city—
king, clerk, knight or knave.   *cleric; servant*

Each man one penny shall pay.
225   Therefore, my beadle, do as I say.   *messenger*
In midst the world by any way   *middle of*
this gamen shall begin.   *process*
The folk of Jews, in good fay,   *Jewish people; truly*
in midst been—that is no nay.   *there's no denying*
230   Therefore thither, day by day!   *go there*
And travail or thou blin.   *keep going; till; stop*

Warn him that there is president   *in charge*
that this is fully mine intent:
that each man appear present,   *at once*
235   his penny for to pay.
And by that penny as well apent   *pertains*
knowledge to be obedient   *acknowledgement*
to Rome, by gift of such a rent,
from that time after ay.   *for ever*

240   When this is done thus in Judee,   *Judea*
that in the midst of the world shall be,

208–11 "Since I was lord, without any lies, I have extended the empire here by
my cleverness more than it ever was." Octavian's reign of peace was often
regarded as the reason for the coming of Christ, the Prince of Peace, at that time.

	to each land, shire, and city!	*go to*
	To Rome make them so thrall!	*similarly subject*
	Warn them, boy—I command thee—	
245	they do the same. Say thus from me.	
	So all this world shall wit that we	*know*
	been sovereign of them all.	*are*

Have done! Boy, art thou not boun?   *enough!; ready*

MESSENGER All ready, my lord, by Mahound!
250   No tail-less tupp in all this town   *ram*
                   shall go further, without fail.*   *certainly*

OCTAVIAN   Boy, therefore by my crown
                   thou must have thy warrison!   *reward*
                   The highest horse beside Boughton*
255   take thou for thy travail.   *labour*

MESSENGER Gramercy, lord, perdy;   *thanks; indeed*
                   this hackney will well serve me—
                   for a great lord of your degree   *rank*
                   should ride in such array.
260   Thee been high in dignity,   *you are*
                   and also high and swift is he!
                   Therefore, that reverence takes ye,   *place of honour*
                   my dear lord, I you pray.

                   But your errand shall be done anon.   *at once*
265   First into Judee I will gone   *Judea; go*
                   and summon the people everychone,   *every one*
                   both shire and eke city.   *also*

OCTAVIAN   Boy, there been ladies many one;   *many a one*
                   among them all choose thee one.
270   Take the fairest, or else none,
                   and freely I give her thee.

250–51 The reference appears to be to a breeding ram with docked tail in search
of ewes to mount.

254 I.e., the gallows of the city of Chester, which were at Boughton Heath, some
two miles to the southeast of the city.

1ST SENATOR	My lord Octavian, we be sent	
	from all Rome with good intent.	*purpose*
	Thy men there have each one i-meant	*decided*
275	as god to honour thee.	*a god*
	And to that point we be assent,	*on; agreed*
	poor and rich in parliament.	
	For so loved a lord, verament,	*truly*
	was never in this city.	

2ND SENATOR	Yea, sicker, sir, their will is this:	*certainly*
282	to honour thee as god with bliss,	*joyfully*
	for thou did never to them amiss	*wrong*
	in word, thought, ne deed.	*nor*
	Peace hath been long, and yet is.	*still*
285	No man in thy time lost ought of his.	*anything*
	Therefore their will is so, iwiss,	*indeed*
	to quite you thus your meed.	*repay; due*

OCTAVIAN	Welcome, my friends, in good fay,	*faith*
	for you be bainable to my pay.	*obedient; pleasure*
290	I thank you, all that ever I may,	*as best I can*
	the homage ye do to me.	*for the homage*
	[But folly it were by many a way	*in many respects*
	such sovereignty for to assay,	*attempt*
	sith I must die—I wot not what day—	*since; know*
295	to desire such dignity.]	*high position*

	For all of flesh, blood and bone	
	made I am, born of a woman;	
	and sicker other matter none	*certainly; material*
	showeth not right in me.	*not at all*
300	Neither of iron, tree ne stone	*nor*
	am I not wrought, you wot each one.	*created; know*
	And of my life, most part is gone—	
	age shows him so, I see!	*manifests himself*

	And godhead asks in all thing	*requires*
305	time that hath no beginning	
	ne never shall have ending;	*nor*
	and none of these have I.	
	Wherefore, by very proof showing,	*true*
	though I be highest worldly king,	
310	of godhead have I no knowing.	*knowledge*
	It were unkindly.	*it would be unnatural*

— not good!
paganism.

But yet enquire of this will we
at her that has grace for to see   *of*
things that afterward shall be
315   by ghost of prophecy.   *a spirit*
And, after her lore, by my lewty,
discussing this difficulty
work; and take no more on me   *act*
than I am well worthy.*   *properly*

320   Sibyl the sage, tell me this thing,
for thou wit has as no man living;   *understanding*
shall ever be any earthly king
to pass me of degree?   *surpass; in condition*

SIBYL   Yea, sir, I tell you without leasing   *truly*
325   a barn born shall be, bliss to bring,   *child*
the which that never has beginning   *the same who*
ne never shall ended be.   *nor*

OCTAVIAN   Sibyl, I pray thee specially,   *particularly*
by sign thou would me certify   *confirm for me*
330   what time that lord so royally
to reign he shall begin.

        Sibyl speaketh:

SIBYL   Sir, I shall tell you witterly   *certainly*
his signs when I see verily;   *portents; truly*
for when he comes, through his mercy
335   on Mankind he will min.   *think*

Well I wot, forsooth iwiss,   *know; truly indeed*
that God will bring Mankind to bliss,
and send from Heaven—lieves well this—   *believe*
his Son, our saviour.
340   Jesus Christ, nothing amiss,   *appropriately*
called he shall be, and is;
to overcome the Devil and his cointise,   *cunning*
and be our conqueror.   *conqueror for us*

316–19 "And, by my faith, I shall act according to her instruction as she considers this problem and take no more upon myself than I fully deserve."

	But what time, sir, in good fay	truly
345	that he will come can I not say.	
	Therefore in this place I will pray	
	to greatest God of might.	
	And if I see ought to your pay	pleasure
	ghostly by any way,	at all spiritual
350	warn you I shall anon this day,	alert; at once
	and show it in your sight.	display it to you

Then Sibyl prays, and the Messenger shall speak in a loud voice:

MESSENGER	Peace I bid, king and knight,	ask
	men and women and each wight;	every person
	till I have told that I have tight,	what I have prepared
355	stand still, both strong and stout.	stand; sturdy
	My lord Octavian, much of might,	great in power
	commands you should be ready dight:	prepared
	tribute he will have in height	at once
	of all this world about.	from

360	He will have written each country,	a record made of
	castle, shire and eke city,	also
	men and women—lieve you me—	believe
	and all that be therein.	
	A penny of each man have will he—	from
365	the value of ten pence it shall be—	
	to knowledge that he has sovereignty	acknowledge
	fully of all Mankind.	

JOSEPH	Ah, Lord! What does this man now here?	is his business
	Poor men's weal is ever in were.	prosperity; doubt
370	I wot by this boaster's bere	know; din
	that tribute I must pay—	
	and for great age and no power	lack of strength
	I won no good this seven year.	earned no wealth
	Now comes the king's messenger	
375	to get all that he may.	

| | With this axe that I bear, | |
| | this percer and this nauger* | |

---

377 The actor here displays the tools of the carpenter's trade. The piercer and

	and this hammer all in fere,	*all together*
	I have wonnen my meat.	*earned my food*
380	Castle, tower, ne rich manor	*nor*
	had I never in my power;	
	but, as a simple carpenter,	
	with these what I might get.	

	If I have store now anything,	*anything saved up*
385	that must I pay unto the king.	
	But yet I have a liking,	*a source of pleasure*
	the angel to me told:	
	he that should Man out of bale bring	*torment*
	my wife had in her keeping.	
390	That seems all good to my liking,	*totally; pleasure*
	and makes me more bold.	

	Ah, lief sir, tell me, I thee pray:	*dear*
	shall poor as well as rich pay?	
	By my fay, sir, I hope nay.	*indeed; not*
395	That were a wondrous wrong.	

MESSENGER	Good man, I warn thee in good fay	*truly*
	to Bethlehem to take the way,	
	lest thou in danger fall today	
	if that thou be too long.	*take*

JOSEPH	Now sith it may none other be,	*since*
401	Mary, sister, now hie we.	*companion; hasten*
	An ox I will take with me	
	that there shall be sold.	
	The silver of him, so mote I thee,	*from; so may I thrive*
405	shall find us in that city,*	*support*
	and pay tribute for thee and me;	
	for thereto we been hold.	*constrained*

Then Joseph shall tie the ox and the harness of the ass, and

---

auger are both instruments for boring wood. Joseph was a carpenter and the play is performed by the Wrights.

400–5 The ox and ass are not part of the biblical account but belong with later tradition. They are familiar figures at the Christmas crib and are introduced here in preparation for the tableau at 447+SD, to which the Expositor refers at 619–20.

shall gather Mary up on to the ass; and when she shall have
come to the stable, Mary shall say:

MARY	Ah Lord! What may this signify?	
	Some men I see glad and merry	
410	and some sighing and sorry.	
	Wherefore soever it be?	*Why ever*
	Sith God's Son came, Man to forbuy—	*since; redeem*
	is comen through his great mercy—	*come*
	methink that Man should kindly	*naturally*
415	be glad that sight to see.	

ANGEL	Mary, God's mother dear,	
	the tokening I shall thee lere.	*significance; teach*
	The common people, as thou seest here,	
	are glad—as they well may—	*may be*
420	that they shall see of Abraham's seed	
	Christ come to help them in their need.	
	Therefore they joyen withouten dread	*rejoice; fearlessly*
	for to abide this day.	*experience*

	The mourning men—take this in mind—	*remember*
425	are Jews that shall be put behind,	*displaced*
	for they passed out of kind	
	through Christ at his coming.*	
	For they shall have no grace to know	
	that God for Man shall light so low;	*come down*
430	for shame on them that soon shall show.	*disgrace*
	Therefore they been mourning.	*are*

teaching on Jews

JOSEPH	Mary, sister, sooth to say,	*companion; truth to tell*
	harbour, I hope, get we ne may;	*lodging; think; not*
	for great lords of stout array	*with strong retinue*
435	occupy this city.	
	Therefore we must in good fay	*truly*
	lie in this stable till it be day.	
	To make men meek, lieve I may,	*I may believe*
	show him here will he.	*appear*

426–27 "For they abandoned their natural moral feeling because of Christ at his
coming"; or "because they passed out of the role of (God's chosen) race through
Christ at his coming."

MARY	Help me down, my lief fere,	*dear husband*
441	for I hope my time be near.	*think*
	Christ in this stable that is here	
	I hope born will be.	*expect*

Then Joseph shall take Mary in his arms.

JOSEPH	Come to me, my sweet dear,	
445	the treasure of Heaven without were!	*doubt*
	Welcome in full meek manner!	*most humbly*
	Him hope I for to see.	*expect*

Then he shall place Mary between the ox and the ass.

JOSEPH	Mary, sister, I will assay
	to get two midwives if I may;
450	for though in thee be God verray—
	and comen against kind—
	for usage here of this city
	and manners' sake, as thinks me,
	two I will fetch anon to thee
455	if I may any find.*

JOSEPH (*to the midwives*)

	Women, God you save and see!	*watch over*
	Is it your will to go with me?	
	My wife is comen into this city	*has come*
	with child, and time is near.	*pregnant;her time*
460	Helps her now for charity,	*love*
	and be with her till day be;	*it is*
	and your travail, so mot I thee,	*work;so may I thrive*
	I shall pay you right here.	*pay you for*

TEBEL	All ready, good man, in good fay!	*truly*
465	We will do all that ever we may.	
	For two such midwives, I dare well say,	

448-55 "Mary, dearest, I shall try to get two midwives, if I can; for though the true God is within you—and though he is come in a way contrary to Nature—I will fetch two right away to you, if I can find any, because of the usual practice and conventions here in this city, as it seems to me"; *sister* is a term of endearment, suggestive of the close but platonic relationship of Joseph and Mary. The Midwives are found in the apocryphal Nativity gospels; their inclusion is defended in the Post-Reformation Banns.

are not in this city.

SALOME	Come, good man, lead us the way.	*for us*
	By God's help, or it be day	*before*
470	that we can good thy wife shall say—	*know our job well*
	and that thou shalt well see!	

JOSEPH	Lo, Mary, heart, brought I have here	*beloved*
	two midwives for the manner,	*according to custom*
	to be with thee, my darling dear,	
475	till that it be day.	

MARY	Sir, they be welcome without were.	*certainly*
	But God will work of his power	*by*
	full soon for me, my lief fere,	*dear husband*
	as best is now and ay.	*always*

Then for a little while they are quiet.

MARY	Ah, Joseph, tidings aright!	*true*
481	I have a son, a sweet wight.	*dear fellow*
	Lord, thanked be thou full of might,	
	for preved is thy posty.	*proved; power*
	Pain none I felt this night.	
485	But right so as he in me light,	*descended*
	comen he is here in my sight—	*come; before my eyes*
	God's Son, as thou may see.	

*Then the star shall appear.**

JOSEPH	Lord, welcome, sweet Jesu!	
	Thy name thou hadst or I thee knew.	*before*
490	Now lieve I the angel's words true,	*believe*
	that thou art a clean may.	*pure virgin*
	For thou art comen Man's bliss to brew	*come; bring*
	to all that thy law will shew.	*profess*
	Now Man's joy begins to new	*renew*
495	and noy to pass away.	*misery*

487+SD Evidence from the subsequent plays suggests that the star is carried by the angel. The repetition at 525+SD may be an error, or may suggest that the star alone is seen here and that subsequently the angel carrying it reveals himself.

MARY   Lord, blessed mayst thou be
               that simple born art, as I see;
               to prive the Devil of his posty,   *deprive; power*
               comen thou art today,   *come*
500   Diversory is none for thee.   *lodging-place*
               Therefore thy sweet body free   *noble*
               in this cratch shall lie with lee,   *cradle; joy*
               and lapped about with hay.   *be wrapped*

TEBEL   Ah, dear Lord, Heaven-king,
505   that this is a marvellous thing!   *what a* (exclam.)
               Withouten teen or travailing *without pain or labour*
               a fair son she has one.
               I dare well say, forsooth iwiss,   *in all truth*
               that clean maiden this woman is,   *pure virgin*
510   for she hath born a child with bliss;   *pleasure*
               so wist I never none.   *know*

SALOME   Be still, Tebel, I thee pray,
               for that is false, in good fay.   *truly*
               Was never woman clean may   *pure virgin*
515   and had child without man.
               But never the later, I will assay *nevertheless; test*
               whether she be a clean may,   *pure virgin*
               and know it if I can.

Then Salome shall attempt to touch Mary in her private parts,
and at once her hands shall dry up; and crying out she shall
say:

SALOME   Alas, alas, alas, alas!
520   me is betide an evil case!*
               My hands be dried up in this place,
               that feeling none have I.   *so that*
               Vengeance on me is now light,   *descended*
               for I would tempt God's might.
525   Alas, that I came here tonight
               to suffer such annoy.   *harm*

Then the star shall appear and the Angel shall come, saying as
follows:

---

520 "A dreadful thing has happened to me."

ANGEL	Woman, beseech this child of grace	*for*
	that he forgive thee thy trespass;	*sin*
	and ere thou go out of this place	
530	holpen thou may be.	*helped*
	This miracle that now thou seest here	
	is of God's own power,	
	to bring Mankind out of danger	
	and mend them, lieve thou me.	*restore; believe*

SALOME	Ah, sweet child, I ask mercy	
536	for thy mother's love, Mary.	
	Though I have wrought wretchedly,	*acted*
	sweet child, forgive it me!	
	Ah, blessed be God! All whole am I!	
540	Now lieve I well and sickerly	*believe; certainly*
	that God is comen, Man to forbuy,	*come; redeem*
	and thou, Lord, thou art he.	

EXPOSITOR	Lo, lordings all, of this miracle here	*gentlemen*
	Friar Bartholomew in good manner*	*appropriately*
545	beareth witness, withouten were,	*assuredly*
	as played is you beforn.	*acted; before*
	And other miracles, if I may,	
	I shall rehearse or I go away,	*before*
	that befell that ilk day	*same*
550	that Jesus Christ was born.	

	We read in chronicles express:	*clearly*
	some time in Rome a temple was	
	made of so great riches	
	that wonder was witterly.	*a marvel it was truly*
555	For all things in it, lieve you me,	*believe*
	was silver, gold, and rich perry;	*gems*
	thrid part the world, as read we,	*a third of*
	that temple was worthy.	*worth*

| | Of each province, that book mind mase, | *makes record* |
| 560 | their god's image set there was; | |

---

544 Friar Bartholomew is alleged to be the authority for the material in the source of this part of the play, *The Golden Legend*. That reference may be to an apocryphal Gospel of St. Bartholomew which has not survived. But the ascription to an authority seems more important than his historical identity.

and each one about his neck has
a silver bell hanging,
and on his breast written also
the land's name and the god's, both two.
565 And set was also in midst of tho   *those*
god of Rome, right as a king.   *just like*

About the house also moving there
a man on horse—stood men to stare—
and in his hand he bare a spear,   *bore*
570 all pure dispitously.   *quite ruthlessly*
That horse and man was made of brass;
turning about that image was.
Save certain priests, there might none pass
for Devil's fantasy.   *fear of the Devil*

575 But when that any land with battle
was ready Rome for to assail,
the god's image withouten fail   *without*
of that land rang his bell
and turned his face dispitously   *mercilessly*
580 to god of Rome, as read I,
in tokening that there were ready
to fighting fresh and fell.   *brave and fierce men*

The image also above standing,
when the bell beneath began to ring,
585 turned him all sharply, showing   *quite abruptly*
toward that land his spear.
And when they see this tokening,   *saw; sign*
Rome ordained without tarrying
an host to keep their coming,   *await*
590 long or they came there.   *before*

And in this manner soothly,   *truly*
by art of necromancy,   *black magic*
all the world witterly   *indeed*
to Rome were made to lout.   *bow*
595 And in that temple there doubtless   *truly*
was called therefore "the Temple of Peace,"
that through this sleight battle can cease   *trick; did*
throughout the world about.

But he that cointly this work cast   *cunningly; designed*

600	asked the Devil or he passed	*before; passed by*
	how long that temple it should last	
	that he there can build.	*had built*
	The Devil answered subtly	*enigmatically*
	and said it should last sickerly	*certainly*
605	until a maiden <u>wemlessly</u>	*spotlessly*
	had conceived a child.	

	They heard, and believed therefore	
	it should endure for evermore.	
	But that time that Christ was bore,	*born*
610	it fell down soon in hie.	*immediately*
	Of which house is seen this day	
	somewhat standing, in good fay.	*part; truly*
	But no man dare well go that way	
	for Fiend's fantasy.	*fear of the Devil*

615	That day was seen verament	*in truth*
	three suns in the firmament,	
	and wondrously together went	*they merged*
	and turned into one.	
	The ox, the ass, there they were lent,	*where; stabled*
620	honoured Christ in their intent;	*will*
	and moe miracles, as we have meant	
	to play right here anon.*	

Then he shall point to the star, and Sibyl shall come to the emperor.

SIBYL	Sir emperor, God thee save and see.	*watch over*
	Look up on high after me.	
625	I tell you sicker that born is he	*for sure*
	that passeth thee of power.	*surpasses; in*
	That barn thou seest so great shall be	*child*
	as none like him in any degree	*in any rank*
	to pass all kings, and eke thee,	*surpass; also*
630	that born are or ever were.	

OCTAVIAN	Ah, Sibyl, this is a wondrous sight,

621–22 "And more miracles were seen, as we have decided to perform here straight away"; *was seen*, from the opening line of the stanza, should be understood in plural form here.

        for yonder I see a maiden bright,   *beautiful*
        a young child in her arms clight,   *held*
        a bright cross in his head.
635   Honour I will that sweet wight   *being*
        with incense throughout all my might,
        for that reverence is most right,
        if that it be thy read.   *advice*

        Incense bring, I command, in hie   *at once*
640   to honour this child, king of mercy.
        Should I be God? Nay, nay, witterly!   *indeed*
        Great wrong iwiss it were.   *truly;would be*
        For this child is more worthy
        than such a thousand as am I.
645   Therefore to God most mighty
        incense I offer here.

> *Then the Angel shall sing "Haec est ara Dei caeli," etc. (Let the setting be according to the judgement of the performer.)*[*]

OCTAVIAN   Ah, Sibyl, hears not thou this song?
        My members all it goeth among.[*]
        Joy and bliss makes my heart strong
650   to hear this melody.
        Sicker it may none other be   *certainly*
        but this child is prince of posty   *power*
        and I his subject, as I see.
        He is most worthy.

SIBYL   Yea, sir, thou shalt lieve well this;   *believe*
656   somewhere on earth born he is,
        and that he comes for Man's bliss—
        his tokening this can show.   *sign*
        Reverence him, I read iwiss,   *advise indeed*
660   for other God there none is;
        that hopes otherwise doth amiss,   *whoever believes*

646+SD Latin "This is the altar of the God of heaven," etc. This piece has not been identified with any liturgical piece of music. Possibly it was composed specially for this play, and its length adjusted by the performer for suitable dramatic effect.

648 "It goes through my whole body."

	but him for Christ to know.	*to acknowledge*

OCTAVIAN Sir senators, goes home anon *go; immediately*
and warn my men everychone *every one*
665 that such worship I must forgone *forgo*
as they would do to me.
But this child worship each mon *must*
with full heart, all that you con, *are able*
for he is worthy to lieve upon; *believe*
670 and that now I will see.

1ST SEN- Ah, lord, whatever this may be!
ATOR This is a wondrous sight to see—
for in the star, as thinks me, *it seems to me*
I see a full fair queen. *most beautiful*
675 Sir, shall this child pass ye *surpass*
of worthiness and dignity? *in*
Such a lord, by my lewty, *by my faith*
I wend never had been. *thought*

EXPOSITOR Lordings, that this is verray *sirs; true*
680 by very sign know ye may; *true*
for in Rome in good fay, *certainly*
thereas this thing was seen, *where*
was built a church in noble array *splendid fashion*
in worship of Mary, that sweet may, *maiden*
685 that yet lasts until this day,
as men know that there have been.

And for to have full memory *remembrance*
of the angel's melody
and of this sight sickerly *certainly*
690 the emperor there knew, *(which)*
the church is called "St. Mary,"
the surname is "Ara Caeli," *added name*
that men know now well thereby
that this was fully true.* *entirely*

695 Another miracle I find also

691–94 The church of Santa Maria in Ara Caeli was included in the tourist sights of Rome at the time. It was allegedly within the room in which Octavian saw the vision.

at Christ's birth that fell tho—   *then*
when Salome attempted to know
whether she was a may.   *virgin*
Her hand rotted, as you have seen;
700   whereby you may take good teen   *warning*
       that unbelief is a foul sin,   *lack of faith*
       as you have seen in this play.

                    THE END

PLAY 7: THE SHEPHERDS

Performed by the Printers

Play 7, the *Shepherds' Play*, was a popular piece, sometimes abstracted for independent performance before visiting dignitaries. Its basic material comes from Luke 2.8–20, but as the Post-Reformation Banns say, the account is very limited and much had to be invented. What emerges is partly an affectionately humorous view of the local Welsh shepherds by the "townies" of Chester, and partly a symbolic action in which the literal contemporary shepherds are transformed by their visit to the stable into spiritual pastors seeking vocations within the religious life. Modern directors must consider how far the symbolic reading can and should be carried back into the earlier scenes of feasting and discord and whether the change of vocation can and should be achieved without comic effect.

A great deal of the action up to the angel's song seems to take place at ground-level. At the start the shepherds seem to have come into Chester in search of their sheep driven from the nearby Welsh hills by storms. They gather from different directions, and their boy Trowle sits at some distance from them.

We have some company accounts for this play, and it has been suggested that the amounts of food purchased may indicate that the shepherds shared their feast with the audience. Modern productions suggest that a considerable amount of space is needed for the wrestling-matches, again indicative of ground-level performance. The audience also seems to be encouraged to join in the shepherds' song. In the midsummer show the shepherds went on stilts, and references to "styltes" in the company play-accounts indicate that this may have been a feature of the play also. The waggon presumably serves as location for the angels, and we know from the accounts that the company hired choristers from the cathedral—the Post-Reformation Banns requirement that the *Gloria* be sung "merrily" suggests that a professional performance of this key text was needed. Presumably curtains opened to reveal the stable. The shepherds finally regroup at ground-level to take their leave and go their different ways through the audience as they had entered.

The giving of gifts by the shepherds is not biblical, but seems to follow the model of presentation of gifts by the Magi. The scene is always effective in the shepherds' touching unease about protocol, their comically simple presents and awkward devotion. In our version of the play (but not the 1607 text) the action is extended by including the gifts of the shepherds' boys.

The play relies primarily upon its evocation of local rural activities—the contemporary place-names, the strange herbs, the local delicacies of the feast, the country sport of wrestling (which requires careful choreography), and the singing, which (perhaps significantly) fails to imitate the angels' song and descends into modern "pop." There is, however, also a sense of the hardships of the shepherd's life and the poverty of existence—cold, rags, the simple pastimes and love of company, the poor gifts. The shepherds are countrymen with their sacks, horns and bottles. Trowle has a dog with him and, according to the accounts, two whistles; he also had specially made shoes. Joseph and Mary are as they were in the previous play. Some modern productions have successfully risked using an alert and unfretful baby for the infant Christ; cryptic Account items such as "for Thomas Poolles child, bycose he pled not our God...iiiid" may suggest that this was also a sixteenth-century practice.

Cast   FIRST SHEPHERD (HANKIN), SECOND SHEPHERD (HARVEY), THIRD SHEPHERD (TUDD), TROWLE, ANGEL, MARY, JOSEPH, FIRST BOY, SECOND BOY, THIRD BOY, FOURTH BOY.

1ST SHEP-	On wolds have I walked full wild	*moors*
HERD	under buskes my bower to build,	*bushes; shelter*
	from stiff storms my sheep to shield,	
	my seemly wethers to save.	*beautiful*
5	From comely Conway unto Clwyd*	

---

5 *Conway* is the name of a north Wales river and town 45 miles west of Chester; *Clwyd* is another north Wales river on which stand the towns of Ruthin and

	under tilds them to hide,	*shelters*
	a better shepherd on no side	
	no earthly man may have.	

	For with walking weary I have me rought;	*made myself*
10	beside the such my sheep I sought.	*marsh*
	my titeful tups are in my thought,	*nimble rams*
	them to save and heal	
	from the shrewd scab, it sought,	
	or the rot, if it were wrought.	
15	If the cough had them caught	
	of it I could them heal.*	

	Lo, here be my herbs safe and sound,	
	wisely wrought for every wound—	*prepared*
	they would a whole man bring to ground	*fit; to his grave*
20	within a little while—	
	of henbane and horehound,	
	tib-radish and egermond,*	
	which be my herbs safe and sound	
	meddled on a row.	*assembled*

	Here be more herbs, I tell it you.	
25	I shall reckon them on a row;	*count them up*
	finter, fanter, and fetterfow,	
	and also pennywort.	
	This is all that I know.	
30	For be it wether or be it ewe,	*ram*
	I shall heal them on a row	
	clean from their hurt.	*completely; disease*

Denbigh, respectively 15 and 20 miles west of Chester. North Wales is a sheep-raising area.

12–16 "To save and heal them from the cursed sheep-scab, once traced, or the sheep-rot, if it were formed. If the cough (i.e., pseudotuberculosis) had taken hold of them, I could heal them of it." Scab, rot and cough are three diseases to which sheep are especially prevalent.

21–29 The shepherd lists a number of medicinal herbs, all apparently authentic. They are henbane, horehound, (?)ribwort, agrimony, fumitory, (?)fan-weed, feverfew and pennywort (spelt *pennywrit* in the manuscripts, to the detriment of rhyme). Like the list of diseases, these names attest a professional skill and are more important for their occupational connotations than for their individual reference.

Here is tar in a pot
to heal them from the rot;   *sheep-rot*
35   well I can and well I wot   *am able; know how*
the talgh from them take.   *tallow*
And if sworn it had the Thurse,   *even if; Devil*
yet shall the talgh be in my purse   *tallow; bag*
and the sheep never the worse
40   to run on the rake.   *path*

But no fellowship here have I   *companionship*
save myself alone, in good fay;   *truly*
therefore after one fast will I cry.   *someone*
But first will I drink, if I may.

Here the First Shepherd drinks.

1ST SHEP-   How, Harvey, how!
HERD   Drive thy sheep to the low.   *hill*
47   Thou may not hear except I blow,
as ever have I heal.   *good fortune*

*Then he blows on his horn and cries "Aho! Io! O!" Then the
Second Shepherd comes, carrying a crow's feather and wearing
somewhat old clothes.*

2ND SHEP-   It is no shame for me to show
HERD   how I was set for to sew   *ready*
51   with the feather of a crow
a clout upon my heel.   *patch*

Sits down.

Fellow, now be we well met.
And though methink us need is,[*]
55   had we Tudd here by us set
then might we sit and feed us.

1ST SHEP-   Yea, to feed us friendly in fay,   *faith*
HERD   how might we have our service?[*]

---

54 "And though it seems to me that we lack some things."

57–58 "Yes, truly how could we have the service due to us in order to have a
friendly meal together?"

| | Cry thou must loud, by this day. | *loudly* |
| 60 | Tudd is deaf and may not well hear us. | |

The Second Shepherd cries in a low voice "How, Tudd, Tudd!"

| 2ND SHEP-
HERD | How, Tudd! Come, for thy father's kin. | *for the sake of* |

1ST SHEP- HERD	Nay, fay! Thy voice is wondrous dim.	*quiet*
	Why, knows thou not him?	
	Fie, man, for shame!	

Then he calls in a resonant voice, as before.

1ST SHEP- HERD	Call him "Tudd, Tibby's son!"	
	and then will the shrew come.	*wretch*
67	For in good faith, it is his won	*custom*
	to love well his dame's name.	*mother's*

| 2ND SHEP-
HERD | How, Tudd, Tibby's son! | |

3RD SHEP- HERD	Sir, in faith now I come,	*truly*
	for yet have I not all done	
72	that I have to done;	*do*
	to seeth salve for our sheep	*boil ointment*
	and—lest my wife should it weet—	*know*
	with great gravel and grit	*large stone*
	I scour an old pan.	

77	Hemlock and hayrife—take keep—	
	with tarboist must been all tamed,	
	pennygrass and butter for fat sheep;*	
80	for this salve am I not ashamed.	

Ashamed am I not to show

77–79 "Hemlock and goosegrass—take heed—must be completely mixed with
tar-ointment, pennywort, and butter for fat sheep." *Butter* is here used in the
sense of "ingredient in medicines; cure for diseases, venom, etc." (MED *buter(e)*,
1(b)).

no point that longeth to my craft;*
no better—that I well know—
in land is nowhere laft.   *remaining*

85   For, good men, this is not unknown
to husbands than been here about:
that each man must to his wife bown,   *submit*
and commonly, for fear of a clout.   *generally; blow*

Thus for clouts now care I;   *blows; worry*
90   all is for fear of our dame-kin.   *womenfolk*
Now will I cast my ware hereby,   *wares*
and hie fast that I were at Hankin.   *hurry; be with*

Hankin, hold up thy hand and have me,   *grip me*
94   that I were on height there by thee.   *the hill*

1ST SHEP-   Gladly, sir, and thou would be by me.   *if*
HERD   for loath me is to deny thee.   *I am unwilling*

2ND SHEP-   Now sithen God has gathered us together,   *since*
HERD   with good heart I thank him of his grace.   *for*
Welcome be thou, well fair wether!   *(joc) my fine ram*
100   Tudd, will we shape us to some solace?   *prepare; fun*

3RD SHEP-   Solace would best be seen   *pleasure*
HERD   that we shape us to our supper;   *in that; get ready for*
for meat and drink, well I deem,   *food; consider*
to each deed is most dear.   *for*

1ST SHEP-   Lay forth each man ilich   *set out; alike*
HERD   what he hath left of his livery.   *from; provisions*
107   And I will put forth my pitch   *portion*
with my part first of us all three.   *share*

2ND SHEP-   And such store as my wife had
HERD   in your sight soon shall you see,   *a verb*
111   at our beginning, us for to glad;   *make happy*
for in good meat there is much glee.   *food; delight*

Here is bread this day was baken,   *baked*
onions, garlick, and leeks,

81–82 "I am not ashamed to demonstrate any special skill that pertains to my occupation."

115	butter that bought was in Blacon,*	
	and green cheese that will grease your cheeks.*	

3RD SHEP-HERD	And here ale of Halton I have,*	
	and what meat I had to my hire;	*food; wage*
	a pudding may no man deprave,	*sneer at*
120	and a jannock of Lancastershire.	*Lancashire oat-cake*

	Lo here, a sheep's head soused in ale,	*pickled*
	and a groin to lay on the green,	*pig's snout* – ?
	and sour milk. My wife had ordained	*curds; planned*
124	a noble supper, as well is seen.	

1ST SHEP-HERD	And as it is well seen, ye shall see	
	and that somewhat I have in my sack:	*if; anything*
127	a pig's foot I have here, perdy,	*indeed*
	and a paunch-clout in my pack—	*tripe*

	a womb-clout, fellows, now have I!	*tripe*
130	a liveras, as it is no lack;	*(?)liver; shortage*
	a chitterling—boiled shall be.	*entrails; they be*
	This burden I bear on my back.	

2ND SHEP-HERD	Now will I cast off my cloak	
	and pull out part of my livery,	*provisions*
135	put out that I have in my poke,	*bag*
	and a pig's foot from pudding's puree.*	

3RD SHEP-HERD	Abide, fellows, and ye shall see here	
	this hot meat—we serven it here—	*food; serve*
	gambons and other good meat in fere,	*hams; food; together*
140	a pudding with a prick in the end.	*skewer*

1ST SHEP-HERD	My satchel to shake out	
	to shepherds I am not ashamed—	

---

115 *Blacon* is a village about a mile and a quarter northwest of Chester.

116 *Green cheese* is fresh, unripened cheese with a high fat content.

117 *Halton* is a village ten miles northeast of Chester.

136 "A puree made from sausages" has been questionably proposed!

| | and this tongue pared round about | *cut* |
| | with my teeth it shall be atamed! | *subdued* |

Then they shall eat together, and the First Shepherd shall say:

1ST SHEP- HERD 147	Bid me do gladly, and I thee, for by God here is good grousing! Come eat with us, God of Heaven high— ✓ but take no heed though here be no housing!	*if I thrive* *eating*
2ND SHEP- HERD 151	Housing enough have we here while that we have heaven over our heads. Now to wet our mouths time were; this flacket will I tame, if thou read us.	*it were* *flask; reduce* *recommend us*
3RD SHEP- HERD 155	And of this bottle now will I bib, for here is bowls of the best. Such liquor makes men to live; this game may nowhere be lest.	*drink* *pleasure; lost*
1ST SHEP- HERD 160	Fellows, now our bellies be full, think we on him that keeps our flocks. Blow thy horn and call after Trowle, and bid him some of our bitlocks.	*offer; left-overs*
2ND SHEP- HERD	Well said, Hankin, by my sooth, for that shrew, I suppose, us seeks. My horn to lill I will not less till that lad have some of our leeks.	*truly* *wretch* *sound; cease*
3RD SHEP- HERD 167	Leeks to his livery is liking; such a lad nowhere in land is. Blow a mote for that miting while that horn now in thy hand is.	*portion; pleasing* *horn-note; youth*
1ST SHEP- HERD 171	With this horn I shall make a "How!" that he and all Heaven shall hear. Yonder lad that sits on a low the lote of this horn he shall hear.	*(imit.)* *hill* *sound*

Then Trowle shall sing and say:

| TROWLE | Good Lord, look on me |

	and my flock, here as they fed have.	
175	On this wold walk we;	*moor*
	are no men here, that no way!	*by no means*
	All is plain, perdee.	*flat land; indeed*
	Therefore, sheep, we mon go.	*must go on*
	No better may be	
180	of beasts that blood and bone have.	*among animals*

	Wot I not, day or night,	*know*
	necessaries that to me be needing—	*may be requisite*
	nettle, tarboist and tarboll,	
	small hans that to me be needing,	
185	hemlock and butter abiding,	
	and my good dog Dottynoll	
	that is nothing choice of his chiding.*	

	If any man come me by	
	and would wit which way best were,	*know*
190	my leg I lift up whereas I lie	*where*
	and wish him the way east and west-where.	*-wards*
	And I rose where I lay,	*if*
	me would think that travail lost.	*it would seem; labour*
	For king ne duke, by this day,	*nor*
195	rise I will not, but take my rest here.	

	Now will I sit here adown	
	and pipe at this pot like a pope!	
	Would God that I were down	
	harmless, as I hastily hope.	*uninjured; believe*
200	At me all men learn mon	
	this "golgotha" grimly to grope.*	
	No man drink here shall	
	save myself, the devil of a sop.	*drink*

| | All these lotes I set at lit— | *horn-calls; don't care about* |
| 205 | nay, ye lads, set I not by ye! | |

181–87 "Nettle, a tar-box, a tar-ball, small items of clothing that I need, hemlock and the remaining butter (i.e., salve), and my good dog Dottynoll, who isn't choosy who he barks at."

200–1 "All men may learn from me how to handle this 'golgotha' seriously." The *golgotha* is probably a skull-shaped cup.

	For you have I many a foul fit.	*rotten time*
	Thou foul filth, though thou flite,	*rage*
	I defy thee!	

1ST SHEP-	Trowle, take tent to my talking.	*pay attention*
HERD	For thy tooth here is good tugging.	
210	While thy wethers been walking,	
	on this loin thou may have good lugging.	*gnawing*

TROWLE	Fie on your loins and your livery,	*portions of food*
	your liverasts, livers and longs,	*victuals; lungs*
	your sauce, your souse, your savoury,	*pickled meat*
215	your sitting without any songs!	

	On this hill I hold me here.	*remain*
	No hap to your hot meat have I.	*chance of; food*
	But flyte with my fellows in fere,	*argue; together*
	and your sheep full sickerly save I.	*most securely*

2ND SHEP-	For thou saves our sheep,	
HERD	good knave, take keep;	*servant; heed*
222	sithen thou may not sleep,	*since*
	come, eat of this souse.	*pickled meat*

TROWLE	Nay, the dirt is so deep	
225	stopped therein for to steep	*stamped; soak*
	and the grubs thereon do creep	
	at home at thy house.	

	Therefore meat, if I may,	*food*
	of your dighting today	*prepared by you*
230	will I nought, by no way,	
	till I have my wage.	
	I wend to have been gay,	*thought; resplendent*
	but see! So ragged is mine array!	*dress*
	Ay pinches is your pay	*always scanty*
235	to every poor page.	*servant*

3RD SHEP-	Trowle, boy, for God's tree,	*cross*
HERD	come eat a morsel with me—	
	and then wrestle will we	
	here on this wold.	*moor*

| TROWLE | That shall I never flee! | *refuse* |

241	Though it be with all three	
	to lay my livery,	*wager; portion*
	that will I hold.	*keep to*

Then he shall go to his masters and shall say:

TROWLE	Now comes Trowle the True;	
245	a turn to take have I tight	*planned*
	with my masters. Or I rue,	*before I repent*
	put him forth that most is of might.	

| 1ST SHEP- | Trowle, better thou never knew. | |
| HERD | Eat of this—meat for a knight! | *food fit for* |

| TROWLE | Nay, spare! Though I spew, | *give up* |
| 251 | all upon your heads shall it light. | *fall* |

| 2ND SHEP- | How should we suffer this shame, | |
| HERD | of a shrew thus to be shent? | *wretch; destroyed* |

| 3RD SHEP- | This lad lusts to be lame | *desires* |
| HERD | and lose a limb or he went. | *before; goes* |

TROWLE	Have done! Begin we this game!	
257	But ware lest your golions glent!*	
	That were little dole to our dame,	*would be; grief*
	though in the midst of the Dee	*River Dee*
	ye were drent!	*drowned*

1ST SHEP-	False lad, fie on thy face!	
HERD	On this ground thou shall have a fall.	
262	Hent on and hold that thou has,	
	if thou hap has. All go to all!*	

TROWLE	And this, sirs, here to solace!	*take this; for comfort*
265	Hankin. shepherd, shame thee I shall.	
	Wroth thou art, worse than thou was.	*angry*
	Ware lest thou walter here by the wall.	*beware; lie*

---

257 "But beware lest your balls drop off!"

262–63 "Take a grip and keep hold of what you have, if you have good fortune. Winner takes all!"

Then he throws the First Shepherd, and the Second Shepherd shall say:

2ND SHEP- HERD 270	Boy, lest I break thy bones, kneel down and ask me a boon. Lest I destroy thee here on these stones, cease, lest I shend thee too soon.	*favour* *kill*
TROWLE 275	Gole, thee, to groins and groans! Good were thee thy old rags to save soon! Little doubt of such drones, lither tike, for thy deeds done!*	

Then the Second Shepherd is thrown.

3RD SHEP- HERD	Out, alas! He lies on his lends. But let me go now to that lad. Shepherds he shames and shends, for last now am I out shad.	*limbs* *destroys* *isolated*
TROWLE 281	Both your backs here to me bends; For all your boasts, I hold you two bad! Hold your arses and your hinder lends; then hope I to have as I have had.*	*esteem* *backsides*
 285	The better in the bore as I had before of this boveart. Yea, hope I more. Keep well thy score, for fear of a fart.	*(?)against the fool* *braggart* *expect* *hold your mark*

Then he shall throw the Third Shepherd, and Trowle shall say:

TROWLE 291	Lie there, lither, in the lake. My livery now will I latch: this curry, this clout, and this cake,	*cur* *portion; seize* *offal; tripe*

271–75 "Howl on, you, with grimaces and groans! It would be a good idea for you to save your old rags at once. Hateful cur, there's small fear from such idlers as you on the evidence of what you've done in the past."

283 "Then I expect to have the same luck as I have had already."

	for ye be cast, now will I catch.	*thrown; take*
	To the Devil I you all betake,	*commit*
295	as traitors attaint of your tach!	*convicted; crime*
	On this wold with this will I wake.	*moor; watch*
	All the world wonder on the watch!*	

And thus Trowle shall withdraw and the First Shepherd shall say:

1ST SHEP- HERD	Fellows, this a foul case is,	*situation*
	that we been thus cast of a knave,	*thrown by; servant*
300	All against our wills he has his;	*his (will)*
	but I must needs hold the harms that I have.	*injuries*

2ND SHEP- HERD	That I have, needs must I hold.	
	Of these unhappy harms oft hear I.	*unfortunate injuries*
	Therefore will I wait on this wold	*watch; moor*
305	upon the weather, for I am weary.	

3RD SHEP- HERD	Though we be weary, no wonder!	
	What between wrestling and waking.	*watching*
	Oft we may be in, though we be now under.*	
	God amend it with his making.	*by his contriving*

Then they shall sit down, and the star shall appear; and the First Shepherd shall say:

1ST SHEP- HERD	What is all this light here	
	that blazes so bright here	
312	on my black beard?	
	For to see this light here	
	a man may be afright here,	*afraid*
315	for I am afeared.	*scared*

2ND SHEP- HERD	Feared for a fray now	*afraid; terrifying thing*
	may we be all now;	
	and yet it is night—	
	yet seems it day now.	
320	Never, soothly to say now,	*truly*

---

297 "Let all the world marvel at the watchman!"

308 "We may often be on top, though this time we are beaten."

	see I such a sight.	*saw*
3RD SHEP- HERD	Such a sight seeming and a light leeming lets me to look.	*appearing* *shining* *stops me looking*
325	All to my deeming, from a star streaming it to me stroak.	*judgement* *struck*
TROWLE	That star if it stond to seek will I fond,	*stands still* *attempt*
330	though my sight fail me. While I may live in lond, why should I not fond, if it will avail me?	 *the land* *make the attempt*

Then Trowle, looking towards the firmament, shall say:

TROWLE 335	Ah, God's mighties! In yonder star light is. Of the sun this sight is, as it now seems.	*powers* *from*
1ST SHEP- HERD 340	It seems, as I now see, a bright star to be, there to abide. From it we may not flee but ay glow on the glee, till it down glide.	 *ever; stare; joyful thing* *descends*
2ND SHEP- HERD 346	Fellows. will we kneel down on our knee after comford to the true Trinity, . for to lead us for to see our elders' Lord?	 *asking for comfort* *the God of our forefathers*
3RD SHEP- HERD 352	Our Lord will us lere in our prayer whereto it will apent; and why on high here the air is so clear, now we shall be kent.	*teach* *pertain* *bright* *informed*

TROWLE	Lord, of this light	
	send us some sight	
	why that it is sent.	
	Before this night	
360	was I never so afright	*afraid*
	of the firmament.	

1ST SHEP-	Nay, fie! By my fay,	*faith*
HERD	now is it nigh day;	*almost*
	so was it never.	
365	Therefore I pray	
	the sooth us to say,	*truth*
	or that we desever.	*before; depart*

Then the Angel shall sing "Gloria in excelsis Deo et in terra
pax hominibus bonae voluntatis."*

1ST SHEP-	Fellows in fere,	*together*
HERD	may ye not hear	
370	this muting on high?	*singing*

2ND SHEP-	In "glore" and in "glere"?	
HERD	Yet no man was near	
	within our sight.	

3RD SHEP-	Nay, it was a "glory."	
HERD	Now I am sorry	*sad*
376	bout more song.	*without*

TROWLE	Of this strange story	*in*
	such mirth is merry.	*rejoicing; delightful*
	I would have among.	*be part of it*

1ST SHEP-	As I then deemed,	*judged*
HERD	"selsis" it seemed	
382	that he sang so.	

367+SD "Glory to God in the highest, and on Earth peace, good will toward
men," Luke 2.14ff., the angel's song mentioned in the Post-Reformation Banns;
this is the verse of the first responsory at Matins on Christmas Day.

2ND SHEP-	While the light leemed,	*shone*
HERD	a wreaking me weened;	*I expected a vengeance*
385	I wist never who.	*knew; who (it was)*

3RD SHEP-	What song was this, say ye	
HERD	that he sang to us all three?	
	Expounded it shall be	
	ere we hethen pass;	*hence*
390	for I am eldest of degree	*in rank*
	and also best, as seems me,	*it seems to me*
	it was "grorus glorus" with a "glee."	
	It was neither more nor lass.	*less*

TROWLE	Nay, it was "glorus, glarus, glorius";	
395	methink that note went over the house.	*it seems to me*
	A seemly man he was, and curious;	*strange*
	but soon away he was.	

1ST SHEP-	Nay, it was "glorus, glarus" with a "glo,"	
HERD	and much of "celsis" was thereto.	*with it*
400	As ever have I rest or woe,	
	much he spake of "glass."	

| 2ND SHEP- | Nay, it was neither "glass" nor "gly." | |
| HERD | Therefore, fellow, now stand by. | *stand aside* |

3RD SHEP-	By my faith, he was some spy,	
HERD	our sheep for to steal—	
406	or else he was a man of our craft,	*occupation*
	for seemly he was, and wonder daft.	*amazingly skilful*

| TROWLE | Nay, he came by night—all things laft— | |
| | our tups with tar to teal.* | |

1ST SHEP-	Nay, on a "glor" and on "glay" and a "gly"	
HERD	gurt Gabriel when he so so gloried.*	
412	When he sang, I might not be sorry.	*sad*

408–9 "No, he came by night, when all's said and done, to mark our rams with tar"; i.e., to change the ownership-markings.

410–11 "No, Gabriel spoke out on a 'glor' and on 'glay and a gly' when he sang his song of glory."

Through my breast-bone bleating he bored.   *singing*

2ND SHEP-   Nay, by God, it was a "gloria"   *"glory"*
HERD   said Gabriel when he began so.
416   He had a much better voice than I ha,   *have*
         as in Heaven all other have so.

3RD SHEP-   Will ye hear how he sang "celsis"?   *"on high"*
HERD   For on that sadly he set him.   *seriously; applied to*
420   Neither sang "sar," nor so well "cis,"
         ne "Pax merry Maud" when she had met him.*

TROWLE   One time he touched on "Tarre,"   *"Earth"*
         and thereto I took good intent.   *to that; heed*
         All Heaven might not have gone harre,   *higher*
425   that note on high when he up hent.   *lifted up*

1ST SHEP-   And after, of "pax" or of "peace"   *"peace"*
HERD   up as a pie he piped;   *jay*
         such a loden—this is no leas—   *voice; lie*
         never in my life me so liked.   *pleased me*

2ND SHEP-   Upon "hominibus" he muted;   *"to men"; sang*
HERD   that much marvel to me was.
432   And ay I quoke when he so hooted;   *ever; shook; cried*
         I durst not heed where that it was.   *what note*

3RD SHEP-   Yet, yet he sang more than all this,
HERD   for some word is worthy a fother.   *a great deal*
436   For he sang "bonae voluntatis":   *"of good will"*
         that is a crop that passeth all other.   *valuable thing*

TROWLE   Yet, and yet, he sang more to;   *in addition*
         from my mind it shall not start.   *go out*
440   He sang also of a "Deo."   *"God"*
         Methought that healed my heart.   *it seemed to me*

         And that word "Terra" he tamed—   *"Earth"; subdued*
         thereto I took good intent.   *to that; heed*

420–21 "Sang neither 'Sara' nor 'Cicely' nor 'Kiss of peace, Merry Maud'" when
she had met him." The allusion is evidently to contemporary—though so far
unidentified—popular songs of a bawdy kind.

	And "pax" also may not be blamed.	*"peace"*
445	For that, to this song I assent.	*agree*

1ST SHEP-	Now pray we to him with good intent,	*will*
HERD	and sing I will, and me unbrace:	*give forth*
	that he will let us to be kent,	*allow; taught*
	and to send us of his grace.	

2ND SHEP-	Now, sith I have all my will—	*since; desire*
HERD	for never in this world so well I was—	*happy*
452	sing we now, I read us, shrill	*advise; clearly*
	a merry song, us to solace.	*make us happy*

TROWLE	Sing we now—let see,	
455	some song will I assay.	*attempt*
	All men now, sings after me,	*sing*
	for music of me learn ye may.	*from me*

*Then they shall sing here "Trolly, lolly, lolly, lo." At this
point the Angel shall appear and shall say:*

ANGEL	Shepherds, of this sight	
	be ye not afright,	*afraid*
460	for this is God's might.	
	Takes this in mind:	
	to Bethlem now right!	*to Bethlehem go now at once*
	There ye shall see in sight	
	that Christ is born tonight	
465	to cover all Mankind.	*deliver*

3RD SHEP-	Now wend we forth to Bethlem—	*go; Bethlehem*
HERD	that is best our song to be—	
	for to see the star-gleam,	
	the fruit also of that maiden free.	*noble*

1ST SHEP-	Now follow we the star that shines	
HERD	till we come to that holy stable.	
472	To Bethlem boin the limbs;	*bend your limbs*

457+SD The words are those of a popular refrain. Richard Rastall has suggested
a three-part piece by William Cornish, of about 1515: "Trolly lolly lolly lo, sing
trolly lolly lo! My love is to the greenwood gone. Now after will I go. Sing trolly
lolly lo." 454–45 suggest that the audience is to join in with the shepherds.

follow we it without any fable.   *any more talk*

2ND SHEP- Follow we it, and hies full fast;   *hurry*
HERD   such a friend loath us were to fail.   *let down*
476   Launch on! I will not be the last
           upon Mary for to mervail.   *marvel*

TROWLE   To Bethlem take we the way,
           for with you I think to wend,   *go*
480   that Prince of Peace for to pray
           Heaven to have at our end.

           And sing we all, I read,   *advise*
           some mirth to his majesty,   *joyful song*
           for certain now see we it indeed—   *certainly*
485   the King's Son of Heaven is he.

           Here they shall go towards Bethlehem.

3RD SHEP- Stint now! Go no moe steps,   *stop; more*
HERD   for now the star beginneth to stond.   *stand*
488   Harvey, that good been our haps   *fortunes*
           we seen by our Saviour fond.   *found*

1ST SHEP- Sim, sim, securely*   *certainly*
HERD   here I see Mary,
492   and Jesus Christ fast by,
           lapped in hay.   *wrapped*

2ND SHEP- Kneel we down in hie   *at once*
HERD   and pray we him of mercy,   *for*
496   and welcome him worthily
           that woe does away.   *puts*

3RD SHEP- Away all our woe is
HERD   and many man's moe is.   *more*
500   Christ, Lord, let us kiss
           the cratch or the clothes.   *cradle*

TROWLE   Solace now to see this   *joy*

---

490 *Sim, sim* seems meaningless. It perhaps indicates some exclamatory noise of
surprise.

	builds in my breast bliss—	
	never after to do amiss,	*wrong*
505	thing that him loath is.	*a thing;hateful to him*

1ST SHEP-   Whatever this old man that here is!   *whatever's*
HERD   Take heed how his head is hore.   *gray*
             His beard is like a busk of briers   *bush*
             with a pound of hair about his mouth and more.

2ND SHEP-   More is this marvel to me now,   *a greater wonder*
HERD   for to nap greatly him needs.   *sleep;he needs*
512   Heartless is he now   *listless*
             for ay to his heels he heeds.   *ever;looks down*

3RD SHEP-   Why, with his beard—though it be row—   *rough*
HERD   right well to her he heeds.   *attends*
516   Worthy wight, wit would we now.   *sir;know*
             Will ye warn us, worthy in weeds?*   *refuse*

MARY   Shepherds, soothly I see   *truly*
             that my Son you hither sent
520   through God's might in majesty
             that in me light and here is lent.   *alighted;remains*
             This man married was to me
             for no sin in such assent;   *by such agreement*
             but to keep my virginity,   *protect*
525   and truly in none other intent.   *for;purpose*

JOSEPH   Good men, Moses take in mind:
             as he was made through God Almight,   *led;almighty*
             ordained laws us to bind
             which that we should keep of right;   *rightly*
530   man and woman for to bind
             lawfully, them both to light;   *delight*
             to fructify, as men may find,   *multiply*
             that time was wedded every wight.   *person*

             Therefore wedded to her I was
535   as Law would, her for to lere—   *required;instruct*
             for noise nor slander nor trespass—   *not for;gossip;sin*
             and through that deed the Devil to dere,   *harm*

---

517 "Will you refuse to teach us, worthy in your array?"

as told me Gabriel full of grace.
When I had trussed all my gear   *packed; belongings*
540   to flee, never to see her face,   *nevermore*
by him was I arrested there.   *stopped*

For he said to me sleeping
that she lackless was of sin.   *blameless*
And when I heard that tokening,   *sign*
545   from her durst I no way twin.   *separate by no means*
Therefore goes forth and preach this thing,   *go*
all together and not in twin: *separately*
that you have seen your Heavenly King
comen on all Mankind to min.   *come; think*

1ST SHEP-   Great God, sitting in thy throne,
HERD   that made all thing of nought,
552   now we may thank thee each one:
this is he that we have sought.

2ND SHEP-   Go we near anon   *at once*
HERD   with such as we have brought.
Ring, brooch, or precious stone—
557   let see if we can proffer ought.

3RD SHEP-   Let us do him homage.
HERD

1ST SHEP-   Who shall go first? The page?   *boy*
HERD

2ND SHEP-   Nay, ye be father in age,   *foremost*
HERD   therefore ye must first offer.

1ST SHEP-   Hail, King of Heaven so high,
HERD   born in a crib;
Mankind unto thee
565   thou hast made full sib.   *close kin*

Hail, King, born in a maiden's bower.   *i.e., womb*
Prophets did tell thou should be our succour;
this clerks do say.   *clerics*
Lo, I bring thee a bell.
570   I pray thee, save me from Hell
so that I may with thee dwell
and serve thee for ay.   *ever*

2ND SHEP- HERD 575	Hail, the Emperor of Hell and of Heaven als. The Fiend shalt thou fell, that ever hath been false.	*also* *cast down*

580	Hail, the maker of the star that stood us beforn. Hail, the blessedsfull barn that ever was born. Lo, son, I bring thee a flacket. Thereby hangs a spoon for to eat thy pottage with at noon, as I myself full oft-times have done. With heart I pray thee to take it.	*before* *most blessed child* *flask* *broth* *with all my heart*
585		

3RD SHEP- HERD	Hail, Prince withouten any peer, that Mankind shall relieve. Hail, the foe unto Lucifer, the which beguiled Eve.	*without; equal* *free*

590	Hail, the granter of hope, for on Earth now thou dwells. Lo, son, I bring thee a cap, for I have nothing else.

595	This gift, son, that I give thee is but small; and though I come the hindmost of all, when thou shalt men to thy bliss call, good Lord, yet think on me.

TROWLE 600	My dear, with drury unto thee I me dress, my state on fellowship that I do not lose; and for to save me from all ill-sickness, I offer unto thee a pair of my wife's old hose.	*love* *present myself* *position*

605	For other jewels, my son, have I none thee for to give that is worth anything at all— but my good heart while I live and my prayers till death doth me call.	*precious things*

1ST BOY	Now to you, my fellows, this do I say: for in this place, or that I wend away,	*before; go*

	unto yonder child let us go pray	
610	as our masters have done us beforn.	*before*

2ND BOY	And of such goods as we have here,	
	let us offer to this prince so dear,	
	and to his mother, that maiden clear,	*pure*
	that of her body has him borne.	

| 1ST BOY | Abide sirs! I will go first to yonder king. |

| 2ND BOY | And I will go next to that lording. | *lord* |

3RD BOY	Then will I be last of this offering;	
618	this can I say, no more.	

1ST BOY	Now, Lord, for to give thee have I nothing—	
620	neither gold, silver, brooch, ne ring,	*nor*
	nor no rich robes meet for a king	*fit*
	that I have here in store.	
	But though it lack a stopple,	*stopper*
	take thee here my well fair bottle,	*most splendid*
625	for it will hold a good pottle;	*drink*
	in faith, I can give thee no more.	*truly*

2ND BOY	Lord, I know that thou art of this virgin born,	
	in full poor array sitting on her arm.	*garb*
	For to offer to thee have I no scorn,	*make offering; shame*
630	although thou be but a barn.	*child*
	For jewel have I none to give thee	
	to maintain thy royal dignity,	
	but my hood—take it thee,	*to you*
	as thou art God and man.	

3RD BOY	O noble child of thy Father on high,	
636	alas, what have I for to give thee?	
	Save only my pipe that soundeth so royally,	*splendidly*
	else truly have I nothing at all.	
	Were I in the rocks or in the valley alow,	*below*
640	I could make this pipe sound, I trow,	*trust*
	that all the world should ring	
	and quaver as it would fall.	*vibrate*

4TH BOY	Now, child, although thou be comen from God	*come*
	and be thyself God in thy manhood,	*human form*

645	yet I know that in thy childhood	
	thou wilt for sweetmeat look.	*sweet foods*
	To pull down apples, pears, and plums,	
	old Joseph shall not need to hurt his thumbs	
	because thou hast not plenty of crumbs.	*morsels*
650	I give thee here my nuthook.	

1ST SHEP- HERD	Now farewell, mother and may,	*maiden*
	for of sin nought thou wottest.	*know*
	Thou hast brought forth this day	
	God's Son, of mighties most.	*greatest in powers*

655	Wherefore men shall say:	
	"Blessed in every coast and place	*region*
	be thou, memorial for us all."	*example*
	And that we may from sin fall	*fall away*
	and stand ever in thy grace,	
660	our Lord God be with thee.	

2ND SHEP- HERD	Brethren, let us all three	
	singing walk homewardly.	*homewards*
	Unkind will I never in no case be,	
	but preach ever that I can, and cry,	*know; proclaim it*
665	as Gabriel taught by his grace me.	
	Singing, away hethen will I.	*hence*

3RD SHEP- HERD	Over the sea, and I may have grace,	*if*
	I will gang and about go	*go*
	to preach this thing in every place;	
670	and sheep will I keep now no moe.	*more*

TROWLE	I read we us agree	*counsel; agree among us*
	for our misdeeds amends to make,	
	for so now will I;	
	and to the child I wholly me betake	*commit myself*
675	for ay securely.	*for ever certainly*
	Shepherd's craft here I forsake;	*occupation*
	and to an anker hereby	*hermitage*
	I will, in my prayers watch and wake.	*will go; watch*

1ST SHEP- HERD	And I an hermit	
	to praise God, to pray,	
681	to walk by sty and by street,	*path and road*
	in wilderness to walk for ay.	*ever*

And I shall no man meet
but for my living I shall him pray,   *sustenance*
barefoot on my feet.
685   And thus will I live ever and ay.   *always*

For ay, ever, and once,   *always; once for all*
this world I fully refuse,   *completely reject*
my miss to amend with moans.   *sin; atone*
690   Turn to thy fellows and kiss,
I yield, for in youth   *urge*
we have been fellows iwiss.   *comrades indeed*
Therefore lend me your mouth,
and friendly let us kiss.   *as friends*

2ND SHEP-   From London to Louth*
HERD   such another shepherd I not where is.   *do not know*
697   Both friend and couth,   *acquaintance*
             God grant you all his bliss!

3RD SHEP-   To that bliss bring you
HERD   great God, if that thy will be.
701   "Amen" all sing you.
             Good men, farewell ye!

TROWLE   Well for to fare, each friend,
             God of his might grant you;
705   for here now we make an end.
             Farewell, for we from you go now!

THE END

---

695 *Louth* is a market town twenty-six miles east-northeast of Lincoln on a road
by the River Lud where it flows out of the Wolds. It is apparently used here for
alliteration only.

PLAY 8: THE THREE KINGS

Performed by the Vintners

THE SERIES OF PLAYS dealing with the birth of Christ continues in play 8 with the coming of the three Magi to the court of king Herod as described in Matthew 2.1–9. Legends had grown up around these strange men from the East who had been led to Jerusalem by a star, and their bodies were believed to be preserved at Cologne. According to legend, they were kings, Gentiles who knew of Balaam's Messianic prophecy and had, like their ancestors, kept vigil for the appearance of the star. They even had names and realms, which are mentioned at the end of the play.

King Herod the Great, to whose court they came for information, was not a Jew by birth but by faith, as his Doctor reminds us. There was a long tradition, found in the Latin drama of the Church, which made Herod a comically irascible character, given to spectacular rages on stage, and in his warning to the kings, Herod's messenger raises the audience's expectations of such an outburst. Herod's first speech shows a progressive breakdown of the façade of kingly dignity as he works himself into a fearsome temper at the assumed threat to his power. Small wonder that the Counsellor is nervous when asked to read through the Scriptures for information about a Messiah; Herod again grows in fury until he drives the hapless Counsellor from the stage. The part is a splendid opportunity for an exhibitionist performance.

Underlying the play is a concern with the nature of kingship, which will continue throughout the rest of the cycle. The Kings, presumably dressed in "oriental" manner, have regal bearing, address Herod in French characteristic of the upper classes (to which he similarly responds), and bear his onslaught with dignity. They have only one prophecy to guide them, but they have kept a firm belief in it. Herod is really an imposter, insecure in his position, whose idea of kingship comprehends only temporal power and who therefore cannot understand that Christ represents no threat to him. He has the whole series of Jewish Messianic prophecies to guide him but resists their obvious truth and plots in treacherous fashion the destruction of the Kings and of the infant Christ while feigning friendship and devotion. We see him at the end reclining luxuriously and drinking—perhaps a reminder that the performing company is that of the Vintners.

The waggon-set was obviously the court of Herod, decked out in rich hangings, with Herod and his servants richly arrayed. He wears a gold crown, two gowns (one to replace the one that slips from his shoulders in his rage), and bears a great sword which he flourishes, and a "staff"—perhaps a sceptre. The Kings ride up on horses through the crowd to meet at the Mount Victorial—perhaps a separate set, or again an area in front of the curtained-off stage. They may have other attendants, for a servant holds the horse of one of them. Their journey to Herod and meeting with the Messenger is evidently at ground level, and they ride there on dromedaries; dromedaries also featured in Chester's midsummer show and were specially constructed machines which were part of the play's spectacle. The star, which is said to bear the image of a Virgin and Child and seems to be like the one seen by Octavian in play 6, is carried ahead of the Kings by an angel.

Minstrels are required to play when the Messenger goes to Herod, and possibly at other times. Presumably they were required to produce a rather raucous and second-rate sound appropriate to Herod's character!

Cast   FIRST KING, SECOND KING, THIRD KING, ANGEL, MESSENGER, HEROD, COUNSELLOR.

1ST KING	Mighty God in majesty	
	that rules the people of Judee,	*Judea*
	when thou on Man wilt have pity	
	and his sins forbuy,	*redeem*
5	send some tokening, Lord, to me,	*sign*
	that ilk star that I may see	*same*
	that Balaam said should rise and be	
	in his prophecy.	
	For well I wot, forsooth iwiss,	*know; truly*

10	that his prophecy sooth is.	*true*
	A star should rise, tokening of bliss,	*a sign*
	when God's Son is born.	
	Therefore these lords and I in fere	*together*
	in this mount make our prayer	
15	devoutly once a year.	
	for thereto we been sworn.	*to it*

2ND KING   Yea, we that been of Balaam's blood ?
that prophesied of that sweet food   *child*
when Balaack, that king so wood,   *angry*
20   to curse would he have made   *have had [them] cursed*
God's people of Israel.
But power failed him every deal;   *entirely*
to prophesy Mankind's heal   *well-being*
that time hap he had—   *fortune*

25   therefore we kings of his kind,   *race*
I read we take his words in mind,   *advise*
grace in him if we may find
that God's Son shall be.
And go we pray, both one and all,
30   into the Mount Victorial.
Peradventure such grace may fall   *occur*
that star that we may see.

3RD KING   Sir, sickerly ye read on right:*
unto that hill I will me dight   *go*
35   and there beseech God Almight
on us for to have mind,
and of that star to have some sight.
Worship we all that sweet wight   *person*
that Balaam to us behight,   *promised*
40   that shall forbuy Mankind.   *redeem*

Say, fellow, take this courser   *steed*
and abide me right here.   *await*
Go we, sirs, to our prayer,
I read now in good fay.   *advise;faith*
45   I have done this many a year,
and my ancestors that before me were,

---

33 "Sir, certainly you counsel rightly."

High God, prince of power,
thou comfort us today!

*Here they shall dismount from their horses and shall go into
the mountain.*

1ST KING	Lord, what time is it thy will	
50	Balaam's prophecy to fulfill,	
	thou give us grace, both loud and still,	*at all times*
	and by some sign us show.	

2ND KING	Yea, Lord, though we be unworthy,	
	on thy men thou have mercy;	*servants*
55	and of thy birth thou certify	*give assurance*
	here to thy kings three,	

[handwritten: now would they know ?]

3RD KING	Lord God, leader of Israel,	
	that die would for Mankind's weal,	*well-being*
	thou come to us, and not conceal,	*remain hidden*
60	but be our counsellor.	

1ST KING	Of all this world thou art the well	*source*
	that shall be called "Emmanuel."	
	Deem thee, Lord, with us to dwell,	*resolve*
	and grant us our prayer.	

Then the star shall appear.

1ST KING	Ah, sire roi, si vous plait,
66	regardes sous sur votre tete.

2ND KING	Une etoile ici est
	qui sur vous replait.

3RD KING	Aloues, soit la un semblant
70	d'une virgine portante,
	comme le semble, d'un enfant
	en bras apertement.*

65–72 First King: "Ah, sir king, if it please you, look up above your head."
Second King: "There is a star there that shines upon you." Third King: "See,
there is an image of a virgin bearing, as it seems, a a child in her arms, clearly."

1ST KING	Ah, Lord, blessed most thou be,	*may*
	that on thy people has pity.	
75	Witterly now witten we	*surely; know*
	that wrought is our asking.	*our prayer is answered*

2ND KING	That our prayer heard has he	
	I lieve full well, by my lewty;	*believe; faith*
	for in the star a child I see	
80	and verray tokening.	*true sign*

3RD KING	Lords, I read we hethen hie,	*advise; hence; hasten*
	for I dare say, and nothing lie,	
	fulfilled is Balaam's prophecy	
	by this, we may well know.	

1ST KING	Yea, lest this be some fantasy	*illusion*
86	yet pray we all specially;	
	for if he be born verily	*truly*
	more signs he will us show.	

*Then the kings again shall kneel, and the Angel carrying the
star shall say:*

ANGEL	Rise up, ye kings three,	
90	and come anon after me	*at once*
	into the land of Judee	*Judea*
	as fast as ye may hie.	*hasten*
	The child ye seek there shall ye see,	
	born all of a maiden free,	*noble*
95	that King of Heaven and Earth shall be	
	and all Mankind forbuy.	*shall redeem*

Here the kings rise up.

1ST KING	Lords, hie we hethen anon.	*hasten we hence at once*
	Now we been bidden thither gone,	*to go*
	I will never bide—by my pon—	*stop; (?) head*
100	till I at him be.	*with*

2ND KING	Yea, sirs, I read us everychone	*advise; every one*
	dromedaries to ride upon,	
	for swifter beasts be there none.	
	One I have, ye shall see.	

3RD KING 106	A dromedary, in good fay,	*truly*
	will go lightly on his way	*easily*
	an hundred miles upon a day;	
	such beasts now take we.*	*animals*
1ST KING 110	Lords, <u>and I lieve well may</u>	*believe*
	<u>that child would shorten well our way</u>	*journey*
	that bringen presents to his pay	*bring;pleasure*
	and most is of degree.	*highest of rank*

Then they go down to the beasts and ride about.

1ST KING	Alas, where is this star i-went?	*gone*
	Our light from us away is glent.	*slipped*
115	Now wot I not where we been lent,	*know;placed*
	nor whitherward lies our way.	
2ND KING	Pray we to God with good intent,	*resolve*
	to whom we bring our present.	
	He will never suffer us to be shent;	*destroyed*
120	that dare I boldly say.	
3RD KING	It is good that we enquire	
	if any the way can us lere.	*tell*
	Say, belamy that rides there,	*fellow*
	tell us some tiding.	
MESSENGER	Sir, tell me what your will were.	*desire might be*
1ST KING	Can thou ought say what place or where	*say anything about*
	a child is born that crown shall bear	
	and of the Jews be king?	
2ND KING 130	We saw the star shine verray	*truly*
	in the east in noble array.	*gloriously*
	Therefore we come now this way	
	to worship him with win.	*joy*

105–8 The reference to the dromedary or one-humped racing camel derives from the *Legenda Aurea* via *Stanzaic Life*. The emphasis on speed serves to explain how the Kings were able to arrive at the stable so soon after the birth of Jesus. The commemoration of their visit, the Feast of the Epiphany, is on 6 January.

MESSENGER	Hold your peace, sirs, I you pray!	
	For if King Herod hear you so say,	*should hear*
135	he would go wood, by my fay,	*mad; truly*
	and fly out of his skin.	

3RD KING And sith a king is so near,   *since*
       go we to him in all manner.   *by all means*

MESSENGER Ye may well see he wonies here,   *dwells*
140   a palace in to dwell.
       But may he wot withouten were *know; without doubt*
       that any is born of more power,
       you bring yourselves in great danger
       such tidings for to tell.

Here the Messenger must go to the king. Minstrels here must play.

MESSENGER O noble king and worthy conqueror,
146   crowned in gold, sitting on high,
       Mahound thee save long in honour!   *preserve*
       Licence I require to speak to thee.
       Tidings now, my lord, I shall you tell
150   that these three kings do show unto me.
       From whence they been I know not well; *are*
       yonder they stand, as ye may see.

1ST KING Sir roi real et reverent,
       Dieu vous garde omnipotent.

2ND KING Nous sommes venus comoplent,
156   nouvelles d'enquire.*

     Staff.*

HEROD   Bien sois venus, rois gents.
       Me dites tout votre entent.

153–56 First King: "Sir king royal and revered, may God preserve you, all-powerful one." Second King: "We have come together to seek tidings."

156+SD This is the first of several one-word cues relating to objects seized by Herod or to his actions as he speaks.

| 3RD KING
160 | Enfant enquirons-nous de grand parent,
et roi de Ciel et Terre.* | |

HEROD	Sirs, advise you what you sayn!	*take care; say*
	Such tidings make my heart unfain.	*unhappy*
	I read you, take those words again	*advise; retract*
	for fear of villainy.	*(a charge of) treachery*

Sword.

165	There is none so great that me dare gain,	*oppose*
	to take my realm and to attain	
	my power, but he shall have pain	
	and punished apertly.	*openly*

	I king of kings, none so keen;	*brave*
170	I sovereign sire, as well is seen;	*lord*
	I tyrant, that may both take and teen	*harass*
	castle, tower and town!	
	I wield this world withouten ween;	*rule; without doubt*
	I beat all those unbuxom been;	*who are disobedient*
175	I drive the devils all bedene	*immediately*
	deep in Hell a-down.	

	For I am king of all Mankind;	
	I bid, I beat, I loose, I bind;	
	I master the moon. Take this in mind—	*remember*
180	that I am most of might.	

	I am the greatest above degree	*above the hierarchy*
	that is, or was, or ever shall be;	
	the sun it dare not shine on me	
	and I bid him go down.	*if*
185	No rain to fall shall none be free;	
	nor no lord have that liberty	
	that dare abide and I bid flee,	*remain; if*
	but I shall crack his crown.	

| | Nor far nor near, that doth me noy— | *(he who); injury* |
| 190 | who wraths me—I shall him destroy; | *angers* |

157–60 Herod: "Welcome, gracious kings. Tell me your full purpose." Third
King: "We seek a child of high lineage, and king of heaven and earth"

for every freke I dare defy   *man;fight*
that nill me pay ne please.   *will not;please;nor*
But ye be bain, I shall you beat;   *unless;obedient*
there is no man for you shall treat.   *plead*
195   All for wrath, see how I sweat!
My heart is not at ease.

    Staff.

For all men way wot and see—   *know*
both he and you all three—   *(i.e., the Messenger)*
that I am king of Galilee,
200   whatsoever he says or does.   *(i.e., Jesus)*

    Sword.

What the devil should this be!
a boy, a groom of low degree   *urchin;youth;rank*
should reign above my royalty   *royal estate*
and make me but a goose

    Cast up.

205   that rings and reigns so royally!   *rules*
All grace and goodness I have to guy.   *govern*
There is no prince but he shall ply   *bend*
to do my heart's ease.

    Staff and another gown.

But now you may both hear and see
210   that I reckoned up my royalty.   *summed up my power*
I read you all, be ruled by me   *advise*
and fond me for to please.   *contrive*

1ST KING   Vidimus stellam eius in oriente et venimus cum
munribus adorare eum.*

Sir, we see the star appear   *saw*
in the east, withouten were   *certainly*

212+Latin "We have seen his star in the east and are come with gifts to worship
him." The quotation is from Matthew 2.2.

215   in a marvellous manner,
       together as we can pray.   *prayed*

2ND KING   We see never none so clear;   *saw*
       by it the way we could lear.   *learn*
       But when we came to your land here
220   then vanished it away.

3RD KING   By prophecy well wotten we   *know*
       that a child born should be
       to rule the people of Judee,   *Judea*
       as was said many a year.   *(for) many a year*

HEROD   That is false, by my lewty,   *faith*
226   for in mauger of you all three,   *despite*
       this realm moves all of me;   *operates entirely from*
       other kings none shall be here.

       But sithen you speak of prophecy,   *since*
230   I will wit anon in high   *know immediately*
       whether ye say sooth or lie.   *truth*
       My clerk soon shall see.   *cleric*
       Sir Doctor, that chief art of clergy,
       look up thy books of prophecy
235   of Daniel, David and Isay,   *Isaiah*
       and what thou seest say thou me.   *to me*

       These kings be come a far way
       to seek a child, I heard them say,
       that should be born in this country
240   my kingdom to destroy.
       Seek each leaf, I thee pray,
       and what thou findest in good fay   *faith*
       tell now here, for I dare lay   *wager*
244   that all these lords lie.

COUN-   Nay, my lord, be ye bold;
SELLOR   I trow no prophets before would   *trust*
       write anything your heart to cold   *chill*
       or your right to deny.
       But sith your grace at this time would   *since*
250   that I the prophets declare should,
       of Christ's coming as they have told,
       the truth to certify,   *establish*

	I beseech your royal majesty	
	with patience of your benignity	
255	the truth to hear, and pardon me	
	their sayings to declare.	

HEROD	Nay, my true clerk, that will not I	*cleric*
	debate with thee; therefore in hie	*at once*
	look well on every prophecy.	
260	For nothing that thou spare,	

	but search the truth of Isay,	*Isaiah*
	Ezechiel, Nahum and Jeremy,	*Jeremiah*
	Micah, Abdas and Zechary,	*Obadiah; Zechariah*
	of Christ what they do say.	
265	Look also upon Malachi,	
	Haggai, Hosea and Sophony,	*Zephaniah*
	Joel, Amos and Habakkuk in hie;	*immediately*
	look none be left away.	

COUN-SELLOR	"Non auferetur sceptrum de Juda, et dux de femore eius, donec veniat qui mittendus est; et ipse erit expectatio gentium." Genesis cap. 49, v. 10.*	

	The Holy Scripture maketh declaration	
270	by patriarchs and prophets of Christ's nativity,	
	when Jacob prophesied by plain demonstration—	
	said the realm of Juda and eke the royalty	*also*
	from that generation never taken should be	
	until he were come that most mighty is,	
275	sent from the Father, king of heavenly bliss.	

	And now fulfilled is Jacob's prophecy;	
	for King Herod that is now reigning	
	is no Jew born, nor of that progeny,	*race*
	but a stranger—by the Romans made their king;	
280	and the Jews know none of their blood descending	
	by succession to claim the sceptre and regality;	*rule*
	wherefore Christ is now born, our King	

268+Latin "The sceptre shall not depart from Juda, nor a law-giver from between his feet, until he come who must be sent; and unto him shall the gathering of the people be."

and Messy.*   *Messiah*

A bill.   *sword*

HEROD	That is false, by Mahound full of might!
	That old vieillard Jacob, doted for age, *ancient; stupid*
285	shall withhold by no prophecy the title and right
	of Romans' high conquest which to me in heritage
	is fallen for ever, as prince
	of high parentage. *noble ancestry*
	If any other king or messy intend is to win, *Messiah*
	his head from his body with this sword
	I shall twin. *separate*

And he shall say, "Read on!"

COUN- SELLOR	"Cum venerit sancta sanctorum, cessabit unctio vestra." Daniel cap. 9.*
290	Daniel, fulfilled with heavenly grace,
	prophesied also by divine inspiration
	that when he was come that of all holy was
	most holiest, in Earth to take his habitation
	in the womb of a virgin, and by his blessed incarnation
295	out of Satan's bond to deliver Mankind
	whom sin original most piteously did bind—*
	then both unctions, sacrifices, and rites ceremonial
	of the Old Testament, with legal observation,
	shall utterly cease and take their end final
300	through Christ's coming, which for Man's salvation
	a New Testament should ordain by divine operation,
	offering himself in sacrifice for Mankind's offence,

276–82 Although Herod had adopted the Jewish faith, he was by birth an Idumaean; hence the Counsellor is correct.

289+ Latin "When the holy of holies shall have come, your unction shall cease." There is no exact biblical correspondence to this text; cf. Daniel 9.24.

295–96 All who died after the Fall of Man were tainted by Adam's Original Sin and could not go to heaven. Those who were obedient to God's word were held by the Devil in the Limbo of the Patriarchs from which they were released when Christ harrowed hell. See play 17.

which from Heaven was exiled through his great
negligence.

Cast down the sword.

HEROD	Fie on that dream-reader! Such dotards never shall—
305	ne no sleepy sluggard—make my right title cease.* *nor*
	But I shall knightly keep it, whatsoever shall befall,
	against that young gedling. And if he once do press *villain*
	this kingdom to claim, or put me to distress, *trouble*
	his head off shall I hew. Yet look thou find there
310	where this boy is born for whom these kings enquire.
COUN-	"Et tu Bethlem quidem terra Juda nequaquam minima
SELLOR	es in principibus Judae. Ex te enim exiet dux qui reget
	populum meum Israell." Micah cap. 5 and Matthew
	cap. 2.*

Micah, inflamed with ghostly inspiration,   *spiritual*
prophesied that Bethlem should a child forth bring.
Ruler of God's people and of the Jews' nation
should he be, born of Israel to be king.

315   Also Isay and Jeremy, full virtuous of living, *Isaiah; Jeremiah*
with diverse others moe fulfilled with grace,   *more*
of Christ's coming prophesied
   while their living was.   *in their lifetime*

"Ambulabunt gentes in lumine tuo et reges in splendore
ortus tui." Isaiah cap. 60.*

Isay, to whom the spirit of prophecy   *Isaiah*
was singularly given through the Holy Ghost,   *uniquely*
320   in his time prophesied that kings witterly   *indeed*
and folks of strange nations and from
   sundry coasts—   *regions*

304–5 Daniel was given power by God to understand all dreams and visions;
later, Daniel himself was granted visions, hence the reference to *sleepy sluggard.*

310+Latin "And thou Bethlehem, in the land of Juda, art not the least among the
princes of Juda; for out of thee shall come a Governor that shall rule my people
Israel" (Matthew 2.6).

317+Latin "And the Gentiles shall come to thy light, and kings to the brightness
of thy rising." Isaiah 60.3.

that Prince's birth to magnify, which of might is most—
should walk in great light; and brightness should appear,
as did unto these kings, in a bright star shining clear.

Cast down the sword.

HEROD   "Effundam super parvulum istum furorem meum et super
consilium juvenum; disperdam parvulos de fores, et
juvenes in plateis morientur gladio meo."[*]

325   Alas! What presumption should move that
     peevish page   *ill-humoured*
or any elvish gedling to take   *magic-making villain*
     from me my crown?
But, by Mahound, that boy for all his great outrage
shall die under my hand, that elf   *mysterious being*
     and vile congeon.   *scoundrel*
And all his partakers I shall slay and beat down,
330   and both of him and his, final destruction make.
Such vengeance and eke cruelty on them all will I take   *also*
that none such a slaughter was seen or heard beforn *before*
sith Athalia here reigned, that fell   *since; fierce*
     and furious queen,[*]
that made slay all men-children that of
     king's blood were born
335   when her son was dead. So for to wreak   *avenge*
     my teen   *anger*
I shall hew that harlot   *villain*
     with my bright brand so keen   *sword; sharp*
into pieces small. Yet look and search again
if these kings shall him find, and his presence attain.

COUN-   "Reges Tharsis et Insulae munera offerent; reges
SELLOR   Arabum et Saba dona adducent." Psalm 71.[*]

324+Latin "I will pour that fury of mine out upon the children. I will cut off the
children from without and the young men in the streets will die by my sword."
Cf. Jeremiah 6.11, and 9.20–21.

333–35 *Athalia* was the daughter of Jezebel and Ahab who introduced the
worship of Baal into the southern kingdom of Israel after her marriage to
Jehoram. 2 Kings 11.1 describes how she had the royal children murdered to
secure her own power. 2 Chronicles 23.12–14 offers the lesson Herod overlooks—
her death at the hands of Jehoiada's men.

338+Latin "The kings of Tarshish and of the isles shall bring presents; the kings

David, of all prophets called
   most prepotent,   *supremely powerful*
340   prophesied that kings of Tharsis and Araby
          with mystical gifts shall come and present
          that Lord and Prince, that King and high Messy,   *Messiah*
          of Abraham's seed descending lineally—
          which kings with great treasure here in presence
345   to seek him as sovereign, and laud his magnificence!

          My lord, by prophecy is proved you beforn   *before*
          that in Bethlem should be born
          a child to save that was forlorn   *what; utterly lost*
          and rule all Israel.

          Break a sword.

HEROD   By Cock's soul, thou art forsworn!   *God's*
351   Have done! Those books were rent and torn! *cease; should be*
          For he shall be no king in crown,
          but I fully in my weal.   *splendour*

          And mauger David, that shepherd with his sling,* *despite*
355   Isay, Jeremy with all their offspring   *Isaiah; Jeremiah*
          here get no other Messy nor king,   *Messiah*
          from my right title to expel.   *expel (me)*

          Cast up.

          What a devil is this to say:
          that I should be disproved and put away—
360   sith my right is so verray—   *since; true*
          for a boy's boast!
          This realm is mine, and shall be ay,   *always*
          manfully to maintain it while I may,   *sustain*
          though he bring with him today
365   the Devil and all his host.

          Cast up. Staff and another gown.

---

of Sheba and of Seba shall offer gifts" (Psalms 71 [AV 72].10).

354 *David* was a shepherd boy who with his sling killed Goliath, the giant champion of the Philistines. He later became king of Israel.

	But goes you forth, you kings three,	*go*
	and enquire if it so be.	
	But algates come again by me,	*in any case*
	for you I think to feed.	
370	And if he be of such degree,	*rank*
	him will I honour as done ye,	*do*
	as falls for his dignity	*befits*
	in word, thought and deed.	

| 1ST KING
375 | Beleve, sir! And have good day,
till we come again this way. | *at once* |

| 2ND KING | And of his riches and his array
from you we shall not lain. | *conceal* |

| 3RD KING | Sir, as soon as ever we may—
and as we seen, so shall we say. | *see* |

| HEROD
381 | Farewell, lords, in good fay—
but hie you fast again. | *truly*
hasten |

The boy and pig when the kings are gone.   *jug*

	Out, alas! What the devil is this?	
	For shame almost I fare amiss	*become ill*
	for was I never so woe, iwiss;	*miserable;indeed*
385	for wrath I am near wood.	*almost mad*
	For every man may well say this—	
	that I maintain my realm amiss,	*govern;wrongly*
	to let a boy inherit my bliss	
	that never was of my blood.	

Staff.

390	But yet, the less it grieves me	
	that I let go those kings three;	
	for I shall know now which is he	
	when they comen again.	*come*
	Then will they tell me in what country	*region*
395	that this boy then born is he;	
	then shall be taken both they and he	
	and that will make me fain.	*happy*

Sword.

By Cock's soul, come they again   *God's*
all three traitors shall be slain,
400   and that ilk swaddling swain—*
I shall chop off his head.
God's grace shall them not gain,   *avail*
nor no prophecy save them from pain.
That rocked ribald, and I may reign,
405   ruefully shall be his read.*

By Mahound full of mights,
tomorrow I will send after my knights,
to rule my realms and my rights
against this boy's boast,
410   and raze the country on every side,   *land*
all that ever may go or ride.   *walk*
So shall this boy lose his pride,   *be humiliated*
for all his greatest boast.

    Cast up.

This boy doth me so greatly annoy   *trouble*
415   that I wax dull and pure dry.   *weary;very thirsty*
Have done, and fill the wine in hie—   *at once*
I die but I have drink.   *unless*
Fill fast and let the cups fly,
and go we hethen hastily;   *hence*
420   for I must ordain curiously   *plan craftily*
against these kings' coming.   *for the coming of*

THE END

---

400 "And that same peasant wrapped in swaddling clothes."

404–5 "That cradled scoundrel, if I may reign, his fate shall be a sorrowful one."

PLAY 9: THE OFFERINGS OF THE THREE KINGS

Performed by the Mercers

CHESTER DEVOTES a whole play to the presentation of gifts by the Magi to the infant Christ and the angel's warning. The immediate biblical source, Matthew 2.9–12, offers only the outline for the play, which consists largely of long speeches by the Magi explaining the appropriateness of their gifts. The source for these allegorical interpretations is *The Golden Legend*, mediated through the fifteenth-century *Stanzaic Life of Christ*, which was composed in Chester. Some influence from the equivalent episode in the Coventry cycle has been postulated on the closing stanzas of farewell in the play.

From the Pre- and Post-Reformation Banns it appears that the play was produced in a spectacular manner which, when it ended the first day's performance, would constitute a memorable and triumphal conclusion; it also foreshadows the massacre of the Innocents with which the next day's performance would begin. The Mercers were evidently a wealthy company and presumably dressed the play lavishly. Certainly their waggon was decorated with rich cloths, and the Post-Reformation Banns contrast its splendour with the poverty of the stable in which Christ was born and which presumably provided the set carried on the waggon.

The action of the play is formal and slow. The Magi apparently enter on ground level and contemplate the Holy Family on the waggon above. Displaying their gifts, they explain to the audience immediately in front of them why the gifts are appropriate, then mount the waggon to make their offerings. Their rich gifts and learned expositions contrast with the poor presents bestowed on the spur of the moment by the shepherds in play 7. Joseph in response to the Magi emphasises Mary's virginity. Then, we may assume, the Magi descend and lie down in weariness on the ground, to be roused from sleep by the star-bearing angel. Alternatively, but unusually, the warning may be given to them by the angel before they leave the stable. They then formally take leave of each other, as the shepherds had done, and go their separate ways to their kingdoms.

———————

Cast   FIRST KING, SECOND KING, THIRD KING, MARY, JOSEPH, ANGEL.

1ST KING	Mighty God and most of main,	*power*
	to honour thee we may be fain;	*eager*
	the star I see it comen again	*come*
	that was out of our sight.	

2ND KING	Thy lordship to us thou ne lain,	*do not conceal*
6	that for Mankind would suffer pain.	
	Thou send us grace, if thou be gain,	*well disposed*
	to come to thee tonight.	

3RD KING	Ah, Lord, honoured be thou ay,	*ever*
10	for now we shall know well the way.	
	I will follow it, in good fay,	*faith*
	my forward to fulfill.	*agreement; carry out*

1ST KING	I hope without dread today	*expect certainly*
	to see that child and his array.	
15	But methinks, lords, by my fay,	*it seems to me; truly*
	the star it standeth still.	

2ND KING	That is a sign we be near—	*that we are*
	but high hall see I none here.	
	To a child of such power	*for*
20	this housing standeth low.	*poor*

3RD KING	Now wot I well, withouten were,	*know; without doubt*
	without pride he will appear	
	to make men meek, in such manner	
	an example us to show.	

1ST KING	The star yonder over the stable is.	
26	I wot we be not gone amiss,	*know; astray*
	for it stirred ever or this	*moved; before*
	and now there it is glent.	*moved*
2ND KING	I wot he wons here, iwiss,	*know; dwells; indeed*
30	and this simple house is his.	
	Ordain we now that King of bliss	*decide; for that king*
	apertly our present.	*clearly; gift*
3RD KING	What present best will for him fall	*befall*
	cast we here amongst us all;	*let us think*
35	for though he lie in an ox stall,	
	his might is never the less.	
1ST KING	"King of Jews" we shall him call;	
	therefore of me have he shall—	*from*
	that am his subject and his thrall—	*servant*
40	gold, or I pass.	*before; depart*
	For in our land is the manner	*custom*
	to approach no king near	
	bout dainty gifts rich and dear	*without; fine*
	after his dignity.	*according to his noble rank*
45	And for a king, gold clean and clear	*pure*
	is most commendable. Therefore now here	
	to relieve him in this manner	*help; way*
	he shall have that of me.	
	Also it seems by this place	
50	that little treasure his mother has.	
	Therefore to help her in this case	*situation*
	gold shall be my present.	
2ND KING	And I will offer through God's grace	
	incense that noble savour has.	*perfume*
55	Stink of the stable it shall waste,	*disperse*
	thereas they be lent.	*where; placed*
3RD KING	And myrrh is best my offering to be:	
	to anoint him, as thinks me—	*it seems to me*
	the child's members, head and knee	*limbs*
60	and other limbs all.	
	Thus shall we honour him all three	

with things that falls to his degree, *befit his rank*
touching manhood and deity. *pertaining to humanity*
These gifts will well befall. *suit*

1ST KING You say well, lords, witterly. *indeed*
66 As touching gold, prove may I,
it should be given him duly
because of temporality. *temporal power*
Sith he shall be king most mighty, *since*
70 tribute he must have truly;
and gold therefore witterly *certainly*
is best, as thinks me. *it seems to me*

2ND KING And sith he hath in him godhead, *since*
methinks best—as eat I bread— *it seems to me*
75 incense to give him through my read *advice*
in name of sacrifice,
for that may no way be led. *set aside*
Sith he of Holy Church is head, *since*
more due gifts, if I should be dead, *fitting*
80 I cannot devise.

3RD KING You say full well, sirs, both two.
And myrrh is good, methinks also. *it seems to me*
sith he for Man will suffer woe *since*
and die on rood-tree— *the cross*
85 myrrh that puts sin him fro *from*
and saves Man from rotting woe; *sad decay*
for it is best to balm him tho, *embalm; then*
that shall he have of me. *from*

1ST KING By these gifts three of good array *appearance*
90 three things understand I may:
a king's power, sooth to say, *truth*
by gold here in my hand;
and for his godhead lasteth ay, *for ever*
incense we must give him today;
95 and bodily death also in good fay *truly*
by myrrh I understand.

2ND KING Gold love also may signify,
for it men given not commonly *generally*
but those they loven heartfully— *to those; sincerely*
100 this child as we done all; *do*

and incense tokeneth, lieve I,   *signifies; believe*
orisons and prayers done devoutly;
myrrh, death that Man hath bodily.
And all these shall him fall.   *to him*

3RD KING   By gold that we to bring are boun,   *ready*
106   that richest metal of renown,
skilfully understand we mon   *reasonably; may*
most precious godhead;
and incense may well be said   *called*
110   a root of great devotion;   *source*
by myrrh, that waives corruption,   *removes*
clean flesh, both quick and dead.   *living*

And sickerly this knowen we: *certainly; know*
he wants none of these three;   *lacks*
115   for full godhead in him has he   *complete*
as gold may signify.
And soul devout in him must be
to come out of the Trinity;
and clean flesh we hopen to see   *sinless; expect*
120   in him full hastily.   *very quickly*

1ST KING   Now we have proved it here
these gifts to him be most dear,
go we forth in good manner   *gladly*
and make we our present.   *offering*

2ND KING   The star it shines fair and clear
126   over this stable ay entire.   *always; fully*
Here is his wonning withouten were,   *dwelling; doubtless*
and herein is he lent.   *placed*

3RD KING   A fair maiden yonder I see,
130   an old man sitting at her knee,
a child also; as thinks me,   *it seems to me*
three persons therein arn.   *are*

1ST KING   I say in certain this is he   *certainty*
that we have sought from far country.
135   Therefore now with all honesty   *sincerity*
honour I will that barn.   *child*

Then he shall take a vessel with gold.

1ST KING	Hail be thou, Lord, Christ and Messy,	*Messiah*
	that from God art comen kindly,	*come; by nature*
	Mankind of bale for to forbuy	*from; torment; redeem*
140	and into bliss bring.	
	We know well by prophecy	
	of Moses, David and Isay,	*Isaiah*
	and Balaam of our ancestry,	*forefathers*
	of Jews thou shalt be king.	
145	Therefore, as falleth for thy crown,	*befits*
	gold I have here ready boun	*prepared*
	to honour thee with great renown	
	after thy royalty.*	
	Take here, Lord, my intention	*purpose*
150	that I do with devotion,	
	and give me here thy benison	*blessing*
	ere that I go from thee.	*before*
2ND KING	Hail be Christ Emmanuel!	
	Thou comen art for Man's heal	*come; well-being*
155	and for to win again that weal	*happiness*
	that Adam put away.	*cast aside*
	Prophets of thee every one tell,	
	both Isay and Ezechiel;	*Isaiah*
	and Abraham might not conceal	
160	the truth of thee to say.*	
	Bishop I wot thou must be;	*priest; know*
	therefore now, as thinks me,	*it seems to me*
	incense will fall best for thee;	*be most fitting*
	and that now here I bring	
165	in tokening of thy dignity	*sign; high position*
	and that office of spirituality.	
	Receive here, Lord, at me	*from*
	devoutly my offering.	
3RD KING	Hail, Conqueror of all Mankind!	*champion*
170	To do mercy thou has mind,	*intend*

---

148 "In accordance with your royal condition."

159–60 "And Abraham was not able to keep the truth about you from being told." The exact allusion is not clear.

Anti-Jewish? polemic?

the Devil's bond to unbind
and relieve all thine.   *release*
A full fair way thou can find   *have found*
to hance us and put him behind,   *exalt*
175 through thy Passion to unbind
thy people that be in pine;   *torment*
for thou shalt mend us through thy might,   *restore*
die and rise the third night,
to recover again our right,   *what is rightfully ours*
180 and break the Devil's band.   *bond*
Myrrh to thee here have I dight   *prepared*
to balm thy body fair and bright.   *embalm; beautiful*
Receive my present, sweet wight,   *child*
and bless me with thy hand.

MARY   You royal kings in rich array,
186   the high Father of Heaven I pray
          to yield you your good deed today,   *reward you for*
          for his mickle might;   *great*
          and give you will now and alway
190   to yearn the life that lasteth ay,   *desire; for ever*
          and never to fall out of the fay   *faith*
          that in your hearts is pight.   *fixed*

          And lieves, lords, withouten were,   *believe; doubt*
          that to my Son you shall be dear,
195   that him today hath honoured here
          and me also for his sake.
          When time is come entere   *fully*
          to prove his strength and his power,
          to him you shall be lief and dear—   *beloved*
200   that dare I undertake.   *guarantee*

JOSEPH   You kings all comely of kind,   *noble by nature*
          full faithfully you shall it find—
          this mensky that God will have in mind   *reverence*
          and quite you well your meed.   *repay; reward*
205   And lieves well; of no man's strind   *believe*
          is he, not gotten by leave of kind;*
          that so believen are full blind,   *whoever; believe*
          for I know it in deed.   *as fact*

205–6 "Of no man's lineage is he, not begotten by consent of Nature."

	This maiden was betaken me	*entrusted to me*
210	when I had lost my jollity,	*sexual appetite*
	and failed might and posty	*lacked; power*
	sin for to assay.	*attempt*
	But for God would in chastity	
	that we should together be,	
215	keeper of her virginity	
	I have been many a day.	

	Therefore I wot, forsooth iwiss,	*know; most truly*
	clean maiden that she is	*pure virgin*
	and with man did never amiss;	*committed sin*
220	and thereof be you bold.	*confident*
	But of the Holy Ghost this is,	*this (child)*
	for to bring Mankind to bliss.	
	And this child is verray his;	*truly*
	so Gabriel me told.	

ANGEL	I warn you, comely kings three,	*fair*
226	my Lord would not you spill-ed be.	*killed*
	Therefore he sends you word by me	
	to turn another way.	*return*
	Herod's fellowship you shall flee;	
230	for you, harm ordained has he.	
	Therefore goes not through his country,	*go*
	ne the gate you came today.	*nor; the way*

1ST KING	Ah, high Lord that we honour here,	
	that warns us in this manner!	
235	Else had we wend withouten were	*gone; doubt*
	to him that would us spill.	*destroy*

2ND KING	Yea, Lord, as thou can us lere,	*teach*
	we will do to our power.	*as best we can*

3RD KING	Go we hethen all in fere,	*hence; together*
240	and his bidding fulfill.	

1ST KING	Farewell, Sir Jasper, brother, to you,

---

241 The names of the Magi are not biblical but traditional. In addition to Jasper and Balthasar named here, the king here unnamed was Melchior. One manuscript supplies that name as a gloss in the margin at this point. The kingdoms are

King of Tharsis most worthy.
Farewell, Sir Balthasar; to you I bow.
I thank you of your company.   *for*
245   He that made us to meet on plain   *caused*
and offer to Mary in her gesine,   *childbed*
send us safe and sound again
to the lands that we came fro.   *from*

2ND KING   You kings, I say you verament: *tell; truly*
250   sith God of his grace us hither sent,   *since*
we will do his commandment   *carry out*
whatsoever befall.
Therefore stand we not in doubt   *we do not fear*
for to walk our lands about,
255   and of his birth that we may moot   *speak*
both to great and small.

3RD KING   Farewell, sir kings, both in fere;   *together*
I thank you both of your good cheer.   *companionship*
But yet my wit is in a were   *mind; confusion*
260   lest Herod make us some tray.   *prepare some ambush*
He that shope both sea and sand   *created*
send us safe into our land!
Kings two, give me your hand.
Farewell, and have good day.

THE END

---

named from Psalms in the text cited by the Doctor to Herod in the preceding
play.

PLAY 10: THE MASSACRE OF THE INNOCENTS

Performed by the Goldsmiths

THE ANGEL'S WARNING TO the Magi at the end of the previous play is fulfilled in play 10, which usually began the second day's performance. It deals with events narrated briefly in Matthew 2.13–18, namely the flight of the Holy Family into Egypt; the killing of the male infants by Herod's soldiers; Herod's death; and the return of the Holy Family to their own home. The play is, however, really about Herod the Great.

Herod's insecurity, evident in play 8, becomes more pronounced in this sequel. His opening vaunt of power is undercut at once by the failure of the Magi to return as he had commanded. His anger and fear at this disobedience leads him wilfully to set aside his moral consciousness (line 23) and to order the murder of the children. Accompanied by his cringing priest and surrounded by sycophantic soldiers, he seeks to state his purpose rationally, but his intense emotions persist in breaking down his pretence of order and reason and overwhelm even his stylistic decorum. His knights, though flatterers, are appalled by his plan, and agree only when told that the slaughter will be of epic scale. But since the angel has already warned the Holy Family, who escape into Egypt to the symbolic harmony of the angel's song, the massacre demonstrably fails in its purpose from the outset.

The playwright draws upon legendary sources in his treatment of Herod's punishments. First, in an ironic reversal of his intention, Herod's own son is killed, a detail found in the *Golden Legend* and the derivative *Stanzaic Life*. Next, drawing upon accounts that originate with the Jewish historian Josephus, the playwright shows Herod's horrible death, in some way rotting away on the stage. Finally, his body is removed to hell by the Devil who anticipates his torment with considerable relish and

threatens the audience—a convenient means of clearing the stage before
the Holy Family returns to establish a mood of harmony confirmed by
the angel's second song. Herod thus becomes a warning example and a
means of affirming that, despite the apparent injustice of the innocents'
slaughter, God's justice prevails and is indeed manifest here on earth
even before death.

The focus upon Herod was evidently maintained by the waggon set,
which presumably represented Herod's court. The Goldsmiths, responsible for this play, who by 1531 or 1532 shared their waggon with the
Vintners (play 8) and from that date with the Dyers (play 23), were
wealthy enough to produce a set of some splendour and to dress the
play richly. Herod wears a gold crown (line 89), and his infant son is
decked in silk, gold and precious stones (lines 401–10). His Messenger
receives a splendid cloak (line 80). The soldiers, too, seem well equipped.
In contrast, most of the women (excluding, presumably, the nurse) would
be poorly dressed.

The play requires a number of locations in addition to the court—
the place from which the slumbering soldiers are summoned; the place
where the angel warns the Holy Family; Egypt, their place of exile; and
the site of the slaughter. Egypt is the scene of a special stage-effect; an
idolatrous statue is to collapse as the Holy Family passes (288+SD).

The slaughter, at least, seems to take place at ground level, the
mothers being, as it were, of the contemporary audience. Modern productions have demonstrated that the pathos of the slaughter is intensified
by the mothers' oscillations between grief and angry violence and that
there is no need to overplay the soldiers as comic cowards.

Cast   HEROD, MESSENGER, FIRST KNIGHT, SECOND KNIGHT, PRIEST,
ANGEL, JOSEPH, MARY, FIRST WOMAN, SECOND WOMAN.

HEROD	Princes, prelates of price,	*worth*
	barons in blauner and bise,	*ermine and rich linen*
	beware of me, all that been wise,	*who are*
	that wields all at my will.	
5	Say no man anything is his	*let no man say*
	but only at my device;	*devising*
	for all this world under me lies	
	to spare—and eke to spill!	*also to destroy*

My subjects all that here been set—   *who are*
10   barons, burgess and baronet—
be bain to me, or you is let,*
and at my bidding be.
For lieves this withouten let,   *believe; without doubt*
that I will do as I have het—   *promised*
15   mar that misbegotten marmoset   *inflict damage on*
that thinks to mar me.   *harm*

And those false traitors that me behight   *promised*
to have comen again this same night   *come*
by another way have taken their flight;
20   this way durst they not take.
Therefore that boy, by God Almight,
shall be slain soon in your sight,
and—though it be against the right—   *what is right*
a thousand for his sake.

25   Alas, what purpose had that page   *lad*
that is so young and tender of age,
that would bereave my heritage,   *take away*
that am so mickle of might?   *great in power*
Forsooth that shrew was wondrous sage   *wretch; wise*
30   against me any war to wage!
That recked ribald for all his rage   *wretched rascal*
shall not reave me my right.   *rob me of*

But sith it may no other be
but these kings are gone from me,
35   that that shrew would have my sovereignty
I think to put him again.
All the knave-children in this country
shall buy his guile, so mote I thee.*
Because I know not which is he,
40   all for his sake shall be slain.

---

11 "Be obedient to me, or there will be restraint (i.e., imprisonment) for you."

33–38 "But since there is no other explanation but that the kings have gone away from me, I intend to bring against him the charge that that wretch would have my sovereign power. All the male children in this region shall pay for his trickery, so may I thrive."

How! Pretty Prat, my messenger!   *clever*
Come hither to me withouten were!   *fearlessly*
For thou must go with hasty bere   *noisy haste*
into Judee this day   *Judea*
45   after my doughty and comely knights   *for; sturdy*
and bid them hie with all their mights   *hasten*
and that they let for no fights.   *stop*
Bring them without delay.

MESSENGER   Yes, my lord of great renown,
50   to do your hest I am boun,   *command; ready*
lightly to leap over dale and down
and speed if I were there.   *prosper; might be*
Farewell, my lord in majesty,
for on my journey I will hie me.   *hasten*

HEROD   Now mighty Mahound be with thee,
56   and ever to dwell in fere.   *together*

MESSENGER   How! awake out of your sleep,
Sir Grimbald and Sir Lancherdeep!
And to me you take good keep,   *heed*
60   for hither I am sent.
My lord, King Herod, begins to sown   *swoon*
for a shrew would have his crown   *wretch*
and thus bereave him of his renown,   *deprive*
and soon would have him shent.   *destroyed*

1ST KNIGHT   Welcome, messenger that art so gent.   *courteous*
66   These tidings which my lord hath sent—
they be welcome, verament.   *truly*
With thee now will I wend.   *go*

2ND KNIGHT   Messenger, I will, in good fay,   *certainly*
70   wend with you this ilk way   *go; same*
to hear what my lord will say,
of this matter to make an end.

MESSENGER   Hail, comely king sitting in see!   *on a throne*
Here been thy knights comen to thee   *are; come*
75   that be men of great degree   *are; high rank*
to hear of your talent.   *purpose*

HEROD   Messenger, for thy good deed

	right well shall I quite thy meed:	*pay your reward*
	have here of me to do thee speed	*to make you prosper*
80	right a gay garment.	*very splendid*

MESSENGER	Gramercy, lord regent;	*reigning*
	well am I pleased to mine intent.	*my way of thinking*
	Mighty Mahound that I have meant	*held in mind*
	keep you in this stead!	*preserve; place*

| 1ST KNIGHT | Sir Lancherdeep, what say ye? | |
| 86 | This is the fairest king that ever I see. | *saw* |

| 2ND KNIGHT | This day under the sun shining |
| | is there none so seemly a king. |

1ST KNIGHT	Hail, comely king crowned in gold!	
90	Each king and kaiser kens not your bet.*	
	If any were that with your grace fight would,	
	such strokes for your sake full sore	*most sorely*
	should be set.	*placed*

2ND KNIGHT	If him we may take or get,	
	the Devil ought him debt;	*owes him a debt*
95	and so he shall be quit	*repaid*
	such masteries for to make.	*deceptions; contrive*

HEROD	Welcome, our knights that be so gent!	*courteous*
	Now will we tell you our intent,	*intention*
	what is the cause we for you sent	
100	so soon and hastily.	
	Yesterday to this city	
	when we were in our royalty,	*royal state*
	there came to us kings three	
	and told us their intent	*purpose*

105	to seek a child that born should be,	
	that was said by prophecy	*related*
	that should be king of Judee	*Judea*
	and many another land.	
	We gave them leave to search and see	
110	and come again to this city;	

---

90 "Each king and emperor knows none better than you."

and if he were of such degree,   *rank*
we would not him withstand.

But and they had comen again,   *if; come*
all three traitors should have been slain,
115   and also that lither swain—   *deceitful youth*
and all for his sake.
Out, alas! What may this be?
For I know not which is he!
Therefore all knave-children in this country,   *male*
120   on them shall fall the wreak.   *vengeance*

For we know not that child well,
though we therefore should go to Hell,
all the children of Israel
we deem them to be slain.   *condemn*
125   Counsellor, what is thy read?   *advice*

PRIEST   Deem them, lord, for to be dead—   *condemn*
for that is best, as eat I bread,
to catch that lither swain.   *deceitful youth*

Command your knights anon to hie,   *at once to hasten*
130   to go to the land of Galilee
and into the land of Judee,   *Judea*
to slay all that they may find.

HEROD   That was well said, my counsellor.
But yet I burn as doth the fire—   *does*
135   what for wrath, what for ire—
till this be brought to end.

Therefore, my knights good and keen,
have done beleve; go wreak my teen.*
Go slay that shrew; let it be seen   *wretch*
140   and you be men of main.   *if; might*
Preves manfully what they been,   *prove; what sex; are*
that none away from you fleen.   *so that; flee*
Drive down the dirty-arses all bedene   *immediately*
and soon, that they were slain!   *should be*

---

138 "Have done at once; go, avenge my suffering!"

145	So shall I keep that vile congeon*	
	that thus would reave me of my crown.	*deprive*
	Therefore, my bachelors, make you boun	*knights; ready*
	and fond to save my right.	*attempt*
	You must hie you out of this town	*hasten*
150	to Bethlehem as fast as you mon.	*may*
	All knave-children, by my crown,	*male-children*
	you must slay this night.	

1ST KNIGHT	Alas! My lord and king of bliss,	
	sent you after us for this?	
155	A villainy it were, iwiss,	*villainous act; indeed*
	for my fellow and me	
	to slay a shitten-arsed shrew;	*wretch*
	a lad his head might off hew!	*a mere boy*
	For ribalds are not in this row,	*rascals; line*
160	but knights of great degree.	*high rank*

2ND KNIGHT	My lief lord of great renown,	*dear*
	we shall wreak you if we mon—	*avenge; may*
	whether he be knight, or champion	
	stiffer than ever Samson was,	*stronger*
165	sickerly I shall drive them down.	*certainly*
	But for to kill such a congeon	*brat*
	me shames sore, by Saint Mahoun,	*I'm sorely ashamed*
	to go in any place.	

HEROD	Nay, nay, it is neither one nor two	
170	that you shall slay, as mote I go,	*as I may walk*
	but a thousand, and yet moe.	*still more*
	Take this in your mind:	
	Because I know not which this shrew is,	*wretch*
	therefore, lest you of him miss,	*in case; miss him*
175	you must slay, forsooth iwiss,	*truly indeed*
	all that you may find.	

	You shall walk far and near	
	into Bethlehem. Spare for no bere	*outcry*
	all knave-children within two year	*male-children*
180	and one day old.	
	Slay them down both one and all.	*strike*

---

145 "That's how I shall take care of that vile brat."

	So shall you meet with that stall	*thief*
	that would my kingdom claim and call,	*demand*
	and my wealth also wield.	*control*

1ST KNIGHT	It shall be done, lord, in hie;	*in haste*
186	shall none be left, witterly.	*certainly*
	We shall go search by and by	
	in Bethlehem all about,	
	and wreak your teen full tenderly,*	
190	leave none unslain, sickerly.	*certainly*
	So shall we soon that shrew destroy,	*wretch*
	and keep him in the rout.	*contain; crowd*

1ST KNIGHT	But look you rich you to array;	*prepare for muster*
	to Bethlehem, that borough, I am boun.	*town; ready*
195	With this spear I think to assay	*attempt*
	to kill many a small congeon.	*little brat*
	If any blab-lipped boys be in my way,	*swollen-lipped*
	they shall rue it, by Mahoun;	
	though all the world would say "Nay,"	
200	I myself shall ding them all down.	*strike*

	If you will wit what I hight,	*know; am called*
	my name is Sir Waradrake the knight.	
	Against me dare no man fight,	
	my dints they so dread.	*blows*

205	But fain would I fight my fill,	*eagerly*
	as fain as falcon would fly,	*eagerly*
	my lord to wreak at his will	*avenge; desire*
	and make those dogs to die.	*cause*
	Those congeons in their clouts I will kill	*brats; cloths*
210	and stoutly with strokes them destroy.	
	Shall never one scape by my will;	*escape; wish*
	all babes for that boy, full sore shall they buy.*	

	Shall never none overpass	*get past*
	of two years age and less;	
215	and this boy that king crowned was	

---

189 "And avenge your anguish most feelingly."

212 "All babes shall full sorely pay the penalty for that brat."

shall not scape without scathe.	*escape unharmed*

2ND KNIGHT And I also, without boast— *bragging*
though the King of Scots and all his host
were here—I set by their boast *put aside; boasting*
220 to drive them down bedene. *quickly*
I slew ten thousand upon a day
of kemps in their best array; *champions; finest armour*
there was not one escaped away
my sword it was so keen.* *sharp*

225 Therefore to me you take good keep; *pay good heed*
my name is Sir Grimbald Lancherdeep.
They that me teen I lay to sleep *anger*
on everich a side. *every side*
I slew of kemps, I understand, *champions*
230 more than an hundred thousand
both on water and on land.
No man dare me abide. *endure*

Through Bethlehem I will spring,
for I must now at your bidding;
235 right all down shall I ding *strike*
these lads everychone. *every one*
And then that false gedling *base fellow*
that born was so young,
he shall not for nothing *anything*
240 away from us gone. *go*

1ST KNIGHT Farewell, my lord, and have good day,
for hardily thus dare I say— *boldly*
not for no boast; in good fay, *truly*
it is not my manner!— *habit*
245 I would I might find in my way
Samson in his best array,
to look whether I durst affray, *see; attack*
to fight with him right here.

HEROD Nay, nay! I know well, or thou swear, *before*
250 that thou art a doughty man of war; *valiant*

217–24 Perhaps an allusion to the Battle of Flodden (1513) in which some 10,000 Scots were killed in the English victory.

and though Samson were here,
soon he should be slain.
But yet, my wit is in a were   *mind; confusion*
whether you shall find that losinger.   *deceiver*
255   But speeds you fast for my prayer,   *hurry; request*
and hie you fast again.   *hasten; back again*

Then the knights shall go, and the Angel shall come.

ANGEL   Joseph, arise, and that anon;   *do that at once*
into Egypt thou must gone—   *go*
and Mary also—from your fone.   *foes*
260   This is my Lord's will.
There stay, lest this child be slain,
till I warn thee to come again.   *advise*
False Herod would have you fain,   *gladly*
Jesus for to spill.   *kill*

JOSEPH   Ah, Lord, blessed most thou be.
266   Thider anon we will flee.   *thither at once*
Have we company of thee,   *if we have your company*
we will hie on our way.   *hasten*

ANGEL   Yea, company we shall you bear
270   till that you be comen there.   *until; have come*
Herod busks him you to dere   *prepares; harm*
as fast as ever he may.

JOSEPH   Mary, sister, now we must flit;   *move on*
upon my ass shall thou now sit,
275   into Egypt till we hit.   *enter*
The angel will us lead.

MARY   Sir, evermore, loud and still,   *in all circumstances*
your talent I shall fulfill.   *wish*
I wot it is my Lord's will;   *know*
280   I do as you me read.   *advise*

ANGEL   Come now forth in God's name.
I shall you shield from all shame;
and you shall see, my lief dame,   *honoured lady*
a thing to your liking;
285   for mahomets both one and all,   *idols*
that men of Egypt "gods" can call,   *do call*

at your coming down shall fall
when I begin to sing.

or idolatry ↗

*Then they shall go, and the Angel shall sing: "Ecce dominus
ascendet super nubem levem, et ingrediatur Egiptum, et move-
buntur simulachra Egipti a facie domini exercituum"; and if
it can be done, some statue or image shall fall.*

1ST KNIGHT	Have done, fellows, hie fast,	*hasten*
290	that these queans were down cast,	*sluts; might be*
	and the children in thrast;	*stabbed*
	and kill them all to cloutes!	*cut them all to pieces*
2ND KNIGHT	Yea, sir, we dwell too long;	*stay*
	therefore, go we them among.	*let us go*
295	They hopen to have some wrong	*expect; harm*
	that gone so fast about us.	*who go*
1ST WOMAN	Whom callest thou "quean," scabbed bitch?	*slut*
	Thy dame, thou dastard, was never such?	*mother; coward*
	She burned a kiln, each stitch—*	
300	yet did I never none.	*any such thing*
2ND WOMAN	Be thou so hardy, I thee behet,	*bold; promise*
	to handle my son that is so sweet,	
	this distaff and thy head shall meet	
	or we hethen gone.	*before we go hence*
1ST KNIGHT	Dame, abide, and let me see	*mother; wait*
306	a knave-child if that it be.	*male-child*
	The king has commanded me	
	all such for to arrest.	*seize*
1ST WOMAN	"Arrest"? Ribot, forthy	*seize; rogue; therefore*
310	thou lies, by my lewty.	*by my faith*
	Therefore I read fast that thou flee	*advise*
	and let me have my peace.	

288+SD "Behold, the Lord rideth upon a swift cloud, and shall come into Egypt;
and the idols of Egypt shall be moved at his presence." The text is from Isaiah
19.1; it is unidentified as a liturgical text.

299 "She burned a kiln, every bit"—i.e., she was probably a common ale-wife.

2ND WOMAN	Say, rotten hunter with thy goad,	
	stitton stallion, stick-toad!*	
315	I read that thou no wrong us bode	*advise; offer*
	lest thou beaten be.	
	Whereto should we longer fode?	*pretend*
	Lay we on them large load.	*rain heavy blows on*
	Their basnets be big and broad;	*helmets*
320	beat on now, lets see.	
2ND KNIGHT	Dame, thy son, in good fay,	*mother; truly*
	he must of me learn a play:	*game*
	he must hop, or I go away,	*before*
	upon my spear-end.	
1ST WOMAN	Out, out and wail-away!	*alas*
326	That ever I abode this day!	*lived to see*
	One stroke yet I will assay	*attempt*
	to give or that I wend.	*before; go*
2ND WOMAN	Out, out on thee, thief!	
330	My love, my lord, my life, my lief,	*beloved*
	did never man or woman grief	*caused*
	to suffer such torment!	
	But yet wroken I will be.	*avenged*
	Have here one, two, or three.	
335	Bear the king this from me—	
	and that I it him sent.	
1ST KNIGHT	Come hither to me, Dame Parnell,	*i.e., slut*
	and show me here thy son snell.	*quickly*
	For the king has bid me quell	*kill*
340	all that we find mon.	*may find*
1ST WOMAN	My son? Nay, strong thief,	
	for—as I have good preef—	*proof*
	do thou my child any grief.	*if you cause*
	I shall crack thy crown.	

313–14 "Say, corrupt hunter with your goad, stubborn(?) stallion, frog-stabber!"
rotten-hunter may also be "rat-catcher"; *stallion* is equivalent to the slang *stud*,
"man kept for sexual services"; *stitton* is not otherwise recorded and its meaning
is doubtful.

Then the knight shall transfix the first male-child and lift it on his spear.

1ST WOMAN	Out, out, and woe is me!	
346	Thief, thou shall hang-ed be.	
	My child is dead; now I see	
	my sorrow may not cease.	
	Thou shall be hanged on a tree	
350	and all thy fellows with thee.	*companions*
	All the men in this country	
	shall not make thy peace.	

	Have thou this, thou foul harlot!	*coward*
	And thou, knight, to make a knot!	*to complete it*
355	And one buffet with this bot	*bundle of cloth*
	thou shalt have to boot.	*as reward*
	And thou this! And thou this!	
	Though thou both shit and piss!	*i.e., with fear*
	And if thou think we do amiss	
360	go busks you to moot.*	*hasten; a law-proceeding*

2ND KNIGHT	Dame, show me thy child there;	*mother*
	he must hop upon my spear.	
	And it any pintel bear,	*if; penis*
	I must teach him a play.	*game*

2ND WOMAN	Nay, freke, thou shalt fail;	*knight*
366	my child shalt thou not assail.	*attack*
	It has two holes under the tail;	*i.e., penis and anus*
	kiss, and thou may assay.	*test it*

	Be thou so hardy, stick-toad,	*bold; toad-stabber*
370	to bide any wrong, or bode?	*endure; offer*
	For all thy speech and thy goad	
	I read ye do but good.	*advise; only*
	For, and thou do me any harm	*if*
	or my child upon my arm,	
375	I shall found to keep thee warm,	*manage; make you sweat*
	be thou never so wood.	*however angry you are*

Then the Second Knight shall transfix the second male-child.

356–60 The woman evidently strikes the two knights alternately.

2ND WOMAN Out, out, out, out!

You shall be hanged, the rout.   *the lot of you*

Thieves, be you never so stout,   *bold*

380   full foul you have done.

This child was taken to me   *entrusted*

to look to. Thieves, who been ye?   *are*

He was not mine, as you shall see.

He was the king's son.

385   I shall tell while I may drey;   *endure*

his child was slain before my eye.

Thieves, you shall be hang-ed high,

may I come to his hall.   *if I may*

But or I go, have thou one!   *before*

390   And thou another, Sir John!*   *i.e., the priest*

For to the king I will anon   *at once*

to plain upon you all.   *lodge a complaint against*

Then she shall go to Herod.

2ND WOMAN Lo, lord, look and see—

the child that thou took to me,   *entrusted*

395   men of thy own meny   *company*

have slain it—here they been.   *are*

HEROD (*enraged*)

Fie, whore, fie! God give thee pine!   *torment*

Why didst thou not say that child was mine?

But it is vengeance, as drink I wine,

400   and that is now well seen.

2ND WOMAN Yea, lord, they see well aright   *saw very well*

thy son was like to be a knight,

for in gold harness he was dight,   *armour; clad*

painted wondrous gay.

405   Yet was I never so sore afright,   *sorely frightened*

when they their spears through him thright;   *thrust*

lord, so little was my might

when they began to fray.   *attack*

---

390 The woman strikes knight and priest in turn. *Sir John* is a familiar or contemptuous way of referring to a priest.

HEROD	He was right sicker in silk array,	*most secure*
410	in gold and perry that was so gay.	*precious stones*
	They might well know by this day	
	he was a king's son.	
	What the Devil is this to say?	
	Why were thy wits so far away?	
415	Could thou not speak? Could thou not pray,	
	and say it was my son?	
	Alas, my days been now done!	
	I wot I must die soon.	*know*
	Bootless is me to make moan,	*useless; for me; complain*
420	for damned I must be.	
	My legs rotten and my arms,	*rot*
	that now I see of fiends swarms—	
	I have done so many harms—	*harmful deeds*
	from Hell coming after me.	
425	I have done so much woe	*caused*
	and never good sith I might go;	*since; move*
	therefore I see now coming my foe	
	to fetch me to Hell.	
	I bequeath here in this place	
430	my soul to be with Satanas.	*Satan*
	I die now. Alas, alas!	
	I may no longer dwell.*	*remain*

*Then he shall make a sign as if he dies and the Demon shall
come.*

DEMON	Ware, ware! for now unwarily	*beware; unexpectedly*
	wakes your woe!	
	For I am swifter than is the roe.	*roe-deer*
435	I am comen to fetch this lord you fro,	*come; from*
	in woe ever to dwell.	
	And with this crooked camrock your	*hooked stick*
	backs shall I clow;	*claw*
	and all false believers I burn and low,	*set alight*
	that from the crown of the head to the right toe	

417–32 Accounts of the death of Herod originate in the Jewish historian Josephus.
But the death, regarded by homilists as punishment for the killing of the children, occurred some time after the Massacre.

440   I leave no right whole fell.   *fully intact skin*

From Lucifer, that lord, I am sent
to fetch this king's soul here present
into Hell to bring him, there to be lent,   *placed*
ever to live in woe.

445   There fire burns bloe and brent,   *dark and high*
he shall there be, this lord, verament.   *truly*
His place evermore therein is hent,   *taken*
his body never to go fro.   *depart*

No more shall you trespass. By my lewty,   *sin; faith*
450   that fills their measures falsely*   *whoever*
shall bear this lord company;
they get none other grace.
I will you bring thus to woe,
and come again and fetch moe   *more*
455   as fast as ever I may go.
Farewell, and have good days.

Exit Demon.

ANGEL   Joseph, arise, and that in hie!   *in haste*
For dead is now your enemy.
Take Jesus the child, and eke Mary   *also*
460   and wend into Judee.   *go; Judea*
Herod, that would have had you slain,
he is marred, both might and main.   *entirely destroyed*
Therefore hies you home again;   *hasten*
in peace now you shall be.

JOSEPH   Ah, Lord that madest all of nought,
466   it is skill thy will be wrought.   *wise that; done*
Now is he dead that us has sought.
We shall never cease   *stop*
till that we at home be
470   again in our country.
Now hope we well to live in lee   *happiness*
and in full great peace.

---

450 The Devil directs his warning specifically against the ale-wives and tapsters
who serve false measures of ale. See also the ending of play 17.

	Mary, sister, we must go	
	to our land that we came fro.	*from*
475	The angel has bidden us so,	
	my own dear sweet.	*sweetheart*
	On my ass thou shalt be,	
	and my mantle under thee,	
	full easily, sister, lieve thou me,*	
480	and that I thee behete.	*promise*

MARY   I thank you, sir, as I can.   *as best I can*
        Help me that I were upon.   *might be on the ass*
        He that is both God and man
        keep us in this tide!   *at this time*

JOSEPH   Come hither, dear heart-root;   *darling*
486   I shall soon be thy boot.   *help*
        Thou shalt soon ride each foot,   *all the way*
        and I will go by thy side.

ANGEL   Now you be ready for to go—
490   Joseph, and Mary also—
        forsooth, I will not depart you fro   *from*
        but help you from your foe.
        And I will make a melody,
        and sing here in your company
495   a word was said in prophecy   *that was said*
        a thousand years ago:

        "Ex Egipto vocavi Filium meum, ut salvum faciet populum
        meum."*

THE END

---

479 "Quite comfortably, dearest, believe me."

496+Latin "Out of Egypt have I called my son, that he may save my people."
The text combines elements of Matthew 2.15 and Matthew 1.12. It is a Magnificat
antiphon and also a Vespers antiphon on the Friday of the first week in Advent.

PLAY 11: THE PURIFICATION OF THE VIRGIN MARY, and CHRIST'S APPEARANCE BEFORE THE DOCTORS

Performed by the Blacksmiths

PLAY 11 brings abruptly together two widely-separated episodes in Christ's childhood which occurred in the temple at Jerusalem and which are similarly brought together in Luke 2.22–51, though with a linking passage that has no parallel in Chester. The first is the purification of the Virgin Mary (verses 22–39). The Pre-Reformation Banns call the waggon "Candilmas dey" after the Feast of Candlemas commemorating the purification. Since by Jewish law the ritual cleansing of the mother after the "impurity" of childbirth must take place at least forty days after the birth, it was more usual to locate this episode before the flight of the Holy Family into Egypt. Here, perhaps, the desire to utilise the temple-set fully and to suggest a comparison between attitudes in the two episodes may have additionally determined its location. The second episode, when Jesus remained behind in Jerusalem and was discovered debating with the Priests (verses 41–51), occurred twelve years later, when the boy Jesus went to Jerusalem for the Feast of the Passover. There is nothing in the text to mark this transition, but the text in all manuscripts is very corrupt at this point.

The central figure in the purification is Simeon, who is presented as an old but rather sceptical man, inclined to doubt the word of the Scriptures. The "book-miracle," in which he attempts to alter the text and finds it miraculously restored by an angel, is found only here and in *Stanzaic Life*, again indicating the strong link between the two texts. It achieves comic effect as Simeon, under the disapproving eye of Anna, a widow and prophetess, repeats his attempt and is amazed by the result. The ceremonies in the temple begin with the presentation of offerings as required by the law (though Joseph carefully emphasises that the law does not apply to Mary's situation) and continues with the inspired creation and singing of the liturgical *Nunc dimittis.* The episode ends with Anna—and presumably the whole group—worshipping the infant.

The second episode is a version shared with the cycles of Coventry and York and with the Towneley manuscript, from which the deficiencies of our text can be made good. The Bible does not indicate what passed between the Doctors and Christ in the Temple and the dramatist here suggests that Christ simply displayed his knowledge of the Decalogue. This was not, in itself, a notable achievement for a twelve-year-old and provokes excessive amazement from the somewhat patronising Doctors who draw from it conclusions which seem hardly justified. The refusal of the aged Joseph to approach the Doctors, leaving it all to Jesus's mother, provides a nice human touch towards the end of the play.

Six sets of play-accounts for the Blacksmiths' company are extant, the earliest being of 1550. They indicate that the face of the boy Jesus was gilded; that Mary wore a crown; and that wigs were used. The play involved much music. The references in the Post-Reformation Banns to minstrels with "pipe, tabret, and flute" are confirmed by payments to the minstrels in the accounts. Additionally, choristers were hired from the cathedral, presumably for singing at moments such as the angel's entrances. Simeon is required to sing, and the part seems on occasion to have been taken by a cathedral singing-man. The 1567 accounts, which contain no payment for hiring choristers, mention a *regalls*, a small portable organ. Payment to the Clerk for the loan of a cope, altar-cloth and an ecclesiastical garment in 1572 suggests the source and nature of the ecclesiastical costumes.

Cast   SIMEON, ANNA, ANGEL, MARY, JOSEPH, FIRST DOCTOR, CHRIST, SECOND DOCTOR, THIRD DOCTOR.

SIMEON	Mighty God, have mind on me,	
	that most art in majesty,	*regal power*
	for many a winter have I be	*been*
	priest in Jerusalem.	
5	Much teen and incommodity	*suffering; inconvenience*
	followeth age, full well I see;	*pursues old age*

	and now that fit may I not flee,	*condition*
	think me never so swem.*	
	When I am dead and laid in clay,	
10	wend I mot the same way	*I must go*
	that Abraham went, the sooth to say,	*truth*
	and in his bosom be.*	
	But Heaven-bliss after my day?	*life*
	Till God's Son come, the sooth to say,	*may come; truth*
15	to ransom his folk, in better array	*condition*
	to bliss come never we.	*may come*
	That Christ shall come well I wot,	*know*
	but day nor time may no man wot.	*know*
	Therefore my book look I mot,	*I must examine*
20	my heart to glad and light.	*gladden and rejoice*
	When Isay saith I will see,	*Isaiah*
	for well I wot how it shall be;	*know*
	or I died well were me	
	of him to have a sight.*	

*Then, examining his book, he shall read the prophecy: "Ecce virgo concipiet et pariet filium," etc.**

SIMEON	Ah, Lord, much is thy power;*	
26	a wonder I find written here.	
	It saith a maiden clean and clear	*virgin; pure*
	shall conceive and bear	
	a son called "Emmanuel."	
30	But of this lieve I never a deal;	*believe; not a bit*
	it is wrong written, as have I heal,	*so may I prosper*

---

8 "However much it grieves me."

11–12 Abraham's bosom was traditionally the limbo of the patriarchs, where the saints of the Old Covenant remained until the coming of Christ to harrow hell. It derives from Luke 16.22, where the dead beggar Lazarus is transported to Abraham's bosom.

23–24 "Happy might I be to have a glimpse of him before I died."

24+SD Latin "Behold, a virgin shall conceive and bear a son" (Isaiah 7.14).

25ff. The miracle of the emended text is found only here and in the *Stanzaic Life*.

or else wonder it were.

	He that wrote this was a fon	*fool*
	to write "a virgin" hereupon	
35	that should conceive without help of man!	
	This writing marvels me!	*scripture; amazes*
	I will scrape this away anon;	*immediately*
	thereas "a virgin" is written on	*where*
	I will write "a good woman"—	
40	for so it should be!	

Then he shall scrape the book as if he were deleting this word "virgin"; and then he shall place the book upon the altar. And the angel shall come and shall take the book, making a sign as if he were writing; and he shall close the book and disappear; and the prophetess Anna shall speak.

ANNA*	Simeon, father, sooth I see—	*the truth*
	that Christ shall come, our boot to be,	*remedy*
	from the Father in majesty	
	on Mankind for to min.	*think*
45	And when he comes, lieves you me,	*believe*
	he will have mercy and pity	
	on his folk, to make them free,	*people*
	and salve them from their sin.	*cure*

SIMEON	The time of his coming know I nought;	*not at all*
50	yet many book-es I have sought.	*searched through*
	But wonderly he this writing wrought,	*wondrously*
	and marvel think-es me—	*it seems a marvel to me*
	my book to look if I find ought	
	what manner Mankind shall be bought	
55	and what time it shall be.*	

Then he shall take the book and shall say in wonderment:

40+SH *Anna* is described in Luke 2.36–38 as a prophetess and a widow of about 84 years of age. Her role here is enlarged, and her faith counters Simeon's scepticism.

53–55 "To examine my book to see if I may find anything about how Mankind shall be redeemed and what time it shall be." The stanza lacks a line—evidently the one immediately preceding this passage, which must have contained the verb on which *to look* depended.

Ah, Lord, how may this be? Today
that I wrote last I find away   *what; gone*
and of red letters in stout array   *in; bold hand*
"a virgin" written thereon.
60   Nay, fay, after I will assay   *no; truly; next; test*
whether this miracle be verray,   *genuine*
and scrape this word written so gay   *erase; brightly*
and write "a good woman."

Then he shall scrape it a second time as he did previously.

SIMEON   Dame Anne. thou may see well here
65   this is emended in good manner;   *properly*
for a wonder thing it were   *marvellous; would be*
to fall by any way.   *happen; by any means*
Therefore, as it was amiss,   *wrong*
I have written that soother is: *what is more true*
70   that "a good woman" shall iwiss   *indeed*
conceive, and not a may.   *virgin*

Then he shall place the book upon the altar, and the angel
shall do as he did before.

ANNA   Sir, marvel you nothing thereon;   *at that*
forsooth, God will take kind in Man.*
Through his godhead ordain he can
75   a maid a child to bear.   *virgin*
For to that high comely king   *noble*
impossible is nothing.
Therefore I lieve it no leasing   *believe; lie*
but sooth, all that is here.   *truth*

SIMEON   My fay, yet eft will I see   *by my faith; again*
81   whether my letters chang-ed be.

He shall take up the book.

SIMEON   Ah, high God in Trinity,
honoured be thou ay!   *for ever*
For golden letters, by my lewty,   *by my faith*
85   are written through God's posty   *power*

---

73 "Truly, God will assume natural form in Man."

	sith I laid my book from me	*since;put*
	and my writing away,	*gone away*
	thereas "a good woman" written was	*where*
	right now before my face.	*just now*
90	Yet stirred I not out of this place	
	and my letter changed is!	*what I wrote*
	This must be needs by God's grace,	*necessarily be*
	for an angel this written has.	
	Now lieve I a maid in this case	*believe;circumstance*
95	shall bear a barn of bliss.	*son*
	Now, Lord, sith that it so is —	*since*
	that thou wilt be born with bliss	*joy*
	of a maid that never did amiss—	*virgin;wrong*
	on me, Lord, thou have mind.	*may you remember me*
100	Let me never death taste, Lord full of grace,	
	till I have seen thy child's face	
	that prophesied is here in this place	
	to cover all Mankind.	*restore*

ANGEL	Simeon, I tell thee sickerly	*for certain*
105	that God's own ghost am I,	*spirit*
	comen to warn thee witterly:	*come;advise;certainly*
	death shall thou never see	
	till thou have seen Christ verray	*the true Christ*
	that born is of maiden Mary	*the virgin*
110	and comen Mankind to forbuy	*come;redeem*
	from God in majesty.	

SIMEON	Ah, Lord, I thank thee of thy grace	*for*
	that thy ghost sent to me has.	*spirit*
	Now hope I sickerly in this place	*surely*
115	thy Son for to see,	
	that of a virgin must be born	
	to save Mankind that was forlorn,	*lost*
	as Isay's books told me beforn.	*Isaiah's;before*
	Lord, blessed must thou be.	

Then Simeon shall sit, looking for consolation; from another
location far from the temple Mary shall speak:

MARY	Joseph, my own true fere,	*husband*
121	now read I—if your will were—	*suggest;if it were*

	sith forty days are gone entire,	*since*
	the temple that we go to,	
	and, Moses' Law for to fulfill,	
125	my son to offer Simeon till.	*to Simeon*
	I wot well that it is God's will	*know*
	that we now so do.	

JOSEPH	Yea, Mary, though it be no need—	
	sith thou art clean in thought and deed—	*since*
130	yet it is good to do as God bede	*commands*
	and work after His saw,*	
	and to the temple that we go	
	and take with us dove-birds two	
	or a turtle to offer to,	*turtle-dove*
135	and so fulfill God's law.*	

MARY	Rightwise Simeon, God thee see!	*righteous; watch over*
	Here am I comen now to thee	*come*
	purifi-ed now to be	
	with mild heart and meek.	*gentle*
140	Receive my son now at me	*from*
	and to my offering birds three,	*for*
	as falls, sir, for your degree,	*befits your rank*
	and for your office eke.	*also*

JOSEPH	A sign I offer here also	
145	of virgin wax, as other moe,	*another in addition*
	in tokening she has lived oo	*token; always*
	in full devotion.	*in total piety*
	And, Sir Simeon, lieve well this:	*Father; believe*
	as clean as this wax now is,	
150	as clean is my wife, iwiss,	*so pure; indeed*
	of all corruption.	*from*

Then Simeon shall take the boy in his arms.

| SIMEON | Welcome, my Christ, my saviour! | |
| | Welcome, Mankind's conqueror! | *champion* |

---

131 "And act according to His word."

133–35 The offering of the poor, in Leviticus 12.8, is either two turtle-doves or two young pigeons. The text here seems confused.

155	Welcome, of all fruits the flower!	
	Welcome, with all my heart!	
	To thee worship, joy, and honour!	*(be given)*
	For now I see my saviour	
	is comen to leech my langour	*come; cure; misery*
	and bring me unto bliss.	

160	Though I bear thee now, sweet wight,	*child*
	thou rulest me as it is right;	
	for through thee I have main and might,	*strength*
	more than through way of kind.	*natural means*
	Therefore a song, as I have tight,	*planned*
165	and lauds to thee with heart right	*praises; true*
	I will show here in thy sight;	
	of me, Lord, thou have mind.	*remembrance*

*Then he shall sing "Nunc dimittis servum tuum, domine,"
etc.*

	Now, Lord, let thy servant be,	
	after thy word, in peace and lee,	*according to; joy*
170	for with my eyes now I see	
	thou art Mankind's heal.	*succour*
	And thou hast ordained there thy posty	*power*
	to people which thou hast pity.	*on whom*
	Lightening is comen now through thee	*light; come*
175	and joy to Israel.	

	And Mary, mother, to thee I say:	
	thy son that I have seen today	
	is comen—I tell thee in good fay—	*come; truly*
	for falling of many fone;	*the downfall; enemies*
180	and to relieve in good array	*comfort; certainly*
	many a man, as he well may,	
	in Israel or he wend away	*before; goes*
	that shall lieve him upon.	*who; believe*

Many signs he shall show

167+SD "Now lettest thou thy servant, Lord, depart"—the Song of Simeon in
Luke 2.29–32 is evidently sung here in full in Latin. The following lines offer an
English paraphrase. Liturgically, this is a Compline canticle, but more appropri-
ately also an antiphon at Matins on the Feast of the Purification (2 February).

185 in which untrue shall none trow.
  And suffer thou shalt many a throw,
  for sword of sorrow—it shall go
  through thy heart. That men shall know
  thoughts in heart on a row
190 of men that shall contrary you
  and found to work thee woe.*

ANNA And I acknowledge to thee, Lord, here, *pledge*
  to lieve on thee through thy power, *believe in*
  that for four score and four year *you;who*
195 has sent me might and grace
  to live in penance and prayer.
  Now wot I well withouten were *know;without doubt*
  that thou art Christ in Godhead clear,
  in thee wholly thou has. *you have it entirely*

200 And openly here sooth I say *the truth*
  to all thy people that I see may—
  the which have waited many a day *watched*
  after thee, saviour— *for*
  that thou art comen, Christ verray; *come;true*
205 this wot I well by many a way. *know;many means*
  Therefore I honour thee now and ay, *worship;always*
  my Christ, my creator.

JOSEPH Mary, of mirths we may us mean,*
  and truly tell betwixt us two *between*
210 of ferly sights that we have seen *wonderful*
  sith we came the city fro. *since;from*

MARY Dear Joseph, you will not ween *know*

184–91 "Many signs he shall display in which no one who is not of true faith shall believe. And you shall suffer on many occasions, because a sword of sorrow shall pass through your heart. That men shall understand to mean all the thoughts in your heart about the men who shall act against you and contrive to create anguish for you."

208 "Mary, we can talk to each other of happy things." At this point the second episode of "Christ before the Doctors" begins, but there is no indication of the fact in the text. This second incident occurred when Jesus was twelve years old. The Chester text is very corrupt at this transitional section and has here been radically reconstructed from the version of the same play in the Coventry Weavers' pageant, with which it has many lines in common.

	what mirth I make withouten woe	*joy; feel; without*
	sith our child with us hath been	*since*
215	and seen those solemn sights also.	

JOSEPH	Homeward therefore I read we hie	*advise; hasten*
	in all the might that ever we may	*with; power*
	for dread of wicked company	
	lest any us meet upon the way.*	

MARY	Joseph, husband lief and dear,	*beloved*
221	our child is gone upon his way.	*his own way*
	My heart were light and he were here;	*would be; if*
	let us go seek him, I thee pray.	
	For suddenly he went away	
225	and left us both in Jerusalem,	
	greatly in liking many a day,*	
	that will be lord over all the realm.	

1ST DOCTOR	Hear our reason right on a row	*reasoning; together*
	you clerks that be of great cunning:	*clerics; learning*
230	Methinks this child will learn our law—	
	he takes great tent to our talking.	*pays close attention to what we say*

JESUS	You clerks that be of great degree,	*clerics; high rank*
	unto my talking you take good heed!	*words*
	My Father that sitteth in majesty,	
235	he knows your works, in thought and deed.	*activities*
	My Father and I together be	
	in one Godhead, withouten dread.	*certainly*
	We be both one, in certainty,	*assuredly*
	all these works to rule and read.	*direct*

| 1ST DOCTOR | Harks this child in his bourding! | *listen to; joking* |

212–19 Line 212 and the following seven lines are taken from Coventry but incorporate all but two lines in the Chester text; the missing lines seem to have been attempts by a scribe to emend a corrupt exemplar and either break the rhyme or repeat a line. The following speech by Mary, in which she realises Jesus is missing, actually begins the "Doctors" episode in Chester but makes sense only when relocated after the dialogue between Mary and Joseph on leaving Jerusalem, as here.

226 "In high delight for many a day."

241	He weens he kens more than he knows.*	
	Certes, son, thou art over-young	*surely*
	by clergy clean to know our laws.	*true theology*
	Therefore, if thou wouldest, never so fain	
245	further in age till thou have draw.*	
	Yet art thou neither of might nor main	*as yet*
	to know it as a clerk might knaw.	*cleric; know*

2ND DOCTOR	And thou wilt speak of Moses' law,	*if*
	take good heed, and thou may see,	
250	in case be that thou can know,*	
	here in this book that written be.	*what is written*

JESUS	The kingdom of Heaven is in me light	*alighted*
	and hath me anointed as a leech,	*healer*
	and given me plain power and might	
255	the kingdom of Heaven to tell and teach.	*tell of*

	You, that be masters of Moses' Law	
	and worthy doctors of great degree,	*high rank*
	one commandment you to me show	
	that God on Earth bade kept should be.*	*commanded*

1ST DOCTOR	I read this is the first bidding	*suggest; command*
261	and is the most in Moses' Law:	*greatest*
	to love our God above all thing	
	with all our might and all our saw.	*belief*

JESUS	That for to do, look ye be bain	*obedient*
265	with all your heart, with good intent.	*firm resolve*
	Take you not His name in vain.	
	This is my Father's commandment.	

---

241 "He believes that he understands more than he knows."

244–45 "Therefore, even if you want to [know our laws], never be so eager to do so until you have moved on further in age."

250 "Just in case it may be that you do know."

256–63 The Doctor cites Christ's statement in Mark 12.29–30, which was held to be a summary of the First Table, Man's duty to God. Jesus completes the Table with the second and third commandments.

Also, you honour your holy day—
no works save alms-deeds you do.
270   These three, the certain for to say,   *assured truth*
the First Table belongen to.*

Also, father and mother worship ay.   *honour always*
Take no man's goods without the right.   *wrongfully*
All false witness you put away.
275   And slay no man, by day nor night.

Envy do by no woman   *injury*
to do her shame, by night or day.   *cause*
Other men's wives desire you none—
all such desires you put away!
280   Look ye ne steal by night nor day,   *do not*
whatsoever that you be lent.   *whatever is lent*
These words understand you may.
They are my Father's commandment.

2ND DOCTOR Behold, how he has learned our laws*
285   and he learned never on book to read !
Methinks he says subtle saws   *mystical words*
and very truth, if you take heed.

3RD DOCTOR Let him wend forth on his ways;   *go*
for, and he dwell, withouten dread,   *if; stay; certainly*
290   the people full soon will him praise
well more than we, for all our deed.   *much; doings*

1ST DOCTOR This is nothing to my intent;
such speech to spend I read we spare.
As wide in world as I have went,
295   yet found I never so ferly fare.*

---

271 See play 5, lines 49–64. The three commandments on the first table of stone
refer to Man's duty to God, those on the second to his duty to his fellow men.

284–95 These lines are here transposed from their manuscript position preceding
Christ's exposition of the Decalogue. Without that exposition, they have no
reference in the text and have obviously been misplaced. In versions of the same
play in other cycles they also follow that exposition.

292–95 "This is not a bit to my intention; I suggest that we refrain from saying

2ND DOCTOR By matters that this child hath meant   *spoken of*
            to know our laws, both less and more,
            out of Heaven I hope him sent   *believe*
            into the Earth to salve our sore.   *ease our distress*

3RD DOCTOR Sir, this child of mickle price   *great worth*
301   which is young and tender of age,
            I hold him sent from the High Justice   *Great Judge*
            to win again our heritage.

MARY   Now blessed be he us hither brought!   *(God) who brought*
305   In land lives none so bright!   *glorious*
            See where he sits that we have sought,
            among yonder masters mickle of might.   *of great power*
            Wend forth, Joseph, upon your way   *go*
            and fetch our son, and let us fare,   *go*
310   that sitteth with yonder doctors gay,   *fine*
            for we have had of him great care.   *about; worry*

JOSEPH   Mary, wife, thou wots right well   *know very well*
            that I must all my travail teen;   *waste all my effort*
            with men of might I cannot mell,   *power; speak*
315   that sit so gay in furs fine.   *splendid*

MARY   My dearworthy son, to me so dear,   *beloved*
            we have you sought full wonder wide.   *wondrous*
            I am right glad that you be here,   *most; are*
            that we found you in this tide.   *at this time*

JESUS   Mother, full oft I told you till,   *very often; to*
321   my Father's works, for weal or woe,   *better or worse*
            hither was I sent for to fulfill.
            That must I needs do or I go.   *before*

MARY   Thy saws, son, as have I heal,   *words; joy*
325   I can nothing understand.   *in no way*
            I shall think on them full well
            and fond to do that they command.   *try; what*

---

such things. As widely in the world as I have travelled I never yet encountered
such a marvellous situation."

ANGEL   Now have you heard, all in this place,
            that Christ is comen through His grace—   *come*
330   as holy Isay prophesied has—   *Isaiah*
            and Simeon has him seen.
            Lieve you well this, lords of might,   *believe*
            and keep you all his laws of right,   *rightful*
            that you may in his bliss so bright
335   evermore with him to lene.   *rest*

THE END

PLAY 12: THE TEMPTATION OF CHRIST,
and THE WOMAN TAKEN IN ADULTERY

Performed by the Butchers

THE THEME of temptation links the two episodes dramatised in this play. The temptations of Christ by the Devil after his forty-day fast in the desert is taken from the account in Matthew 4.1–11, while the attempt by the Pharisees to trick Christ into theological inconsistency through the case of a woman taken in the act of adultery derives from John 8.1–11. Each temptation concludes with an explanation of its significance by an Expositor who cites authorised commentaries in support of his claims. He uses St. Gregory the Great (line 170) as authority for the parallel that he draws between the three temptations of Christ—in gluttony, vainglory and covetousness—and the threefold temptation to which Adam succumbed in taking the apple at the Fall, thereby presenting Christ as "the second Adam" who redeems the sin of the first. And the Expositor cites St. Augustine (lines 285–89) in pointing the apparent contradiction between the strict justice of Moses' law and the attitude of mercy enjoined by Christ upon his followers. The Pharisees' discomfiture arises from their discovery of their own sins written, without comment, by Christ in the dust.

Chester does not have a play of Christ's baptism by John the Baptist, which marks the start of the "ministry" series in the cycles. That play also motivated the Devil's temptation since traditionally God's declaration at the Baptism that Christ was his Son prompted the Devil to seek proof of Christ's parentage. But, though there is no such link here, the Devil's purpose remains the same (lines 199–200), and he is comically frustrated and baffled as Christ deflects his questions. He retires in some confusion but resolves to gather his resources together.

Although we have no accounts from the Butchers' company, a play-list states that their play is "the pynacle with the woman of canany," indicating that the temple with a high pinnacle was part of the waggon-set. Presumably some form of lifting device was used to move Christ to its top, although ladders are a possibility. The text also requires a further location, the hill, which could be accommodated on the waggon beside the pinnacle. The initial encounter was presumably at ground level, with stones lying around. The location of the action therefore rises progressively throughout the episode, Christ's subsequent descent and the grouping for the following episode being covered by the Expositor's intervention at ground level.

The Post-Reformation Banns refer to "the Devil in his feathers all ragged and rent," suggesting a spectacular feathered costume; the popularity of this figure is indicated by his inclusion in the midsummer show. Jesus's confrontation with this strange creature contrasts with the more "naturalistic" confrontation between the Pharisees and Jesus, perhaps again at ground level. The Pharisees seem usually to have been dressed in clerical robes, and they have a ready point of entry from the temple. The woman (played by a boy) would be dressed in contemporary fashion, perhaps even as a respectable lady in the community. Her role is very limited; as in the Bible, she makes no comment and asks for no mercy until the Pharisees have left. The important feature here is the theological confrontation and Christ's second victory over temptation. The Expositor's final explanation seems to be delivered in front of the tableau of the woman kneeling in worship before Christ.

Cast   DEVIL, GOD, EXPOSITOR, FIRST PHARISEE, SECOND PHARISEE, ADULTERESS.

DEVIL	Now, by my sovereignty I swear	
	and principality that I bear	*high office*
	in Hell-pain when I am there,	
	a gamen I will assay.	*trick; attempt*
5	There is a dozebeard I would dere	*idiot; harm*
	that walks abroad wide-where.	*far and wide*
	Who is his father I wot nere,	*I've no idea*
	the sooth if I should say.	*truth*
	What master mon ever be this	*sort of teacher; may*

10	that now in world comen is?	*come*
	His mother, I wot, did never amiss,	*know; sinned*
	and that now marvels me.	*amazes*
	His father cannot I find, iwiss,	*indeed*
	for all my craft and my cointise.	*skill and cunning*
15	It seems that Heaven all should be his,	
	so stout a sire is he.	*strong; lord*
	He is man from foot to crown,	*human*
	and gotten without corruption!	*conceived; sinfulness*
	So clean of conversation	*pure in speech*
20	knew I none before.	
	All men of him marvel mon,	*must marvel at him*
	for as man he goeth up and down,	*like a man*
	but as god with devotion	*like a god; worship*
	he has been honoured yore.	*of old*
25	Sithen the world first began	*since*
	knew I never such a man	
	born of a deadlich woman,	*mortal*
	and he yet wemless!	*nevertheless spotless*
	Among sinful, sin does he none, ✳	*sinful people*
30	and cleaner than ever was anyone;	*(he is) purer*
	blotless eke of blood and bone	*also entirely sinless*
	and wiser than ever man was.	
	Avarice nor any envy	
	in him could I never espy.	
35	He has no gold in treasury	
	ne tempted is by no sight.	*nor; any*
	Pride has he none, ne gluttony,	*nor*
	ne no liking of lechery.	*nor any*
	His mouth heard I never lie	
40	neither by day nor night.	
	My highness he puts ay behind,	*majesty; always*
	for in him fault none can I find.	
	If he be God in Man's kind,	*human form*
	my craft then fully fails.	*power*
45	And more than man I wot he is,	*human; know*
	else something he did amiss;	*or; would have done*
	save only hunger he has, iwiss	*except that; truly*
	else wot I not what him ails.	*know; what else; troubles*

And this thing dare I soothly say: *truly*
50   if that he be God verray   *the true God*
hunger should grieve him by no way;
that were against reason.   *would be; contrary to*
Therefore now I would assay   *attempt*
with speech of bread him to betray,   *talk about bread*
55   for he has fast now many a day;   *fasted*
therefore bread were in season!   *would be*

The Devil speaks (to Christ):

Thou man, abide, and speak with me!
God's Son if that thou be,
make of these stones—now let see—   *let us see*
60   bread through thy blessing.   *by blessing them*

GOD   Satan, I tell thee sickerly,   *certainly*
bread Man lives not only by,
but through God's word, verily,   *truly*
of His mouth coming.   *from*

65   Therefore thou pines thee, Satanas,   *torment yourself*
to supplant me of my place   *from*
by meat, as sometime Adam was,   *food*
of bliss when he was brought.   *out of joy*
Deceived he was that time through thee,
70   but now must fail thy posty;   *power*
therefore, to meve that thing to me   *raise; topic*
it shall serve thee of nought.   *not avail you*

Satan, through thine enticement   *temptation*
hunger shall nought turn my intent,*
75   for God's will omnipotent
is my meat without fail,   *unfailing source of food*
and His word perfect sustenance
to me always, without distance;   *without delay*
for thou shalt find no variance   *inconstancy*
80   in me that shall thee avail.

DEVIL   Out, alas! What is this?
This matter fares all amiss;   *is all going wrong*

---

74 "Hunger shall in no way deflect my resolve."

	hungry I see well he is,	
	as Man should kindly be.	*by nature*
85	But through no craft ne no cointise	*no skill or cunning*
	I cannot turn his will, iwiss;	*deflect; truly*
	that need of any bodily bliss	*carnal pleasure*
	in him nothing has he.	*none at all*

	For he may suffer all manner of noy	*trouble*
90	as man should, well and stiffly;	*a man; bravely*
	but ay he winneth the victory	
	as godhead in him were.	*as if divinity*
	Some other sleight I mot espy	*trick; must*
	this disobedient for to destroy;	
95	for of me he has the mastery	
	unhappily now here.	*by misfortune*

	Adam, that God himself wrought,	*formed*
	through my deceit in bale I brought;	*into torment*
	but this sire that I have sought	
100	born of a woman—	
	for no need that himself has,	
	with no counsel in this case	
	to grieve him I may have no grace	
	for no craft that I can.*	

	Yet will I seek some subtlety.	*look for; trickery*
105	Come forth, thou Jesu, come with me	
	to this holy city!	
	I have an errand to say.	*message*
	Very God if that thou be	*true*
110	now I shall full well see,	
	for I shall shape honour for thee	*contrive*
	or that thou wend away.	*before; go*

Then Jesus shall be set on top of a pinnacle of the temple, and the Devil shall say:

	Say thou now that sits on height:	*on high*
	if thou be God's Son, by sleight	*clever trick*

99–104 "But this lord that I have sought out, born of a woman—I may have no grace to harm him by any words of advice in this instance, by any power that I know, because of any need that he has."

115	come down, and I will say in sight	*in sight of all*
	thou didst a fair mastery.*	
	Thine own angels mon keep to thee	*must take care of*
	that thou hurt no foot ne knee.	*so that; nor*
	Show thy power; now let see,	*let us see*
120	that thou may have mastery thereby.	*domination*

Jesus speaks to the Devil.

JESUS	Satan, sickerly I thee say	*certainly; to you*
	it is written that thou ne may	*may not*
	tempt God, thy Lord, by no way,	
	what matter soever be moved.	*broached*

As he descends from the pinnacle, the Devil shall speak.

DEVIL	Alas, that me is woe today!	*what woe is mine*
126	Thus have I failed of my prey.	*missed*
	Was I never rent in such array	*torn; fashion*
	ne half so foul reproved.	*foully rebuked*

Then Satan shall lead Jesus up on to a mountain, and the Devil shall say:

DEVIL	Yet, fellow, if it be thy will,	
130	go we play us to a hill;	*to disport ourselves*
	another point I must fulfill	*issue; clear up*
	for ought that may befall.	*whatever*
	Look about thee now and see	
	of all this realm the royalty;	*splendour*
135	for to kneel down and honour me	*for kneeling*
	thou shalt be lord of all.	

JESUS	Go forth, Satanas, go forth, go!	*Satan*
	It is written, and shall be so:	
	"Thy Lord God thou shalt honour oo	*for ever*
140	and serve Him"—though thee nye!	*it grieves you*

DEVIL	Out, alas! that me is woe!	*what woe is mine*
	For found I never so great a foe.	
	Though I to threpe be never so throw,	*injure; fierce*

---

116 "You gave a splendid display of your supremacy."

I am overcomen thrie.   *overcome thrice*

145   Alas, my sleight now am I quit.   *repaid for my guile*
      Adam I founded with a fit,   *tempted; experience*
      and him in cumbrance soon I knit   *sin; bound*
      through cointise of my craft.   *cunning; power*
      Now soon of sorrow he mon be shut   *must be rid*
150   and I punished in Hell-pit.   *(must be) punished*
      Knew I never man of such wit   *intellect*
      as him that I have laft.   *left*

      Alas, for shame I am shent!   *destroyed*
      With hell-hounds when I am hent   *seized*
155   I must be ragged and all to-rent   *ripped and torn*
      and driven to the fire.
      In sorrow and woe now am I brought,
      and all my cunning is set at nought;
      endless pain must I have, unsought,
160   to my reward and hire.

      But I am now of good intent   *resolve*
      to hold a court full diligent   *most diligently*
      and call my servants, verament,   *truly*
      shortly for to appear;   *promptly*
165   them to reward with dignity   *honour*
      that all their life have served me.
      In burning bliss there shall they be
      and sit with Lucifer.

EXPOSITOR   Lo, lordings, God's righteousness,   *sirs*
170   as Gregory makes mind express:*
            Since our forefather overcomen was   *i.e., Adam; overcome*
            by three things to do evil—
            gluttony, vainglory (there been two), *are*
            covetousness of highness also—   *high position*
175   by these three points, bout moe,   *issues; no more*
            Christ has overcomen the Devil.   *overcome*

      That Adam was tempted in gluttony
      I may well prove apertly,   *clearly*
      when of that fruit falsely

---

170 "As St. Gregory expressly states," *In Evangelia*, Homily 16.

180 the Devil made him to eat.
And tempted he was in vainglory
when he hight him great mastery, *promised; domination*
and have godhead unworthily *that he would have*
through eating of that meat. *food*

185 Also he was tempted in avarice
when he hight him to be wise, *promised; he would be*
know good and evil at his device *desire*
more than he was worthy.
For covetousness, Gregory saith express, *expressly*
190 sins nought only in riches *not at all*
but in willing of highness *desire of lordship*
and state unskilfully. *unadvisedly*

Also Christ in these sins three
was tempted, as ye might well see;
195 for in gluttony—lieve ye me— *believe*
he moved him sleightly here *tempted; cunningly*
when he enticed him through his read *counsel*
to turn the stones into bread,
and so to move his godhead *provoke his divinity*
200 which he was in a were. *of which; in doubt*

In vainglory he tempted him also,
when he bade him down to go
the pinnacle of the temple fro— *from*
an unskilful gate! *a profitless course*
205 And in covetousness he tempted was
when he showed him such riches
and hight him lands more and less, *promised*
and that through great estate. *high rank*

Thus overcome thrice in this case
210 the Devil, as played was in this place,
of the three sins that Adam was
of weal into woe waived.*
But Adam fell through his trespass, *sin*
and Jesu withstood him through his grace;

209–12 "Thus was the Devil overcome three times in this situation, in the three sins for which Adam was cast from joy into sorrow, as was enacted in this place."

215　　　for of his godhead soothness　　　　　*of the truth about*
　　　　that time was clean deceived.　　　　*the Devil was deceived*

Then shall two Pharisees come, leading a woman taken in adultery.

1ST PHAR-　Master, I read by God Almight　　　　*suggest*
ISEE　　　that we lead this wretched wight,　　　*person*
　　　　that was taken thus tonight
220　　　in foul adultery,
　　　　before Jesu in his sight;
　　　　for so to tempt him I have tight　　　*planned*
　　　　to wit whether he will deem the right　*know; judge*
224　　　or else unlawfully.

2ND PHAR-　That is good read, fellow, by my fay.　*counsel*
ISEE　　　So mon we catch him by some way;　　*may*
　　　　for if he do her grace today,　　　　*should show*
　　　　he does against the Law,
　　　　and if he bid punish her sore,　　*should command (us)*
230　　　he does against his own lore　　　*acts; teaching*
　　　　that he has preached here before:
　　　　"To mercy men should draw."　　　　*incline*

Then they lead the woman between them before Jesus.

1ST PHAR-　Master, this woman that is here
ISEE　　　was wedded lawfully two year;
235　　　but with another than her fere　　　*husband*
　　　　we found her do amiss.　　　　　*commit sin*
　　　　And Moses' Law bids us stone
　　　　all such as been unclean.　　　　　*are*
　　　　Therefore to thee we can us mean　　*have come*
240　　　to give a doom of this.　　　*a judgment about*

JESUS　　Now which of you everichon　　　　*all*
　　　　is bout sin, busk him anon,　*without; hasten quickly*
　　　　and cast at her the first stone—
244　　　believe, or that ye blin.　*at once; before; stop*

Then Jesus shall write upon the ground.

1ST PHAR-　Speak on, master, and somewhat say.
ISEE　　　Shall she be stoned, or else nay?

> Or do her mercy, as thou may,   *show*
> to forgive her this sin?

2ND PHAR- Master, why art thou so still?
ISEE   What writest thou, if it be thy will?   *if you please*
251   Whether shall we spare or spill   *put to death*
           this woman found in blame?   *caught in guilt*
           What writest thou, master? Now let me see.

Then he looks at the writing.

255   Out, alas! that woe is me!   *what woe is mine*
           For no longer dare I here be
           for dread of worldly shame.

And he shall flee, and then the First Pharisee shall speak.

1ST PHAR- Why fleest thou, fellow, by thy fay?   *faith*
ISEE   I will see soon and assay.   *test it*

Then the second (Pharisee) inspects the (writing).

           Alas, that I were away
260   Far beyond France!
           Stand you, sibyl, him beside!   *witch*
           No longer here dare I abide
           against thee for to chide,   *complain*
           as have I good chance.   *good fortune*

And he shall flee; and Jesus shall speak to the woman.

JESUS   Woman, where been these men eachone   *are; all*
266   that putten this guilt thee upon?   *lay this charge*
           To damn thee now there is none   *condemn*
           of those that were before.

ADULTERESS Lord, to damn me there is none.   *condemn*
270   for all they been away gone.   *are*

JESUS   Now I damn thee not, woman.   *condemn*
           Go forth, and sin no more.

ADULTERESS Ah, Lord! Blessed must thou be,
           that of mischief has holpen me.   *from misfortune; helped*

275	Hethenforth filth I will flee	*henceforth; sin; shun*
	and serve thee in good fay.	*true faith*
	For godhead full in thee I see	*complete divinity*
	that knowest all works that done we.	*deeds; have done*
	I honour thee, kneeling on my knee,	
280	and so will I do ay.	*always*

EXPOSITOR	Now, lords, I pray you take heed!	*sirs*
	The great goodness of God's deed	
	I will declare, as it is need —	*necessary*
	this thing that played was.	*enacted*
285	As Augustine speaketh expressly	*specifically*
	of it in his Homily	
	upon St. John's Evangely,*	*Gospel*
	this he says in that case:	*matter*

	Two ways they casten him to annoy,	*plotted; trouble*
290	since he had preached much of mercy	
	and the Law commandeth expressly	
	such women for to stone	
	that trespassen in adultery.	*sin*
	Therefore they hoped witterly	*indeed*
295	variance in him to espy	*inconsistency*
	or blemish the Law clean.	*dishonour; entirely*

	That wist Jesu full well their thought,	
	and all their wits he set at nought—	
	but bade which sin had not wrought	
300	cast first at her a stone;*	
	and wrote in clay—lieve ye me—	*believe*
	their own sins, that they might see,	
	that eachone fain was to flee	*so that; each; eager*
	and they left her alone.	

305	For eachone of them had grace	
	to see their sins in that place;	
	yet none of them wiser was,	

---

287 I.e., St. Augustine of Hippo, *Tractatus in Iohannem* 33.

297–300 "Jesus knew very well that was their thinking, and he turned all their cleverness to nothing—but asked whoever had not committed sin first to cast a stone at her."

but his sins each man knew.
And fain they were to take the way   *eager; depart*
310   lest they had damned been that day.
Thus helped that woman in good fay   *truly*
our sweet Lord Jesu.

THE END

PLAY 13: THE HEALING OF THE BLIND MAN, and THE RAISING OF LAZARUS

Performed by the Glovers

THE THEME of this play, announced in Jesus's opening speech to his disciples and the audience, is of the transition from spiritual death to spiritual life. It is conveyed through two very different actions which show Jesus's compassion for human suffering and his power over earthly affliction and the Devil. In the first action, taken from John 9.1–38, Jesus heals a blind man whose restoration to sight from the darkness of blindness emblematises his spiritual redemption; he has done what Jesus commanded, and sees his Saviour. In the second, taken from John 11.1–46, Jesus raises his friend Lazarus from death after three days and nights in the tomb, drawing him out from the limbo of the patriarchs in hell.

The first episode also confirms the Pharisees in their enmity towards Jesus, for he heals the blind man on the sabbath in defiance of the law. Behind the accusation of the blind man and the summoning of his parents lie the practices of the contemporary ecclesiastical courts, whose activities were not popular. In defying the Pharisees (who are described as the oppressors of the poor,) therefore, the blind man and his parents would be voicing a popular criticism; simultaneously, they indicate a gulf between the "oppressive" Jewish authorities and the ordinary Jewish people, a recurring idea in the cycle. To raise Lazarus, Jesus re-enters this hostile society and works his miracle to the jeers of Jewish onlookers (who could be doubled with the Pharisees). Their sneers have something in common with the mockery directed at Jesus on the cross in play 16. Moreover, the raising of Lazarus was traditionally held to figure the death and resurrection of Christ, and—as Jesus states at the end of the play—he is about to undertake his journey to Jerusalem, where he will be put to death. In play 14 the charges of breaking the sabbath and of raising Lazarus will be brought against him.

The action moves between the ground and the waggon. Jesus, perhaps with all twelve disciples (although only two speak), addresses the audience at ground level. Through the crowd comes a "contemporary" blind man led by a boy, asking for alms, who is observed by the disciples and becomes the object of enquiry and demonstration. The action perhaps moves to the front of a curtained waggon for the inquisition. The parents are presumably summoned from the audience. Jesus perhaps re-appears on the waggon as the blind man and Pharisees are descending to the ground; his subsequent disappearance as the Pharisees stoop to gather their stones could be effected by simply stepping within the curtain.

That curtain would then open to mark the start of the second action, revealing what the Pre-Reformation Banns call "the toumbe of Lazarey." The tomb, like the medieval representations of the tomb of Christ, is probably a table-tomb, at which Mary awaits the return of Martha from her dialogue at ground-level with Jesus and his disciples. The comment at lines 426–29 suggests that Jesus weeps naturalistically at the tomb before adopting a stylised attitude, first addressing God and then, in a loud voice, commanding Lazarus to rise. The raising of Lazarus is a slow and eerie process as the tomb-lid lifts and the figure bound in grave-cloths rises. Though there is no stage-direction to suggest it, it would be appropriate for this climactic moment of rising to be accompanied by music. The play ends with the tableau of Mary and Martha, probably Lazarus, and possibly the whole cast, kneeling to Jesus in front of the empty tomb.

Cast   JESUS, BOY, BLIND MAN, PETER, JOHN, FIRST NEIGHBOUR, SECOND NEIGHBOUR, FIRST PHARISEE, SECOND PHARISEE, MESSENGER, MOTHER, FATHER, FIRST JEW, SECOND JEW, MARY, MARTHA, LAZARUS.

JESUS   "Ego sum lux mundi. Qui sequitur me non ambulat in tenebris sed habebit lumen vitae."[*]

Latin before line 1 "I am the light of the world; he that followeth me shall not walk in darkness, but shall have the light of life" (John 8.12).

Brethren, I am Filius Dei, the light of this world. *Son of God*
He that followeth me walketh not in darkness
but hath the light of life; the Scriptures so record;
as patriarchs and prophets of me bearen witness,
5   both Abraham, Isaac, and Jacob in their sundry
testimonies,
unto whom I was promised before the world began
to pay their ransom and to become man.

"Ego et Pater unum sumus":
my Father and I are all one,*
which hath me sent from the throne
sempiternall   *everlasting*
10   to preach and declare his will unto Man
because he loveth him above his creatures all
as his treasure and darling most principal—
Man, I say again, which is his own elect
above all creatures peculiarly select.*

15   Wherefore, dear brethren, it is my mind and will
to go to Bethany that standeth hereby,
my Father's hests and commandments to fulfill. *promises*
For I am the Good Shepherd that putteth
his life in jeopardy
to save his flock, which I love so tenderly;
20   as it is written of me—the Scripture beareth witness:
"Bonus pastor ponit animam suam pro ovibus suis."*

Go we therefore, brethren, while the day is light,
to do my Father's works, as I am fully minded;
to heal the sick and restore the blind to sight,
25   that the prophecy of me may be fulfilled.
For other sheep I have which are to me committed.
They be not of this flock, yet will I them regard,
that there may be one flock and one shepherd.

---

8 "I and my Father are one" (John 10.30).

13–14 "Man, I say once more, who is chosen to be his (i.e., God's) own, specially chosen above all created things."

21 "The good shepherd giveth his life for his sheep" (John 10.11).

But or we go hence, <u>print these sayings</u>   *before*
  in <u>your mind and heart,</u>
30 <u>record them</u>, and keep them in memory.
  Continue in <u>my</u> word; from it do not depart.
  Thereby shall all men know most perfectly
  that you are my disciples and of my family.
  Go not before me, but let my word be your guide;
35 then in your doings you shall always well speed. *prosper*

not translated → "Si vos manseritis in sermone meo, veri discipuli mei
  eritis, et cognoscetis veritatem, et veritas liberabit vos."*

BOY (*leading a blind man*)
  If pity may move your gentle heart,
  remember, good people, the poor and the blind,
  with your charitable alms <u>this poor man</u> to comfort.
  It <u>is your own neighbour</u> and of your <u>own</u> kind.

BLIND MAN Your alms, good people, for charity,
41 to me that am blind and never did see,
  your neighbour, born in this city!
  Help or I go hence. *before*

PETER Master, instruct us in this case
45 why this man born blind was.
  Is it for his own trespass *sin*
  of else for his parents'? *i.e., his parents' sin*

JOHN Was sin the cause original,
  wherein we be conceived all,
50 that this blind man was brought in thrall,
  or his forefathers' offence?*

JESUS It was neither for his offence,
  neither the sin of his parents,
  or other fault or negligence

35+Latin "If ye continue in my word, then are ye my disciples indeed; and ye shall know the truth, and the truth shall make you free" (John 8.31–32).

48–51 "Was Original Sin, in which we are all conceived, the cause that this blind man was brought into bondage, or was it the sin of earlier generations?" Original Sin is the common legacy of Man from the fall of Adam. The visitation of the sins of the fathers upon the children to the third and fourth generations is mentioned in the Fourth Commandment, Exodus 20.5.

55   that he was blind born;
     but for this cause specially:
     to set forth God's great glory,
     his power to show manifestly,   *clearly*
     this man's sight to reform.   *restore*

60   While the day is fair and bright,
     my Father's works I must work, right   *perform*
     until the coming of the night
     that light be gone away.   *when*
     In this world when I am here,
65   I am the light that shineth clear.
     My light to them shall well appear
     which cleave to me alway.   *hold fast*

Then Jesus shall spit on the earth and make a paste, and rub the eyes of the blind man with his hands. And then he shall speak.

JESUS   Do, man, as I say to thee.
     Go to the water of Silo-ee.
70   There wash thine eyes, and thou shalt see.
     And give God the praise.

Then the blind man shall seek the water and Jesus shall depart.

BLIND MAN   Lead me, good child, right hastily
     unto the water of Silo-ee.

Then he shall wash, and then shall say:

     Praised be God Omnipotent
75   which now to me my sight hath sent.
     I see all things now here present.
     Blessed be God always.

     When I had done as God me bade,
     my perfect sight forthwith I had;
80   wherefore my heart is now full glad   *most*
     that I doubt where I am.   *I don't know*

1ST NEIGH-   Neighbour, if I the truth should say,
BOUR   this is the blind man which yesterday
     asked our alms as we came this way.

85   It is the very same!

2ND NEIGH-   No, no, neighbour, it is not he—
BOUR   but it is the likest to him that ever I see!
             One man to another like may be,
             and so is he to him.

BLIND MAN   Good men, truly I am he
91   that was blind, and now I see.
             I am no other, verily;   *truly*
             enquire of all my kin.

1ST NEIGH-   Then tell the truth, we thee pray.
BOUR   How this is happened, to us say—
96   thou that even yesterday
             couldst see no earthly thing
             and now seest so perfectly!
             No want of sight in thee we see.   *failure*
100   Declare therefore to us truly,
             without more reasoning.   *speculation*

BLIND MAN   The man which we call Jesus,
             that worketh miracles daily with us
             and whom we find so gracious,
105   anointed my eyes with clay;
             and to the water of Silo-ee
             he bade me go immediately
             and wash my eyes, and I should see—
             and thither I took my way.

110   When the water on my eyes light,   *fell*
             immediately I had my sight.
             Was there never earthly wight   *person in this world*
             so joyful in his thought.

2ND NEIGH-   Where is he now, we thee pray?
BOUR

BLIND MAN   I know not where he is, by this day.

2ND NEIGH-   Thou shalt with us come on this way
BOUR   and to the Pharisees these words say.
             But if thou would these things deny,   *unless*
             it shall help thee right nought.   *in no way at all*

120   Look up, lordings and judges of right!   *lords; rightful*

We have brought you a man that had no sight
and on the Sabbath day through one man's might
was healed and restored forsooth.   *truly*

1ST NEIGH-   Declare to them, thou wicked wight,   *fellow*
BOUR   who did restore thee to thy sight,
126   that we may know anonright   *immediately*
               of this matter the truth.

BLIND MAN   Jesus anointed my eyes with clay
               and bade me wash in Silo-ee,
130   and before I came away
               my perfect sight I had.

1ST PHAR-   This man, the truth if I should say,
ISEE   is not of God—my head I lay—   *wager*
               which doth violate the Sabbath Day.
135   I judge him to be mad.

2ND PHAR-   It cannot enter into my thought
ISEE   that he which hath this marvel wrought   *performed*
               should be a sinner—I lieve it nought;   *believe*
               it is not in my creed.   *within my belief*
140   Say what is he that did thee heal.

BLIND MAN   A prophet he is, without fail.   *definitely*

1ST PHAR-   Surely thou art a knave of kind* = by nature
ISEE   that feignest thyself for to be blind;
               wherefore now this is my mind,
145   the truth to try in deed.   *test in practice*

               His father and mother both in fere   *together*
               shall come declare the matter here,   *to declare*
               and then the truth shall soon appear
               and we put out of doubt.   *shall be put*
150   Go forth, messenger, anon in hie,   *at once quickly*
               and fetch his parents by and by.
               This knave can nought but prate and lie;*
               I would his eyes were out.

---

142 "Assuredly you are one of Nature's rogues."

152 "This rogue knows nothing at all except how to invent stories and to tell lies."

MESSENGER	Your bidding, master. I shall fulfill,	
155	and do my duty as is good skill,	*it is right*
	for this day hither I know they will,	*will come*
	and I shall spy them out.	*if*

Then he shall look around, and shall speak to them.

	Sire and dame, both in fere,	*both together*
	you must afore the Pharisees appear.	*before*
160	What their will is, there shall you hear.	
	Have done, and come your way.	*stop what you're doing*

MOTHER	Alas, man, what do we here?	
	Must we afore the Pharisees appear?	*before*
	A vengeance on them, far and near!	
165	They never did poor men good. ✳	

FATHER	Dame, there is no other way	
	but their commandment we must obey,	
	or else they would without delay	
	curse us, and take our good.	*anathematize; goods*

MESSENGER	Here have I brought, as you bade me,	
171	these two persons that aged be.	
	They be the parents of him truly	
	which said that he was blind.	

1ST PHAR-	Come near to us, both two,	
ISEE	and tell us truly or that you go	*before*
176	whether this be your son or no—	
	look no deceit we find!	*take care*

FATHER	Masters, we know certainly	
	our son he is—we cannot deny—	
180	and blind was born undoubtedly.	
	And that we will depose.	*formally swear*

	But who restored him to his sight	
	we be uncertain, by God Almight.	*almighty*
	Wherefore of him, as is right,	
185	the truth you must enquire.	

MOTHER	For he has age his tale to tell,	*is old enough*
	and his mother-tongue to utter it well!	

Although he could never buy nor sell, ?
let him speak, we desire.

1ST PHAR-ISEE 192	Give praise to God, thou crafty knave,	*rogue*
	and look hereafter thou do not rave	*talk wildly*
	nor say that Jesus did thee save	
	and restored thee to thy sight.	

1ST PHAR-
ISEE
192

Give praise to God, thou crafty knave,　　　*rogue*
and look hereafter thou do not rave　　　*talk wildly*
nor say that Jesus did thee save
and restored thee to thy sight.

2ND PHAR-
ISEE
196

He is a sinner, and that we know,
deceiving the people to and fro.
This is most true that we thee show.
Believe us, as is right.

BLIND MAN

If he be sinful I do not know,
but this is truth that I do show:
when I was blind and in great woe
200　he cured me, as ye see.

1ST PHAR-
ISEE

What did he, thou lither swain?　　　*lying wretch*

BLIND MAN

I told you once—will you hear it again?
Or his disciples will you become,
205　of all your sins to have remission?

2ND PHAR-
ISEE

Oh cursed caitiff, ill mot thou thee!*
Would thou have us his disciples to be?
No, no! Moses' disciples been we,　　　*are*
for God with him did speak.

210　But whence this is we never knew.　　　*this man (Jesus)*

BLIND MAN

I marvel of that, as I am true—　　　*am amazed at*
that you know not from whence he should be
that me cured that never did see—
knowing this most certainly:
215　God will not sinners hear.
But he that honoureth God truly,
him will he hear by and by
and grant his asking graciously,　　　*request*
for that man is to him dear.

---

206 "O accursed wretch, may ill-fortune fall on you!"

220	And to this, I dare be bold,	*in addition to this*
	there is no man that ever could	
	restore a creature to his sight	
	that was blind born and never saw light.	
	If he of God were not, iwiss,	*truly*
225	he could never work such things as this.	

1ST PHAR- What, sinful knave! Wilt thou teach us
ISEE   which all the Scriptures can discuss

and of our living be so virtuous?   *in our way of life*
We curse thee. Out of this place!   *anathematize*

JESUS   Believest thou in God's Son truly?

BLIND MAN   Yea, gracious lord. Who is he?

JESUS   Thou hast him seen with thine ee.   *eye*
He is the same that talketh with thee.

BLIND MAN   Then here I honour him with heart free,   *open*
235   and ever shall serve him until I die.

1ST JEW   Say, man that makest such mastery,
or thou our souls do annoy,*
tell us here apertly   *clearly*
Christ if that thou be.

JESUS   That I spake to you openly   *spoke*
241   and works that I do, verily,   *truly*
in my Father's name Almighty
beareth witness of me.

	But you believe not as you seen,	*what you see*
245	for of my sheep ye ne been;	*are not*
	but my flock, withouten ween,	*without doubt*
	hear my voice alway.	
	And I know them well eachone,	*all*
	for with me alway they gone;	*go*
250	and for them I ordained in my wone	*dwelling*
	everlasting life for ay.	*for ever*

236–37 "Say, you fellow who performs such acts of power, before you cause
harm to our souls."

No man shall reave my sheep from me,   *steal*
for my Father in majesty
is greater than been all ye,   *are*
255   or any that ever was.

2ND JEW   Thou shalt abie, by my bones,   *stay*
or thou hethen pass.   *before; hence*

Help, fellow, and gather stones
and beat him well, by Cock's bones.   *God's bones*
260   He scorns us cointly for the nonce   *slyly now*
and doth us great annoy.   *causes; grievance*

Then they shall gather stones.

Yea, stones now here I have
for this ribald that thus can rave.   *rogue; talk wildly*
One stroke, as God me save
265   he shall have soon in hie.   *at once*

JESUS   Wretches, many a good deed
I have done you in great need;   *in time of necessity*
now quite you foul my meed*
to stone me on this manner.

1ST JEW   For thy good deed that thou hast wrought
271   at this time stone we thee nought,
but for thy leasing, falsely wrought,   *lying*
thou shewest apertly here.   *which you clearly display*

Thou, that art man as well as I,   *human*
275   makes thyself God here openly.   *make out to be*
There thou lies foul and falsely,   *in that matter*
both in word and thought.

JESUS   But I do well and truly   *perform*
my Father's bidding by and by.
280   Else may you hope well I lie,   *otherwise; rightly think*
and then lieves you me nought.   *believe*

But sithen you will not lieve me,

_____

268 "Now you repay my reward wickedly."

	believe my deeds that you may see,	
	to them believing takes ye,	
285	for nothing may be soother.	*more true*
	So may you know well and verray	*truly*
	in my Father that I am ay,	*always*
	and he in me, sooth to say,	*truth*
	and either of us in other.*	

Then they shall gather stones, and Jesus shall suddenly vanish.

2ND JEW	Out, out, alas! Where is our fone?	*foe*
291	Cointly that he is hethen gone!	*how cunningly; hence*
	I would have taken him, and that anon,	*at once*
	and foul him all to-frapped.	*wickedly; beaten*
	Yea, make we never so much moan,	*however much grief*
295	now there is no other wone,	*hope*
	for he and his men everychone	*all*
	are from us clearly scaped.	*escaped*

1ST JEW	Now by the death I shall on die,	*in*
	may I see him with my eye,	*if I may*
300	to Sir Caiaphas I shall him wrye	*betray*
	and tell that shall him dere.	*what; distress*
	See I never none, by my fay,	*saw; truly*
	when I had stones, so soon away.	
	But yet, no force! Another day	*no matter*
305	his tabert we shall tear.	*tabard*

MARY*	Ah, Lord Jesu. that me is woe	*how sorrowful I am*
	to wit my brother sickly so!	*know; is so ill*
	In feeble time Christ yode me fro.	*wretched; went; from*

282–89 "But since you will not believe me, address yourselves in a spirit of belief to my deeds that you can see."

305+SH In Luke 10.38–42 Jesus visits Mary and Martha and Mary sits attentively at his feet while her sister Martha is busy with household chores. Mary anointed Jesus's head (Matthew 26.7) and feet (John 12.3). A similar episode, involving an unnamed woman is described in Luke 7.36ff. as occurring in the house of Simon (see next play) and has led to her identification with that woman, a notorious sinner. That sinner, in turn, was traditionally identified with Mary Magdalen. The brother mentioned is Lazarus, although the identification is not made until 315.

Well were we and he were here!   *happy; if*

MARTHA   Yea, sister. About I will go
311   and seek Jesu to and fro.
              To help him he would be throw   *eager*
              and he wist how it were.   *if; knew; things stood*

Then Jesus shall come.

              Ah, my Lord, sweet Jesus! Mercy!
315   Lazar, that thou loved tenderly,   *Lazarus*
              lieth sick a little hereby   *near here*
              and suffreth much teen.   *distress*

JESUS   Yea, woman, I tell thee witterly,   *certainly*
              that sickness is not deadly   *mortal*
320   but God's Son to glorify.   *in order to glorify*
              Lo! I am him, as may be seen.

Then Martha shall go to Mary.

MARY   Ah, Martha, sister, alas, alas!
              My brother is dead sith thou here was.   *since*
              Had Jesus, my Lord, been in this place,
325   this case had not befall.   *situation; happened*

MARTHA   Yea, sister, near is God's grace!
              Many a man he holpen has.   *has helped*
              Yet may he do for us in this case   *he may still do so*
              and him to life call.

MARY   Here will I sit and mourning make   *grieve*
331   till that Jesu my sorrow slake.   *until*
              My teen to heart, Lord, thou take   *suffering*
              and leech me of my woe.   *heal*

MARTHA   In sorrow and woe here will I wake,   *watch*
335   and lament for Lazar my brother's sake.
              Though I for cold and penance quake,   *anguish*
              hethen will I not go.   *hence*

*Then they shall sit side by side beside the sepulchre weeping,
and Jesus shall be far off.*

JESUS   Brethren, go we to Judee.   *Judea*

PETER   Master, right now thou well might see
340   the Jews would have stoned thee;
               and yet thou wilt again?   *will go back*

JESUS   Wot you not well this is verray,   *know; true*
               that twelve hours are in the day   *daylight*
               and whoso walketh that time his way   *goes on his way*
345   trespasseth not, the sooth to say?   *strays; truth*

               He offendeth not that goeth in light;   *spiritual light*
               but whosoever walketh about in night,
               he trespasseth all against the right   *sins; truth*
               and light in him is none.
350   Why I say this, as I have tight,   *planned*
               I shall tell you soon in height.   *at once*
               Have mind on it through your might   *heed it carefully*
               and think well thereupon.   *upon it*

               To the day myself may likened be,
355   and to the twelve hours all ye
               (that lightened be through following me ⌐   *enlightened*
               that am most liking light.   *most like*
               For world's light I am verray,   *the true light*
               and whoso followeth me, sooth to say,   *truth*
360   he may go no thester way,   *road of darkness*
               for light in him is dight.   *set*

not   "Oportet me operari opera eius qui misit me donec dies
translated   est; venit nox quando nemo potest operari. Quamdiu
               sum in mundo, lux sum mundi."*

               Brethren, I tell you tiding;   *a piece of news*
               Lazar my friend is sleeping.
               Thither we must be going,
365   upon him for to call.

JOHN   Lord, if he sleep, safe he may be,   *may sleep*

361+Latin "I must work the works of him that sent me, while it is day; the night
cometh, when no man can work. As long as I am in the world, I am the light of
the world" (John 9.4–5).

for in his sleep no peril is he. *in no danger*
Therefore it is not good for thee
go thither for so small. *to go; a little thing*

JESUS   I tell you brethren certainly: *for sure*
371   Lazar is dead, and thither will I. *will I go*
Fain I am, you wot, that I *happy; know*
was not there, that you may see. *so that; understand*
Go we thither anon in hie. *at once*

THOMAS   Follow him, brethren, to his annoy, *to his peril*
376   and die with him devoutly,
for other it will not be. *otherwise*

*Then Jesus shall go towards the place where Mary and Martha
are sitting, and Martha shall go to meet him.*

MARTHA   Ah, Lord Jesu, haddest thou been here led, *brought*
Lazar my brother had not been dead; *would not have*
380   but well I wot thou wilt us read, *know; advise*
now thou art with us here.
And this I lieve and hope aright: *believe; trust*
what thing thou askest of God Almight, *almighty*
he will grant it thee in height *at once*
385   and grant thee thy prayer.

JESUS   Thy brother, Martha, shall rise, I say.

MARTHA   That lieve I, Lord, in good fay, *believe; truly*
that he shall rise the last day;
then hope I him to see.

JESUS   Martha, I tell thee without nay, *certainly*
391   I am rising and life verray; *resurrection; true life*
which life shall last for ay *for ever*
and never shall ended be.

Whosoever lieveth steadfastly *believes*
395   in me—I tell thee truly—
though he dead be, and down lie,
shall live and fare well. *prosper*
Lieves thou, woman, that this may be? *do you believe*

MARTHA   Lord, I lieve, and lieve mon, *believe; must believe*

400	that thou art Christ, God's Son,	
	is comen into this world to won,	*who has come; dwell*
	Man's boot for to be.	*remedy*
	This have I lieved steadfastly;	*believed*
	therefore on me thou have mercy,	
405	and on my sister eke, Mary.	*also*
	I will fetch her to thee.	

Then Martha shall go and shall call Mary.

MARTHA	Ah, Mary, sister lief and dear,	*beloved*
	hie thee quickly and come near.	*make haste*
	My sweet Lord Jesu, he is here	
410	and calleth thee him to.	

MARY	Ah, well were we and it so were!	*happy; if*
	But had my lovely lord of lere	*lovely of countenance*
	seen my brother lie on bier,	
	some boot might have been do.	*remedy; done*

415	But now he stinketh, sooth to say,	*truth*
	for now this is the fourth day	
	sith he was buried in the clay,	*since*
	that was to me so lief.	*dear*
	But yet my Lord I will assay,	*make trial of*
420	and with all my heart him I pray	
	to comfort us, and that he may,	*if*
	and mend all our mischief.	*amend; misfortune*

Then Mary, seeing Jesus, prostrates herself at his feet, saying:

	Ah, Lord Jesu! Haddest thou been here	
	Lazar my brother. thine own dear,	*darling*
425	had not been dead in this manner.	
	Much sorrow is me upon.	

JESUS	Where have ye done him? Tell-es me.	*put*

MARY	Lord, come hither and thou may see,	
	for buried in this place is he	
430	four days now agone.	*passed*

Then the Jews shall come, the First of whom shall speak.

1ST JEW	See, fellow, for Cock's soul	*God's*
	This freke beginneth to ream and yowl	
	and make great doel for a ghoul	
	that he loved well before.*	

2ND JEW	If he had cunning, methink he might	*power*
436	from death have saved Lazar by right,	*rightly*
	as well as send that man his sight	*sending*
	that which so blind was bore.	*born*

JESUS	Have done, and put away the stone.	*stop*

MARTHA	Ah, Lord, four days be agone	*passed*
441	sith he was buried, blood and bone.	*since*
	He stinks, Lord, in good fay.	*truly*

JESUS	Martha, said I not to thee,	
	if thou fully lieved in me	*believed*
445	God's grace soon shalt thou see?	
	Therefore, do as I thee say!	

Then they shall lift the stone from the sepulchre, and Jesus, turning his back and with hands upstretched, shall say:

	Father of Heaven, I thank it thee,	*you for this*
	that so soon has heard me.	*quickly*
	Well I wist, and soothly see,	*know; in truth*
450	thou hearest mine intent.	*my will*
	But for this people that stand hereby	
	speak I the more openly,	
	that they may lieve steadfastly	*believe*
	from thee that I was sent.	

455	Lazar! Come forth! I bid thee!	*Lazarus*

LAZARUS	Ah, Lord! Blessed most thou be,	*may*
	which from death to life hast raised me	
	through thy mickle might.	*great power*
	Lord, when I heard the voice of thee,	

432–34 "This fellow begins to weep and howl and make great sorrowing for an idiot that he formerly loved dearly."

460	all Hell failed of their posty,*	*in their power*
	so fast from them my soul can flee;	*fled*
	all devils were afraid.	

JESUS   Loose him now, and let him go.

MARTHA	Ah, Lord, honoured be thou oo	*for ever*
465	that us hast saved from much woe	
	as thou hast oft beforn.	*before*
	For well I wist it should be so,	*knew*
	when ye were full far us fro.	*very far from us*
	Thee, Lord, I honour, and no moe,	*no others*
470	kneeling upon my kneen.	*knees*

MARY	Ah, Lord Jesu, much is thy might!	
	For now my heart is glad and light	
	to see my brother rise in my sight	
	here before all these men.	
475	Well I hoped that soon in height	*believed; at once*
	when thou came it should fare aright.	*work out well*
	Thee, Lord, I honour with all my might,	
	kneeling upon my kneen.	*knees*

	Ah, Lord Jesu, I thank thee	
480	that on my brother has pity.	
	By very sign now men may see	*true*
	that thou art God's Son.	
	With thee ever, Lord, will I be	
	and serve thee with heart free	*willing heart*
485	that this day has gladded me,	*made me joyful*
	and alway with thee won.	*dwell*

JESUS	Have good-day, my daughter dear.
	Wherever you go, far or near,
	my blessing I give you here.
490	To Jerusalem I take the way.

THE END

---

460 Dying before Christ's redeeming sacrifice, Lazarus went to the limbo of the patriarchs; see play 17.

PLAY 14: CHRIST AT THE HOUSE OF SIMON THE LEPER, CHRIST AND THE MONEYLENDERS, and JUDAS'S PLOT

Performed by the Shoemakers

THE FEAR AND HOSTILITY OF the Jewish leaders towards Jesus which have been realised during the preceding two plays find focus in play 14 in the coming of Jesus to Jerusalem, as heralded at the end of play 13, to celebrate the Feast of the Passover. Jesus's entry is a great public event, greeted with joy by the citizens, though Jesus himself foretells the downfall of the city because it will not ultimately acknowledge him. He further provokes the antagonism of the Jewish leaders by driving the traders out of the temple. In contrast to these public scenes, the High Priests meet in private council to consider how to counter this threat to their authority and resolve to take steps to silence Jesus. Their opportunity comes when Judas arrives to betray his master.

Judas links the scenes of the entry and of the betrayal to the opening scene of the play, in which Jesus, at the house of Simon the Leper, is anointed by Mary Magdalen. This action, by a lady regarded as a notorious sinner (though not identified as Mary Magdalen in the Gospels), shocks Simon, who fears for Jesus's reputation. Judas, however, is horrified at the waste of money involved and, as it transpires later, at the loss of income to himself. The explanation that he sold Jesus for thirty pieces of silver because he customarily robbed his master of a tenth of all he received was conventional—his reputation as a thief derives from John 12.6, and he is here identifiable by the purse he carries—but it provides motivation for his subsequent action.

The various events are all taken from the Gospel accounts. But the anointing (Matthew 26.6–14; Mark 14.3–9; Luke 7.36–50; John 12.1–9), the entry (Matthew 21.1–16; Mark 11.1–10, 15–19; Luke 19.29–46; John 12.12–19 and 2.12–16), and the council (Matthew 26.3–5, 14–16; Mark 14.1–2, 10–11; Luke 22.1–6; John 11.47–53) are separated in the Gospels and are here brought together in telling conjunction.

Both sets of Banns refer to the waggon as the "Jerusalem carriage." There is a set of accounts for the Shoemakers, the company responsible for the play's production, in 1550. Though those accounts suggest a somewhat different play from that now extant, they refer to the setting up of a steeple—presumably to represent the temple. One assumes that the "private" actions in the house of Simon and of the Priests with which the play opens and closes took place on the waggon, together with the cleansing of the temple, but that Jesus descended to ground level to collect and ride the ass. The citizens who greeted him would then be equally the citizens of Jerusalem and the citizens of Chester. As indicated above, the entry encompasses a number of different moods—rejoicing, sorrow, and violent anger. The scenes which frame it form a telling contrast between the emotional and powerful act of the anointing, where Jesus disposes of criticisms of Mary's action, and the harsh political and commercial considerations which govern the deliberations of the Priests. While Mary speaks of love, the Priests speak of expediency, and it is on their note of political confidence that the play ends, leaving the audience to await the continuation.

The accounts speak of the hiring of minstrels. Though one might also have expected payment to boy-choristers for the singing of the "Hosanna," no such payment appears. Nevertheless, it is clear that the spectacular entry requires liturgical song, as well as the waving of branches and strewing of garments.

Cast   JESUS, PETER, PHILIP, SIMON, LAZARUS, MARTHA, MARY MAGDALEN, JUDAS, JANITOR, FIRST CITIZEN, SECOND CITIZEN, THIRD CITIZEN, FOURTH CITIZEN, FIFTH CITIZEN, SIXTH CITIZEN, FIRST BOY, SECOND BOY, FIRST MER-CHANT, SECOND MERCHANT, CAIAPHAS, ANNAS, FIRST PHARISEE, SECOND PHARISEE.

JESUS	Brethren, go we to Bethany	
	to Lazar, Martha and Mary;	*Lazarus*
	for I love much that company.	
	Thither now will I wend.	*go*

5	Simon the Leper hath prayed me*	
	in his house to take charity.	*receive hospitality*
	With them now it liketh me	*pleases*
	a while for to lend.	*stay*

PETER
10	Lord, all ready shall we be	
	in life and death to go with thee.	
	Great joy they may have to see	
	thy coming into their place.	

PHILIP
	Lazar thou raised through thy pity,	
	and Simon also—measel was he—	*leprous*
15	thou cleansed, Lord, that wotten we,	*healed; we know*
	and holp them through thy grace.	*helped*

Then they shall go towards the house of Simon the Leper.

SIMON
	Welcome, Jesu, full of grace,	
	that me that foul and measel was	*leprous*
	all whole, Lord, thou healed has,	
20	over all to show.	*to display it everywhere*
	Well is me that I may see thy face	*happy am I*
	here in my house, this poor place.	
	Thou comforts me in many a case	*many situations*
	and that I full well know.	

LAZARUS
26	Welcome, Lord, sweet Jesu.	
	Blessed be the time that I thee knew.	
	From death to life through thy virtue	
	thou raised me not yore.	*not long ago*
	Four days in earth when I had lain	
30	thou grantedst me life, Lord, again.	
	Thee I honour with all my main	*power*
	now and evermore.	

MARTHA
| | Welcome, my lovely Lord and lere! | *beautiful* |
| | Welcome, my dearworth darling dear! | *beloved* |

---

5 *Simon the Leper* is said to be the host at the feast in Matthew 26.6, Mark 14.3. Despite the reference at 17–29, we know of no healing miracle involving Simon. Because John 12.2 refers to Martha serving and, on the assumption that the reference is to the same event as in the other gospels, Simon was assumed to have some relationship to Mary—perhaps her father or husband.

35   Fain may thy friends be in fere   *happy; together*
           to see thy freely face.   *noble*
           Sits down, if your will were,   *it might be your wish*
           and I shall help to serve you here
           as I was wont in good manner   *accustomed; fittingly*
40   before in other place.

Then Jesus shall sit, and all the rest with him; and Mary
Magdalen shall come with a box of ointment and shall speak
in sorrowing fashion.

MAGDALEN   Welcome, my lovely Lord of leal!   *truth*
           Welcome, my heart! Welcome, my heal!   *health*
           Welcome, all my world's weal,   *prosperity*
           my boot, and all my bliss!   *remedy*
45   From thee, Lord, may I not conceal
           my filth and my fault-es fele. = vie l   *many sins*
           Forgive me that my flesh so frail
           to thee hath done amiss.   *sinned against*

           Ointment I have here ready
50   to anoint thy sweet body.
           though I be wretched and unworthy,
           waive me not from thy wone.   *send away; dwelling*
           Full of sin and sorrow am I,
           but therefore, Lord, I am sorry.   *for it*
55   Amend me through thy great mercy
           that makes to thee my moan.   *who; lament*

Then she shall open the box, and shall give an indication of
anointing; and she shall wet Jesus's feet with tears and shall
dry them with her hair.

SIMON   Ah, Judas, why doth Jesus so?
           Methink that he should let her go,
           this woman full of sin and woe,
60   for fear of world's shame.   *public scandal*
           And if he very prophet were,   *if; true*

40+SD The woman, named only as Mary in John 12.3, was traditionally identified
both as Martha's sister (see play 13 305+SH) and as the Mary Magdalen of Luke
8.2 from whom Christ expelled seven devils. The spoken text here does not name
her for the audience.

	he should know her life here	*way of life*
	and suffer her not to come him near,	
	for pairing of his fame.	*damaging; good name*

JUDAS*
66

Nay, Simon, brother, sooth to say,   *truth*
it is nothing to my pay.   *not at all; pleasure*
This ointment goeth too fast away
that is so much of price.   *of such great cost*
This ilk boist might have been sold   *same box*

70   for three hundred pennies told   *in total*
and dealt to poor men, whosoever would,
and whosoever had been wise.*

JESUS

Simon, take good heed to me.
I have an errand to say to thee.   *message*

SIMON
76

Master, what your will may be
say on, I you beseech.

JESUS

By an example I shall thee show,   *parable*
and to this company on a row.   *together*
Whereby I say, thou may know   *by what*

80   to answer to my speech.   *how to reply*

Two debtors sometime there were
oughten money to a usurer.   *owed; money-lender*
The one was in his danger   *power*
five hundred pennies told;   *for five hundred; in all*

85   the other fifty, as I say here.
For they were poor, at their prayer   *entreaty*
he forgave them both in fere,   *together*
and nought take of them he would.   *from*

Whether of these two, read if thou can,   *which; guess*
90   was more beholden to that man?

SIMON

Lord, as much as I can thereon,   *as best I know of it*

64+SH *Judas Iscariot*, the betrayer of Jesus, was the only one of the twelve who was not a Galilean.

71–72 "And doled out to poor men by anyone who wanted to, if anyone had had any sense."

	shall say or I pass.	*before I go*
	Five hundred is more than fifty.	
	Therefore methink skilfully	
95	that he that he forgave the more party	
	more holden to him he was.*	

JESUS		
	Simon, thou deems soothly, iwiss.	*judge most truly*
	Sees thou this woman that here is?	
	Sicker, she hath not done amiss	*certainly*
100	to work on this manner.	*act in this way*
	Into thy house here thou me get;	*invited me*
	no water thou gave me to my feet.	*for*
	She washed them with her tears wet	
	and wiped them with her hair.	

105	Kiss sith I came thou gave none,	*since*
	but sith she came into this wone	*since; dwelling*
	she hath kissed my feet eachone;	*both*
	of weeping she never ceased.	
	With oil thou hast not me anoint,	*anointed*
110	but she hath done, both foot and joint.	
	Therefore I tell thee one point,	*one fact*
	much sin is her released.	*from her*

To Judas Iscariot.

	And, Judas, also to thee I say:	
	whereto wouldest thou thee mispay	
115	with this woman by any way*	
	that eased me thus has?	*comforted*
	A good deed she hath done today,	
	for poor men you have with you ay,	*always*
	and me ye may not have, in fay,	*truly*
120	but a little space.	*except for a short time*

To Mary Magdalen:

94–96 "Therefore it seems reasonable to me that he to whom he forgave the greater share was more beholden to him."

114–15 "To what end would you be displeased with this woman in any way?"

Therefore, woman, witterly,   *truly*
for thou hast loved so tenderly,
all thy sins now forgive I;
belief hath saved thee.   *faith*
125   And all that preach the Evangely   *Gospel*
through the world by and by   *in due course*
of thy deed shall make memory   *shall recall*
that thou has done to me.

MAGDALEN   My Christ, my comfort and my king,
130   I worship thee in all thing,
for now my heart is in liking,   *in happiness*
and I at mine above.   *at my highest point*
Seven devils now, as I well see,
thou hast driven now out of me,
135   and from foul life unto great lee   *great happiness*
relieved me, Lord, for love.   *released*

Then Jesus shall stand up, and as he stands, he shall speak as
follows:

JESUS   Peter and Philip, my brethren free,   *noble*
before you a castle you may see.
Go you thither, and fetch anon to me   *at once*
140   an ass and foal also.   —follows Mcttha
Loose them, bring them hither anon.   *at once*
If any man grudge you as ye gone,   *object to; go*
and you say that I will ride thereon,   *if; on it*
soon will they let them go.

PETER   Master, we shall do your bidding
146   and bring them soon for anything.   *regardless of*
Philip, brother, be we going   *let us be*
and fetch those beasts two.

PHILIP   Brother, I am ready boun.   *all ready*
150   Hie that we were at the town.   *make haste; may be*
Great joy in heart have we mon   *may*
on this errand for to go.

Then they shall go into the city, and Peter shall speak to the
Janitor.   (i.e., keeper of the city gate)

PETER   How, how! I must have this ass.   *Hey there!*

JANITOR
155

Here thou gettest neither more nor lass   *nothing*
but thou tell me or thou pass   *unless; before*
whither they shall gone.   *go*

PHILIP

My master Jesu, lieve thou me,   *believe*
thinks to come to this city
and bade both brought to him should be,
160   himself to ride upon.

JANITOR

All ready, good men, in good fay!   *indeed*
And sith he will come today,   *since*
all this city I will say   *tell*
and warn of his coming.
165   Take ass and foal and go your way,
for each man of him marvel may   *at*
Lazar, that four days dead lay,   *Lazarus*
he raised at his calling.

[margin, handwritten: person — for the crowd]

Then the Janitor shall go to the citizens.

Tidings, good men every one!
170   The prophet Jesus comes anon.   *immediately*
Of his disciples yonder gone   *there go*
twain that were now here.   *two; just now*
For his marvels lieve ay upon   *always believe*
that he is very God's Son   *Son of the true God*
175   although he in this world won,   *may dwell*
for else it wonder were.   *otherwise; would be*

1ST CITIZEN

Ah, Lord, blessed most thou be!   *may you be*
Him will I go now and see;
and so I read, that all we   *thus I propose*
180   thitherward take the way.   *go in that direction*

2ND CITIZEN

Fellows, I lieve that Christ is he,   *believe*
comen from God in majesty;   *come*
else such marvels, as thinks me,   *otherwise; it seems*
he ne did day for day.   *would not have done daily*

3RD CITIZEN

Lazar he raised, as God me save,
186   that four days had been in grave.
Therefore devotion now I have
to welcome him to this town.

4TH CITIZEN   Branches of the palm-tree
190   eachone in hand take we,   *all*
               and welcome him to this city
               with fair procession.   *fine*

5TH CITIZEN   With all the worship that I may*
               I welcome him will today,
195   and spread my clothes in the way
               as soon as I him see.

6TH CITIZEN   These miracles preven apertly   ✸ — Is This the
               that from the Father Almighty   teaching in church?
               he is comen. Mankind to buy;   *clearly prove*
200   it may none other be.   *come; redeem*

1ST BOY   Fellows, I heard my father say
               Jesu the prophet will come today.
               Thither I read we take the way   *suggest*
               with branches in our hand.

2ND BOY   Make we mirth all that we may   *joyful music*
206   pleasant to that Lord's pay.   *pleasure*
               "Hosanna!" I read, by my fay,   *suggest; truly*
               to sing that we fand.   *try*

               Then the boys shall go towards Jerusalem singing "Hosanna!"
               with branches of palm-trees in their hands. And the citizens
               shall lay out their garments in his path: "Hosanna, filio
               David! Benedictus qui venit in nomine Domini! Hosanna in
               *excelsis!"**

               Then Jesus, sitting upon the ass, seeing the city, shall weep
               and shall say:

JESUS   Ah, Jerusalem, holy city!
210   Unknown today it is to thee
               that peace thou hast—thou canst not see—

---

193 "With all the honour that I may contrive."

207+SD "Hosanna to the son of David. Blessed is he that cometh in the name of
the Lord; Hosanna in the highest"; Matthew 21.9—a Palm Sunday antiphon,
evidently sung here by cathedral choristers.

but bale thou shalt abide.*
Much must thou dreigh yet some day   *suffer still*
when woe shall fall on every way,   *everywhere*
215   and thou beguiled, sooth to say,   *deluded; truth*
with sorrow on all side—   *sides*

destroyed, dolefully driven down.   *sadly cast down*
No stone with other in all this town
shall stand, for that they be unlieven   *unbelieving*
220   to keep Christ's come   *observe; coming*
and God's own visitation,
done for Mankind's salvation;
for they have no devotion,   *reverence*
ne dreaden not his doom.   *nor fear; judgment*

*Then Jesus shall ride towards the city and all the citizens shall
lay down their garments in the way. And when he comes to
the temple, he shall say to the merchants as he descends from
the ass with a whip:*

225   Do away, and use not this thing,   *stop*
for it is not my liking.   *pleasure*
You make my Father's wonning   *dwelling-place*
a place of merchandise.   *trade*

1ST MER-   What freke is this that makes this fare*
CHANT   and casteth down all our ware?
231   Came no man hither full yare   *for very long*
that did us such annoys.   *harms*

2ND MER-   Out, out, woe is me!
CHANT   My table with my money
235   is spread abroad, well I see,   *scattered*
and nought dare I say.
Now it seems well that he
would attain royalty;   *wants to become a king*
else thus bold durst he not be   *otherwise*
240   to make such array.   *put on such a display*

210–12 "You do not know what peace you have—you cannot see it—but you
shall endure misery."

229 "What fellow is this that creates this disturbance?"

1ST MER- CHANT	It seems well he would be king	
	that casteth down thus our thing	*belongings*
	and says his father's wonning	*dwelling*
	in this temple is.	
245	Say, Jesus, with thy jangling	*idle talk*
	what evidence or tokening	*sign*
	showest thou of thy reigning,	
	that thou darest do this?	

2ND MER- CHANT	What signs now showest thou here	
251	that preves such power	*validates*
	to shend our ware in such manner	*destroy*
	masterly, through thy main?	*like a lord;power*

JESUS	This temple here I may destroy	
	and through my might and my mastery	*power*
255	in days three it edify	*build*
	and build it up again.	

1ST MER- CHANT	Aha, Jesus! Wilt thou so?	
	This word, as ever mot I go,	*may*
	shall be rehearsed before moe.	*repeated;more people*
260	Caiaphas I shall tell.	

Then Jesus shall eject the buyers and sellers with his whip.

JESUS	Hie you fast this temple fro,	*hasten;from*
	for merchandise shall be here no moe.	*trading;no more*
	In this place, be you never so throw,	*fierce*
	shall you no longer dwell.	

JUDAS	By dear God in majesty	
266	I am as wroth as I may be,	
	and some way I will wreak me	*avenge*
	as soon as ever I may.	
	My master Jesu, as men might see,	
270	was rubbed head, foot and knee	
	with ointment of more dainty	*finer quality*
	than I see many a day.	

	To that I have great envy	*moreover*
	that he suffered to destroy	
275	more than all his good thrie—*	

273–75 "Moreover, I hate him greatly because he has allowed goods to be

and his dame's, too!   *mother's*
Had I of it had mastery,   *command*
I would have sold it soon on hie   *at once*
and put it up in treasury   *money-store*
280   as I was wont to do.   *accustomed*

Whatsoever was given to Jesu
I have kept since I him knew;
for he hopes I be true,   *thinks; am*
his purse I alway bear.*
285   Him had been better, in good fay,
had spared ointment that day,
for wroken I will be some way   *revenged*
of waste that was done there.   *for*

Three hundred pennies-worth it was
290   that he let spill in that place.   *allowed to waste*
Therefore God give me hard grace
but himself shall be sold
to the Jews, or that I sit,   *before*
and for the tenth penny of it;
295   and thus my master shall be quit   *paid back for*
my grief an hundredfold.

Sir Caiaphas and his company
conspiren Jesus to annoy.   *plot; harm*
Their speech anon I will espy,   *counsel; at once*
300   with falsehood to foul him.   *do him down*
And if they gladly will do why,   *make recompense*
I shall teach them to him in hie,   *direct; at once*
for of his counsel well know I.   *Jesus's plan*
I may best beguile him.   *betray*

Then Judas shall for a time go away, and Caiaphas shall speak.

CAIAPHAS   Lordings, lookers of the law,   *gentlemen; guardians*
306   harkens hither to my saw.   *what I say*

---

destroyed that are three times more valuable than all his possessions."

281–84 Judas was in charge of the common purse (John 13.29) and stole from it
(12.4). That his greed at the wasted ointment prompted his betrayal of Christ was
a commonplace.

	To Jesu all men can draw	*have drawn*
	and liking in him has.	*take pleasure*
	If we letten him long gone,	*allow; to go about*
310	all men will lieve him upon;	*believe in him*
	so shall the Romans come anon	*at once*
	and prive us of our place.	*deprive*

	Therefore it is fully my read	*advice*
	we cast how he best were dead;	*think; might be*
315	for if he long on life be led	*may continue*
	our Law goeth all to nought.	
	Therefore, say eachone his counsel,	*let all speak*
	what manner of way will best avail	
	this ilk shrew for to assail—	*same cursed wretch*
320	some sleight there must be sought.	*cunning trick*

ANNAS	Sir, you say right skilfully;	*most reasonably*
	but needsly men must espy	*necessarily*
	by him we catch no villainy	*get no scandal*
	to fond, and foul to fail.	*by trying; badly failing*
325	For you know as well as I,	
	oft have we fonded to do him annoy;	*tried; harm*
	but ever he hath the victory—	
	that no way may avail.	*no way can succeed*

1ST PHAR-ISEE	Yea, sir, in temple he hath been,	
	and troubled us with much teen,	*misery*
331	and when we wended and did ween	*thought and expected*
	of him to have had all our will,	
	or ever we wist, he was away.	*before; knew*
	This maketh the people, in good fay,	*truly*
335	to lieve that he is Christ verray,	*believe; true*
	and our Law for to spill.	*destroy*

2ND PHAR-ISEE	Yea, lords, one point may do gain;	*matter; help*
	that lourden Lazar should be slain	*rascal Lazarus*
	for he raised him up again	
340	that four days had been dead.	
	For that miracle much of main,	*of great power*
	to honour him eachone is fain;	*everyone; eager*
	and Lazar, that dead was, will not lain	*lie*
	and he on life be led.	*if he continue alive*

| CAIAPHAS | No more, forsooth, will many moe | *indeed; more* |

346   that he has made to speak and go;
and blind that have their sight also
loven him steadfastly
and followen him both far and near,   *follow*
350   preaching to the people his power.
Therefore my wit is in a were,   *mind; confusion*
to ordain remedy.

ANNAS   And remedy must ordained be
before this great solemnity,*
355   or else may other as well as we
truss and take our way.   *pack up*
For when he came to this city,
all the world, as you might see,
honoured him upon their knee
360   as God had comen that day.   *as if; come*

1ST PHAR-   Also, lordings, you saw there   *gentlemen*
ISEE   how that he fared with chaffer—   *went on with trade*
cast it down, God give him care,
that was of so great price!   *worth*
365   And also, loudly he can lie—   *lied*
called the temple apertly   *openly*
his Father's house, full falsely,
right as it had been his!   *as if*

2ND PHAR-   Lordings, there is no more to say—   *gentlemen*
ISEE   but lost is our Law, I dare lay,   *wager*
371   and he come on our Sabbath day   *if; should come*
that now approacheth nigh.
Heal he any, less or more,   *if he should heal*
all men will lieve on his lore.   *believe; teaching*
375   Therefore it is good to slay him before,   *in advance*
if that we will be sly.   *secretive*

CAIAPHAS   Among our wits let us see   *brains*
to take him with some subtlety.   *cunning trick*
He shall have silver, gold and fee,   *wealth*
380   this thing that would fulfill.   *accomplish*

---

354 I.e., the Jewish Feast of the Passover commemorating the liberation of the
Israelites from slavery in Egypt.

JUDAS   Lords, what will you give me   *sirs*
              and I shall soon help that he   *if*
              slyly betrayed be
              right at your own will?   *just as you desire*

CAIAPHAS   Welcome, fellow! As have I row,   *peace*
386   that bargain fain would I go to.   *eagerly accept*

JUDAS   Let see what ye will do—
              and lay down silver here!
              For the Devil swap off my swire   *cut off my neck*
390   and I do it without hire,   *if;payment*
              other for sovereign or for sire.   *either;king;knight*
              It is not my manner.   *way*

CAIAPHAS   Say on. What shall we give thee
              to help that he taken be?   *may be*
395   And here is ready thy money
              to pay thee or thou pass.   *before you go*

JUDAS   As ever mote I thrive or thee,   *may;prosper*
              and I show my subtlety,   *if;cunning trick*
              thirty pennies ye shall give me
400   and not a farthing lass.*   *less*

1ST PHAR-   Yea, but thy troth thou must plight   *pledge*
ISEE   for to serve us aright   *properly*
              to betray thy master through thy might,
              and have here thy money!

JUDAS   Have here my troth, as I have tight.   *promised*
406   Or Friday that it be night
              I shall bring you to his sight
              and tell which is he.*

1ST PHAR-
ISEE   Ye been brethren on a row.   *are; together*

---

400 *farthing*—i.e., a coin worth a quarter of a penny.

406–8 "Before it is night-time on Friday I shall bring you where you may have sight of him and tell you which he is." Judas is conscious of the need to effect the capture before the Jewish Sabbath on the Saturday. Accordingly, he acts during the hours of darkness on Friday morning while Jesus waits and prays in Gethsemane.

410   Which is he I cannot know.

JUDAS   No? A very sign I shall you show.   *true*
                  Aspies who I kiss,   *watch*
                  and that is he, sooth to say.   *truth*
                  Takes him manly as you may,   *manfully*
415   and lead him slyly away   *secretly*
                  whither your liking is.   *wherever; pleasure*

CAIAPHAS   Now look thou serve us truly,
                  thy master's coming to espy.

JUDAS   Trust well thereto and sickerly   *on that; certainly*
420   that he shall not eschew.   *escape*
                  And would God Almighty
                  the King of France might so afie   *have such faith*
                  in this realm and barony   *i.e., England*
                  that they were all so true! *

425   On Friday in the morning
                  espies all on my coming,
                  for where that he is walking
                  I will go and espy.
                  With him I think to eat and drink;
430   and after, tidings to you bring
                  where he shapes his dwelling,   *plans to stay*
                  and come and tell you in hie.   *speedily*

                       THE END

421–24 Judas seems to suggest that his loyalty is of a kind that the King of France
might welcome from the people of England—i.e., that they would betray their
King to him. England retained possessions in France until the loss of Calais in
the reign of Mary, 1558.

PLAY 15: THE LAST SUPPER,
and THE BETRAYAL OF CHRIST

Performed by the Bakers

AFTER HIS TRIUMPHAL entry into Jerusalem, Jesus prepares to celebrate the Feast of the Passover with his disciples, knowing that Judas is going to betray him. At this Last Supper with his friends he gives to them bread and wine, which he identifies as his body and blood, and urges them to think on him whenever they share these elements. This meal establishes the form and significance of the central sacrament of the Christian religion, the Eucharist (Mass or Holy Communion). After this act, Jesus reveals that he knows the identity of his betrayer, and Judas leaves to carry out his treachery. Peter vows loyalty but Jesus foretells that he will disclaim knowledge of Jesus before cockcrow. Jesus and his disciples then go to the garden of Gethsemane, where Jesus prays while awaiting the arrival of Judas and the High Priests' men. The play dramatises events from Matthew 26.17–57, Mark 14.12–50, and Luke 22.7–51. It incorporates into those accounts the example that Jesus gives of humility in washing his disciples' feet and the dialogues which he utters, from John 13 and 14.1–19.

The Bakers' company who, appropriately, performed the play are urged in the Post-Reformation Banns to "cast God's loaves abroad," evidently sharing the Supper with the audience. They provided a waggon called in the Pre-Reformation Banns "The Maunday," from Maundy Thursday, the day before Good Friday. Evidently the waggon carried the fair parlour (line 29) with paved floors and windows bright (lines 53–54) displayed by the mysterious owner to whom Peter and John are led by the man with the waterpot. It contained a table which is prepared by the two disciples, presumably with benches, allowing the party to group

itself in the manner of paintings of the Last Supper. The action would
therefore seem to begin with Jesus and his followers entering on
ground-level, then ascending to the waggon for the central act of the
meal. Possibly, after Judas's exit, the table is removed at Jesus's "take up
this meat anon" (line 137). Later, without indication in the text apart
from Jesus's "Rise up and go hethen" (line 257), all move to another
location, Gethsemane. Possibly the set was curtained with an appropriate
backdrop or the action reverted to ground-level. But wherever Jesus
prays, it would be effective for Judas and the High Priests' officers to
enter at ground level and for the disciples to scatter through the crowd
while the soldiers force a way out for their prisoner.

The movement of the play up to the entry of the soldiers is slow.
Time is taken to prepare the room. Jesus's actions in blessing and dis-
pensing the bread and wine must be slow, clear and deliberate, a solemn
ritual. The meal itself proceeds for a while until Jesus foretells his betrayal, when each disciple must protest in turn. The washing of the feet, too,
is a lengthy and slow business; not only does Jesus wash the feet of each
disciple but the disciples then wash each other's feet. The movement to
Gethsemane is probably processional, and the three prayers are punctuat-
ed by Jesus's journeys to and from his drowsy disciples. Though there is
no indication of music, it seems impossible that some of these actions
would not have been accompanied by solemn music, perhaps also—
particularly for the journey to Gethsemane—by sacred song.

With the sudden entry of the soldiers, the mood changes. Peter's
angry and instinctive response and the horror of the excised ear (however effected) heralds the new strain of violence and cruelty that is to
continue in the following play.

Cast   JESUS, PETER, SERVANT, OWNER, JOHN, ANDREW, JAMES, JUDAS,
THOMAS, PHILIP, MALCHUS, FIRST JEW.

JESUS	Brethren all, to me right dear,	*most*
	come hither to me and ye shall hear!	
	The feast of Easter you know draweth near*	
	and now it is at hand.	
5	That feast needs keep must we	

---

3 *Easter*—the Christian festival commemorating the Resurrection of Christ.

with very great solemnity.
The paschal lamb eaten must be[*]
as the Law doth command.

Therefore, Peter, look that thou go—
10   and John with thee shall be also—
prepare all things that longeth thereto,[*]
according to the Law.

PETER   Lord, thy bidding do will we.
But tell us first where it shall be   *only*
15   and we shall do it speedily,
and thither we will draw.   *go*

JESUS   Go into the city which ye do see,
and there a man meet shall ye
with a water-pot that beareth he,
20   for so you may him know.
Into what house that he shall go,   *whichever*
into the same house enter ye also
and say the Master sent you two
his message for to show.   *make clear*

25   Say "The Master to thee us sent
to have a place convenient
the paschal lamb to eat"—there is my intent,
with my disciples all.
A fair parlour he will you show.   *private room*
30   There prepare all things due   *appropriate*
where I with my retinue
fulfill the Law we shall.

PETER   All ready, Lord. Even thy will
shortly we two shall fulfill,   *quickly*
35   and the fair city we shall go till   *to*
as fast as we may.

---

7 *The paschal lamb* was a male yearling lamb which, according to Exodus 12.3–10, was to be eaten roasted. All that remained was to be burnt by morning. The blood of the lamb had been used to mark the doorposts of the Israelites in their captivity in Egypt so that the Lord would pass over them in his retribution upon the Egyptians. See also note to 83 below.

11 "In order to prepare all things that pertain to that feast."

Then Peter and John shall go, and they shall speak to a man
carrying a brick-coloured pitcher of water.

PETER	All hail, good fellow, heartily!	*greetings; warmly*
	To thy master's house I pray thee hie;	*hasten*
	and we must keep thee company	
40	our message for to say.	

SERVANT	Come on your way and follow me;	
	my master's house soon shall you see.	
	Lo, here it is, verily.	*truly*
	Say now what ye will.	

Then they shall enter the house.

PETER	Sir, the Master saluteth thee	*greets*
46	and as messengers sent we be.	
	Therefore we pray thee heartily	*sincerely*
	take heed us until.	*to take; to us*

	The Master hath sent us to thee.	
50	A place prepare for him must we.	
	The paschal lamb there eat will he	
	with his disciples all.	

OWNER	Lo, here a parlour all ready dight,	*prepared*
	with pav-ed floors and windows bright.	
55	Make all things ready as you think right,	
	and this have you shall.	

JOHN	Now, brother Peter, let us hie	*hasten*
	the paschal lamb to make ready;	
	and to our Master then will we	*will go*
60	as fast as we may.	

Then they shall deck out the table and return.

PETER	Thy commandment, Lord, done have we.
	The paschal lamb is made ready.
	Therefore, come on and you shall see,
	and we shall lead the way.

Then they shall go.

JESUS	Now, brethren, go to your seat.	*seats*
66	this paschal lamb now let us eat,	
	and then we shall of other things entreat	
	that be of great effect.*	
	For know ye <u>now, the time is come</u>	
70	<u>that signs and shadows be all done.</u>	*are ended*
	Therefore make haste, that we may soon	
	all figures clean reject.*	*completely*

<u>For now a new Law I will begin</u>
to help Mankind out of his sin
75 so that he may Heaven win,
the which for sin he lost.
And <u>here,</u> in presence of you all,
<u>another sacrifice begin I shall,</u>
to bring Mankind out of his thrall,   *bondage*
80 for help him need I most.   *necessarily; must*

Then Jesus shall recline, and John shall sleep in his bosom.

Brethren, I tell you, by and by   *from time to time*
with great desire desired have I
this Passover to eat with you, truly,*
before my Passion.
85 For I say to you sickerly,   *certainly*
my Father's will Almighty
I must fulfill meekly
and ever to be boun.   *ready*

Then Jesus shall take bread, break it, and give it to his disciples, saying:

67–68 "And then we shall concern ourselves with other things which have greater effectiveness."

69–72 A sign is something that stands for something else; a figure is similarly an image or a prefiguration (as, for example, the events of play 4 are interpreted by the Expositor). Jesus here says that the time of images and parables is passed and the clear truth will be shown.

80+SD On this detail, see further, play 22, 173–76.

83 The Feast of the Passover was the Jewish commemoration of the slaying of the Egyptian first-born and the sparing of the exiled Israelites by the Angel of God, described in Exodus 12.21–27.

This bread I give here my blessing.
90   Take, eat, brethren, at my bidding,
for, lieve you well, without leasing,   *believe; truly*
this is my body
that shall die for all Mankind
in remission of their sin.
95   This give I you, on me to min,   *remember*
ay after evermore.   *always*

*Then he shall take the chalice in his hands, with eyes turned
to Heaven, saying:*

Father of Heaven, I thank thee
for all that ever thou dost to me.   *for*
Brethren, take this with heart free;   *joyful*
100 that is my blood
that shall be shed on the tree.
For more together drink not we   *we may not drink*
in Heaven-bliss till that we be
to taste that ghostly food.   *spiritual*

*Then he shall eat and drink with the disciples, and Judas
Iscariot shall have his hand in the dish.*

105 Brethren, forsooth I you say: *truly; to you*
one of you shall me betray
that eateth here with me today
in this company.

PETER   Alas, alas, and weal-away!   *misery*
110 Who that may be, know I ne may—   *may not know*
for I it is not, in good fay,   *truly*
that shall do such annoy.   *cause such harm*

ANDREW   Hard it is for us all
to whom this case shall befall.   *misfortune*
115 We be but twelve within this hall.
Lord, tell if it be I.

JAMES   Sorrowful for these words be we.
Who it is I cannot see.   *determine*
If this case shall fall to me,   *misfortune*
120 Lord, tell me hastily.

Then Judas shall reach into the dish.

JESUS

Through his deceit I am but dead
that in my cup wets his bread.
Much woe for his wicked read   *counsel*
that wretch must thole, iwiss.   *suffer; truly*
125   Well were him had he been unborn,   *it would be good for*
for body and soul he is forlorn   *utterly lost*
that falsely so hath done beforn—   *before*
and yet in will he is.*

JUDAS

Lief Master, is it not I   *dear*
130   that shall do thee this villainy?

JESUS

Thou hast read, Judas, readily,   *said truly*
for sicker thou art he.   *certainly*
That thou shalt do, do hastily.   *what*

JUDAS

Farewell, all this company!
135   For on an errand I must hie;   *hasten*
undone it may not be.

JESUS

Brethren, take up this meat anon!   *food; quickly*
to another work we must gone.   *deed; proceed*
Your feet shall washen be eachone   *washed; all*
140   to show all charity.   *complete love*
And first myself—I will begin,
and wash you all that be herein,
on this deed that you may min   *have mind*
and meeker for to be.   *and may therefore be*

Then Jesus shall gird his body with a towel.

PETER

Ah, Lord! Shalt thou wash my feet?   *must you*

JESUS

That do I, Peter, I thee behete,
the while more thou shalt not weet,
but thou shalt afterward.*

PETER

Nay, Lord, forsooth in no manner!   *indeed by no way*

---

128 "And yet he is still of that intention."

146–48 "What I do, Peter, I promise you, you shall not understand any more for
the time being, but you shall understand it afterwards."

150   My feet shalt thou not wash here.

JESUS   But I wash thee, withouten were,   *unless; truly*
              of joy gets thou no part.

PETER   Nay, Lord, my feet may well be laid;   *neglected*
              but wash my hands and my head.

JESUS   All is clean. Therefore do I read
156   thy feet shall washen be
              and you clean. But not all!*

PETER   Lord, of weal thou art the wall,   *joy; well-spring*
              and though it do not well befall,   *is not fitting*
160   have here my feet to thee.   *for you*

        *Then he shall wash the feet of all, one at a time, and take off
the towel.*

JESUS   My dear brethren, well wit ye   *know*
              that "Lord" and "Master" you call me;
              and well you say, as it should be—
              I am, and have been yore.   *for a long time*
165   Sith I have washen your feet here—   *since; washed*
              Lord and Master—in meek manner,   *humbly*
              do eachone so to other in fere   *each; together*
              as I have done before.

        Then all in turn shall wash the feet of the others.

              My little children, and my brethren free,   *noble*
170   little while may I with you be,   *for a short time*
              but thither shall you not go with me
              as I am now in way.   *going*
              But this soothly is my bidding: *truly*
              you love together in all thing   *love one another*
175   as I before, without fletching,   *wavering*
              have loved you truly ay.   *always*

              So all men may know and see

155–57 "The rest is clean. Therefore I propose that your feet must be washed and you become fully clean. But not all here are pure."

	my disciples that you be,	
	falsehood if you always flee	*shun*
180	and loven well in fere.	*love; together*

PETER	Lord, whither art thou in way?	*going*

JESUS	Peter, thither as I go today,	
	come, sickerly, thou ne may	*certainly; may not*
	this time, in no manner.	*at this time by no means*

185	But thou shalt thither go.	

PETER	Why shall it not, Lord, be so?	
	My life I will put in woe	*in jeopardy*
	and for thy sake be slain.	

JESUS	Peter, I say thee sickerly,	*tell; for certain truth*
190	or the cock have crowen thrie	*before; crowed; thrice*
	thou shalt forsake my company	
	and take thy word again.	*recant your words*

	Brethren, let not your hearts be sore,	*sad*
	but lieve in God evermore	*believe*
195	and in me, as you have before,	
	and care not in this case.	*don't worry; situation*
	For in my Father's house there is	
	many wonnings of great bliss,	*dwellings*
	and thither I will go now, iwiss,	*truly*
200	to purvey you a place.	*prepare in advance*

	And though I go from you away	
	to purvey a place to your pay,	*prepare; pleasure*
	I come again another day	*shall come*
	and take you all with me.	

THOMAS	Lord, we wot not, in good fay,	
206	what manner of gate thou wilt assay.*	
	Tell us, that we know may	
	that gate, and go with thee.	*road*

205–6 "Lord, we do not know, truly, what kind of road you intend to set out upon."

JESUS	Thomas, I tell thee, without strife,	*contradiction*
210	in me is way, soothness, and life.	*truth*
	and to my Father no man ne wife	*nor woman*
	may come without me.	
	And if you know me verily,	*in truth*
	my Father you might know in hie.	*at once*
215	From henceforth, I say you sickerly,	*for certain*
	know him all shall ye.	
PHILIP	Lord, let us see thy Father anon	*at once*
	and it sufficeth us everychone.	*will satisfy; all*
JESUS	A long time you have with me gone,	
220	Philip—why sayest thou so?	
	Sickerly, who seeth me	*certainly; sees*
	seeth my Father, I tell it thee.	
	Why willest thou my Father to see	*do you desire*
	while I with you go?	
225	Philip, lieves thou not this:	*do you not believe*
	that my Father in me is,	
	and I in him also, iwiss,	*indeed*
	and both we be one?	*we are both one Being*
	The works that I do are his,	
230	for his help I may not miss.	*lack*
	Therefore, to win you Heaven-bliss,	*for yourselves*
	my deeds you lieve upon!	*believe in my works*
	Whatsoever ye ask my Father dear	
	in my name in good manner,	*in the proper way*
235	to fulfill it I have power—	
	all that is to my pay—	*everything; at my pleasure*
	that my Father in majesty	*so that*
	by me glorified may be;	
	and either, as I say to thee,	
240	for one have been ay.*	
	If that you love me heartfully,	*with all your heart*
	keep my bidding truly,	*do what I ask sincerely*

239–40 "And each of us, as I say to you, has always been glorified for the one
God." The dramatist is anxious throughout to stress the indivisibility of the
Persons of the Trinity whose nature was defined at the very start of the cycle.

and to my Father pray will I
to send you the Holy Ghost *
245   to abide with you evermore;
for the world knoweth not his lore,   *knowledge*
but you, that have knowen me yore—   *known;very long*
in you he shall be most.   *strongest*

Though I go now to distress,   *suffering*
250   I will not leave you comfortless;
but lieves this well and express: *believe; clearly*
eft I will come again.   *once more*
And then your hearts on a row   *collectively*
shall gladly be, my bliss to know,   *happy*
255   which joy no man shall take you fro,   *from you*
would he never so fain.   *however eager he may be*

Rise up and go hethen anon.   *hence; at once*
To my prayer I must gone.   *go*
But sit you still everychone,   *all of you*
260   my Father while I call.
Wakes, and have my benison   *keep watch; blessing*
for falling into temptation.   *against*
The spirit ay to bale is boun !   *always; for evil; ready*
and the flesh ready to fall.

*Then Jesus shall go to pray; and the disciples shall fall asleep
because of their distress.*

265   Father of Heaven in majesty,
glorify, if thy will be,   *it may be*
thy Son, that he may glorify thee
now, or I hethen wend.   *before; go hence*
In Earth thou hast given me posty,   *power*
270   and I have done with heart free   *willing heart*
the work that thou charged me   *placed upon*
and brought it to an end.

Thy name have I made men to know   *caused*
and spared not thy will to show

---

244 *The Holy Ghost*—i.e., the third Person of the Trinity (with the Father and the
Son). Modern translations call it "the Holy Spirit." Its coming at Pentecost is
dramatised in play 21.

275   to my disciples on a row   *in a company*
    that thou hast given me.   *whom*
    And now they know verily   *truly*
    that from the Father sent am I.
    Therefore, I pray thee especially:
280   save them through thy mercy!

Then he shall come to the disciples and shall find them sleeping; and he shall say:

What! Sleep you, brethren all, here?
Rise up and make your prayer
lest temptation have power
to make you for to fall.
285   The flesh is, as I said before,
inclining ay to sin sore,   *always; sadly*
and ghost occupied evermore.   *the spirit; preoccupied*
Therefore now wakes all!   *keep watch*

Then he shall go a second time to prayer, and shall say in a loud voice:

My heart is in great misliking   *distress*
290   for death that is to me coming.
Father, if I dare ask this thing:
put this away from me!
Each thing to thee possible is.
Nevertheless, now in this
295   at your will I am, iwiss.   *truly*
As thou wilt, let it be.

Then he shall return again to his disciples.

Ye sleepen, brethren, yet, I see.   *sleep; still*
Sleeps on now, all ye!   *sleep*
My time is comen taken to be.   *come*
300   From you I must away.   *go away*
He that hath betrayed me,
this night from him will I not flee.
In sorry time born was he,
and so he may well say.

Then Judas shall come there with a company of soldiers, with lanterns, torches and arms.

JESUS	You men I ask, whom seek ye?	
MALCHUS*	Jesus of Nazareth, him seek we.	
JESUS	Here, all ready—I am he.	
	What have you for to say?	
JUDAS	Ah, sweet Master, kiss thou me,	
310	for it is long sith I thee see,	*since; saw*
	and together we will flee	
	and steal from them away.	
JESUS	What seek you men with such a breath?	*outcry*
1ST JEW*	We seek Jesus of Nazareth.	
JESUS	I said yore, and yet I say,	*before; still*
316	I am he, in good fay.	*truly*
	Suffer these men to go their way	*i.e., the disciples*
	and I am at your will.	
MALCHUS	False thief, thou shalt gone	*go*
320	to Bishop Caiaphas, and that anon,	*at once*
	or I shall break thy body and bone	
	and thou be too late.	*if; are*
PETER	Thief! And thou be so bold	*if*
	my master so for to hold,	
325	thou shalt be quit an hundredfold—	*repaid*
	and onward take thou that!	*take that on account*
	Be thou so bold, as thrive I,	*so may I thrive*
	to hold my master here in hie,	*seize; hastily*
	full dear thou shalt it abuy.	*dearly; pay for*
330	But thou thee hethen dight,	
	thy ear shall off, by God's grace,	

305+SH Malchus is named in John 18.10 where he is said to be the servant of the High Priest. He is not identified by name for the audience of the play. It is clear from the Gospels' account that the ear was not completely severed. Luke, the physician, is the only evangelist to mention its healing.

313+SH The speaker leads the company; there is no "second" Jew!

or thou pass from this place.*

*Then he shall draw out a sword and shall cut off the ear of
Malchus.*

Go plaint now to Caiaphas   *make a formal complaint*
and bid him do thee right.   *give you justice*

MALCHUS   Out! Alas, alas, alas!
336   By Cock's bones, my ear he has!   *God's;he's got*
           Me is betide a hard case
           that ever I come here!*

JESUS   Peter, put up thy sword in hie!   *at once*
340   Whosoever with the sword smiteth gladly   *exultantly*
           with sword shall perish hastily,
           I tell thee withouten were.   *without doubt*

Then Jesus shall touch the ear and shall heal it.

MALCHUS   Ah, well is me, well is me!
           My ear is healed now, I see.
345   So merciful a man as is he
           knew I never none.

1ST JEW   Yea, though he have healed thee,   *may have*
           shut from us shall he not be,   *protected*
           but to Sir Caiaphas, as mot I thee,   *so may I thrive*
350   with us shall he gone.   *go*

JESUS   As a thief you came here
           with swords and staves and armere   *weaponry*
           to take me in foul manner   *cruel fashion*
           and end your wicked will.   *accomplish*
355   In temple with you when I was ay,   *always*
           no hand on me would you lay;
           but now is comen time and day   *come*
           your talent to fulfill.   *purpose*

330–32 "Unless you're ready to go hence, your ear'll be off, by the grace of God,
before you go from this place."

337–38 "A cruel fortune has befallen me that I ever came here."

1ST JEW	Come, caitiff, to Caiaphas,	*wretch*
360	or thou shalt have a hard grace.	*fate*
	Trot on upon a prouder pace,	*brisker rate*
	thou vile popelard.	*hypocrite*
	Though Beelzebub and Satanas	*Satan*
	come to help thee in this case,	*may come; situation*
365	both thy hands that thou has	
	shall be bounden hard.	*bound tight*

THE END

PLAY 16, Part 1: THE TRIAL
AND FLAGELLATION OF CHRIST*

Performed by the Fletchers, Bowers, Coopers and Stringers*

PLAY 16 presents a particular problem, since it is clear from both manuscript and external evidence that sometimes *The Trial and Flagellation* and *The Crucifixion* were performed as a single play and sometimes as two separate plays. Indeed, the responsibility for the two plays—as they then clearly were—is an issue in the earliest record of Chester's cycle, in 1422. The Post-Reformation Banns, however, indicate that the actions constitute a single play under the responsibility of several companies. They lay particular emphasis upon it as a central play in the cycle because it contains the main article of Christian belief. The events leading up to and including Christ's Passion are thus seen as theologically central, and they are certainly dramatically powerful.

The material in the play comes directly from the accounts in the four gospels. It is diverse and involves numerous changes of location, particularly in the first part where the constant movements are the counterpart to the growing sense of urgency as the Priests seek to secure

---

Title The 1607 manuscript presents this action of *The Trial and Flagellation* and the following action of *The Crucifixion* as a single play; the other manuscripts present them as two separate plays but do not assign a number to *The Crucifixion*. In the EETS edition *The Trial and Flagellation* is numbered 16 and *The Crucifixion* 16A. Here they are presented as two parts of the same play under a single number.

Guild-ascription "The arrow-makers, bow-makers, barrel-makers, and bow-string makers." The Coopers' Company of Chester still possesses a copy of *The Trial and Flagellation*, which was made by George Bellin, their clerk, in 1599.

the condemnation and execution before the sabbath dawns. Jesus appears first before the High Priests, who seek to establish whether he is guilty of blasphemy, an offence worthy of death under their law. Since, however, they are not allowed to administer capital punishment, they take him to the Roman governor, Pontius Pilate, and seek to demonstrate that he is guilty of an offence under Roman law, that of treason by stirring the people to insurrection. Pilate is obviously sceptical and seizes an opportunity to pass Jesus on to Herod Antipas, son of the Herod the Great of plays 8 and 10, tetrarch of Galilee and Peraea (a referral found only in Luke 23.6–12). Herod finds no case against Jesus and returns him to Pilate. Here the action proceeds to judgement, with Pilate addressing the people, taking Jesus to one side to talk to him (found only in John 18.33–8), and trying to come to a private arrangement with the Priests, before finally washing his hands (only in Matthew 27.24) and condemning Jesus.

The second part is more narrowly focused. Jesus follows the road to Calvary, and Simon of Syrene is compelled to bear his cross. At Calvary a series of incidents—the dicing for the clothes, the placing of the superscription, the laments of the Maries, the dialogue with the thieves and Jesus's words to his mother and to John—go on around the cross. After Jesus's death, the centurion voices his belief and, in reponse, the unbiblical legend of Longinus, the blind soldier who is given his sight when he pierces Jesus's side, is played. Finally the body is removed for burial.

Although the actions are diverse, the staging is comparatively simple. The first part requires only a court setting with seats for the judges to be occupied in turn by the Priests, by Pilate, and by Herod. The stage is vacated for the journeys, which serve to emphasise the episodic divisions for the audience and allow a new judge to occupy the waggon. The repeated journeys and the sequence of judges makes visual a thematic point about authority and victim. Pilate's invitation to the Priests to "come up" (line 146) suggest that they are on ground level. Similarly, the journey to Calvary must require a further descent to ground level, allowing the waggon to be re-set for the hill of the Crucifixion.

The action of the play is a grim mixture of formality and violence. Christ is buffeted and scourged at the will of the judges and mocked by Herod. Bloodstained and weary, he is driven to exhaustion along the way to Calvary and is nailed to the cross, being, as tradition suggested, stretched upon it. The audience is spared none of the gleeful violence and humiliation of these events. It is a brutal and shocking spectacle in which we, like a medieval audience at an execution, witness a fellow human being suffering and recognise, moreover, that this is our God. The text does not really indicate the considerable length of time over which these acts of violence are played, or specify the laughter and shouts that must accompany them from tormentors and soldiers. Attention focuses upon Jesus, who must through expression, voice-tone and body-position communicate his suffering to the audience without overplaying it. At the same time, two thieves are crucified with him and must communicate similar sufferings if the tableau is to be convincing. Possibly supplementary actors were required to attach the thieves to their crosses and to remove them.

The growing humiliation of Christ, King of Kings, who is first dressed as a mock king and then stripped to a loin-cloth for crucifixion, contrasts with the splendour of the authorities around him—the Priests in clerical robes, Pilate and Herod in rich and elaborate costumes, the glittering armour of the soldiers, for whose benefit this spectacle is performed. The judges are all different in "character." The Priests are the guardians of their law, deeply anxious for its protection and full of anger against the "blasphemer" Jesus. Pilate is a dignified and rational pagan Roman, suspicious of the Jews and gaining an increasing respect for Jesus, whom he questions with speculative curiosity and seeks vainly to save. Pilate had two reputations in the Middle Ages—as an evil man who condemned Jesus, and as a well-intentioned man who tried to save him. It is the latter role that is stressed in our play. Herod is a shallow, vain man, anxious to have some entertainment from one whom he seems to regard as the equivalent of a stage conjuror, his frustration at Jesus's silence grows in its comic effect, but fails to explode into the violence characteristic of his father.

It must be emphasised that the mechanical process of attaching an actor to a cross and raising him is itself a very dangerous and difficult business. Should the top-heavy cross slip, as indeed it could before being inserted in its specially prepared boring in the waggon floor, the actor would be seriously injured. Hence the mechanics of this operation are part of the play's interest. Similarly, the removal of the body is also a fascinating mechanical process which occupies time. It should be done from a ladder behind the corpse, using slings to lower the sagging body of the actor to the arms of someone below. There is therefore good practical reason for having two actors here—Joseph of Arimathea and Nicodemus—to undertake this action.

The play ends on an affirmative note. The centurion is a Roman witness to Jesus's claims, yet another example of the rational pagan. Longinus, emblem of the Gentiles led from darkness to light in a way reminiscent of the blind man of play 13, is the occasion of a miracle which must be realised by the piercing of a concealed bladder of coloured liquid behind the actor on the cross. The final speeches of Joseph and Nicodemus express calm certainty and look forward to the Resurrection in play 18.

Cast FIRST JEW, SECOND JEW, ANNAS, CAIAPHAS, THIRD JEW, FOURTH JEW, JESUS, PILATE, HEROD.

> *And at the start the Jews shall come, leading Jesus to Annas and Caiaphas.*

1ST JEW	Sir Bishops, here we have brought	
	a wretch that much woe has wrought	*misery; caused*
	and would bring our Law to nought—	
	for it he hath spurned.	*despised*

2ND JEW	Yea, wide-where we have him sought,	*widely*
6	and dear also we have him bought,	*at high price*
	for here many men's thought	*minds*
	to him he has turned.	

ANNAS	Ah, jangling Jesus, art thou now here?	*argumentative*
10	Now thou may prove thy power,	*demonstrate*
	whether thy cause be clean and clear;	*if; right*
	thy Christhood we must know.	*claim to be Christ*

CAIAPHAS	Methink a mastery that it were	
	other for penny or prayer	
15	to shut him of his danger	
	and such sleight to show.*	

ANNAS	Sir Caiaphas, I say sickerly	*for certain*
	we that been in company	*are together here*
	must needs this dozebeard destroy	*idiot*
20	that wickedly has wrought.	

CAIAPHAS	Sir, it is needful—this say I—	
	that one man die, witterly,	*should die; certainly*
	all the people to forbuy	*redeem*
	so that they perish nought.	

3RD JEW	Sir Caiaphas, harken now to me!	
26	This babble-a-vaunt would our king be.	*braggart*
	Whatsoever he says now before thee,	

13–16 "It seems to me that whether for monetary gain or at our entreaty, it would be a demonstration of power for him to free himself from his peril and show such cleverness."

	I heard him say full yore	*long ago*
	that prince he was, of such posty	*power*
30	destroy the temple well might he	*(that) he might*
	and build it up in days three	
	right as it was before.	

4TH JEW	Yea, sicker, that I heard him say.	*certainly*
	He may not deny by no way!	
35	And also, that he was God verray,	*true*
	Emmanuel and Messy.*	*Messiah*
	He may not nick this ne say nay,	*deny; nor; no*
	for more than forty, in good fay,	*truly*
	that in the temple were that day	
40	hearden as well as I.	*heard*

CAIAPHAS	Say, Jesu, to this what sayen ye?	*say*
	Thou wottest now what is put on thee.	
	Put forth, prince, thy posty	
	and perceive what they preven.*	
45	What Devil! One word speaks not he!	
	Yet, Jesu, here I conjure thee;	*compel by oath*
	if thou be God's Son, before me	
	answer to that they meven.	*put forward*

JESUS	As thou sayest, right so say I—	
50	I am God's Son Almighty;	
	and here I tell thee truly	
	that me yet shall thou see	
	sit on God's right hand him by	
	Mankind in clouds to justify.	*pass judgement upon*

CAIAPHAS	"Justify!" Marry, fie, fie on thee, fie!	
56	Witness of all this company	*let all bear witness*
	that falsely lies he!	
	Ye hearen all what he says here.	*hear*
	Of witness now what need were?	*would there be*
60	For before all these folk in fere	*together*

---

36 *Emmanuel*, meaning "God with us," is the name given to the Messiah in Isaiah 7.14. Isaiah's prophecy, with the name, is applied to Jesus in Matthew 1.23.

43–44 "Display your power, prince, and take cognisance of the proof that they advance."

| | loudly thou lies! | |
| | What say you men that now been here? | *are* |

1ST JEW	Buffets him that makes this bere,	*beat; boast*
	for to God may he not be dear	
65	that our Law so destroys.	

CAIAPHAS	Destroy shall he not it,	
	ye wretches—ye wanten wit!	*you lack intelligence*
	Fond that freke a fit	
	and gurd him in the face.*	

ANNAS	Despise him, spurn and spit!	
71	Let see, or you sit,	*before*
	who has hap to hit	*the good fortune*
	that thus us harmed has.	*him who*

Then the Jews shall set Jesus up in a chair, and the First Jew shall speak as the process of torture goes on.

1ST JEW	For his harming here	*in order to harm him*
75	nigh will I near	*approach*
	this fameland frere	*stuttering friar*
	that makes our Law false.	

2ND JEW	He is, without were,	*doubt*
	to the Devil full dear.	*very*
80	Spit we all in fere	*together*
	and buffet him als.	*beat; also*

3RD JEW (*spitting*)

	Ye hearden in this place now,	*heard*
	how he lied has now.	
	In midst of his face now	*full in his face*
85	foul will I file him.	*foully; smear*

4TH JEW (*spitting*)

| | Pass he shall a pace now.* | |
| | For God he him mase now, | *because; makes himself* |

68–69 "Contrive something unpleasant for that fellow and hit him in the face."

86 Either "He shall go through his paces now," or "He shall pass quickly from one of us to another."

gets he no grace now	
when I may beguile him.	*outwit*

1ST JEW (*delivering a blow*)

90	Fie upon thee, freke!	*fellow*
	Stoop now and creak.	*croak*
	Thy brains to break	
	am I ready boun.	*prepared*

Then the Second Jew delivering a blow while covering the face of Jesus:

2ND JEW

95	His face will I steek	*cover*
	with a cloth, er he creak,	*before*
	and us all wreak	*avenge*
	with my warrison.	*curse*

3RD JEW

	And thou be Messy	*if; Messiah*
	and loath for to lie,	*reluctant*
100	who smote thee?—cry,	
	if that thou be Christ.	

4TH JEW (*striking*)

	For all his prophecy,	*prophesying*
	yet he fails thrie;	*three times*
	though my fist flee,	*bruises him*
105	gets he a fist.	*a blow*

1ST JEW (*striking*)

	Though he him beshite,	*shits himself*
	a buffet shall bite;	*blow; cut into him*
	may no man me wite,	*blame me*
	though I do him woe.	*cause*

2ND JEW (*striking*)

110	Him fails to flite	*he is unable to complain*
	or ought to despite;	*argue anything against us*
	for he has too lite,	*because; little*
	now must he have moe.	*more*

3RD JEW (*striking*)

	And moe yet I may.	*more; may do*
115	I shall soon assay	*make my attempt*
	and show large pay,	*display a great result*

·

       thou prince, on thy pate.   *head*

4TH JEW   If he say nay,   *even if he may say no*
           I shall, in fay,   *truly*
120   lay on. I dare lay   *add blows; wager*
           it is not too late.

       *Then they shall cease from their blows, and Caiaphas shall
       speak.*

CAIAPHAS   Lordings, what is your best read?   *gentlemen; counsel*
           This man has served to be dead,   *deserved*
           and if he lightly thus be led,   *leniently; treated*
125   our Law clean will sleep.   *entirely; lie dormant*

ANNAS   Sir, it is fully mine advice,
           lead we him to the High Justice.   *let us lead; chief*
           Sir Pilate is both ware and wise*   *prudent*
           and has the Law to keep.   *uphold*

       *Then Caiaphas and Annas and the Jews shall lead Jesus to
       Pilate. Caiaphas shall speak.*

CAIAPHAS   Sir Pilate, here we bring one
131   that false is, and our elders' fone.   *ancestors' foe*
           Tribute may be given none
           to Caesar for him here.
           Wheresoever he and his fellows gone,   *go*
135   they turn the folk to them eachone.   *convert; all*
           Now ask we doom here him upon   *judgement*
           of thee that has power.

ANNAS   Sicker he is our elders' foe.   *certainly*
           Wheresoever he goeth, to or fro,
140   that he is Christ, and king also,
           he preaches apertly.   *openly*
           Wist Caesar that, he would be woe   *if C. knew; grieved*
           such a man and we let go.   *if*
           Therefore to damn him we been throw,   *condemn; are keen*

---

128 *Sir Pilate*, i.e., Pontius Pilate, procurator of Judea, who was responsible for
enforcing the Roman Law. The succeeding trial presumably is set in his head-
quarters, to which the Jews now take Jesus.

145   lest he us all destroy.

PILATE   Come up lordings, I you pray,   *gentlemen*
              and we shall hear what he will say
              among this fellowship here.   *company*

              What sayest thou, man in mis-array?   *wretched state*
150   And thou be King of Jews, say!   *if*

JESUS   So thou sayest; men hear may
              a king that thou me mase.   *makes*

PILATE   No cause find I, in good fay,   *truly*
              to do this man to death today.

CAIAPHAS   Sir, the people—us to mispay—   *to displease us*
156   converted to him all he has.

ANNAS   Yea, all the land of Galilee
              clean turned to him has he.   *completely converted*
              Therefore doom now ask we,   *judgement*
160   this false man to do down.

PILATE   Sith he was born there as sayen ye,   *since; say*
              to Herod sent soon shall he be;   *at once*
              else reft I him his royalty
              and blemish his renown. *

165   Go, leads him to Herod in hie,   *hastily*
              and says I send him to justify   *to him for judgement*
              this man of which he hath mastery   *over; dominion*
              at his own liking.   *however he wishes*

1ST JEW   Him shall he have full hastily,
170   and lead him thither anon will I.   *at once*
              Come thou forth with thy ribaldry   *sacrilegious talk*
              and speak with our king.

161–64 "Since he was born where you say, he shall at once be sent to Herod;
otherwise I would be depriving him of his royal position and impair his reputation." This Herod is Herod Antipas, son of the Herod the Great who died in play
10. He was tetrarch of Galilee and Persaea, but not a king. The account of Jesus's
appearance before Herod is found only in Luke 23.8–12.

Then the two Jews shall go, leading Jesus to Herod; and the First Jew shall speak.

1ST JEW	Sir King, here Pilate hath you sent	
	a shrew that our Law has shent,	*wretch; destroyed*
175	for to have his judgement	*verdict*
	or he hethen wend.	*hence; go*
HEROD	Ah, welcome, Jesu, verament!	*sincerely*
	And I thank Pilate of his present,	*for*
	for oft-times I have been in that intent	*of that mind*
180	after thee to have send.	*sent*
	Jesu, much have I heard of thee.	
	Some virtue fain now would I see.	*power; desire to*
	If thou from God in majesty	
	be comen, tell us here.	*come*
185	I pray thee, say now to me,	*speak*
	and prove some of thy posty,	*power*
	and much the gladder would I be,	
	truly, all this year.	

Jesus shall make no reply.

HEROD	What! I ween that man is wood,	*think; mad*
190	or else dumb, and can no good.	*knows nothing good*
	Such a stalwart never before me stood,	*determined man*
	so stout and stern is he.	*strong; menacing*
	Speak on, Jesu, for Cock's blood,	*God's*
	for Pilate shall not, by my hood,	
195	do thee none amiss. But mend thy mood	
	and speak somewhat with me.*	
	Alas, I am nigh wood for woe.	*almost mad for anguish*
	Methinks this man is wondrous throw,	*fierce*
	deaf and dumb as a doted doe,	
200	or frantic, in good fay.	*deranged truly*
	Yet sithen that Pilate has done so,	*since*
	the wrath that was between us two	*ill-feeling*
	I forgive—no more his foe	

194–96 "For Pilate shall not do you any harm, on my life. Only modify your attitude and talk a little with me."

to be after this day.

205   Clothe him in white, for in this case
to Pilate it may be solace,   *a source of pleasure*
for Jews' custom before was
to clothe men that were wood   *mad*
or mad, as now he him mase,   *makes himself to be*
210   as well seems by his face;
for him that has lost his grace   *state of grace*
this garment is full good.   *very appropriate*

> *Then the Jews shall dress him in a white garment; and the*
> *First Jew shall speak.*

1ST JEW   Have this, Jesu, upon thee—
a worshipful weed, as thinks me,   *noble garment; seems*
215   of the king's livery
that now is on thee light!   *descended*

2ND JEW   Put thee forth. Thou may not flee.   *come on out*
Now thou art in thy royalty—   *regal dress*
Sir Herod, king, by leave of thee!
220   And gramercy this gift!   *thanks for*

> *Then the two Jews shall leave, leading Jesus in the white*
> *garment to Pilate; and the First Jew shall speak.*

1ST JEW   Sir Pilate, here the King hath sent
Jesu again, and sith we went,   *since*
he has forgiven his mal-intent   *ill-will*
for thy deed today.

PILATE   Yea, fault in him can I find none,
226   ne Herod, as seems hereupon.   *nor; it seems by this*
Therefore is best we let him gone   *it is; go*
whither he will his way.   *wherever he wants*

2ND JEW   Nay, all, all we cryen with one voice,   *cry*
230   nail him, nail him to the cross.

PILATE   Ye men, for shame! Let be your noise!   *stop*
My counsel will I say.
Ye knowen eachone the manner: *know all; custom*
delivered must be a prisoner—

| 235 | this feast that now approaches near— | *at this feast* |
| | for honour of the day. | |

Will ye Jesus delivered be?

3RD JEW	Nay, suffer the death worthy is he,	*to suffer*
	and thereupon all cryen we,	*cry for that*
240	and Barabbas reserved.*	*kept alive*

| PILATE | What shall I do with Jesu here | |
| | that Christ is called, and King in fere? | *as well* |

| 4TH JEW | Nail him on the cross in all manner, | *at all events* |
| | for so he hath deserved. | |

PILATE	Now, sithen I see you so fervent,	*since; angry*
246	and shapen that he shall be shent,	*agreed; killed*
	wash I will here in your present,	*presence*
	wax ye never so wood.	*however mad you grow*
	Ye shall all wit verament	*know truly*
250	that I am clean and innocent	*pure*
	and for to shed in no intent	*in no mind*
	this rightwise man's blood.	*righteous*

*Then Pilate shall wash his hands. And Caiaphas and Annas
shall withdraw with Pilate, and Pilate shall speak.*

| PILATE | Ye prelates here everychone, | *all* |
| | what will ye do? Let him gone? | *go* |

| CAIAPHAS | Nay! Nail him to the cross anon— | *at once* |
| 256 | and deem him or thou leave. | *sentence; before* |

| PILATE | Takes ye him, that been so grim, | *you who are* |
| | and after your Law deem ye him. | *according to; sentence* |

| ANNAS | Nay, that is not lawful, lith ne limb | *joint; nor* |
| 260 | for us no man to reave. | *deprive of* |

---

240 *Barabbas* is described in the Gospels as a robber and a noted criminal who
had led an insurrection in Jerusalem and had committed murder. Pilate here
follows the custom of offering to release a prisoner of the people's choice as a
conciliatory gesture at the Passover season.

PILATE   What devil of Hell is this to say?*
          Jesu, tell me, I thee pray,
          art thou King—say "yea" or "nay"—
          of Jews by ancestry?   *lineage*

JESUS   Whether, hopes thou it so be   _   *which is it; think*
266   or other men told it thee?   *did others tell*

PILATE   Nay, fay! Thyself may know and see   *no; truly*
          that no Jew am I.

          Men of thine own nation
270   showen for thy damnation   *argue; condemnation*
          with many an accusation
          and all this day so han.   *have done so*
          Art thou king—say, for all their cry?   *despite*

JESUS   My realm in this world, as say I,
275   is not—but were it, witterly   *indeed*
          with Jews were I not tane.   *would not be captured*

          And if my realm in this world were,   *should be*
          strive I would with you now here
          and lead with me such power
280   should prive you of your prey.*
          But my might in this manner   *form*
          will I not prove, ne now appear   *nor*
          as worldly king; my cause unclear   *earthly; tainted*
          were then, in good fay.   *truly*

PILATE   Ergo, a king thou art, or was?   *therefore*

JESUS   That thou sayest, it is no less.   *lies*
          But now I tell thee here express   *directly*
          that king I am and be may.
          In world I came to bear witness
290   of soothness, and therefore born I was.   *truth; for that*
          And all that lieven soothness   *believe the truth*

---

261 "What the hell kind of talk is that!"

279–80 "And bring such forces with me that I should deprive you of your victim."

take heed to that I say.

PILATE   What is soothness? Tell thou me.   *truth*

JESUS   Soothness came from God's see.   *the throne of God*

PILATE   In Earth then hath truth no posty   *power*
296   by thine opinion?

JESUS   How should truth on Earth be
              while so deemed in Earth is he   *thus judged*
              of them that have none authority   *by*
300   in Earth? Against reason!   *it's irrational*

PILATE   Lordings, I find no cause, iwiss,   *gentlemen; indeed*
              to damn this man that here is.   *condemn*

CAIAPHAS   Pilate, he hath done much amiss.
              Let him never pass.   *get away*
305   By Moses' Law liven we   *live*
              and after that Law dead shall he be,   *according to*
              for apertly preached has he   *openly*
              God's Son that he was.

ANNAS   Yea, Pilate, he that makes him a peer
310   other to king or king's fere
              withsayeth Caesar of his power,
              and so we have done with him.*
              And whoso calls himself a king here
              reaves Caesar of his power.   *deprives*

PILATE   Anon go scourge this losinger   *scoundrel*
316   and beat him, lith and limb.   *joint*

1ST JEW   Come now with care,   *sorrow*
              freke, for thy fare.   *fellow; behaviour*
              On thy body bare
320   strokes shalt thou bear.

309–12 "Yes, Pilate, he that makes himself an equal either to a king or to the
consort of a king gainsays Caesar his power, and so we have proceeded with the
case of this man."

2ND JEW	Cast of thy ware,	*clothing*
	all thy clothes, yare!	*quickly*
	Start now and stare!	*flinch; be amazed*
	This stalwart I would steer.	*strong fellow; restrain*

Then they shall strip him and shall bind him to a pillar; and the Third Jew shall speak.

3RD JEW	Now he is bounden.	*tied up*
326	Be he never so wandon,	*however rebellious*
	soon shall he be founden	*tested*
	with flaps in fere.	*with a rain of blows*

4TH JEW	In woe is he wounden	
330	and his grain is grounden.	
	No lad unto London	
	such law can him lere.*	

Then after they have scourged him. then they shall dress him in purple and sit him on a chair; and the First Jew shall speak.

1ST JEW	Now, sith he king is,	*since*
	quaint his clothing is.	*elegant*
335	Beggar, I bring thee this,	
	thee for to wear.	*for you to wear*

Then the Second Jew, placing a crown of thorns upon his head, shall speak.

2ND JEW	All in lithing this is	
	that of old sprung is.*	
	Of thorns this thing is,	
340	thee for to wear.	*for you*

329–32 "He is wrapped in sorrow and his fate is sealed. No lad from here to London can teach him such a law as I can." *his grain is grounden*, literally "his corn is ground," seems to be a colloquialism, but the text and the idiom are both obscure.

337–38 "All by way of healing this is, which has come down from of old"; *lithing* is a word recorded only from one other medieval text, and its meaning here is doubtful. The sense seems to be, ironically, that the crown of thorns is an ancient remedy.

3RD JEW   Now thou has a weed,   *garment*
                   have here a reed.

                   He shall hand him a reed.

                   A sceptre I thee bede,   *offer*
                   a king for to be.

4TH JEW   Harvey, take heed!*
346   Thus must I need
                   for my foul deed
                   kneel upon knee.

                   Then they shall kneel.

1ST JEW   Hail, King of Jews!
350   That so many men shows,   *what; prove*
                   ribald, now thee rues,   *scoundrel; makes you regret*
                   with all thy reverence.   *the honour done to you*

2ND JEW   With iron on him hews,   *cut*
                   and his hide hews.   *cut*
355   Anointment thee news   *revives you*
                   for thine offence.

3RD JEW   To write in his face—
                   thou that thee king mase,
                   now my nose has.
360   Good spice of the new!*

4TH JEW   With a hard grace   *ill-fortune*
                   thou came to this place.
                   Pass thou this race,   *if you escape this battle*
                   sore shalt thou rue.   *sorely repent*

PILATE   Lordings, here you may see   *gentlemen*
366   your king in all his royalty.   *regal splendour*

---

345 *Harvey* is presumably the name of one of the other Jews, though it may be a
familiar address to Jesus himself.

357–60 "To paint on his face—you who make yourself out to be a king, now you
have what's in my nose. Good spice, newly made!" Nasal mucus is here dis-
charged upon Jesus. The last line sounds rather like the street-cry of a spice-
seller.

CAIAPHAS   Nay, sir, forsooth, no king have we   *truly*
                save the Emperor of Rome, pardee;   *indeed*
                and but thou nail him to the tree,   *unless*
     370   the Emperor full wrath will be.

ANNAS   All we sayen right as says he.   *say*
                Deem him while thou hast time.   *pass judgement on*

PILATE   Whether of them will ye han,   *which of the two;have*
                Jesus Christ or Barabban?   *Barabbas*

CAIAPHAS   Nay! Jesus, this traitor that is tane,   *captured*
     376   must nailed be to the tree.
                And let Barabban go his way.   *Barabbas*

PILATE   Take him to you now, as I say,
                for save him I ne may,   *may not*
     380   undone but I would be.   *unless;overthrown*

1ST JEW   This doom is at an end.   *judgement*
                Now read I that we wend   *propose;go*
                this shrew for to shend   *wretch;kill*
                a little here beside.

                The Second Jew, placing the cross on Jesus's back, shall speak.

2ND JEW   Here shalt thou not lend.   *stay*
     386   Come hither, and be hend   *courteous*
                thy back for to bend.
                Here may thou not abide.

                Then they shall go towards the Mount of Calvary.

                              THE END*

The End Finis appears at the end of *The Trial and Flagellation* in the four earliest
manuscripts, but the action evidently proceeded without a break to the second
part, *The Crucifixion*. A misplaced fragment of sixteen lines containing Peter's
Denial of Christ is interpolated between the two parts in the four earliest manuscripts but is here omitted. The episode of the Denial is not otherwise dramatised
in the cycle.

PLAY 16, Part 2: THE CRUCIFIXION

Performed by the Ironmongers

Cast CAIAPHAS, ANNAS, SIMON, FIRST JEW, FIRST WOMAN, SECOND WOMAN, JESUS, SECOND JEW, THIRD JEW, FOURTH JEW, PILATE, MARY, MARY MAGDALEN, MARY JACOBI, MARY SALOME, FIRST THIEF, SECOND THIEF, JOHN, CENTURION, LONGINUS, JOSEPH OF ARIMATHEA, NICODEMUS.

CAIAPHAS	Now of this sedger we been sicker.	
	Against us boots him not to bicker.	
	Though he fleer, flatter and flicker,	
	this fist shall he not flee.*	
5	Thou, Jesu, would be our king!	
	Go forth! Evil joy thee wring!	*ill-luck; torture*
	For wroken on thee at our liking	*avenged; pleasure*
	full soon shall we be.	
	Gurd on fast and make him go,	*beat*
10	this freke that is our elders' foe;	*fellow*
	for all his wiles, from this woe	
	shall no man him were.	*protect*
ANNAS	Him seems weary of his way.*	

1–4 "Now we are certain of this fellow. It doesn't help him to attack us. Though he may sneer, flatter, or change his tune, he won't escape my fist."

13 "His way seems wearisome to him!"

	Some help to get I will assay,	*try*
15	for this cross, in good fay,	*truly*
	so far he may not bear.	
	Come hither, Simon of Surrey,*	*Cyrene*
	and take this cross anon in hie.	*immediately*
	Unto the Mount of Calvary	
20	help that it were borne.	*might be*
SIMON	The Devil speed this company!	*prosper*
	For death he is not worthy!	
	For his sake, sickerly,	*certainly*
	I hold you all forlorn.	*utterly lost*
25	To bear no cross am I intent,	*of a mind*
	for it was never mine assent	
	to procure this prophet's judgement,	*condemnation*
	full of the Holy Ghost.	*(who is); Spirit*
CAIAPHAS	Simon, but thou will be shent	*unless; want to; killed*
30	and suffer pain and imprisonment,	
	this cross upon thy back thou hent	*take up*
	and let be all thy boast.	*put aside*
SIMON	Alas, that ever I hither come!	*came*
	Would God I had been in Rome	
35	when I the way hither nome,	*took*
	thus to be annoyed.	*troubled*
	But God I take to witness	*as*
	that I do this by distress.	*under compulsion*
	All, iwiss, through your falseness	*indeed*
40	I hope will be destroyed.	*think*

Then he shall take up the cross.

ANNAS	Have done! Bring forth those thieves two!	
	On either half him they shall go.	*side of him*
	This freke shall be handled so	*fellow*
	with fellowship in fere.	*in a company together*

---

17 Simon of Cyrene was said by Luke 23.26 to have been travelling out of the country when he was compelled to take up Christ's cross and carry it to the place of crucifixion, Mount Calvary. Nothing more is known of him.

45	Take them here, bound fast,	
	while this whipcord may last,	*stay intact*
	for the prime of the day is past.	*i.e., 6.00 a.m.*
	How long shall we be here?	

Then they shall lead out Jesus and the two thieves, and the women shall come, the first of whom shall speak.

1ST WOMAN	Alas, alas, and woe is me!	*how sorrowful am I*
50	A doleful sight this is to see.	*sorrowful*
	So many sick saved hath he	
	and now goeth thus away.	

2ND WOMAN	Sorrowful may his mother be	
	to see the flesh so fair and free	*noble*
55	nailed so foul upon a tree,	*wickedly*
	as he mon be today.	*must*

JESUS	Ye women of Jerusalem,	
	weep not for me, ne make no swem;	*nor; grief*
	but for your own barm-team	*children*
60	ye mon ream tenderly.	*must weep*
	For time shall come, withouten were,	*without doubt*
	ye shall bless belly that never child bear,	*womb; bore*
	and pap that never milk came near,	*breast*
	so nigh is your annoy.	*distress*

CAIAPHAS	Have done! You tormenters, tite,	*torturers; quick*
66	and spoil him that hath done us spite!	*strip; scorn*

1ST JEW	Yea, though he both groan and shite,	
	out he shall be shaken.	
	Be thou wroth or be thou fain,	*like it or not*
70	I will be thy chamberlain.	*valet*
	This coat gets thou never again	
	and I may be waken.	*if; watching out*

2ND JEW	This coat shall be mine,	
	for it is good and fine	
75	and seam is there none therein	
	that I can see.	

3RD JEW	Yea, God give me pine	*torment*
	and that shall be thine,	*if*

	for thou art ever incline	*inclined*
80	to draw towards thee.	*pull things your way*

4TH JEW   Nay, fellows, by this day,
           at the dice we will play,
           and there we shall assay   *attempt*
           this weed for to win.   *garment*

1ST JEW   Ah, fellow, by this day,
86   well can thou say!   *have you said*
           Lay forth those clothes—lay
           on board or we blin!   *before; stop*

           *Then they shall strip Jesus of his clothes and he shall stand
           naked until they have played their game of chance.*

2ND JEW   Fellows, now let see—
90   here are dice three!—
           which of all we
           shall win this ware.

3RD JEW   Nay, parted they shall be,   *shared out*
           for that is egally.   *fair*
95   Therefore, as mote I thee,   *so may I thrive*
           or we hethen fare—   *before we go hence*

4TH JEW   This coat bout seam,   *without*
           to break it were shame,   *split; would be a pity*
           for in all Jerusalem
100   is none such a garment.

1ST JEW   His dame now may dream
           for her own barm-team;*
           for nother aunt nor eem   *neither; uncle*
           gets this gay garment.   *fine*

2ND JEW   His other clothes all
106   to us four can fall.
           First part them I shall,   *share out*
           and after play for this.   *play (dice)*
           This kirtle mine I call.   *tunic*

101–2 "His mother may speculate vainly on behalf of her own family."

110	Take thou this pall.	*cloak*
	Each man in this hall	
	wots I do not amiss.	*knows*

To the Third:

This kirtle take to thee—   *tunic*

To the Fourth:

	and thou this to thy fee.	*for your wage*
115	Each man now may see	
	that all we be served.	

3RD JEW	Yea, now I read that we	*advise*
	sit down, as mot I thee,	*so may I thrive*
	and look whose this shall be	
120	that is here reserved.	*set aside*

Then all shall sit down and the First Jew shall speak, throwing the dice.

1ST JEW	Now will I begin	
	for to cast, or I blin,	*before; stop*
	this coat for to win	
	that is both good and fine.	

He throws and loses.

2ND JEW	By my father's kin,	
126	no part has thou therein!	
	But, or I hethen win,	*before I go hence*
	this coat shall be mine.	

	Take! Here, I dare lay,	*check; wager*
130	are doublets in good array.	*sets of two; fine fashion*

He throws and loses.

3RD JEW	Thou fails, fellow, by my fay,	*indeed*
	to have this to thy fee,	*for your wage*
	for here is quatre-trais.	*i.e., three fours*

He throws and loses.

	Therefore go thou thy way,	
135	and as well thou may,	*as best you can*
	and leave this with me.	

4TH JEW	Fellows, verament,	*truly*
	I read we be at one assent.*	
	This gay garment	*fine*
140	that is bout seam,	*without*
	you give by judgement	
	to me this vestment,	*item of clothing*

He throws and wins.

| | for cinques God hath me sent, | *sets of five* |
| | think you never so swem. | *however grieved you are* |

1ST JEW	As I have good grace,	
146	well won it thou has,	
	for cinques there was	*sets of five*
	that every man might see.	

CAIAPHAS	Men, for Cock's face,	*God's*
150	how long shall <u>pee-wee arse</u>	*pissy-arse*
	stand naked in that place?	
	Go nail him on the tree!	

2ND JEW	Anon, master, anon.	*at once*
	A hammer have I won.*	*obtained*
155	As far as I have gone	*travelled*
	is none such another.	*there is*

3RD JEW	And here are, by my pon,	*by my head*
	nails good won	*a good quantity of*
	to nail him upon	*on him*
160	and he were my brother.	*even if*

| 4TH JEW | Go we to as fast. | |
| | This caitiff have I cast. | |

---

138 "I propose that we be unanimous."

154 Hammer and nails were, of course, the products of the Ironmongers who performed the play.

He shall be wrung wrast
or I wend away.*

1ST JEW 166	Here is a rope will last for to draw at the mast. This popelard never passed so perilous a play.*	

2ND JEW 170	Lay him thereupon, this ilk mased mon, and I shall drive on this nail to the end.	*on it* *this same crazy man* *in*

3RD JEW 175	As broke I my pon, well cast him I con and make him full wan or I from him wend.	*head* *cast him down* *very pale* *before; go*

Then they shall place Jesus on the cross.

4TH JEW 180	Fellows, will ye see how sleight I shall be this fist, or I flee, here to make fast?	*skilful* *before I rush off* *secure*

1ST JEW	Yea, but, as mote I thee, short-armed is he. To the boring of this tree it will not well last.	*so may I thrive* *hole bored* *i.e., his arm; extend*

2ND JEW 186	Ah, therefore care thee nought. A sleight I have sought. Ropes must be bought to strain him with strength.	*don't worry* *trick; discovered* *force*

3RD JEW 190	A rope, as I bethought, ye shall have in brought.	*took thought*

161–64 "Let's get to it quickly. I've untied this wretch. He'll be cruelly twisted before I go away."

165–68 "Here's a rope that'll bear the strain to stretch him to the beam. This hypocrite never endured such a terrible act."

Take it here, well wrought,   *made*
and draw him a length.   *stretch*

Then they shall tie the cord to his left hand because the right
was nailed in earlier.

4TH JEW   Draws, for your father's kin,   *pull*
              while that I drive in
195   this ilk iron pin   *same*
              that I dare lay will last.   *wager; hold*

1ST JEW   As ever have I win,   *joy*
              his arm is but a fin.   *no thicker than a fin*
              Now drive on bouten din   *without more debate*
200   and we shall draw fast.   *pull hard*

Then three shall pull and the fourth shall drive the nail
through.

2ND JEW   Fellow, by this light,
              now were his feet dight,   *if his feet were fixed*
              this gamen went on right   *entertainment; properly*
              and up he should be raised.

3RD JEW   That shall be done in height   *at once*
206   anon in your sight,   *immediately*
              for, by my truth I plight,   *pledge*
              I serve to be praised.   *deserve*

Then they shall nail through his feet.

4TH JEW   Fellows, will you see
210   how I have stretched his knee?
              Why praise ye not me
              that have so well done?

1ST JEW   Yea, help now, that he
              on height raised be,*   *may be*
215   for, as mot I thee,   *so may I thrive*
              almost it is noon.   *the ninth hour*

---

214 Presumably at this point the cross is raised from its horizontal position on
the ground to the vertical.

Then Pilate, holding a tablet in his hand, shall speak.

PILATE	Come hither thou, I command thee.	
	Go nail this table unto the tree.	*tablet*
	Sithen he will King of Jews be	*since*
220	he must have a cognisance.	*identification*
	"Jesu of Nazareth" men may see;	
	"King of Jews"—how likest thee?—	*does it please*
	is written thereon, for so said he	
	without variance.	*unswervingly*
2ND JEW	Nay, Sir Pilate, to us bede.	*talk*
226	King is he none, so God me speed.	*prosper*
	Therefore thou dost a sorry deed;	
	this writing many a man rues.	*regrets*
	Thou should write that men might read	
230	how he lies to each lede	*person*
	and told overall thereas he yede	*everywhere; went*
	that he was King of Jews.	
PILATE	That that is written I have written.	*what*
3RD JEW	And in good faith that is foul written,	*badly*
235	for every man may well witten	*know*
	that wrong thou has wrought.	*done*
	What the Devil! King is he none!	
	But falsely thereas he hath gone	*wherever*
	he has told leasings many one,	*many lies*
240	that dear they should be bought.	*so that; paid for*

Then they shall all make merry in front of the cross; and Mary shall come, weeping.

MARY	Alas, my love, my life, my lee!	*joy*
	Alas now, mourning, woe is me!	*in my grief*
	Alas, son, my boot thou be!	*be my remedy*
	Thy mother that thee bare	*bore*
245	think on, my fruit. I fostered thee	*child; suckled*
	and gave thee suck upon my knee.	
	Upon my pine thou have pity!	*torment*
	Thou failest no power.	*lack*
	Alas, why nill my life forlorn	*will not; be forfeit*
250	to find my son here me beforn	*before*

tugg-ed, lugg-ed, and all to-torn[*]
with traitors now this tide,   *by; time*
with nails thrust, and crown of thorn?   *pierced*
Therefore I mad, both even and morn,   *grow demented*
255   to see my birth that I have borne   *child*
this bitter bale to bide.   *suffering; endure*

My sorrow, sweet son, thou cease,[*]   *bring to an end*
or of my life thou me release.   *from*
How should I apaid be or in in peace,   *contented*
260   to see thee in such penance?   *suffering*
Sith thou me to thy mother chose,   *since; for*
and of my body born thou was,
as I conceived thee wemless,   *sinlessly*
thou grant me some legiance.   *relief*

265   Alas, the sorrow of this sight
mars my mind, main and might,   *destroys; power*
but ay my heart methink is light   *always; seems to me*
to look on that I love.   *what*
And when I look anonright   *straightway*
270   upon my child that thus is dight,   *arrayed*
would death deliver me in height,   *at once*
then were I all above.   *would be; beyond everything*

Alas, my sorrow when will thou slake   *assuage*
and to these traitors me betake   *commit*
275   to suffer death, son, for thy sake,
and do as I thee say?
Alas, thieves, why do ye so?
Slays ye me, and let my son go—   *slay*
for him suffer I would this woe—
280   and let him wend away.   *go*

MARY MAGD. Alas, how should my heart be light
to see my seemly Lord in sight   *gracious*

---

251 "Tugged about, dragged round and torn to pieces."

257–72 This and the following stanza are found only in the 1607 manuscript.
They express the special role of the Virgin Mary as the elect of God, entitled to
special favour, and participant in the Passion of Jesus. Possibly, therefore, their
omission in the other manuscripts indicates Protestant censorship.

	dolefully drawn and so dight	*pulled; arrayed*
	that did never man grievance?	
285	Marred I am main and might	*destroyed; power*
	and for him fails me to fight;	*I am unable*
	but God, that rules ay the right,	*always; what is right*
	give you mickle mischance.	*great misfortune*

MARY	Alas, sorrow sits me sore!	*lies sorely upon*
JACOBI*	Mirth of thee I get no more.	*joy*
291	Why wouldst thou die, Jesu, wherefore,	
	that to the dead gave life?	
	Help me, Jesu, with some thing	
	and out of this bitter bale me bring,	*suffering*
295	or else slay me for anything	
	and stint me of this strife.	*keep me from; anguish*

MARY	Come down, Lord, and break thy bands!	*bonds*
SALOME*	Loose and heal thy lovely hands!	
	Or tell me, Jesu, for whom thou wonds,	*hesitates*
300	sith thou art God and Man.	*since*
	Alas, that ever I born was	
	to see thy body in such a case.	*situation*
	My sorrow will never slake nor cease,	*slacken*
	such sorrow is me upon.	

ANNAS	Now this shrew is hoven on height	*wretch; raised; high*
306	I would see, for all his sleight,	*cunning*
	for his crown how he can fight	
	and far from us to flee.	*(how he can) flee*
	He that has healed so many one	
310	now save himself, if that he can,	*should now save*
	and then all we shall lieve him upon	*believe*
	that it is soothly so.	*truly*

JESUS	Father of Heaven, if thy will be,	
	forgive them this they done to me;	*do*

288+SH *Mary Jacobi* is the mother of James the Less and of Joseph (see Mark 15.40) and may in fact be another name for Mary Cleopas, wife of the Cleopas who is possibly to be identified with one of the disciples on the road to Emmaus (see play 19).

296+SH *Mary Salome* is said by Mark to have ministered to Christ in Galilee and was a witness of the empty tomb (see Mark 16.1).

315	for they be blind and may not see	
	how foul they done amiss.	*wickedly they do wrong*
CAIAPHAS	If thou be of such posty,	*power*
	and God's Son in majesty,	
	come down, and we will lieve on thee	*believe*
320	that it soothly so is.	*truly*
1ST THIEF	If thou be Christ verray	*the true Christ*
	and God's Son, now as I say,	
	save us from this death today	
	and thyself also.	
2ND THIEF	Ah, man, be still, I thee pray!	
326	Dread God, I read thee, ay,	*fear; advise; always*
	for follily thou speakest, in fay.	*foolishly; truly*
	Make not thy friend thy foe.	
	Man, thou wottest well, iwiss,	*know; indeed*
330	that rightwisely we suffer this,	*rightfully*
	for he hath not done so much amiss	*such great wrong*
	to suffer so great annoy.	*torment*
	But, Lord, I beseech thee,	
	when thou art in thy majesty,	*position of power*
335	then that thou wilt think on me,	
	and on me have mercy.	
JESUS	Man, I tell thee, in good fay,	*truly*
	for thy belief is so verray,	*faith; true*
	in Paradise thou shalt be today	
340	with me there in my bliss.	
	And woman, to thee also I say ,	*i.e., Virgin Mary*
	by thee thy son there thou see may	*your own son*
	that clean virgin has been ay	*pure; always*
	right as thyselven is.	*you yourself are*
345	And John, there thy mother thou may see.	
JOHN	Yea, Lord. Her keeper I shall be.	*guardian*
	Welcome Mary, mother free;	*noble*
	together we must go.	
MARY	Alas, my heart will brast in three!	*break*
350	Alas, Death, I conjure thee!	*solemnly invoke*

	The life, son, thou take from me	
	and twin me from this woe.	*separate*

JOHN	Comfort thee now, sweet Mary,	
	for though we suffer this annoy,	*unhappiness*
355	sister, I tell thee sickerly,	*certainly*
	on live thou shalt him see	*alive*
	and rise with full victory	
	when he has fulfilled the prophecy.	
	Thy son thou shalt see, sickerly,	*certainly*
360	within these days three.	

JESUS	Eloi, eloi, eloi, eloi!	
	My God, my God, I speak to thee!	
	Eloi lama sabachthani!	
	Why has thou thus forsaken me?*	

| 1ST JEW | Ah, hark, hark how he crieth upon Ely* | |
| 366 | to deliver him of his annoy. | *trouble* |

| 2ND JEW | Abide, and we shall see in hie | *quickly* |
| | whether Ely dare come here. | |

| JESUS | My thirst is sore, my thirst is sore. | |

3RD JEW	Yea, thou shalt have drink therefore	*for it*
371	that thou shalt list to drink no more	*desire*
	of all this seven year.*	*for*

JESUS	Mighty God in majesty,	
	to work thy will I would never wand.	*hesitate*
375	My spirit I betake to thee;	
	receive it, Lord, into thy hand.	

Consummatum est.*

361–64 Quoted from Mark 15.34.

365 *Ely* is misinterpreted by the Jews as a reference to the prophet Elijah.

370–72 Evidently here Jesus is offered the sponge of vinegar and hyssop; see Matthew 27.48, and John 19.29.

376+Latin I.e., "It is finished," John 19.30.

CENTURION	Lordings, I say you sickerly,*	*gentlemen; for sure*
	this was God's Son Almighty.	
	No other, forsooth, lieve will I,	*truly; believe*
380	for needs so it must be.	*necessarily*
	I know by manner of his cry	
	he has fulfilled the prophecy	
	and godhead showed apertly	*shown clearly*
	in him—all men may see.	
CAIAPHAS	Centurio, as God me speed,	*centurion; prosper*
386	thou must be smutted—thou canst not read!	*cracked; give advice*
	But when thou seest his heart bleed,	
	let's see what thou can say.	
	Longeus, take this spear in hand*	
390	and put from thee—look thou ne wand.*	
LONGINUS	Ah, lord, I see ne sea ne land	*have seen; neither; nor*
	this seven year, in good fay.	*truly*
4TH JEW	Have this spear and take good heed.	
	Thou must do, as the Bishop thee bede,	*commands*
395	a thing that is of full great need.	*necessity*
	To warn I hold thee wood.	*resist; mad*
LONGINUS	I will do as ye bid me,	
	but on your peril it shall be.	*at*
	What I do I may not see,	
400	whether it be evil or good.	

Then Longinus shall pierce Christ's side with a spear, saying:

	High King of Heaven, I thee here.	*praise*
	What I have done well wot I nere,	*know; never*
	but on my hand and on my spear	

377ff There is a different version of the same episodes here following in the 1607 manuscript; see Lumiansky-Mills 1974, Appendix 1C.

389 John 19.34 mentions the piercing of Christ's side by a soldier, but it is the apocryphal Gospel of Nicodemus that names the soldier as Longinus. Legends accumulated around him. Here he becomes a type of the Gentiles, redeemed from spiritual blindness by Christ's Passion and their faith.

390 "Strike away from you—look that you don't hesitate."

	out water runneth throw;	*flows out strongly*
405	and on my eyes some can fall	*has fallen*
	that I may see both one and all.	
	Ah, Lord, wherever be this wall	*well-spring*
	that this water came fro.	*from*

	Alas, alas, and weal-away!	*misery*
410	What deed have I done today?	
	A man I see, sooth to say,	*truth*
	I have slain in this stid.	*place*
	But this I hope be Christ verray	*think; may be; true*
	that sick and blind has healed ay.	*always*
415	Of mercy, Lord, I thee now pray,	*for*
	for I wist not what I did.*	*knew*

	Jesu, much have I heard speak of thee,	
	that sick and blind through thy pity	
	has healed before in this city	
420	as thou has me today.	
	Thee will I serve, and with thee be,	
	for well I lieve in days three	*believe*
	thou will rise full in posty	*in full power*
	from enemies. Lord, I thee pray.	*pray to*

JOSEPH*	Ah, Lord God, what hearts have ye	
426	to slay this man that I here see	
	dead, hanging upon rood-tree,	*a cross*
	that never yet did amiss.	*wrong*
	For, sickerly, God's Son is he.	*certainly*
430	Therefore a tomb—is made for me—	*(that) is*
	therein his body buried shall be,	
	for he is King of Bliss.	

NICODEMUS*	Sir Joseph, I say sickerly	*certainly*
	this is God's Son Almighty.	
435	Go ask at Pilate his body,	*from*

415–16 Compare 313–16 above.

424+SH *Joseph* of Arimathea is praised in all gospels as a Jew and a just man, and a disciple of Christ.

432+SH *Nicodemus* is identified in John 19.29 with a Pharisee who came to Jesus at night and who subsequently defended Jesus against his fellow Pharisees.

	and buried shall he be.	
	I shall help thee, witterly,	*certainly*
	to take him down devoutly,	
	though Caiaphas go horn-wood thereby,	*stark mad at it*
440	and all his meny.	*retinue*

Then Joseph of Arimathia shall come to Pilate and shall say:

JOSEPH	Sir Pilate, special I thee pray	*particularly*
	a boon thou grant me as thou may.	*request*
	This prophet that is dead today,	
	thou grant me his body.	

PILATE	Joseph, all ready, in good fay!	*truly*
446	If that Centurio he will say	*the centurion*
	that he is dead withouten nay,	*without denial*
	him will I not deny.	*refuse*

Centurio, is Jesus dead?

CENTURION	Yea, sir, as broke I my head,	*so may my head break*
451	in him there is no life led,	*remaining*
	for I stood thereby.	*alongside*

PILATE	Joseph, take him then to thee	
	and bury him where thy will be.	*it may be your wish*

JOSEPH	Grammercy, sir, pardee.	*thank you; truly*
456	I thank you heartfully.	*sincerely*

Then Joseph shall go on to the Mount (of Calvary), and shall say:

	Ah, sweet Jesu, sweet Jesu,	
	as thou art God, faithful and true,	
	in a tomb is made full new	*(that) is*
460	thy body shall in be laid.	
	Shouldst thou never have such virtue	
	as thou hast showed since I thee knew	
	but if godhead thy deeds should show	
	as thou before has said.*	

461–64 "You would never have such power as you have displayed since I knew

465   Therewith, Jesu, come hither to me.   *having so said*
                Thy blessed body buried shall be
                with all worship and honesty   *honour;propriety*
                and mensk—all that I may.   *honour*
                Yet hope I within these days three   *think*
470   in flesh and blood alive to see
                thee that art nail-ed on a tree
                unworthily today.   *without justification*

NICODEMUS   Joseph, brother, as I well see,
                this holy prophet is given to thee.
475   Some worship he shall have of me   *from*
                that is of might-es most.   *greatest in powers*
                For as I lieve by my lewty,   *believe;faith*
                verray God's Son is he,   *Son of the true God*
                for wondrous sights men might see
480   when that he yield the ghost.   *gave up his spirit*

                For the sun lost all his light;
                earthquake made men afright;   *afraid*
                the rock that never before had clight   *split*
                clave, that men might know;   *split*
485   graves opened in men's sight;
                dead did rise. Therefore, by right,   *rightly*
                I may say this was God's Son Almight   *almighty*
                that so great signs can show.   *displayed*

                Therefore here brought have I
490   a hundred pounds of spicery.   *spices*
                Myrrh, aloes, and many more thereby   *in addition*
                to honour him with I bring,
                for to balm his sweet body   *anoint*
                in sepulchre for to lie,
495   that he may have on me mercy
                in Heaven where he is King.

THE END

---

you, unless your deeds should demonstrate divinity, as you have said before."

PLAY 17: THE HARROWING OF HELL

Performed by the Cooks

"HE DESCENDED into hell." The stark and rather enigmatic article of the
Apostles' Creed rests on only slight biblical evidence—Jesus's words to
the penitent thief in Luke 23.43; the resurrection of the saints at the time
of Jesus's resurrection in Matthew 27.52–53; and his preaching to the
spirits in prison mentioned in I Peter 3.18–20. But the ultimate authority
is the descent into hell described in the second part of the apocryphal
Gospel of Nicodemus, also called the Acts of Pilate. Like many such
apocryphal writings, this account found a place in the standard lections
of the Church. It is in the *Legenda Aurea* or "Golden Legend," and hence
in *A Stanzaic Life of Christ*, probably the immediate source of Chester's
play. This version furnishes the material for most of the action of the
play, including the encounter in Eden.

As the ending and climax to the second day of performance, the
play affirms the triumph of God over the powers of darkness and evil
and the release of mankind from the bondage of sin. It is a play of
triumph, and one of spectacle also. Its central scene is hell itself with its
great gates, a dungeon of smoke, stench and darkness over which Satan
presides, sitting on his throne. By some unspecified means at the start of
the play, light is introduced into the darkness. Within the area specially
reserved for the prophets and patriarchs, limbo, we see figures from
previous ages—some, such as Adam and Simeon, familiar from earlier
plays. The approach of Jesus throws the diabolical company into confusion. There is a tremendous din, a triumphal shout or a roll or thunder,
as Jesus approaches—a very different figure from the crucified man who
hung on the cross in the previous play. He probably wears a red resurrection robe and carries the cross-staff with its banner that he also bears

in the following play. He must demand entry with authority and at his repeated command the gates of hell fall with a great crash. The first Adam and Jesus, the second Adam, are reconciled, the Devil is bound, and the redeemed leave hell. The procession of the redeemed to heaven is, however, by way of the earthly paradise of Eden where Adam meets the two prophets who will appear in the penultimate play, *Antichrist*, the next day and also the penitent thief who joins the procession in fulfilment of Jesus's promise to him in the previous play. Whether the action envisages a multi-level set in which the redeemed move from the lower hell to the higher Eden; or a separate location apart from the waggon; or a backdrop curtaining off hell, is not clear. There is no necessity to have a further location of heaven; this seems situated offstage.

[handwritten: So Dante]

In the 1607 manuscript, the play ends in triumph as the redeemed leave the stage singing the *Te Deum* while the Devil remains bound in a now empty hell. But in the other manuscripts there is a comic coda, changing the tone, as a Chester ale-wife enters, to receive punishment for her "sins" in contravening Chester's bylaws and defrauding her customers. Since the play was performed by the Cooks and the Innkeepers, this coda has particular immediate reference. It seems to belong to a period in 1533 when Chester's mayor, Henry Gee, re-enforced the laws controlling the quality and sale of alcohol in the city. But the ale-wife was also a figure in the midsummer show and hence introduces a more "popular" element which stands out strongly beside the preceding action and, in particular, the triumphant procession with its liturgical song.

Cast   ADAM, ISAIAH, SIMEON, JOHN THE BAPTIST, SETH, DAVID, SATAN, SECOND DEVIL, THIRD DEVIL, JESUS, MICHAEL, ENOCH, ELIJAH, THIEF, ALE-WIFE.

> *And at the start there shall be physical light in Hell contrived by some device, and then Adam shall speak.*

ADAM   Oh Lord and Sovereign Saviour,
          our comfort and our counsellor,
          of this light thou art author
          as I see well in sight.
5   This is a sign thou wilt succour
          thy folks that liven in great langour,   *people; misery*
          and of the Devil be conqueror,

	as thou hast yore beheight.	*long ago; promised*
10	Me thou madest, Lord, of clay, and gave me Paradise in to play; but through my sin, the sooth to say, deprived I was therefro, and from that weal put away, and here have long-ed sithen ay	*truth of it joy dwelt; since; ever*
15	in thesterness both night and day, and all my kind also.	*darkness lineage*
	Now, by this light that I now see, joy is comen, Lord, through thee, and on thy people thou hast pity	*come*
20	to put them out of pain. Sicker, it may none other be, but now thou hast mercy on me, and my kind through thy posty thou wilt restore again.	*certainly* *lineage; power*
ISAIAH 26	Yea, sickerly, this ilk-e light comes from God's Son Almight, for so I prophesied aright while that I was living. Then I to all men beheight,	*certainly; same almighty rightly* *promised*
30	as I ghostly saw in sight, these words that I shall to my might rehearse without tarrying:	*spiritually beheld as best I can*

"Populus qui ambulabat in tenebris vidit lucem magnam."*

	"The people" I said that time express, "that yeden about in thesterness	*clearly went; darkness*
35	seen a full great lightness" — as we done now eachone. Now is fulfilled my prophecy that I, the prophet Isay, wrote in my book that will not lie,	*have seen; light do; all* *Isaiah*
40	whoso will look thereon.	*whoever wants to look at it*

32+Latin "The people that walked in darkness have seen a great light" (Isaiah 9.2).

SIMEON   And I, Simeon, sooth to say,   *truth*
                will honour God all that I may;   *as much as I can*
                for when Christ child was, in good fay,   *a child; truly*
                in temple I him took   *received*
45   and, as the Holy Ghost that day
                taught me or I went away,   *before*
                these words I said to God's pay   *delight*
                that men may find in book: *in the Bible*

                "Nunc dimittis servum tuum, domine, secundum ver-
                bum tuum, in pace."*

        paraphrase
                There I prayed, withouten leas,   *in truth*
50   that God would let me be in peace,
                for he is Christ that comen was—   *had come*
                I had both felt and seen—
                that he had ordained for Man's heal,   *remedy*
                joy to the people of Israel.   *as a source of joy*
55   Now is it won, that ilk weal,   *same happiness*
                to us, withouten ween.   *for us for certain*

JOHN BAPT.*   Yea, Lord, I am that prophet John
                that baptised thee in Flood Jordan   *the river*
                and prophesied to every nation
60   to warn of thy coming
                to bring the people to salvation
                by merit of thy bitter Passion,
                through faith and penance to have remission
                and with thee to have wonning.   *dwelling*

                "Penitentiam agite! Appropinquat enim regnum caelo-
                rum."*   *not trans*

48+Latin "Lord, now lettest thou thy servant depart in peace, according to thy
word" (Luke 2.29). See also play 11 167+SD-75.

56+SH *John the Baptist* was the son of Elizabeth. a kinswoman of the Virgin Mary;
see play 6. A prophet of the Messiah, his ministry of baptism in the wilderness
is described in all four gospels, and his baptism of Jesus in Matthew, Mark and
Luke. He was subsequently beheaded by Herod. Chester is the only one of the
four extant cycles that does not dramatise Jesus's baptism.

64+Latin "Repent ye; for the kingdom of Heaven is at hand" (Matthew 2.2).

65   And with my finger I showed express,   *clearly*
          when I lived in wilderness
          a lamb in tokening of thy likeness,*
          our ransom for to be.
          At thy coming we had forgiveness;
70   Mercy concluded Righteousness.   *fulfilled. Justice*
          Wherefore these words I do rehearse   *repeat*
          with honour unto thee:

          "Ecce agnus Dei, qui tollit peccata mundi."*
                                    not trans

SETH*   And I, Seth, Adam's son, am here
          that living went, withouten were,   *truthfully*
75   to ask at Paradise a prayer   *make a request*
          at God, as I shall say: *from*
          that he would grant an angel in hie   *quickly*
          to give me oil of his mercy   *out of*
          to anoint my father in his annoy   *distress*
80   in sickness when he lay.

          Then to me appeared Michael
          and bade me travail never a deal,   *labour not a bit*
          and said for reaming nor prayers fele   *grieving; many*
          that grant me not to seek;   *he would not allow; beg*
85   nor of that oil might I have none,   *nor*
          made I never so much moan,   *however much complaint*
          till five thousand years were gone
5,500 ? Yrs.   and five hundred eke.   *also*

          As all kneel, David shall speak.

DAVID   Ah, high God and King of Bliss,
90   worshipped be thy name, iwiss!   *truly*
          I hope that time now comen is   *believe; come*
          delivered to be of langour.   *set free from misery*

---

67 "A lamb as an emblem of what you were like."

72+Latin "Behold the Lamb of God, which taketh away the sin of the world"
(John 1.29).

72+SH *Seth* was the third son of Adam and Eve. The reference here is to the
account, in the apocryphal Gospel of Nicodemus, of his visit to Eden to request
a drop of the oil of mercy to anoint the dying Adam and relieve his pain.

	Come, Lord, come to Hell anon	*quickly*
	and take out thy folks everychone,	*all your people*
95	for the years be all comen and gone	*come*
	sithen Mankind first came here.	*since*

Then Satan, sitting in his throne, shall speak to the devils.

SATAN	Hell-hounds all that been here,	*are*
	makes you boun with boast and bere,	*ready; strife*
	for to this fellowship in fere	*this whole company*
100	there hies a ferly freke.	*hastens; marvellous fellow*
	A noble morsel ye have mon—	*may have*
	Jesu, that is God's Son,	
	comes hither, with us to won.	*dwell*
	On him now ye you wreak.	*take vengeance*

105	A man he is fully, in fay,	*truly*
	for greatly death he dread today,	*feared*
	and these words I heard him say:	
	"My soul is thirst to death."	*thirsty unto death*
	Such as I made halt and blind,	*lame*
110	he has them healed into their kind.	*proper condition*
	Therefore this bluster look ye bind	*blusterer*
	in bale of Hell-breath.	*torment*

2ND DEVIL	Sir Satanas, what man is he	*Satan*
	that should thee prive of thy posty?	*deprive; power*
115	How dare he do against thee	*act*
	and dread his death today?	
	Greater than thou he seems to be,	
	for degraded of your degree	*cast down from; rank*
	thou must be soon, well I see,	
120	and priv-ed of thy prey.	*deprived*

3RD DEVIL	Who is he so stiff and strong	*brave*
	that so masterlike comes us among,	*dominating*
	our fellowship as he would fong?	*company; as if; seize*
	But thereof he shall fail!	*in that*
125	Wait he us with any wrong,	
	he shall sing a sorry song;	
	but on thee, Satan, or it be long,	
	and his will ought avail—*	

125–28 "If he should threaten us from any wrongful position, he shall sing a song

SATAN	Against this shrew that com-es here	*wretch*
130	I tempted the folk in foul manner.	*people; wickedly*
	Easel and gall to his dinner	*vinegar*
	I made them for to dight,	*prepare*
	and sithen to hang him on rood-tree.	*then; cross*
	Now is he dead, right so through me,	*even so*
135	and to Hell, as ye shall see,	
	he comes anon in height.	*immediately*

2ND DEVIL	Sir Satanas, is not this that sire	*Satan; fellow*
	that raised Lazar out of the fire?	*Lazarus*

SATAN	Yea, this is he that would conspire	*plot*
140	anon to reave us all.	*at once; rob*

3RD DEVIL	Out, out, alas, alas!	
	Here I conjure thee, Satanas,	*charge; Satan*
	thou suffer him not come in this place	*to come*
	for ought that may befall.	

2ND DEVIL	Yea, sickerly, and he come here,	*certainly; if*
146	passed is clean our power,	*completely*
	for all this fellowship in fere	*entire company*
	have home away he would;	*i.e., rightful place*
	for at his commandment	*command*
150	Lazar, that with us was lent,	*Lazarus; set*
	mauger our teeth away he hent	*despite our fangs; took*
	and him might we not hold.	

*Then Jesus shall come, and there shall be a cry, or a a great
physical din; and Jesus shall say:* "Attollite portas, principes,
vestras, et elevamini, portae aeternales, et introibit rex glori-
ae."*

JESUS	Open up Hell-gates anon,	*at once*
	ye princes of pine everychone,	*torment; all*
155	that God's Son may in gone,	*go*

---

of sorrow; but on you, Satan, before long, if his will prevails at all...." The threat,
and construction, are unfinished.

152+SD "Lift up your heads, O ye gates, and be ye lift up, ye everlasting doors,
and the King of Glory shall come in" (Psalms 23 [AV 24].7, 9).

and the King of Bliss.

2ND DEVIL	Go hence, popelard, out of this place	*fool*
	or thou shalt have a sorry grace.	*miserable fate*
	For all thy boast and thy menace	*despite; threats*
160	these men thou shalt miss.	*lack*
SATAN	Out, alas! What is this?	
	See I never so much bliss	*saw; joy*
	towards Hell come, iwiss,	*truly*
	sithen I was warden here.	*since; keeper*
165	My masterdom fares amiss,	*supremacy; goes wrong*
	for yonder a stubborn fellow is,	
	right as wholly Hell were his,	*just as if; entirely*
	to reave me of my power.	*rob*
3RD DEVIL	Yea, Satanas, thy sovereignty	*Satan; royal power*
170	fails clean. Therefore thou flee,	*completely*
	for no longer in this see	*seat*
	here shalt thou not sit.	
	Go forth! Fight for thy degree!	*position*
	Or else our prince shall thou not be;	
175	for now passes thy posty	*passes away; power*
	and hethen thou must flit.	*hence; go*

Then Satan, rising from his seat, shall speak.

SATAN	Out, alas! I am shent!	*destroyed*
	My might fail-es, verament.	*power; truly*
	This prince that is now present	
180	will pull from me my prey.	
	Adam by mine enticement,	
	and all his blood, through me were shent.	*lineage; utterly lost*
	Now hethen they shall all be hent,	*hence; taken*
	and I in Hell for ay.	*I (shall be); ever*
DAVID	I, King David, now well may say	
186	my prophecy fulfilled is, in fay,	*truly*
	as now shows in sight verray,	*appears true*
	and soothly here is seen.	*truly*
	I taught men thus here in my life-day	
190	to worship God by all way,	*in every way*
	that Hell-gates he should affray	*attack*
	and win that his hath been.	*those who*

"Confiteantur domino misericordiae eius et mirabilia eius, filiis hominis contrivit portas aereas et vectes ferreas confregit."*

Then Jesus shall speak again.

JESUS	Open up Hell-gates, yet I say,	*still*
	ye princes of pine that be present,	*torment*
195	and let the King of Bliss this way	*(pass) this way*
	that he may fulfill his intent.	

SATAN	Stay! What, what is he, that King of Bliss?

DAVID	That Lord the which Almighty is—	
	in war no power like to his;	
200	of Bliss is greatest King.	*(he) is*
	And to him is none like, iwiss,	*indeed*
	as is soothly seen by this,	*truly*
	for men that sometime did amiss	*once committed sin*
	to his bliss he will them bring.	

At this point the patriarchs are taken out. (Here must God take out Adam.)

JESUS	Peace to thee, Adam, my darling,	
206	and eke to all thy offspring	*also*
	that rightwise were on Earth living.*	
	From me now ye shall not sever.	
	To bliss now I will you bring	
210	there you shall be, without ending.	*where*
	Michael, lead these men singing*	
	to bliss that lasteth ay.	*for ever*

192+Latin "Oh that man would praise the Lord for his goodness, and for his wonderful works to the children of men! For he hath broken the gates of brass, and cut the bars of iron in sunder" (Psalms 106 [AV 107].14–16). The gates evidently fall at the end of Jesus's speech.

207 "Who were righteous while they were living on earth."

211 *Michael* was an archangel (cf. Jude 9) who, as the defender of Israel against the powers of evil, is regarded as the champion of the righteous against the Devil. In play 23 he slays Antichrist.

MICHAEL	Lord, your will done shall be.
	Come forth, Adam, come with me.
215	My Lord upon the rood-tree

MICHAEL   Lord, your will done shall be.
         Come forth, Adam, come with me.
215   My Lord upon the rood-tree   *cross*
         your sins hath forbought.   *redeemed*
         Now shall ye have liking and lee,   *pleasure and joy*
         and be restored to your degree   *position*
         that Satan with his subtlety   *(you) who; cunning*
220   from bliss to bale had brought.   *torment*

*Then Michael shall lead out Adam and the saints to Paradise, and Enoch and Elijah and the Redeemed Thief shall meet them.**

SATAN   Out, alas! Now goes away   *go*
         all my prisoners and my prey,
         and I myself may not start away,   *withdraw*
         I am so straitly tied.   *closely*
225   Now comes Christ. Sorrow I may   *grieve*
         for me and my meny for ay.   *company; ever*
         Never, sithen God made the first day,   *since*
         were we so sore afraid.

*Here Adam must speak to Enoch and Elijah.**

ADAM   Sirs, what manner of men been ye   *kind of; are*
230   that bodily meet us, as I see,   *in the flesh*
         that dead came not to Hell as we,   *being dead*
         sithen all men damn-ed were?   *since*
         When I trespassed, God hight me   *sinned; promised*
         that this place closed should be
235   from earthly men to have entry,   *mortal*
         and yet I find you here.

220+SDff. The encounters in the Earthly Paradise are described in the apocryphal Gospel of Nicodemus and transmitted through the *Legenda Aurea*.

228+SD *Enoch and Elijah* Both these Old Testament figures were assumed bodily into the after-life. The abrupt exit of Enoch, father of Methuselah, in Genesis 5.25, was interpreted by Paul as a bodily translation (Hebrews 11.5); Elijah the Tishbite, the opponent of the priests of Baal, was bodily assumed in a whirlwind, as described in 4 (AV 2) Kings 2.11. Both have here been preserved in the Earthly Paradise of Eden to await the coming of Antichrist (see play 23), and the dialogue that follows clearly occurs when the procession of the redeemed from hell has reached that place.

ENOCH	Sir, I am Enoch, the sooth to say,	*truth*
	put in this place to God's pay;	*at God's pleasure*
	and here have lived ever since ay	*always*
240	at liking all my fill.	*fully at my pleasure*
	And my fellow here, in good fay,	*companion; truly*
	is Ely the prophet, see ye may,	*Elijah*
	that ravished was in this array*	*taken up; guise*
	as it was God's will.	

ELIJAH	Yea, bodily death, lieve thou me,	*physical; believe*
246	yet never suffered we,	
	but here ordained we are to be	
	till Antichrist come with his.*	*shall come; his own*
	To fight against us shall he	*he shall fight*
250	and slay us in the Holy City;	*i.e., Jerusalem*
	but sickerly, within days three	*certainly*
	and half, we shall rise.	

ADAM	And who is this that comes here	
	that lives with you in this manner?	*in this way*

THIEF	I am that thief, my father dear,	
256	that hung on rood-tree.	*a cross*
	For I believed withouten were	*because; without doubt*
	that Christ might save us both in fere,	*together*
	to him I made my prayer,	*offered*
260	the which was granted me.	
	When I see signs full verray	*saw; most true*
	that he was God's Son, sooth to say,	*truth*
	to him devoutly did I pray,	
	in his region when he come	*kingdom; should come*
265	that he would think on me alway;	*always*
	and he answered and said: "This day	
	in Paradise thou shalt with me play."	*rejoice*
	Hitherward I nome.	*here; went*

---

243 *this array*—cf. "He was an hairy man, and girt with a girdle of leather about his loins," 4 (AV 2) Kings 1.8.

248 On *Antichrist*, see further, play 23. The exact reference of *his* is uncertain—"kingdom," "followers" or "deeds" could be understood.

270	Then he betaught me this tokening,	*granted; sign*
	this cross upon my back hanging,	
	to Michael angel for to bring,	*the angel*
	that I might have entry.	

ADAM   Now go we to Bliss, old and young,

      and worship God all-willing;   *who wills everything*

275   and thitherward I read we sing   *going there; propose*

      with great solemnity.

   Then they shall all go, and Michael shall begin "Te Deum
   laudamus." *

ALE-WIFE Woe be the time that I came here!*

      I say to thee now, Lucifer,

      with all thy fellowship in fere,   *company together*

280   that present be in place:

      woeful am I with thee to dwell,

      Sir Satanas, sergeant of Hell.   *Satan; controller*

      Endless sorrow and pains cruel

      I suffer in this case.   *situation*

285   Sometime I was a taverner,   *once*

      a gentle gossip and a tapster, *courteous companion*

      of wine and ale a trusty brewer,

      which woe hath me wrought. *produced misery for me*

      Of cans I kept no true measure.   *pots*

290   My cups I sold at my pleasure, *priced as I liked*

      deceiving many a creature.

      Tho my ale were nought. *then; would be rubbish*

      And when I was a brewer long,

      with hops I made my ale strong;

276+SD "We praise you, Oh God," the opening of a celebratory hymn sung at Matins. The whole hymn would, of course, be sung by the procession of the redeemed.

277ff. The "Ale-wife Episode" is omitted in the 1607 manuscript, perhaps on the grounds of decorum. The Wife was in breach of the Chester bylaws controlling the standards and sale of alcohol as re-enacted in 1533. Her abuses include short measures, excessive pricing for poor-quality ale, and the use of prohibited additives—including hops—to give the illusion of strength to poor ale. Ironically, the performing company included the Chester inn-keepers.

295	ashes and herbs I blend among	*mixed in*
	and marred so good malt.	*such*
	Therefore I may my hands wring,	
	shake my cups, and cans ring.	*pots; rattle*
	Sorrowful may I sike and sing	*sigh*
300	that ever I so dalt.	*dealt*

	Taverners, tapsters of this city	*i.e., Chester*
	shall be promoted here with me	
	for breaking statutes of this country,	*region*
	hurting the common weal,	*harming the general good*
305	with all tippers-tappers that are cunning,	
	mis-spending much malt, brewing so thin,	
	selling small cups money to win,	
	against all truth to deal.*	

	Therefore this place now ordained is	
310	for such ill-doers so much amiss.	*(who do) so much*
	Here shall they have their joy and bliss,	
	exalted by the neck,	*raised high*
	with my master, mighty Mahound,	
	for casting malt besides the comb,	
315	much water taking for to compound,	
	and little of the seck—	

	with all mashers, mengers of wine, in the night	
	brewing so, blending against day-light.*	
	Such new-made claret is cause full right	*certainly*
320	of sickness and disease!	
	Thus I betake you, more and less,*	
	to my sweet master, Sir Satanas,	*Satan*
	to dwell with him in his place	
	when it shall you please.	

305-8 "With all barmen that are good at cheating, wasting much malt, brewing such watery beer, selling short measures to make more profit, trading contrary to all honest practice."

314-18 "For throwing malt so that some falls outside the vat, taking a lot of water to mix the ale and taking little out of the malt-sack—with all brewers, wine-blenders, who so brew during the night in preparation for day-time."

321 "So I commit you, great and small."

SATAN   Welcome, dear daughter, to us all three.
326   Though Jesu be gone with our meny,   *company*
             yet shalt thou abide here still with me
             in pain without end.

2ND DEVIL   Welcome, sweet lady! I will thee wed!
330   For many a heavy and drunken head
             cause of thy ale were brought to bed   *because of*
             far worse than any beast.   *(in a condition)*

3RD DEVIL   Welcome, dear darling, to endless bale!   *torment*
             Using cards, dice and cups small,   *short measures*
335   with many false oaths, to sell thy ale—
             now thou shall have a feast!

THE END

PLAY 18: THE RESURRECTION

Performed by the Skinners

PLAY 18 began the third day's performances at Chester. It opens soon after the burial of Jesus on Good Friday, when a nervous Pilate is advised to set a guard at the tomb to prevent the disciples stealing the body, as briefly indicated in Matthew 27.62–66. After the setting of the watch, the action moves forward without indication to the morning of Easter Sunday following the account of the Resurrection and the visit of the Maries to the tomb in Matthew 28.1–8 and, for the visit of the Maries, Mark 16.1–8 and Luke 24.1–11. The stage-direction at Jesus's rising (154+SD(2)) specifies that he is to tread upon one of the swooning guards, a feature found also in art-representations. The laments of the Maries and the dialogue with the angels at the tomb look ultimately to a liturgical model, *Quem Quaeritis*, from which the earliest Christian drama, a sung Latin play, developed in the tenth century; our play will not have drawn directly upon that early play, but its influence persists in the tradition of vernacular drama.

The play continues with the race to the tomb by Peter and John as described in Luke 24.12 and more fully in John 20.2–10. This incident is used by the playwright to prompt Peter to voice his shame and penitence, which later find an outlet in his meeting with Jesus at the end of the play; that is an elaboration of a meeting mentioned only briefly in Luke 24.34 and 1 Corinthians 15.5. This later scene of repentance and forgiveness incorporates lines which seem to refer to Peter's traditional role as the first pope; possibly the end of the play, found in only two of the five manuscripts, was censored for that reason after the Reformation.

The play also incorporates a dilemma which arises from a conflict in the biblical sources. Whereas the three synoptic gospels describe the visit of the Maries to the tomb, John 20.11–18 concentrates upon what

seems to be a solitary visit by Mary Magdalen and the appearance to her
of the risen Christ whom she at first mistakes for the gardener. Incorpo-
rating both versions, the play presents Mary Magdalen first receiving the
news of the Resurrection, then unexpectedly expressing doubt (lines 364–
65), and finally remaining at the tomb in distress, apparently no longer
understanding the situation. Revision of the text may have produced this
inconsistency; the Post-Reformation Banns say that the play is "not
altered in many points from the old fashion." But a modern actress can
handle this confusion convincingly in terms of psychological stress and
emotion,

The focus of the action is obviously the sepulchre which, from
contemporary art and from the disposition of the soldiers, seems to have
been a table-tomb whose flat top slab lifts or slides to allow Christ to
stand and step out on to one of the soldiers. The two angels who precede
him seem to be choristers dressed in albs who sing an antiphon as the
tomb opens and, after the Resurrection, take up positions at either end of
the tomb. The meeting-place for the Priests and Pilate is a further location; possibly the tomb is curtained off. Their splendid robes contrast
with the garments of the Maries and the disciples. The Maries and
disciples take up positions perhaps at ground level to advance on and
retire from the tomb; and Jesus, with gilded face, now dressed in red and
carrying a cross-staff with a Resurrection banner on top, can re-enter and
leave on the waggon above, or at ground level to address them. The
empty tomb, with Peter kneeling before Jesus, forms the final tableau.

Cast   PILATE, CAIAPHAS, ANNAS, FIRST KNIGHT, SECOND KNIGHT, THIRD
KNIGHT, FIRST ANGEL, SECOND ANGEL, JESUS, MARY MAGDALEN, MARY
JACOBI, MARY SALOME, PETER, JOHN.

PILATE   Per vous, Sir Caiaphas,
                et vous, et vous, Sir Annas,
                et son disciple Judas
                qui le traison fait,
5   et grand luce de lucide
                a moi parfait delivere—
                <u>Notre Dame</u> fuit juge—
                pour louer roi elit.*

1–8 "By you, Sir Caiaphas, and you, and you Sir Annas, and his disciple Judas

You lords and ladies so lovely and lere,
10   you kemps, you known knights of kind,
        harkens all hitherward, my hest-es to hear,
        for I am most fairest and freshest to find,
        and most highest I am of estate;*
        for I am prince peerless,
15   most royal man of riches,
        I may deal and I may dress.   *dispose; set in order*
        My name is Sir Pilate.

        For Caesar, lord most of posty,   *in power*
        honoured my estate and my degree.   *position; rank*
20   When that they sent Jesus to me
        to deliver him to the dead,   *give him up to death*
        they cried on me all, with one voice—
        the Jews on me made piteous noise.
        I gave them leave to hang him on cross.
25   This was through Jews' read.   *advice*

        I dread yet lest he will us grieve,   *still; trouble us*
        for that I saw I may well believe—   *what*
        I saw the stones began to cleave   *split*
        and dead men up can rise.   *arose*
30   In this city all about
        was none so stern ne so stout   *brave; strong*
        that up durst look; for great doubt   *fear*
        they could so soon agrise.   *trembled*

        And therefore, Sir Caiaphas, yet I dread   *still fear*
35   lest there were peril in that deed.   *might be*
        I saw him hang on rood and bleed   *cross*
        till all his blood was shed.
        And when he should his death take,   *receive*
        the weather waxed wondrous black—

---

who committed treason, and the great light of brilliance to me perfectly revealed—Our Lady was judge—to praise the noble king." The language is corrupt and the exact reference of the lines and their appropriateness to the context are obscure.

9–13 "You lords and ladies so fair and beautiful, you champions, you knights renowned by nature, turn your ears this way to hear my commands, for I am the most handsome and splendid that might be found, and I am most noble in my position."

40 layt, thunder—and earth began to quake. *lightning*
 Thereof I am adread. *of that; afraid*

CAIAPHAS And this was yesterday, about noon?

PILATE Yea, Sir Bishop, this is one. *?the very same*
 To speak therefore we have to done. *must*
45 For I let bury him full soon*
 in a tomb of stone.
 And therefore, sirs, among us three
 let us ordain and oversee
 if there any peril be, *may be*
50 or we hence gone. *before; go*

CAIAPHAS Sir Pilate, all this was done,
 as we saw, after soon; *shortly afterwards*
 but betime at afternoon *in due time; in the*
 the weather began to clear.
55 And, sir, if it be your will,
 such words you let be still *unspoken*
 and speak of another skill, *matter*
 lest any man us hear.

ANNAS Yea, Sir Pilate, nought forthy *nevertheless*
60 I saw him and his company
 raise men with sorcery
 that long before were dead.
 For, and there be any more such laft, *if; left*
 which can of such witchcraft, *know*
65 if that body be from us raft, *taken*
 advise you well, I read. *think carefully I advise*

CAIAPHAS Yea, Sir Pilate, I tell you right. *rightly*
 Let us ordain many a hardy knight, *assign*
 well armed to stand and fight
70 with power and with force,
 that no shame to us befall. *so that*
 Let us ordain here among us all *decree*
 and true men to us call *trusty*
 to keep well the corse. *guard; body*

---

45 "For I allowed him to be buried straight away."

PILATE   Now, by Jesu that died on rood,   *the cross*
76   methink your counsel wondrous good.   *seems to me*
     The best men of kin and blood   *lineage*
     anon I will in.   *at once; will (summon)*
     Sir Colphram and Sir Jeragas-
80   Aroysiat, and Sir Jerophas,
     we pray you, sirs, here in this case   *situation*
     anon look you ne blin.   *at once; don't fail*

     Ah, my knights stiff and stern of heart,   *strong*
     you be bold men and smart.   *vigorous*
85   I warn you now at words short,   *in few words*
     with you I have to done.   *business to do*

1ST KNIGHT   Sir, we be here, all and sum,   *the whole company*
     as bold men, ready boun   *prepared*
     to drive your enemies all adown
90   while that we may stand.   *as long as*

     We be your knights everychone.   *are; all*
     Faintness in us there shall be none.   *cowardice*
     We will be wroken upon thy fone   *avenged; foes*
     wherever he may be found—   *i.e., the enemy*
95   and for no dread that we will wand.*

PILATE   That I am well to understand.   *I fully understand*
     You be men doughty of hand;   *strong in hands*
     I love you without lack.   *fail*

     But that prophet that was done and draw
100   through the recounting of your Law—
     but yet something me stands in awe
     of words that he spake.*
     Forsooth, this I heard him say,   *truly*
     that he would rise the third day.
105   Now surely, and he so may,   *if*
     he hath a wondrous tack.   *power of endurance*

---

95 "And we shall not shrink from that for any fear."

99–102 "But that prophet that was put to death and drained of blood because of the reckoning of your Law—but still something about the words that he spoke puts me in fear." The construction is broken.

2ND KNIGHT	Yea, let him rise, if that he dare!	
	For, and I of him be aware,	*if*
	he bode never a worse chare,	*endured; fortune*
110	or that he wend away.	*before; might go*
	I helped to slay him ere-while.	*a time before*
	Weens he to do us more guile?	*does he think; deceit*
	Nay, it is no peril,	*danger*
	my head here dare I lay.	*wager*

3RD KNIGHT	Yea, let him quicken! Hardily,*	
116	whiles my fellows here and I	*whilst*
	may awake and stand him by,	*keep watch*
	he scapeth not uncaught.	*escapes; without capture*
	For, and he once heave up his head,	*if*
120	but that he be soon dead,	*unless*
	shall I never eat more bread	
	ne never more be saught.	*nor; at peace*

1ST KNIGHT	Have good-day, sir! We will be gone.	
	Give us our charge everychone.	*commission; all*

PILATE	Now farewell, the best of blood and bone,	
126	and takes good heed unto my saw.	*what I have said*
	For, as I am a Roman true,	
	if that you any treason sue,	*promote*
	there is none of you shall it eschew	*escape*
130	but he shall be to-draw.	*torn apart*

2ND KNIGHT	Now, fellows, we be charged hie.*	
	Our Prince hath sworn that we shall die	
	without any prophecy	*regardless of*
	or any other enchare	*?miracle*
135	but if we done as the wise.	*unless; act like wise men*
	I read us we right well advise.	*suggest; consider*
	Though he be bold, he shall not rise	*may be*
	but one of us be ware.	*without; being aware*

3RD KNIGHT	Sir, the most wit lieth in thee	*intelligence*

---

115 "Yes, let him come alive! Certainly."

131 "Now, fellows, we are ordered to make haste." The knights evidently leave
Pilate's court at this point to go to the tomb.

Shockingly cavalier attitude upon kead about from kead

140   to ordain and to oversee.

Ye been the eldest of us three,   are
and man of most renown.
The tomb is here at our hand.
Set us thereas we shall stand.   station; where
145   If that he rise, we shall fand   contrive
to beat him adown.

1ST KNIGHT   And I shall now set us so,   station
if that he rise and would go,   should rise
one of us, or else two,
150   shall see of his uprist.   rising
Stand thou there, and thou here,
and I myself in middle mere.   marking the centre
I trow our hearts will not fear   believe
but it were stoutly wist.*

not translated → *Then two angels shall sing "Christus resurgens a mortuis" etc. And Christ shall then rise again; and then, the singing having ended, he shall speak as follows:*

JESUS (*rising again, and he shall stir those knights with his foot*)
155   Earthly man that I have wrought,   mortal; created
awake out of thy sleep.
Earthly man that I have bought,   mortal; redeemed
of me thou take no keep.   take no heed
From Heaven Man's soul I sought
160   into a dungeon deep;
my dear leman from thence I brought,   beloved
for ruth of her I weep.   pity

I am very Prince of Peace   the true
and King of free mercy.   freely dispensed
165   Who will of sins have release,
on me they call and cry;
and if they will of sins cease
I grant them peace, truly,
and thereto a full rich mess   portion of food

---

154 The line seems obscure—?"but they would be known to be valiant."

154+SD "Christ rising from the dead"—both an antiphon and an Alleluia verse for Easter Day.

170   in bread—my own body.

I am very bread of life.   *the true*
From Heaven I light and am send.   *descended; sent*
Who eateth that bread, man or wife,   *woman*
shall live with me without end.
175   And that bread that I you give
your wicked life for to amend,
becomes my flesh through your belief   *faith*
and doth release your sinful bend.   *bond of sin*

And whosoever eateth that bread
180   in sin and wicked life,   *in (a state of)*
he receiveth his own death—
I warn both man and wife;   *woman*
the which bread shall be seen in stead
there joy is ay full rife.*
185   When he is dead, through fools' read   *advice*
then is he brought to pain and strife.   *suffering*

*Then the two angels, after Christ has risen again, shall sit in
the sepulchre; one of them shall sit at the head and the other at
the feet.*

1ST KNIGHT   Out, alas! Where am I?
So bright about is hereby   *it is hereabouts*
that my heart wholly
190   out of slough is shaken.   *out of my skin*
So foul feared with fantasy   *frightened by delusion*
was I never, in none annoy,   *no time of trouble*
for I wot not, witterly,   *know; truly*
whether I be on sleep or waken.   *may be; awake*

Then he shall make his companion get up.

2ND KNIGHT   Where art thou, sir bachelere?   *knight*
196   About me is wonder clear.   *marvellously bright*
Wit me wants, withouten were,

183–84 "This bread shall be displayed in a place where joy is ever fully abun-
dant." Though the general sense is that the effectiveness of the sacrament
pertains only to heaven, the exact meaning of the lines is obscure.

for fearder I never was.*
To remove far or near   *move away*
200   me fails might and power.   *I lack*
My heart in my body here
is hoven out of my breast.   *lifted up*

*Then he shall touch his companion and shall make him rise
from sleep.*

3RD KNIGHT   Alas, what is this great light
shining here in my sight?
205   Marred I am, both main and might;   *weakened; strength*
to move have I no main.   *strength*
These two beasts that are so bright—   *creatures*
power I ne have to rise aright—   *don't have; properly*
me fail with them for to fight,   *I am unable*
210   would I never so fain.   *however eager I might be*

1ST KNIGHT   Yea, we are shent, sickerly,   *ruined; certainly*
for Jesu is risen, well wot I,   *know*
out of the sepulchre mightily,
and thereof I have in mind.   *have it in memory*
215   And as dead here can I lie.   *as if; lay*
Speak might I not, ne espy   *nor*
which way he took, truly—
my eyes they were so blind.

2ND KNIGHT   Yea, I will creep forth upon my knee
220   till I this peril pass-ed be,
for my way I may not see,
neither earth ne stone.   *nor*
Yea, in a wicked time we
nailed him on the rood-tree.   *cross*
225   For as he said, in days three
risen he is and gone.

3RD KNIGHT   Hie we fast we were away   *hasten; that we might be*
for this is God's Son verray.   *true*
Strive with him we ne may   *may not*
230   that master is and more.   *a lord; greater*
I will to Caiaphas, by my fay,   *truly*

197–98 "Reason fails me, truly, for I was never more afraid."

the sooth openly for to say. *truth*
Farewell, sirs, and have good-day,
for I will go before. *ahead*

1ST SOLDIER We to leng here is no boot, *stay; remedy*
236 for needs to Sir Pilate we mot *necessarily; must go*
and tell him both crop and root *the whole story*
so soothly as we wist. *as truthfully; know*
For, and the Jews knew as well as we *if*
240 that he were risen through his posty, *power*
then should the last error be
worse than was the first.

Then they shall go to Pilate.

2ND KNIGHT Harkens, Sir Pilate! The sooth to sayn,*
Jesu that was on Friday slain
245 through his might is risen again.
This is the third day.
There came no power him to fet, *fetch*
but such a sleep he on us set
that none of us might him let *prevent*
250 to rise and go his way. *from rising*

PILATE Now by the oath that I have to Sir Caesar sworn
all you dog's sons beforn tomorn *before tomorrow*
shall die— therefore think no scorn.
If it be on you long,
255 if that you have privily
sold him to his company,
then are you worthy for to die
right in your own wrong.*

3RD KNIGHT Now by the order that I bear of knight,
260 he rose up in the morning light
by virtue of his own might.
I know it well afine. *completely*

---

243 "Listen, Sir Pilate! The truth to tell."

253–58 "Therefore do not regard this as a laughing matter. If the responsibility belongs to you, if you have secretly sold him to his disciples, then you deserve to die justly in your own crime."

	He rose up, as I say now,	
	and left us lying, I wot ne'er how,	*know never*
265	all bemased and in a swow,	*bemused; swoon*
	as we had been sticked swine.	*as if; speared*

PILATE	Fie, thief! Fie, traitor!	
	Fie on thee, thy truth is full bare!	*credibility; thin*
	Fie, fiend, fie, faitour!	*scoundrel*
270	Hie hence—fast I read that thou fare!*	

1ST KNIGHT	That time that he his way took	
	durst I neither speak nor look,	
	but for fear I lay and quoke,	*trembled*
	and lay in sound dream.	*deep trance*
275	He set his foot upon my back	
	and every lith began to crack.	*joint*
	I would not abide such another shack	*shock*
	for all Jerusalem.	

PILATE	Fie, harlot! Fie, hound!	*scoundrel*
280	Fie on thee, thou tainted taken dog!	*rotten captive*
	What! Lay thou still in that stound	*at that time*
	and let that losinger go so on thy rog?*	

	Sir Caiaphas and Sir Annas,	
	what say you to this trespass?	*crime*
285	I pray you, sirs, in this case	*situation*
	advise me of some read.	*with some counsel*

CAIAPHAS	Now, good sir, I you pray,	
	harkens to me what I you say—	
	for much avail us it may—	
290	and do after my spell.	*according to my words*
	Pray them now, sir, pardee,	*indeed*
	as they loven well thee,	*love*
	here as they standen all three,	*stand*
	to keep well our counsel.	

---

270 "Hasten hence—I advise you to travel fast."

282 "And let that liar tread on your back like that"; *rog* is obscure and the meaning of the line is therefore doubtful.

ANNAS	Sir Bishop, I say you verament,	*tell; truly*
296	unto your counsel I fully assent.	
	This foolish prophet that we all to-rent	*tore apart*
	through his witchcraft is stolen away.	
	Therefore let us call our council together	
300	and let us conclude to the whole matter,	*put an end*
	or else our laws are done for ever.	*destroyed*

PILATE	Now in good faith, full woe is me,	*I am most sorrowful*
	and so I trow been all ye,	*believe; are*
	that he is risen thus privily	*secretly*
305	and is from us escaped.	
	Now I pray you, sirs, as ye love me,	
	keep this in close and privity,	*concealed and secret*
	until our council, and till we,	
	have heard how he is scaped.	*has escaped*

Then he shall give them money, and they shall go. And the women shall come weeping and seeking Jesus.

MARY MAGD.	Alas, now lorn is my liking.	*lost; happiness*
311	For woe I wander and hands wring.	
	My heart in sorrow and sighing	
	is sadly set and sore.	*sorrowfully*
	That I most loved of all thing,	*things*
315	alas, is now full low lying.	
	Why am I, Lord, so long living	
	to lose thy lussom lore?	*happy teaching*

MARY	Alas, weal away is went!	*joy; gone*
JACOBI	My help, my heal from me is hent.	*joy; taken*
320	My Christ, my comfort, that me kent,	*taught*
	is clongen now in clay.	*enclosed*
	Mighty God Omnipotent,	
	thou give them hard judgement	
	that my Sovereign hath so shent,	*ruler; destroyed*
325	for so I may well say.	

MARY	Alas, now marred is all my might!	*weakened*
SALOME	My Lord, through whom that I was light	*made happy*
	shamefully slain here in my sight!	
	My sorrow is ay unsaught.	*always inconsolable*
330	Sith I may have no other right	*since*
	of these devils that have my Lord so dight,	*treated*

	to balm his body that is so bright	*anoint;fair*
	boist here have I brought.	*a box*

MARY MAGD.   Sister, which of us everychone   *all*
335   shall remove this great stone
                that lieth my sweet Lord upon,
                for move it I ne may?   *cannot*

MARY   Sister, mastery is it none.   *no great task*
JACOBI   It seems to me as he were gone.   *as if*
340   For on the sepulchre sitteth one,   *someone is sitting*
                and the stone away.   *(is)*

MARY   Two children I see there sitting—
SALOME   all of white is their clothing—
                and the stone besides lying.   *at the side*
345   Go we near and see.

Then they shall go and shall look into the sepulchre.

1ST ANGEL   What seek ye women here
                with weeping and unliking cheer?   *unhappy demeanour*
                Jesus, that to you was dear,
                is risen, lieve you me.   *believe*

2ND ANGEL   Be not afraid of us in fere,   *both*
351   for he is went, withouten were,   *gone;truly*
                as he before can you lere,   *taught*
                forth into Galilee.

1ST ANGEL   This is the place, therefore be apaid,   *content*
355   that Jesu our Lord was in laid.
                But he is risen as he said,
                and hethen went away.   *hence;gone*

2ND ANGEL   Hie you, for ought that may befall,*
                and tell his disciples all;
360   and Peter also say you shall   *tell*
                there find him that you may.   *wherever you may find*

MARY MAGD.   Ah, hie we fast for anything   *hasten;whatever*

---

358 "Make haste, no matter what may happen."

	and tell Peter this tiding.	*piece of news*
	A blessedful word we may him bring,	*blessed*
365	sooth if that it were.	*if it might be true*

| MARY
JACOBI | Yea, walk thou, sister, by one way
and we another shall assay
till we have met with him today,
my dearworth Lord so dear. | *try out*

beloved |

Then they shall leave, and shall walk around for a little while; and then they shall meet the disciples Peter and John.

MARY MAGD.	Ah, Peter and John, alas, alas!	
371	There is befallen a wondrous case.	*situation*
	Some man my Lord stolen has	
	and put him I wot not where.	*know*

| PETER | What? Is he removed out of the place | |
| 375 | in the which he buried was? | |

| MARY MAGD. | Yea, sickerly, all my solace | *certainly* |
| | is gone, and is not there. | |

JOHN	Peter, go we thither anon,	*at once*
	running as fast as we may gone,	*go*
380	to look who hath removed the stone	
	and whether he be away.	*gone*

PETER	Abide, brother, sweet John,	*wait*
	lest we meet with any fone;	*foes*
	but now I see none other one,	*no-one else*
385	to run I will assay.	*try*

Then they shall both run together, but John shall run more quickly than Peter; and he shall not enter the sepulchre.

JOHN	Ah, Peter, brother, in good fay,	*truly*
	my Lord Jesu is away,	*gone*
	but his sudary, sooth to say,	*shroud;truth*
	lying here I find	
390	by itself, as thou see may;	
	far from all other clothes it lay.	
	Now Mary's words are sooth verray,	*really true*
	as we may have in mind.	*may recall them*

PETER	Yea, but as God keep me from woe,	
395	into the sepulchre I will go	
	to look whether it be verray so	*really*
	as Mary to us can say.	*said*

Then he shall go into the sepulchre.

PETER	Ah, Lord, blessed be thou ever and oo,	*always*
	for as thou told me and other moe	*others more*
400	I find thou has overcome our foe	
	and risen art, in good fay.	*truly*

Then Peter shall speak in a sorrowing fashion.

PETER	Ah, Lord, how shall I do for shame—	*be able*
	that have deserved so much blame	
	to forsake thy sweet name—	
405	to meet with thee by any way;	
	I, that in penance and great annoy	*distress; anguish*
	my sweet Lord forsook thrie—	*three times*
	save endless hope of his mercy,	*except for*
	thereto trust I may.*	*in that*

410	For ne it were his great grace	*were it not for*
	and sorrow in heart that in me was,	
	worse I were than was Judas,	*would be*
	my Lord so to forsake.	

JOHN	Peter, comfort thee in this case,	*situation*
415	for sicker my Lord Jesu accepted has	*certainly*
	great repentance for thy trespass;	*sin*
	my Lord in heart will take.	*receive it in his heart*

	Go we seek Jesu anon on hie,	*immediately*
	one way thou, another way I.	

PETER	Yea, well I hope through his might	
421	my penance shall him please.	*repentance*

402–9 The reference is to Peter's denial of his discipleship to Christ after his
capture—an event not dramatised in the cycle, but extant in misplaced and
fragmentary form; see note to end of play 16, part 1.

Then they shall go off, one along one way and the other along another. The women shall come.

MARY MAGD.	Hethen will I never, sickerly.*	
	Till I be comforted of mine annoy	*in my distress*
	and know where he is readily,	*for certain*
425	here will I sit and weep.	

1ST ANGEL	Woman, why weepest thou so ay?	*constantly*

MARY MAGD.	Son, for my Lord is taken away	*because*
	and I wot ne'er, the sooth to say,	*know never; truth*
	who hath done that thing.	
430	Alas, why were I not dead today,	*might be*
	clought and clongen under clay,*	
	to see my Lord that here lay	*in order to*
	once at my liking.*	*once as I wish*

Then Jesus shall come, clad in an alb and carrying a cross-staff in his hands; and Mary Magdalen shall go to meet him as he approaches, speaking.

JESUS	Why weepest thou, woman? tell me why.	
435	Whom seekest thou so tenderly?	

MARY MAGD.	My Lord, sir, was buried hereby	*near here*
	and now he is away.	*gone*
	If thou hast done me this annoy,	*caused; anguish*
	tell me, lief sir, hastily	*good sir*
440	anon this ilk day.	*at once; same*

JESUS	Woman, is not thy name Mary?

MARY MAGD.	Ah, Lord, I ask thee mercy.

---

422 "I will never go away from here, truly."

431 "Held fast and enclosed beneath the ground."

433+SDff) The remainder of the play is found only in the manuscripts of 1600 and of 1607.

433+SD The *alb* is an ecclesiastical vestment of white cloth reaching down to the feet.

JESUS	Mary, touch not my body	
	for yet I have not been	
445	with my Father Almighty;	
	but to my brethren go thou in hie	*hastily*
	and of this thing thou certify	*give assurance*
	that thou hast soothly seen.	

	Say to them all that I will gone	*go*
450	to my Father that I came from—	
	and their Father; he and I all one.	*are entirely*
	Hie! Look that thou ne dwell.	*hasten; don't linger*

MARY MAGD.	Ah! Be thou blessed ever and oo!	*always*
	Now waived is all my woe.	*taken away*
455	This is joy to them and other moe.	*more*
	Anon I will go tell.	*at once*

Mary Magdalen shall go to Mary Jacobi and to Mary Salome.

MARY MAGD.	Ah, women, weal now wonnen is.	*joy; gained*
	My Lord Jesu is risen iwiss.	*truly*
	With him I spake a little ere this	*before now*
460	and saw him with mine ee.	*eye*
	My bale is turn-ed into bliss.	*grief*
	Mirth in mind there may none miss,	*joy; be lacking*
	for he bade warn that was his	
	to Heaven that he would flee.*	
MARY		
JACOBI	Ah, sister, go we search and see	
466	whether these words sooth be.	*may be true*
	No mirth were half so much to me	*joy would be worth*
	to see him in this place.	*(as) to see*
MARY		
SALOME	Ah, sister, I beseech thee	
470	with full mind wend we,	
	for fain methinks me list to flee	
	to see his fair face.*	

463–64 "For he gave orders to inform those who were his followers that he
intended to depart to heaven."

469–72 "Ah, sister, I beg you that we should go with strong resolve, for I seem
to want to fly eagerly to behold his beautiful face."

Then the women shall go, and Jesus shall come to meet them, speaking.

JESUS	All hail, women, all hail!	*greetings*

Then Mary Jacobi, making a curtsy, shall speak.

MARY
JACOBI
476

Ah, Lord, we lieven without fail   *believe; doubt*
that thou art risen us to heal, ≥ save   *gladden*
and waived us from woe.   *banished*

MARY
SALOME

480

Ah, welcome be thou, my Lord sweet!
Let us kiss thy blessed feet
and handle thy wounds that be so weet,   *moist*
or that we hence go.   *before*

JESUS

Be not afraid, women, of me,
but to my brethren now wend ye   *go*
and bid them go to Galilee;
there meet with me they mon.   *may*

MARY
JACOBI
487

Anon, Lord, done it shall be!   *at once*
Well is them this sight to see,   *happy are they*
for Mankind, Lord, is bought by thee   *redeemed*
and through thy great Passion.

MARY
SALOME
491

Peter, tidings good and new!
We have seen my Lord Jesu
on life, clean in hide and hue,[*]
and handled have his feet.

PETER

495

Yea, well is ye that have been true,   *happy are you*
for I forsware that I him knew.   *denied*
Therefore shame makes me eschew   *avoid*
with my Lord for to meet.

500

But yet I hope to see his face,
though I have done so great trespass.   *committed; sin*
My sorrow of heart known he has
and to it will take heed.
Thither as he buried was   *to that place where*

---

491 "Alive, pure in skin and complexion."

I will hie me to run apace   *hasten;fast*
of my sweet Lord to ask grace
of my foul misdeed.   *for*

*Then Jesus shall come to meet Peter. (Here Jesus cometh in
with a cross-staff in his hand.)*

JESUS   Peter, knows thou not me?

PETER   Ah, Lord, mercy I ask thee
             with full heart, kneeling on my knee.   *sincerely*
             Forgive me my trespass.   *sin*
             My faint flesh and my frailty   *weak*
510   made me, Lord, false to be;
             but forgiveness with heart free   *wholeheartedly*
             thou grant me through thy grace!   *please grant*

JESUS   Peter, so I thee behight   *assured*
             thou should forsake me that night.
515   But of this deed thou have in sight   *remember*
             when thou hast sovereignty.   *spiritual power*
             Think on thine own deed today,
             that flesh is frail and falling ay;   *always*
             and merciful be thou alway   *always*
520   as now I am to thee.

             Therefore I suffered thee to fall;   *for this reason*
             that to thy subjects hereafter all   *on*
             that to thee shall cry and call,
             thou may have minning.   *remembrance*
525   Sithen thyself fallen has,   *since*
             the more incline to grant grace.
             Go forth! Forgiven is thy trespass.   *sin*
             And have here my blessing.

THE END

---

516 Traditionally, Peter was the first pope and head of the Universal Church.
This may well be the reference of this and the following lines. It may also
suggest that this final section may have been partially censored in the common
exemplar after the Reformation and thus explain the omission of the last 95 lines
of the play in three of the manuscripts.

PLAY 19: EMMAUS

Performed by the Saddlers

PLAY 19 is a play about recognition. Whereas the first appearances of Jesus after the Resurrection in play 18 were in the context of the garden and the tomb, the three appearances in play 19 are more remote in time and place. The first encounter, with two travellers later the same day, is mentioned briefly in Mark 16.12, but more fully described in Luke 24.13–33. Hence, although Luke names only one of those encountered—Cleophas, perhaps husband of the sister of the Virgin Mary—it is always assumed that the other was Luke himself. The two are travelling to a village called Emmaus which is mentioned in the Latin heading to this play but never named in the text. Jesus joins them and offers reassurance, but they do not recognise him until he is persuaded to eat with them and breaks the bread as he had in the Last Supper; he then disappears. The two disciples return to Jerusalem. According to Mark, Jesus appeared to them "in another form," a phrase which seems to have been the origin of the medieval idea that he was dressed as a pilgrim, a tradition from liturgical drama where the episode was called *Peregrini*, "the pilgrims." Presumably therefore he is in the distinctive guise of a medieval palmer, with scrip and staff and a large hat turned up at the front.

The second problem of recognition arises on the evening of the same day, when Jesus appears to his disciples in a locked room in Jerusalem as described in Mark 16.14–18, Luke 24.33–49, and John 20.19–23. The disciples doubt the evidence of their eyes, fearing that they are seeing a ghost. To convince them, Jesus first displays his wounds, inviting the disciples to touch, and then eats and shares the food with them in a scene reminiscent of the Last Supper. Again he disappears, and the disciples go to Bethany.

Thomas, who was not with the other disciples, meets them and is sceptical of what they report. Accordingly, the third issue of recognition is resolved when Jesus appears in order to convince Thomas, as described in John 20.24–29. John indicates that this event occurred eight days after the previous appearances, but there is no sense of this passage of time in the play. Thomas's conviction through the material proof of feeling Jesus's wounds leads to the play's message for the contemporary audience: "Blessed are they that have not seen, but yet have believed" (John 20.29).

[handwritten margin note: Or in ✗ Most of the plays]

Probably this play once had a different form. The Post-Reformation Banns include in its contents Jesus's "often-speech to the woman," which has no counterpart in our text. The Pre-Reformation Banns call the waggon "The Castell of Emawse," which suggests that the set was the room in which Jesus makes his three appearances, representing locations successively in Emmaus, Jerusalem, and Bethany. The changes of location involve vacating the set and journeying at ground level; significantly, Cleophas and Luke meet the other disciples at a location outside the room, and similarly Thomas meets the disciples as they are journeying to Bethany. The result is three repeated manifestations on the same dramatic set. Jesus's disappearances may perhaps be effected by nothing more elaborate than stepping behind a curtain at the back of the waggon. The second disappearance is very abrupt and the text carries no indication of the disciples' reactions.

Although there are only six speaking parts, the play must require a cast of at least thirteen (Jesus, eleven apostles and Cleophas) for its performance.

Cast   LUKE, CLEOPHAS, JESUS, ANDREW, PETER, THOMAS.

LUKE*	Alas, now weal is went away.	*joy; gone*
	Mourn my master ever I may	
	that is now clongen under clay.	*enclosed*
	That makes my heart in care.	*puts; in sorrow*

Before 1 SH *Luke*, author of the third Gospel, from which the account of the meeting on the road to Emmaus is taken. That Gospel does not mention Cleophas's companion by name, and although it is usually assumed to be Luke by medieval authorities, historically—since Luke was a gentile—this seems unlikely. The speaker is never identified by name for the audience in the play.

5	Sorrow and sighing, the sooth to say,	*truth*
	makes me half dead, that is no nay.	*no denying*
	When I think on him both night and day	
	for doel I droop and dare.	*grief; mourn; tremble*

CLEOPHAS*	Yea, much mirth was in me	*joy*
10	my sweet sovereign when I might see,	
	and his liking lore with lee,*	
	and now so low is laid.	
	Brother, now is days three	
	sith he was nail-ed on the tree.	*since; cross*
15	Lord, whether he risen be,	*could he be*
	as he before hath said?	

LUKE	Lief brother Cleophas,	*dear*
	to know that were a coint case.*	
	Sith he through heart wounded was,	*since*
20	how should he live again?	

Johannine theme.

CLEOPHAS	If that he godhead in him has	
	and comen to buy Man's trespass,	*has come; redeem; sin*
	he may rise through his own grace	
	and his death to us gain.	*may be profitable*

LUKE	A misty thing it is to me	*difficult*
26	to have belief it should so be,	
	how he should rise in days three—	
	such wonders never was wist.	*known*

CLEOPHAS	Sooth thou sayest, now well I see.	*the truth*
30	Lieve may I not by my lewty!	*believe; faith*
	But God may of his majesty	*out of*
	do whatsoever him list.	*pleases him*

*Then Jesus shall come in the dress of a pilgrim and shall speak
to them.*

| JESUS | Good men, if your will were, | *might be* |

9+SH *Cleophas* is mentioned only here in the gospels.

11 "And his pleasant teaching with delight."

18 "To have that knowledge would be a strange thing."

	tell me in good manner	
35	of your talking—that in fere,	
	and of your woe wit I wold.*	

CLEOPHAS	Ah, sir, it seems to us here	
	a pilgrim thou art, as can appear.	*it seems*
	Tidings and tales all entire	*fully complete*
40	thou may hear— what is told	

	in Jerusalem that other day.	
	Thou, that walkest many a way,	
	may thou not hear what men do say	
	about thereas thou yede?	*wherever you go around*

| JESUS | What are those? Tell me, I thee pray. | *i.e., those tidings* |

LUKE	Of Jesus of Nazareth, in good fay,	*truly*
	a prophet to each man's pay	*delight*
	and wise in word and deed!	

	To God and Man wise was he,	*in the eyes of*
50	but bishops—cursen mot they be—*	
	damned him and nailed him on a tree,	*condemned; cross*
	that wrong never yet wrought.	*he who; did*

CLEOPHAS	Witterly, before weened we	*indeed; thought*
	that Israel he should have made free,	
55	and out of pain through his posty	*power*
	the people he should have brought.	

LUKE	Yea, sir, now is the third day	
	sith they made this affray,*	
	and some women thereas he lay	*at the place where*
60	were early in the morn	
	and feared us foul, in fay.	*frightened; truly*
	They told us he was stolen away,	

34–36 "Tell me courteously about your conversation—in company with you I
would like to know that, and about the source of your unhappiness."

50 "May they be accursed."

58 "Since they did this terrible thing."

and angels, as they can say,   *said*
the sepulchre sitting beforn.   *(were); in front of*

CLEOPHAS   Yea, sir, these women that heard I   *whom*
66   said he was risen readily,   *obviously*
and some men of our company   *from our group*
thither anon can go   *went at once*
and found it so, as is told of yore.   *of old*
70   And they said so, neither less nor more.   *exactly*
And yet our hearts are full sore   *sorrowful*
lest it be not so.

JESUS   Ah, fools, and feeble in good fay!   *weak in true faith*
Late to believe unto God's lay!   *slow; law*
75   The prophets before can thus say—   *said*
lieve you on this soothly—   *believe in; truly*
that it needs be alway   *ever be necessary*
Christ to suffer death, the sooth to say,   *(for); truth*
and to joy that lasteth ay   *for ever*
80   bring Man through his mercy.

And first at Moses to begin,
what he saith I shall you min: *remind you of*
that God was a greave within   *= bush (= Mary)*
that burned ay, as him thought;
85   The greave paired nothing thereby.*
What was that but Maid Mary   *the Virgin*
that bare Jesus sinlessly   *bore*
that Man hath now forbought.   *fully redeemed*

Also Isay said this: *Isaiah*
90   "As a woman comforts, iwiss,   *truly*
her child that hath done amiss
to amend, lieve ye me,   *make all well; believe*
so God would Man reconciled here   *desired; (to be)*
through his mercy, in good manner,   *graciously*
95   and in Jerusalem in bitter were   *distress*
forbought they should be."   *fully redeemed*

83–85 "That God was inside a bush that burned constantly, as it seemed to him.
The bush was in no way damaged by that." The ever-burning bush (Exodus
3.2ff.) was traditionally interpreted as a figure of the Virgin Birth.

↑ About trans left

"Quemadmodum mater consolatur filios suos, ita et ego
consolabor vos; et in Jerusalem consolabimini" (Isaiah,
chapter sixty six).*

CLEOPHAS	Ah, Lord give thee good grace,	*may the Lord*
	for greatly comforted me thou has!	
	Go with us to this place.	
100	A castle is hereby.	*village*

JESUS	Now, good men, soothly to say,	*truly*
	I have to go a great way.	
	Therefore at this time I ne may,	*may not (stay)*
	but I thank you heartily.	

LUKE	Sir, you shall in all manner	*in any event*
106	dwell with us at our supper,	
	for now night approacheth near.	
	Tarry here for anything!	*at all events*

Then Jesus shall go with them to the village.

CLEOPHAS	Now God forbid that we were	*should be*
110	so uncourteous to you here	*discourteous*
	for, save my lovely Lord of lere,	*countenance*
	thy lore is most liking.	*teaching; most pleasing*

LUKE	Sit down, sir, here, I you pray,	
	and take a morsel if you may,	
115	for you have walked a great way	
	sith today at noon.	*since*

JESUS	Gramercy, good men, in good fay.	*thank you; truly*
	To bless this bread, sooth to say,	*truth*
	I will anon in good array	*want; forthwith; properly*
120	rightly you beforn.	*in front of*

Then he shall break the bread and shall say:

	Eats on, men, and do gladly	*do (so)*
	in the name of God Almighty,	

96+Latin "As one whom his mother comforteth, so will I comfort you; and ye
shall be comforted in Jerusalem" (Isaiah 66.13).

for this bread blessed have I
that I give you today.

Then Jesus shall vanish.

LUKE   Gramercy, sir, sickerly!   *thank you; assuredly*
126   Now read I you be right merry.   *counsel; to be*
          What! Where is he that sat us by?
          Alas, he is away!

CLEOPHAS   Alas, alas, alas, alas!
130   This was Jesus in this place.
          By breaking the bread I knew his face,
          but nothing there before.   *before that*

LUKE   A burning heart in us he made,   *caused*
          for while he with us here was
135   to know him we might have no grace,
          for all his lussom lore.   *pleasing teaching*

CLEOPHAS   Go we, brother, and that anon,   *at once*
          and tell our brethren everychon.   *all*
          How our master is from us gone,
140   yea, soothly we may say.   *truly*

LUKE   Yea, we may make our moan   *lament*
          that sat with him in great wone   *hope*
          and we no knowledge had him upon   *about*
          till he was passed away.

*Then they shall go to the other disciples assembled together in
another place.*

CLEOPHAS   Ah, rest well, brethren one and all.   *be happy*
146   Wondrously is us befall!   *it has happened to*
          Our Lord and we were in a hall
          and him yet knew not we.

ANDREW   Yea, lieve thou well this, Cleophas,   *believe*
150   that he is risen that dead was
          and to Peter appeared has
          this day apertly.   *clearly*

LUKE   With us he was a long fit,   *period of time*

	and undid his Holy Writ;	interpreted; Scripture
155	and yet our wits were so knit	minds; formed
	that him we might not know. ⌉	

CLEOPHAS	Now sicker away was all my wit	certainly; mind
	till the bread was broken each bit;	
	and anon when he brake it	at once; broke
160	he vanished in a throw.	instant

PETER	Now we brethren all in fere,	together
	I read we hide us somewhere here,	advise; ourselves
	that Jews meet us not in no manner	by no way
	for malice, lieve ye me.	because of; believe

ANDREW	Leng we here in this place.	let us stay
166	Peradventure God will show us grace	perchance
	to see our Lord in little space	in a little while
	and comforted for to be.	

Then they shall all go within the hall, and Jesus shall come, standing in the midst of his disciples; and then he shall speak.

JESUS	Peace among you, brethren fair!	
170	Yea, dread you nought in no manner.	by any means
	I am Jesus, without were,	doubt
	that died on rood-tree.	the cross

PETER	Ah, what is he that comes here	
	to this fellowship all in fere	entire company
175	as he to me now can appear?	has appeared
	A ghost methink I see.	it seems

JESUS	Brethren, why are ye so fraid for nought	
	and noyed in heart for feeble thought? *	
	I am he that hath you forbought	fully redeemed
180	and died for Man's good.	benefit
	My feet, my hands you may see;	
	and know the sooth also may ye,	truth
	soothly that I am he	truly

177–78 "Brethren, why are you so afraid for nothing at all and troubled in your hearts because of your weak-mindedness?"

	that dead was upon a rood.	*cross*
185	Handle me, both all and one,	
	and lieve well this everychone:	*believe; all of you*
	that ghost hath neither flesh ne bone	*nor*
	as you see now on me.	

ANDREW	Ah, Lord, much joy is us upon!	
190	But what he is wot I ne can.	*I do not know*

JESUS	Now sith you lieve I am no man,	*since; believe*
	more signs you shall see.	
	Have you any meat here?	*food*

PETER	Yea, my Lord lief and dear,	*beloved*
195	roasted fish and honey in fere!	*together*
	Thereof we have good won.	*great plenty*

JESUS	Eat we then in good manner.	*properly*
	Thus now you know without were	*doubt*
	that ghost to eat hath no power,	*a ghost*
200	as you shall see anon.	*forthwith*

Then Jesus shall eat, and shall give (food) to his disciples.

JESUS	Brethren, I told you before	
	when I was with you not gain an hour,	
	that needily both less and more	
	must fulfilled be	
205	in Moses' Law as written were,	
	all other prophets as now were.	
	Is fulfilled in good manner	
	of that was said of me.*	
	For this was written in prophecy:	
210	that I must suffer death needily	*necessarily*

201–8 "Brethren, I told you before when I was with you not above an hour ago,
that necessarily those things that were written in Moses' Law, (and in) all other
prophets that have been up to now, must be fulfilled down to the very last point.
What was said of me is duly fulfilled." Compare Luke 24.44, and play 20, 41ff.

	and the third day with victory	
	rise in good array	*in full health*
	and preach remission of sin	
	unto all men that his name doth min.	*call to mind*
215	Therefore, all ye that be herein,	
	think on what I say.	

*Then Jesus shall vanish, and the disciples shall go to Bethany;
and, meeting Thomas, Peter shall speak.*

| PETER | Ah, Thomas! Tidings good and new! | |
| | We have seen the Lord Jesu. | |

THOMAS	Shall I never lieve that this is true,	*believe*
220	by God Omnipotent,	
	but I see in his hands two	
	holes the nails in can go,	*went into*
	and put my finger eke also	*additionally*
	thereas the nails went.	*where*

ANDREW	Thomas, go we all in fere	*together*
226	for dread of enemies. Better were	*it would be*
	than Jews should have us in their danger	*power*
	and all our fraternity.	

THOMAS	Wherever you go, brethren dear,	
230	I will go with you in good manner;	*willingly*
	but this talk you tell me here	
	I lieve not till I see.	*believe*

PETER	Now, Thomas, be thou not away	
	and in hap see him thou may	*perchance*
235	and feel him also, in good fay,	*truly*
	as we have done before.	

THOMAS	Wherever you be, I will be ay;	*always*
	but make me lieve this thing verray	*believe; is true*
	you pine you not! Therefore I you pray	*trouble*
240	to speak of that no more.	

*Then they shall all go again to the house and shall lie down.
And suddenly Jesus shall appear, saying:*

JESUS	Peace, my brethren, both one and all!
	Come hither, Thomas; to thee I call.
	Show forth, for ought that may befall,*
	thy hand and put in here. — *put it; i.e., his side*
245	And see my hands and my feet,
	and put in thy hand—thou ne let. — *do not refuse*
	My wounds are yet fresh and wet — *still*
	as they first were.
	And be thou no more so dreading — *fearful*
250	but ever truly believing.

Then he shall reach out his hand into the side and the wounds.

THOMAS	My God, my Lord, my Christ, my King!
	Now lieve I without weening. — *believe; doubting*
JESUS	Yea, Thomas, thou seest now in me. — *look on*
	Thou lievest now that I am he. — *believe*
255	But blessed must they all be
	that lieve and never see — *believe*
	that I am that same body
	that born was of meek Mary
	and on a cross your souls did buy — *redeem*
260	upon Good Friday.*
	Whoso to this will consent— ~~whosoever~~
	that I am God Omnipotent—
	as well as they that be present — *i.e., the disciples*
	my darlings shall be ay. — *always*
265	Whoso to this will not consent — *whosoever*
	ever to the Day of Judgement,
	in Hell-fire they shall be brent, — *burnt*
	and ever in sorrow and teen. — *(be) always; torment*
	Whosoever on my Father hath any mind — *remembrance*
270	or of my mother in any kind — *in any way*

---

243 "No matter what may happen."

260 Good Friday is the liturgical day commemorating Christ's Passion

in Heaven-bliss they shall it find   *gain reward for*
without any woe.
Christ give you grace to take the way   *i.e., audience*
unto that joy that lasteth ay,   *for ever*
275   for there is no night but ever day—
for all you thither shall go.   *i.e., the disciples*

THE END

PLAY 20: THE ASCENSION

Performed by the Tailors

BOTH SETS OF BANNS refer to play 20 as the play of the Ascension, an event that took place forty days after the Resurrection. It is therefore surprising to find that this episode is prefaced in our text by a repetition of the appearance of Jesus to his disciples on the evening of Easter Day which has formed part of play 19. In Luke the account of this appearance (24.33–49) is followed immediately by the account of the Ascension (50–52) without any indication of time passing, as in the play also. But it seems dramatically improbable that the Tailors should re-play an episode just performed by the Saddlers, and it is more likely that the prefatory account of the appearance was added for some performance in which Emmaus was not played. It represents an alternative available within the cycle.

The central action of the Ascension is drawn ultimately from Mark 16.19, Luke 24.50–52, and Acts 1.9–12. The final instructions which Christ gives to his disciples before the Ascension are taken from Mark 16.15–18 and Acts 1.4–8. But liturgical song makes a major contribution also to the text—the singing of *Ascendo ad patrem meum* and the sung dialogue of the angels and Jesus (from Isaiah 63.1–3) after line 104; *Exaltare domine* which accompanies the reception of Jesus into heaven after line 152; and *Viri Galilei quid aspicitis* addressed by the angels to the apostles below.   Though no accounts are extant for this play, choristers and singing men may well have been employed to perform these items.

Though a short play in terms of the length of text, its playing-time is extended not only by the singing in full of the liturgical items but also by the elaborate action involved. It is difficult to envisage a set which would accommodate both the appearance in the locked room and also the ascent to heaven. Possibly the set—presumably initially as in play 19—can be cleared during a journey at ground-level to Bethany and Jesus's address to the disciples. The stage-direction at line 96 makes it clear that Jesus is to stand in a specific place for the Ascension, strengthening the sense that the waggon contained a lifting device which would raise him in stages from the floor of the waggon to an upper level. Midway is an area "as if above the clouds" which he reaches at the end of the *Ascendo*. At this point, or earlier, the upper level of heaven opens to reveal the angels. When Jesus reaches heaven, the two angels evidently replace him on the lift and descend to the midway-level to address the disciples while the upper level closes to conceal Jesus. No reference is made to the exit of the angels at the end. Possibly the waggon was curtained around them while the disciples left through the audience.

Such an elaborate lifting device would require a specially constructed waggon, capable of taking the necessary machinery, high enough to accommodate the three levels convincingly, yet sufficiently counter-balanced to be stable. Though the disciples could have remained on ground-level for the Ascension, the combined weight of eleven men on the waggon floor would perhaps add "ballast" for Jesus and the angels above. Something of the strength of the waggon may be gauged from the possibility that it may have had to accommodate a maximum of sixteen actors (eleven apostles, four angels and Jesus).

Clear reference is made to Jesus's wounds and to his bloodstained clothing. Possibly this last indicates that he wears a red Resurrection robe.

Cast   JESUS, PETER, ANDREW, JOHN, JAMES THE GREAT, SIMON, PHILIP, FIRST ANGEL, SECOND ANGEL, THIRD ANGEL, FOURTH ANGEL.

> *And first Jesus shall say:* "Pax vobis; ego sum; nolite timere."*

JESUS	My brethren that sitten in company,	*sit together*
	with peace I greet you heartfully.	*sincerely*
	I am he that stands you by—	*it is really me*
	ne dread you nothing.	*don't be at all afraid*

Latin before line 1 "Peace unto you! It is I; do not be afraid."

5	Well I know and witterly	*certainly*
	that ye be in great ecstasy	*bewilderment*
	whether I be risen verily—	*may be; really*
	that makes you sore in longing.	*in deep anxiety*
	You is no need to be annoyed so	*for you; troubled*
10	neither through thought to be in woe.	*nor; puzzlement*
	Your hands puts now you fro	*reach out*
	and feel my wound-es weet.	*moist*
	And lieves this, both all and one,	*believe*
	that ghost hath neither flesh ne bone	*a ghost; nor*
15	as ye may feel me upon	
	on hand-es and on feet.	

"Spiritus quidem carnem et ossa non habet sic me videtis habere."*

PETER	Ah, what is this that standeth us by?	
	A ghost methink he seemeth, witterly.	*certainly*
	Methink lightened much am I	*gladdened*
20	this spirit for to see.	
ANDREW	Peter, I tell thee privily	*in confidence*
	I dread me yet full greatly	*I am in great doubt*
	that Jesu should do such mastery	*perform; a miracle*
	and whether that this be he.	
JOHN	Brethren, good it is to think evermore	
26	what words he said the day before	
	he died on rood—gone is not yore—	
	and be we steadfast ay.*	
JAMES	Ah, John, that makes us in were	
30	that alway when he will appear	
	and when us list best to have him here,	
	anon he is away!*	

16+Latin "For a spirit hath not flesh and bones, as ye see me have" (Luke 24.39).

25–28 "Brethren, it is good to ponder constantly on the words that he said the day before he died on the cross—it is not long passed—and we should always be steadfast."

29–32 "Ah, John, what makes us uncertain (about whether it is really Jesus) is

JESUS	I see well, brethren, sooth to say,	*truth*
	for any sign that I show may	*because of*
35	ye be not steadfast in the fay,	*faith*
	but flitting I you find.	*wavering*
	Moe signs therefore ye shall see.	*more*
	Have you ought may eaten be?	*(that) may be*
SIMON	Yea, Lord, here—meat enough for thee—	*food*
40	or else we were unkind.	*discourteous*
JESUS	Now eat we then for charity,	*out of love*
	my lieve brethren fair and free,	*dear; good*
	for all things shall fulfilled be	
	written in Moses' Law.	*(that are) writtten*
45	Prophets in psalms saiden of me	*said*
	that death I behoved on the rood-tree,*	
	and rise within days three	*had to rise*
	to joy Mankind to draw,	*in order to lead*
	and preach to folk this world within	*had to preach*
50	penance, remission of their sin;	*repentance*
	in Jerusalem I should begin,	
	as I have done for love.	
	Therefore, believe steadfastly	
	and come ye with me to Bethany.	
55	In Jerusalem ye shall all lie	*remain*
	to abide the grace above.	*await; from above*

Luke

Then Jesus shall eat with his disciples, and then Philip shall speak.

PHILIP	Lord, from us thou nought conceal!	*nothing*
	What time that thou art in thy weal,	*when; bliss*
	shalt thou restore Israel	*to Israel*
60	again her realm that day?	
JESUS	Brother, that is not to thee	*for you*
	to know my Father's privity	*hidden purpose*

---

that when he keeps appearing and when we most desire to have him (staying) here, he goes away immediately."

46 "That I had to suffer death upon the cross."

that toucheth to his own posty—   *pertains; power*
wit that ye ne may.   *know; may not*

65   But take ye shall, through my behest,   *receive; promise*
     virtue of the Holy Ghost*   *power; from; Spirit*
     that sent shall be to help you most
     in world where ye shall wend.   *go*
     My witness all ye shall be   *John, Luke*
70   in Jerusalem and Judee,   *Judea*
     Samaria also, and each country,   *every*
     to the world's end.

     Go ye in all the world, and through my grace
     preach my word in each place.   *Matthew*
75   All that steadfast belief has   *have*
     and fullought, saved shall be.   *baptism*
     And whoso believeth not in your lore,   *teaching*
     the words ye preach them before,   *in the words*
     damned shall be for evermore—
80   that pain may them not flee.   *depart from them*

     By this thing you shall well know
     whoso believeth steadfastly in you—
     such signs, soothly, they shall show   *truly; display*
     wheresoever they tide to go.   *chance*
85   In my name well shall they   *readily*
     devils' powers to put away;   *they shall cast out*
     new tongues ye shall have to preach the fay*
     and adders to master also.   *venomous snakes; control*

     And though they poison eat or drink,
90   it shall noy them nothing;   *harm; not at all*
     sick men with their handling   *at their touch*
     shall heal-ed readily be,   *at once*
     such grace shall be in their doing.   *deeds*
     Now to my Father I am going.
95   Ye shall have, brethren, my blessing,
     for to Heaven I must stee.   *ascend*

---

66 The Holy Spirit is the Third Person of the Trinity, the Godhead; see play 21.

87 "New languages you shall have in order to preach the faith."

*Then he shall lead the disciples into Bethany; and when he shall have reached the place, Jesus shall speak as he ascends, standing in the place where he ascends. Jesus shall say: "Data est mihi omnis potestas in caelo et in terra."**

JESUS   My sweet brethren, lief and dear,   *faithful*
               to me is granted full power
               in Heaven and Earth, far and near,
100   for my godhead is most.   *greatest*
               To teach all men now go ye
               that in world will followed be   *baptised*
               in the name of my Father and me
               and of the Holy Ghost.   *Spirit*

*Then Jesus shall ascend, and in the course of ascending, he shall sing. (God singeth alone.)**

JESUS   Ascendo ad Patrem meum et Patrem vestrum, Deum meum
[a]   et Deum vestrum. Alleluia.**

When, however, Jesus has fully sung the hymn, he shall stand in the midst, as if above the clouds, and the Greater Angel shall speak to the Lesser Angel.

1ST ANGEL *shall sing:**
[b]   Quis est iste qui venit de Edom, tinctis vestibus de Bosra?

LESSER ANGEL *shall sing in response:*
[c]   Iste formosus in stola sua, gradiens in multitudine fortitud-
               inis suae?

96+SD "All power is given unto me in heaven and in earth" (Matthew 28.18).

104+SD The bracketed sentence is in English in the manuscripts and seems to be an incorporated production-note.

[a] "I ascend unto my Father and your Father, and to my God and your God" (John 20.17), the Benedictus anthem at Lauds on Ascension Day.

[b]-[f] The sung Latin dialogue is based on Isaiah 63.1–3: "'Who is this that cometh from Edom, with dyed garments from Bozrah?' 'This that is glorious in his apparel, travelling in the greatness of his strength?' 'I that speak in righteousness, mighty to save.' '[Wherefore art thou red in thine apparel] and thy garments like him that treadeth in the winefat?' 'I have trodden the winepress alone; and of the people there was none with me.'" No antiphonal equivalent has yet been discovered.

JESUS *shall sing alone:*
   [d]   Ego qui loquor justitiam et propugnator sum ad salvandum.

CHOIR *shall sing:*
   [e]   Et vestimenta tua sicut calcantium in torculari?

JESUS *shall sing alone:*
   [f]   Torcular calcavi solus, et de gentibus non est vir mecum.

The First Angel shall speak in the mother tongue.

1ST ANGEL	Who is this that cometh within	
106	the bliss of Heaven that never shall blin,	*cease*
	bloody, out of the world of sin—	
	and harrowed Hell hath he?	*despoiled*

2ND ANGEL	Comely he is in his clothing,	*handsome*
110	and with full power going,	*total; moving*
	a number of saints with him leading.	
	He seemeth of great posty.	*power*

Then Jesus, pausing in the same place, shall speak.

JESUS	I that spake rightwiseness	*righteousness*
	and have brought Man out of distress,	
115	"Forbuyer" called I am and was	*redeemer*
	of all Mankind through grace.	
	My people that were from me raft	
	through sin and through the Devil's craft,	
	to Heaven I bring—good one never left—	
120	all that in Hell was.*	

3RD ANGEL	Why is thy clothing now so red,	
	thy body bloody, and also head,	
	thy clothes also, all that been led,	*are worn*
	like to pressers of wine?	*those who press*

116–20 "I am bringing to heaven my people, everyone who was in hell, who were stolen away from me through sin and through the cunning power of the Devil—I left not a single virtuous soul."

JESUS	For the Devil and his power	*because of*
126	that Mankind brought in great danger.	*into*
	Through death on cross and blood so clear	
	I have made them all mine.	

	These bloody drops that ye now see	*drops of blood*
130	all they fresh shall reserved be	*kept*
	till I come in my majesty	
	to deem the last day.	*give judgement (on)*
	This blood shall witness bear to me.	*may bear*
	I died for Man on the rood-tree,	*cross*
135	and rose again within days three.	
	Such love I loved thee ay.	*with such love; always*

	These drops now with good intent	*truly*
	to my Father I will present	
	that good men that on Earth be lent	*living*
140	shall know apertly	*clearly*
	how graciously that I them bought,	
	and, for good works, that I have wrought	
	everlasting bliss that they sought,	
	to preve the good worthy;*	

145	and that the wicked may eachone	*all*
	know and see all one	*each one*
	how worthily they forgone	*justly; forgo*
	the bliss that lasteth ay.	*for ever*
	For these causes, lieve ye me,	*believe*
150	the drops I shed on rood-tree,	*the cross*
	all fresh shall reserv-ed be	*preserved*
	ever, till the last day.	

Then he shall ascend, and in the course of ascending the angels shall sing the hymn written below. They shall sing: "Exaltaremus, domine, in virtute tua; cantamus et psallemus virtutes tuas."*

Not trans

142–44 "And shall know that I have obtained the everlasting bliss that they looked for in return for their good deeds which are to prove that the good deserve it."

152+SD (1) "Be thou exalted, Lord, in thine own strength; so we will sing and praise thy power" (Psalms 20.14 [AV 21.13]), an Ascension Day antiphon.

*Then the angels shall descend, and they shall sing: "Viri Galilei, quid aspicitis in caelum?"**

4TH ANGEL	Ye men that been of Galilee,	*are*
	whereupon now wonder ye,	*at what; marvel*
155	waiting him that through posty	*looking for; power*
	is now gone you fro?	*from*

1ST ANGEL	Jesu Christ, lieve ye me,	*believe*
	that steed to Heaven as ye see,	*ascended; saw*
	right so come again shall he	*even in the same way*
160	as ye seen him go.	*have seen*

PETER	Lo, brethren, what these angels sayen—	*say*
	that Jesu, through his great main,	*power*
	to Heaven is gone, will come again	*(and)*
	right as he forth went.	*just*

ANDREW	Many sithen so hight he	*times; promised*
166	to send his Ghost, with heart free;	*Spirit; gladsome*
	and in Jerusalem we shall be	
	till it were to us sent.	*should be*

SIMON	Brethren, I read us, in good fay,	*advise; indeed*
170	that we thither take the way	
	and with devotion night and day	
	leng we to our prayer.	*be constant in*

PHILIP	For know we mon by sign verray	*may; true*
	that he is God's Son, sooth to say.	*truth*
175	Therefore it is good we go to pray	
	as he commanded here.	

JOHN	Now mon we lieve it no leasing,	*may; believe; lie*
	for both by sight and handling,	*touching*
	speaking, eating and drinking	
180	he proves his deity.	*divinity*

JAMES	Yea, also by his up-steying	*ascension*
	he seems fully Heaven-king.	*completely*

152+SD (2) "Ye men of Galilee, why stand ye gazing up into heaven?" (Acts 1.11), an Ascension Day antiphon.

	Who has therein full lieving,	*in that; total faith*
	saved life and soul is he.	
PETER	Go we, brethren, with one assent,	*general agreement*
186	and fulfill his commandment;	*instruction*
	but look that none through dread be blent,	*blinded*
	but lieves all steadfastly.	*believe*
	Pray we all with full intent	*earnestly*
190	that he to us his Ghost will sent.	*Spirit; send*
	Jesus, that from us now is went,	*gone*
	save all this company!	*i.e., the audience*
	Amen.	

THE END

PLAY 21: PENTECOST

Performed by the Fishmongers

after put?

OUR SIXTEENTH-CENTURY records show that Chester's cycle was then performed at Whitsun, the festival commemorating the coming of the Holy Spirit upon the apostles at Pentecost. This play of Pentecost therefore had particular significance. To the events described in Acts 1.15–2.12, covering the election of Matthias to replace Judas and the descent of the Holy Spirit, the play adds the tradition (confirmed in a sermon-series which in the Middle Ages was erroneously attributed to St. Augustine) that the Apostles' Creed was composed under the Spirit's direct influence. The Creed contains the central articles of the Christian faith and, within the cycle, picks up details from several previous plays and looks on to the Judgement.

Line 55

   Like the previous play, play 21 requires a two-level set. The action begins in an inner room where the apostles have gathered, as Jesus commanded in play 20. After recalling Jesus's promise to send his Holy Spirit, the apostles kneel and sing *Veni Creator Spiritus*, appropriately a Whitsun hymn. It is a long hymn, and Richard Rastall has pointed out that since the 1607 manuscript writes out the first verse in full, possibly the apostles sang only that one verse before offering a spoken translation of the hymn in English. Such a curtailment might be a concession to untrained singers; alternatively, a "director" might have the right to decide how much of the hymn should be attempted! Perhaps only at its conclusion would the upper level open to reveal heaven where the Godhead explains the purpose of the gift of the Spirit while the apostles continue to kneel below. It is not clear whether heaven should remain open after the coming of the Holy Spirit, with God looking down upon its effects—as it were, sanctioning the composition of the Creed.

A Whitsun antiphon, *Accipite Spiritum Sanctum*, is apparently sung
in full by the two angels, who may be trained singers, as a prelude to the
descent of the Holy Spirit in tongues of fire. How that effect of fire was
created is not clear. Modern producers have tended to use red streamers
dropped upon the apostles, though the effect is often received in an
unduly literal way by modern audiences. The apostles presumably rise,
in somewhat dazed manner, after the angels' speeches and talk animated-
ly among themselves until Peter calls them to order again.

The creation of the Creed is a very formal action. Each apostle takes
responsibility for one article of faith and declares it in Latin before
offering a translation. The Latin is presumably delivered in a chanting
monotone, as in liturgical performance. The English declaration has to be
made loudly and firmly, with each speaker perhaps coming forward
before the audience. A mood of naturalism breaks into the play finally as
two foreigners enter, presumably in some distinctive dress and from
among the audience, to marvel at the transformation.

Although its text is longer and its cast of speaking parts (eighteen)
more extensive than play 20, play 21 is an occasion for words rather than
action and spectacle. The splendour of heaven and the diversity of the
apostles, each presumably with his particular emblem, do provide visual
appeal, but it is the words of the Creed, now invested with the full force
of the cycle's action, that count. We have witnessed God the Father
presiding over the Old Law. We have witnessed God the Son establishing
the New Law. Now we witness the coming of the Holy Spirit to preside
over the contemporary world of the Church whose belief has been
codified under its authority.

Cast   PETER, MATTHEW, ANDREW, JAMES THE GREAT, JOHN, THOMAS, JAMES
THE LESS, PHILIP, BARTHOLOMEW, MATTHIAS, SIMON, TADEUS, GOD THE SON,
GOD THE FATHER, FIRST ANGEL, SECOND ANGEL, FIRST FOREIGNER, SECOND
FOREIGNER.

And first, standing among the apostles, Peter shall speak.

PETER *(to his fellow disciples)*

My dear brethren everychone,	*all*
you know well, both all and one,	*everyone of you*
how our Lord is from us gone	
to bliss that lasteth ay.	*for ever*

5   Comfort now may we have none - *Goethe*
       save his behest to trust upon.   *promise*
       Therefore lieve we in this won
       that never one wend away.*)

       Leng we stiff in our prayer,   *remain; steadfast*
10   for well I wot, withouten were,   *know; without doubt*
       he will send us a counsellor,
       his Ghost, as he behight.   *Spirit; promised*
       Therefore leng we right here,   *remain*
       this faithful fellowship in fere,   *together*
15   till our Lord, as he can us lere,   *taught*
       send us of Heaven light.   *from; enlightenment*

       Then Peter, standing up in the midst of the brotherhood, shall
       speak.

       My dear brethren fair and free,   *fine and noble*
       Holy Scripture, lieve ye me,   *believe*
       fully must fulfill-ed be
20   that David said beforn.*   *before*
       All of the Holy Ghost had he   *entirely; from; Spirit*
       touching Judas, witten ye,   *concerning; understand*
       that sold our master for money
       and now is clean forlorn.   *completely lost*

25   Among us numbered that wretch was,
       the faith to preach in each place;
       and now his hire fully he has,   *reward*
       for hanged himself has he.
       His body bursten for his trespass,   *burst open; sin*
30   soul damned as a man without grace.*   *(his) soul*
       Therefore, as the Psalter mind mase,   *recalls*
       fulfilled now must be: *(it) must*

7–8 "Therefore let us who are in this dwelling believe, so that not one of us goes
away."

17–20 The reference is to the text from Psalms quoted at 32+SD below, q.v.

25–30 The reference conflates two different accounts of Judas's death—that he
hanged himself (Matthew 27.5); and that he fell headlong and burst asunder
(Acts 1.18–19).

"Fiat habitatio eius deserta et non sit qui habitet in eo.
Episcopatum eius accipiat alter."*

35	Therefore, men that now been here	*are*
	and fellows that ay with us were	*colleagues; always*
	while Jesus Christ, our master dear,	
	in Earth living was,	
	that ye that seen his power,	*so that; have seen*
	his miracles many in good manner—	*truly*
	dying, rising, both—in fere	*together*
40	may best now bear witness:	

	Matthias, I read, here be one,	*advise; should be*
	and Joseph, that ay with us hath gone,	*always*
	for whom we cast two lots anon	*at once*
	and busk us all to pray	*make haste*
45	whether of them it is God's will	*which*
	this same office to fulfill.	*carry out*

Then all shall speak together:

CHORUS	We assenten us there-till,	*we agree to that*
	for this is the best way.	

Then all the apostles shall kneel and Peter shall speak.

PETER	Thou, Lord, that knowest all thing,	*everything*
50	each heart and will of man living,	*of every man*
	show us here by some tokening	*sign*
	whom that we shall take;	
	and whether of these is thy liking	*which; desire*
	in Judas' stead that be standing,	*place; should be*
55	thy name to preach to old and young;	
	and whether that thou wilt make.	*which; appoint*

*Then Peter shall cast lots, and the lot shall fall upon Matthias;
and Peter shall speak.*

PETER	This lot is fallen, brethren free,	*noble*

32+Latin "Let his habitation be desolate, and let no man dwell therein; and his
bishopric let another take" (Acts 1.20, citing Psalms 68.26, 108.8 [AV 69.25,
109.8]).

| | on Matthew—all men may see.
To us therefore I take thee | *Matthias* |
| 60 | and apostle I thee make. | |

MATTHIAS	Yea, honoured be God in Trinity,	
	though I unworthy thereto be,	*for that (office)*
	that to you have chosen me.	*for which*
	Die will I for his sake.	

ANDREW	Now, Peter, brother, go we and pray,	
66	for evermore I min may	*may remember*
	my Sovereign, how I heard him say	
	here in your company—	

JAMES	he would not leave us, by no way,	*no means*
THE GREAT	fatherless children, in good fay,	*truly*
71	but rich us soon in better array	*prepare us better*
	with his Ghost graciously.	*Spirit*

JOHN	Yea, brethren, also, verament,	*truly*
	to us he said in good intent	*in kindness*
75	in Earth here while he was present	*earth*
	and with us could lend—	*stay*

THOMAS	but if so were that he ne went,	*unless; did not go*
	his Ghost to us should not be sent;	*Spirit*
	and if he yode, where we were lent	*went; staying*
80	it he would us send.	

JAMES	Yea, sweet and liking was his lore,*	
THE LESS	and well ye witten that there wore,	*know; were*
	but a little while before,	*just*
	or he to Heaven steigh—	*before; rose up*

PHILIP	he bade we should not go away	*commanded*
86	from Jerusalem to no country	*any region*
	but there abide, sooth to say,	*await; truth*
	his hest from on high.	*command*

| BARTHOL. | Also he said to us eachone | *all of us* |
| 90 | that his foregoer, St. John, | *predecessor* |

---

81 "Yes, his teaching was sweet and pleasant."

with water baptised many one
while that he was here—

MATTHEW   but we shall baptise, without boast,   *translates*   truly
                 fully with the Holy Ghost   Spirit
95   through help of him that is most,   greatest
                 soon after, without were: certainly

                 "Tunc Johannes quidem baptizavit aqua; vos autem
                 baptazimini Spiritu Sancto non post multos hos dies."*

SIMON   We mind thereon, less and more.   *we all remember that*
                 Yet some that standen him before   *were standing*
                 asked whether he should restore
100   that time all Israel.   *at that time*

TADDEUS   And he answered anonright: *straight away*
                 That time know ye ne might   *could not*
                 that in his Father's will was pight— *means* *set*
                 for that he must conceal.

                 "Non est vestrum nosse tempora vel momenta quae
                 Pater posuit in sua potestate."*

MATTHIAS   Yea, brethren, that time he us behight   *promised*
106   the Holy Ghost should in us light,   *Spirit; descend*
                 that we might tell to each wight   *person*
                 his deeds all bedene   *works; immediately*
                 in Jerusalem and Judee—   *Judea*
110   where in the world soever walked we—   *travelled*
                 and Samary, that men should see, *means*   *Samaria*
                 as after may be seen.   *in later times*

                 "Accipietis virtutem supervenientes Spiritus Sancti in
                 vos, et eritis mihi testes in Jerusalem et in Judea, Samaria
                 et usque ad ultimum terrae."*

96+Latin "For John truly baptized with water; but ye shall be baptized with the
Holy Ghost not many days hence" (Acts 1.5). The reference is to John the Baptist.

104+Latin "It is not for you to know the times nor the seasons which the Father
hath put in his own power" (Acts 1.7).

112+Latin "But ye shall receive power, after that the Holy Ghost is come upon

PETER	Kneel we down upon our knee	
	and to that Lord now pray we.	
115	Soon I hope that he will see	*think; have regard*
	to his disciples all.	

ANDREW	Yea, in life so taught he:	*while he was alive*
	ask, and have with heart free;	*gladsome heart*
	rightwise boon shall granted be	*righteous request*
120	when men will on him call.	

*Then all the apostles, kneeling, shall sing "Veni, Creator
Spiritus." Then James the Great shall speak.*

JAMES	Come, Holy Ghost! come, Creator!	*Spirit*
THE GREAT	Visit our thoughts in this stour—	*enter; time*
	thou art Man's conqueror—	*champion*
	and grant us, Lord, thy grace!	

JOHN	Thou, that art call-ed "Counsellor"	
126	and sent from Heaven as saviour,	*are sent*
	Well of Life, leech our langour	
	that prayen here in this place.*	

THOMAS	Ye that in seven would counsel	
130	grace of thy Ghost about to deal,*	
	as thou promised for Man's heal,	*well-being*
	appear now, since I pray.	

JAMES	Light our wits with thy weal;*	
THE LESS	put life in our thoughts lele;	*faithful*

---

you; and ye shall be witnesses unto me both in Jerusalem, and in all Judea, and in Samaria, and unto the uttermost parts of the earth" (Acts 1.8).

120+SD *Veni Creator Spiritus* is the cue for the singing of the verse-hymn for Whit Sunday (the liturgical commemoration of Pentecost). The hymn is translated in the subsequent speeches.

127-28 "Life-giving spring, heal the sorrow of us who pray here in this place."

129-30 "You who would give counsel that grace should be distributed about from your Spirit in seven forms."

133 "Illumine our minds with your joy."

135	fulsen thy friends that been frail	*strengthen;are*
	with virtues lasting ay.	*everlasting*

PHILIP	Vanish our enemies far away	*remove*
	and grant us peace, Lord, to our pay,	*for our delight*
	for while thou art our leader ay	*for ever*
140	we may eschew annoy.	*escape distress*

BARTHOL.	Through thy might know we may
	the Father of Heaven full, in good fay;
	and yea, his Son, all sooth to say—
	thou art in company.*

MATTHEW	Worshipped be thou ever and oo,	*always*
146	the Father and the Son also.	
	Let thy Ghost now from thee go	*Spirit*
	and faith that we may find.	*and (grant) that*

till here

SIMON	That we asken with heart throw—	*ask;eager*
150	to fulsen us against our foe—	*strengthen*
	grant thy men here, both one and moe,	*all*
	that have thee ever in mind.	

Christ must speak in Heaven.

GOD	Glorious Father fair and free,	*splendid and noble*
THE SON	ye know well of your deity	*in your godhead*
155	that I have done your will.	
	The apostles, that you have chosen to me,	*for*
	with grace, wisdom, and prosperity	
	that you will them fulfill.	*(I pray);perfect*

*Then all the apostles are meditating or praying up to the time
when the Holy Spirit is sent; God the Father shall speak.*

GOD	My Son beloved, lief and dear,
THE FATHER	your healthful asking ever I hear.
161	That you ask is not to arear—

143–44 "And indeed, his Son, to tell the whole truth—you are united with them."
All manuscripts read *ye* for *yea* here.

I know your clean intent.*
With will full liberal and clear   *generous;pure*
my Ghost to them shall appear   *Spirit*
165   to make them wiser than they were.
That is my full assent.   *complete concurrence*

My Ghost to Earth shall go down
with seven gifts of renown,
there to have by devotion,
170   confirm them to be sad,*
that they may be ever ready boun   *so that;prepared*
in Heaven-bliss to wear the crown
ever to reign in possession,   *occupation*
there to be merry and glad.

175   My patriarchs and prophets here
that through your faith to me were dear,   *faith in you*
angels and archangels clear
all in my bliss wonning,   *dwelling*
ye wotten well withouten were   *know;certainly*
180   how I have mended in good manner   *restored;rightly*
Man that was lorn through Lucifer   *lost*
and through his own liking.   *desire*

My Son I sent down from my see   *throne*
into a virgin fair and free   *noble*
185   and manhood took, as liked me   *human form;it pleased*
on Man to have mercy,
that righteousness might sav-ed be   *so that*
since Man had lost his liberty.
I made Man in one degree;   *level of heavenly rank*
190   his bale behoved to buy.*

159–62 "My beloved Son, true and precious, I always listen to your beneficent requests. What you ask is not among the least of my considerations. I know your pure intention." No manuscript contains *I* at line 160.

167–70 "My Spirit shall go down to Earth with seven gifts of splendour, as theirs to have because of their faith, to strengthen them to endure misery." The reference is to the seven gifts of the Holy Spirit (from Isaiah 11.2): wisdom, understanding, counsel, fortitude, knowledge, piety, and fear of the Lord.

190 "It was appropriate to redeem his sin."

GOD   Now Man fully have I bought   redeemed
THE SON*   and out of bale to bliss brought.   torment
              His kind also, as me good thought,   nature; it seemed
              is mixed within my Godhead.
195   Thus Man that I thus made of nought,   Mankind
              that Satanas through sin had sought,   Satan
              by this way I have so wrought   means; so contrived
              none good in Hell been led.   no virtuous one; may be

              But while I was in that degree   condition
200   in Earth wonning, as man should be,   dwelling
              chosen I have a good meny   company
              on which I must have mind.
              Now they have made their moan to me   request ?
              and prayed specially, as I see,   particularly
205   which I must suffice with heart free   satisfy; noble
              or else I were unkind.   would be; untrue to my nature

              Throughout the world they shall gone,   go
              my deeds to preach to many one.   many a one
              Yet steadfastness in them is none
210   to suffer for me annoy.   misery
              Fletching yet they been eachone.   vacillating; are
              But when my Ghost is them upon,   Spirit
              then shall they after be stiff as stone   firm
              my deeds to certify.   affirm

215   Dread of death ne no distress   nor
              shall let them of steadfastness.   hinder them from
              Such love in them, and such goodness
              my Spirit shall ever inspire
              that to speak and express
220   all languages that ever yet was   every language
              they shall have cunning, more and less,   skill; all
              through force of heavenly fire.   power; from heaven

              Also they shall have full power
              to baptise men in water clear
225   that believen in good manner,   believe; properly
              to have full mind on me.   full knowledge of

190+SH Though there is no indication in any manuscript, the speaker here seems
to change from God the Father to God the Son.

	And on all such, withouten were,	*truly*
	the Holy Ghost at their prayer	*Spirit*
	shall light on them, that they may lear	*descend; learn*
230	in faith steadfast to be.	

	Now will I send anon in hie	*at once quickly*
	to my brethren in company	*all together*
	my Ghost, to glad them graciously—*	
	for that is their willing—	*desire*
235	in likeness of fire freely,	*nobly*
	that they may stiffened be thereby,	*strengthened*
	my works to preach more steadfastly,	
	and thereby more cunning.	*(they may be); knowledgeable*

*Then God shall send out the Holy Spirit in the form of fire, and as it is sent, two angels shall sing the antiphon "Accipite Spiritum Sanctum. Quorum remiseritis peccata, remittentur eis," etc. And as they sing they shall throw fire upon the apostles. And when this is done, the (first) angel in Heaven shall speak.**

1ST ANGEL	Rest well, all that been here!	*greetings; are*
240	My Lord you greets, and his Ghost dear.	*Spirit*
	He bids you dread no boast nor bere	*threat; strife*
	of Jews far ne near;	*nor*
	but look ye go anon in hie	*at once quickly*
	into all the world by and by,	*round about*
245	and also preach the faith meekly,	
	and his works so dear.	*precious*

2ND ANGEL	And through this Ghost that I you bring	*Spirit*
	ye shall have understanding	
	of every land speaking,	*of the speech*
250	whatsoever they say;	
	and this world that is fletching	*wavering*
	you shall despise over all thing	*above*
	and Heaven at your ending	
	ye shall have to your pay.	*for your delight*

---

233 "My Spirit, to make them happy through grace."

238+SD "Receive ye the Holy Ghost: Whose soever sins ye remit, they are remitted unto them; and whose soever sins ye retain, they are retained" (John 20.22–23), the Benedictus antiphon on Whit Sunday.

PETER 256	Ah, mercy, Lord full of might! Both I feel and see in sight the Holy Ghost is on us light; of fire this house full is.	*Spirit; descended*

ANDREW 260	Now have we that was us behight, for full of love my heart is pight and wiser than is any wight methink I am, iwiss.	*what; promised* *set* *person* *it seems; indeed*

JAMES THE GREAT 265	Yea, Lord, blessed must thou be, for both I feel and eke I see the Holy Ghost is light on me. Thus quit I am my meed.	*also* *descended* *rewarded with; gift*

JOHN 270	For such love, by my lewty, with this fire in my heart can flee that death to die for my Master free I have no manner of dread.	*faith* *into; sped* *noble* *kind of fear*

THOMAS	And I thank thee, both God and Man, for since this fire light me upon of all languages well I can and speak them at my will.	*descended* *have good knowledge* *when I want*

JAMES THE LESS 277	I, before that was a fon, am waxen as wise as Solomon. There is no science but I can thereon, and cunning to fulfill.*	*fool* *grown*

PHILIP 280	And I that never could speak thing save Hebrew as I learn-ed young, now I can speak at my liking all languages, both low and high.	*anything* *which; as a child* *pleasure* *major and minor*

BARTHOL. 285	And so stiff I am of believing that I doubt neither prince ne king my Master's miracles for to ming and for his love to die.	*firm; in belief* *fear; nor* *tell of* *love of him*

277–78 "There is no branch of knowledge that I do not know of, and the skill to apply it."

MATTHEW   Ah, blessed be my Master dear,
             so little while that can us lere!   *tongues*   time; teach
             All languages that ever were
290   upon my tongue been light.   are easy

SIMON   My belief is now so clear   *steadfast*   faith
             and love in heart so printed here, *fixt*   imprinted
             to move my mind in no manner   resolve; by no way
             there is no man hath might.

TADDEUS   Yea, sithen this fire came from on high   since
296   I am waxen so wondrous sly   grown; marvellously wise
             that all languages, far and nigh, *tongues*   near
             my tongue will speak now aright.   correctly

MATTHIAS   Now sithen my Lord to Heaven stight   since; ascended
300   and sent his Ghost as he behight,   Spirit; promised
             to all distresses now am I dight   *fortitude*
             and die for God Almight.*

PETER   Now, brethren I read us, all in fere   advise; together
             make we the Creed in good manner*   rightly
305   of my Lord's deeds dear
             that gladded us hath today;   made us joyful
             and I will first begin here,
             since Christ betook me his power,*   entrusted to me
             the lewd hereafter that we may lere,   ignorant; teach
310   to further them in the fay.   advance; faith

           Then Peter shall begin: "Credo in Deum, Patrem Omnipoten-
           *tem, Creatorem caeli et terrae."**

301–2 "Now am I prepared for all troubles, and am ready to die for Almighty
God."

304 The *Creed*, or statement of belief, here created is the Apostles' Creed, a title
deriving from the tradition that it was created by the twelve apostles under the
direct influence of the Holy Spirit.

308 The reference here is to the power committed to Peter by Christ in Matthew
16.18–19.

310+SD "I believe in God, the Father Almighty, Maker of heaven and earth."

PETER   I believe in God Omnipotent
that made Heaven and Earth and Firmament,
with steadfast heart and true intent;   *will*
and he is my comford.   *comfort*

ANDREW   "Et in Jesum Christum, Filium eius unicum, dominum
nostrum."*

315   And I believe, where I be lent,   *wherever; dwelling*
in Jesu, his Son, from Heaven sent,
verray Christ, that us hath kent   *true; taught*
and is our elders' Lord.   *forefathers'*

JAMES   "Qui conceptus est de Spiritu Sancto, natus ex Maria
THE GREAT   virgine."*

I believe, without boast,   *sincerely*
320   in Jesus Christ of might-es most,   *greatest in powers*
conceived through the Holy Ghost   *(who was); Spirit*
and born was of Mary.

JOHN   "Passus sub Pontio Pilato, crucifixus, mortuus et sepul-
tus."*

And I believe, as I can see,   *have witnessed*
that under Pilate suffered he,
325   scourged and nailed on rood-tree;   *the cross*
and buried was his body.

THOMAS   "Descendit ad inferna; tertia die resurrexit a mortuis."*

And I believe, and sooth can tell,   *truth*
that he ghostly went to Hell,   *in spirit*
delivered his that there did dwell,   *freed his people*
330   and rose the third day.

314+Latin "And in Jesus Christ, his only Son, our Lord."

318+Latin "Who was conceived by the Holy Ghost, born of the Virgin Mary."

322+Latin "Suffered under Pontius Pilate, was crucified, dead and buried."

326+Latin " He descended into hell; the third day he rose again from the dead."

JAMES
THE LESS
"Ascendit ad caelos; sedet ad dexteram Dei Patris Omni-
potentis."*

And I believe fully this,
that he steighed up to Heaven-bliss   *ascended*
and on his Father's right hand is,
to reign for ever and ay.   *always*

PHILIP
"Inde venturus est judicare vivos et mortuos."*

335
And I believe, with heart steadfast,
that he will come at the last   *the last (day)*
and deem Mankind as he hath cast,   *judge; intended*
both the quick and the dead.   *living*

BARTHOL.
"Credo in Spiritum Sanctum."*

And my belief shall be most   *faith; strongest*
340
in virtue of the Holy Ghost;   *the power; Spirit*
and through his help, without boast,   *certainly*
my life I think to lead.

MATTHEW
"Sanctam Ecclesiam Catholicam, sanctorum communio-
nem."*

And I believe, through God's grace,
such belief as Holy Church has—   *faith*
345
that God's body granted us was
to use in form of bread.

SIMON
"Remissionem peccatorum."*

330+Latin "He ascended into heaven, and sitteth on the right hand of God, the
Father Almighty."

334+Latin "From thence he shall come to judge the quick and the dead."

338+Latin "I believe in the Holy Ghost."

342+Latin "The Holy Catholic Church, the communion of saints"—the latter here
being then translated as "participation in the eucharistic elements" rather than
the alternative "fellowship with holy persons."

346+Latin "The forgiveness of sins."

	And I believe, with devotion,	*devoutly*
	of sin to have remission	*forgiveness*
	through Christ's blood and Passion,	
350	and Heaven when I am dead.	*(to have)*

| TADDEUS | "Carnis resurrectionem."* |

	And I believe, as all we mon,	*must*
	in the general resurrection	
	of each body, when Christ is boun	*ready*
	to deem both good and evil.	*judge*

| MATTHIAS | "Et vitam aeternam."* |

355	And I believe, as all we may,	
	everlasting life , after my day,	*time on earth*
	in Heaven for to have ever and ay,	*always*
	and so overcome the Devil.	

PETER	Now, brethren, I read all we	*advise*
360	go each one to diverse country	*a different country*
	and preach to shire and to city	
	the faith, as Christ us bede.	*commands*

ANDREW	Yea, lief brother, kiss now we	*dear*
	each one another before we die,	
365	for God's will must fulfilled be,	
	and that is now great need.	*a major necessity*

Then two foreigners shall come, one of whom shall speak.

1ST FOR-	Ah, fellow, fellow, for God's pity!	
EIGNER	Are not these men of Galilee?	
	Our language they can as well as we,	*know*
370	as ever eat I bread!	*i.e., as I live*

2ND FOR-	Well I wot, by my lewty,	*know;faith*
EIGNER	that within these days three	
	one of them could not speak with me	

350+Latin "The resurrection of the body."

354+Latin "And the life everlasting."

	for to have been dead!	*i.e., to save his life*
1ST FOR- EIGNER 377	Of all languages that been hereby that come to Mesopotamy, Capadocy and Jury, they jangle without ween— of the Isle of Pontus, and Asye,	*are* *Mesopotamia* *Cappadocia; Judea* *speak; thinking* *Asia*
380	Friseland and Pamphily, Egypt, right into Libye that is beside Cyrene.	*Pamphylia* *Libya*
2ND FOR- EIGNER 385	Yea, also men of Araby and of Greece that is thereby hearden them praise full tenderly God of his great grace; and we hearden them, witterly, praise God fast, both thou and I. Fellow, go we therefore and espy	*Arabia* *heard; feelingly* *for* *heard; truly* *steadfastly*
390	how goes this wondrous case.	*develops; situation*

THE END

PLAY 22: THE PROPHETS OF ANTICHRIST

Performed by the Clothworkers

THE FINAL THREE plays of the cycle concern the last days of the world, when the final prophecies will be fulfilled. This sequence seems to have undergone revision during the period of the cycle's history, for a document of 1429–30 shows the Shearmen, who in the 1607 manuscript are associated with "the Clothiers" as responsible for play 22, sharing the costs of a play with the companies of the Weavers, Walkers ("fullers of cloth") and Chaloners ("blanket-makers"). That play was probably *The Last Judgement*. By 1467–68 the Shearmen were bearing the full costs of a waggon, and by 1500 the Hewsters (Dyers) were probably responsible for a play of *Antichrist* that had been inserted before the final play, *The Last Judgement*, which had by then become the responsibility of the Weavers and the Walkers. A list of companies and plays compiled in 1539–40 calls the Shearmen's play (our play 22) "Profettys afore the Day of Dome," making no reference to Antichrist; but both sets of Banns describe the play as dealing with the prophets of Antichrist and make no reference to prophecies of the Last Judgement! The extant play describes itself as "our play of Antichrist's signs" (338–39), despite the fact that the weight of prophecies lies with the Last Judgement.

These facts perhaps indicate that play 22 was introduced as a series of prophecies of the Last Judgement during re-organisation of the cycle's content and was subsequently adapted to incorporate some mention of Antichrist as the cycle was further extended. These considerations may explain the impression of unevenness left by our version, which splits into two clear sections. The first presents four prophecies—from Ezechiel 37.1–10, Zechariah 6.1–7, Daniel 7, and St. John's Apocalypse (Revelation) 11.3–11—each with an interpretation offered to the contemporary audience by the Expositor. The second is a recital by the Expositor of the

Fifteen Signs which will precede the Day of Judgement. This was a common topic, included in the standard *Legenda Aurea* ("The Golden Legend") from which the version in the play probably derives. The ascription there to St. Jerome, which is repeated in the play, served to give authenticity to the account of the signs, but no work by Jerome dealing with this topic is known.

A play of the prophets of *Christ* was a frequent feature of cyclical and liturgical drama. The version of Chester's cycle given here, which is attested by the four earliest manuscripts, contains no such play. But the 1607 manuscript contains a version of play 5 in which Balaam's Messianic prophecy is the cue for the entry of a series of Jewish prophets prophesying the Incarnation. Play 22, the prophets of Antichrist, would balance that prophet-sequence. As the play stands, however, it serves primarily to authenticate the events set in future time which are performed in plays 23 and 24.

Our play 22 continues and intensifies the formality and direct address of play 21. Each prophet steps forward in turn, delivers his speech and then, presumably, defers to the Expositor who gives his interpretation. Finally, in front of the four prophets, the Expositor recounts the signs before the end of the world. There is no dialogue or action, and no set is specified. The figures are simply mouthpieces for their pronouncements, though each will have his own iconographic dress and/or symbol. But their speeches, telling of wonders beyond normal human comprehension, challenge the actors' skill, and demand total involvement and conviction in their delivery.

Cast   EZECHIEL, EXPOSITOR, ZECHARIAH, DANIEL, JOHN THE EVANGELIST.

EZECHIEL   "Facta super me manus domini et eduxit me spiritus domini, et demisit me in medio campi qui erat plenus ossibus, et circumduxit me per ea in giro." These things are in the Book of Ezechiel, Chapter 37.*

Latin before line 1 "The hand of the Lord was upon me, and carried me out in the spirit of the Lord, and set me down in the midst of the valley which was full of bones, And caused me to pass by them round about" (Ezechiel 37.1–2). The vision was traditionally interpreted as a prophecy of the general resurrection on Doomsday.

Harken, all that loven heal!   *love salvation*
I am the prophet Ezechiel.
What I saw I will not conceal
but as me thought I will tell.   *it seemed to me; relate*
5   God his ghost can with me deal   *shared his spirit*
that led me long with word-es lele   *true*
into a field where bones fele   *plain; many*
all bare, without flesh or fell.   *(lay) bare; skin*

Then spake that ghost unto me   *spirit*
10   and said: "Man's son, how likest thee?   *does it please*
Thinkst thou not well that this may be,   *truly think*
these bones might turn and live?"
Then bade he me tell and prophesy   *commanded*
that he would revive them soon on hie   *speedily*
15   with flesh and sinews and skin thereby   *in addition*
which soon he can them give.   *imparted to them*

After that, ghost he them get,   *life; obtained for*
rise of their graves he them let,
and made them stand upon their feet,
20   speak, go, and see—
this saw I right in my sight—
to know that he was God Almight   *acknowledge; Almighty*
that Heaven and Earth should deal and dight
and never shall ended be.*

EXPOSITOR   Now, that you shall expressly know   *clearly*
26   these prophet's words upon a row,   *in their entirety*
what they do signify I will show   *truly mean*
that much may do you good.   *which; great good*
By them understand may I
30   the Day of Doom skilfully,   *through my knowledge*
when men through God's posty   *power*
shall rise in flesh and blood.

Therefore this prophet said full yare   *long ago*
he saw a field of bones bare,   *plain*
35   and soon that ghost with them can fare,   *spirit; went*
gave them flesh and life.

23–24 "Who should dispose and ordain heaven and earth and who should never
have ending."

Believe this fully withouten ween,   *without doubting*
that all which dead and rotten been   *are*
in flesh shall rise, as shall be seen—
40   man, maid, and wife.

They that shall be saved shall be as bright
as seven times the sun is light;
the damn-ed thester shall be in sight,
their doom to underfo.*
45   Both saved and damned after that day
die they may not by no way.   *any means*
God give you grace to do so ay   *so to act always*
that bliss you may come to.   *heavenly joy*

ZECHARIAH   "Levavi oculos meos et vidi; et ecce, quatuor quadrige
egredientes de medio duorum montium." This is in the
Book of the Prophet Zechariah, chapter 6.*

I, Zachary—men, lieves ye me—   *Zechariah;believe*
50   lift up my eyes a sight to see,   *lifted*
and, as me thought by my lewty,   *it truly seemed to me*
four chariots came anon   *at once*
out of two hills, lieve ye me—   *believe*
silver hills they were, as witten we!   *understand*
55   Great wonder I had in my degree   *state of knowledge*
whither that they would gone.   *go*

Red horses in one were, readily;   *certainly*
another black that went them by;
the third was white, I wot not why;   *know*
60   the fourth of diverse hue.   *various colours*
They were stiff, drawing bigly.*
Then anon answered I   *at once*
to that angel in my body   *attendant spirit*
which told me word-es true—

41–42 "Those who shall be saved shall be as bright as seven times the brightness
of the sun; those who shall be damned shall be dark to look on in readiness to
receive their damnation."

48+Latin "And I turned and lifted up mine eyes, and looked, and behold, there
came four chariots out from between two mountains" (Zechariah 6.1).

61 "They were strong, pulling mightily."

65	I asked him then what it might be	
	and he answered anon unto me.	*at once*
	"These chariots," he said, "which thou dost see,	
	four winds they be iwiss,	*are; certainly*
	which shall blow, and ready be	*are*
70	before Christ, that prince which is of posty.	*power*
	There is none so fell their fit may flee*	
	nor win their will from this."	*gain their desire*

EXPOSITOR	Now, for to moralise aright,	
	which this prophet saw in sight,*	
75	I shall fond through my might	*attempt*
	to you in meek manner,	*humble fashion*
	and declare that soon in hight	*immediately*
	more plainly, as I have tight.	*planned*
	Listen now with hearts light	
80	this lesson for to lear.*	

	Four chariots this prophet see, how they	*saw*
	out of two hills took their way—	
	the hills of silver, the sooth to say,	*truth*
	the horses of diverse hue.	*different colours*
85	Which hills signify may	*may represent*
	Enoch and Hely, in good fay,*	*Elijah; truly*
	that as good silver shall be ay,	*always*
	steadfast men and true.	

	Four chariots he saw, as thinks me,	*it seems to me*
90	skilfully may likened be	*appropriately*
	to saints of four manners of degree	*kinds of rank*
	that then shall suffer annoy.	*tribulation*
	Four horses is also certainty,	
	of diverse hues that he can see;	

---

71 "There is no one so fierce as to escape their peril."

73–74 "Now, to draw the correct moral significance from what this prophet beheld with his physical vision."

79–80ff. The interpretation of the chariots and horses has the authority of St. Jerome, but the interpretation of the hills here as Enoch and Elijah seems unusual and rather awkward.

86 On Enoch and Elijah, see above, play 17.

95	four manner of saints in dignity liken them well may I:*	
	"Martyrs," "Confessors"—there be two;	*are*
	"Men Misbelieving Converted" also	*converted heretics*
	that turned shall be from sin and woe	
100	through Enoch and Hely;	*Elijah*
	"Virgins" also, both one and moe.	*innocents; more*
	Here be diverse hues too	*various colours also*
	that through God's grace shall go	
	for him to suffer annoy.	*tribulation*
105	These red horses call I may	
	all manner of Martyrs in good fay,	*kinds of; truly*
	for red may well betoken ay	*symbolise; always*
	Man's blood-shedding.	*human bloodshed*
	The white he saith tooken their way	*says; took*
110	above the Earth to go astray	*wandering*
	are such that neither night nor day	
	dreaden death nothing.	*have no fear of*
	The black horses which went them by?	
	By them may well signify	*be symbolised*
115	Preachers of God's Word, truly,	
	that confessors shall be.*	
	The skewed horses, by mine intent,*	
	the which into the south forth went	
	I may well liken verament	*compare truly*
120	to Jews and paynims eke.	*pagans also*
	Yet through faith with heart fervent	
	shall turn to good amendment	*(they) shall; reform*
	when Enoch and Hely have them kent	*Elijah; taught*
	salvation for to seek.	

95–96ff. The four chariots are interpreted as four different kinds of saint (martyrs, confessors, converts, innocents). The horses are then also interpreted according to their colours (martyrs, innocents who do not fear death, preachers, and heretics to be converted).

116 *confessors*, i.e., those who profess Christianity in the face of persecution but do not die a martyr's death.

117 "The skewbald horses, according to my understanding."

DANIEL   "Ego, Daniel, videbam in visione mea nocte; et ecce, quatu-
              or venti pugnabant in magno mare, et quatuor bestiae
              gradentes ascendebant de mare." These things are in the
              Book of Daniel, chapter 7.*

125   I, Daniel, as I lay on a night,
              methought I saw a wondrous sight: *it seemed to me*
              four winds—together they can fight   *fought*
              above the sea upon hie;   *hastely*
              four beasts—out of that sea they yede.   *came*
130   To the fourth beast I took good heed,   *close attention*
              for that to speak of now is need.   *it is necessary*
              The other all I will leave.   *all the rest*

              That beast was wondrous stiff and strong,   *mighty*
              of teeth and nails sharp and long,   *with; claws*
135   eating overall that he could fong;
              the remnant he fortrod.*
              Unlike he was to any of lede.   *in the world*
              Ten horns he had upon his head.
              In the midst, one little horn can spread   *extended*
140   above all other on high.

              That horn had mouth to speak and eyes to see,
              and spake great words, lieve you me;   *believe*
              but of the ten, the first three
              soon were consumed away.

145   That one horn had so great posty;   *power*
              the remnant meek to him to be*
              that highest was in that degree,   *rank*
              and endured so many a day.   *remained*

              Then was it told me right there

124+Latin "I saw in my vision by night, and behold, the four winds of heaven
strove upon the great sea. And four great beasts came up from the sea, diverse
from one another" (Daniel 7.2–3).

135–36 "Eating everywhere whatever he could seize; the remainder he utterly destroyed by trampling them down."

146 "The remainder had to be humble towards him." The syntax here is confused.

150	that ten horns ten kings were,	
	but all that one should fear	
	that sprang upward so fast,	
	and that he should work against that King	
	that of nought made all thing—	
155	but little while, without leasing,	*truly*
	that king his might should last.	*king's power*

EXPOSITOR	By this beast understand I may*	
	the world to come next Doomsday;	*Judgement Day*
	and by that horn, in good fay,	*truly*
160	in midst the ten can spring,	*(that) sprang up*
	Antichrist I may understand,	
	that then great lord shall be in land	
	and all the world have in hand	*in his power*
	three years and half during.	*for a period of*

"Tradentur in manu eius usque ad tempus et tempora et dimidium temporis, et usque ad annum duos annos et dimidium anni." These things are in the Book of Daniel, chapter 7.*

165	Ten horns ten kings in land shall be,	
	of which Antichrist shall slay three.	
	The other seven this case shall see	*situation*
	and put them to his grace.	*themselves; into*
	This shall befall, witterly,	*truly*
170	by the understanding that have I	*according to*
	of Daniel's prophecy	
	that here rehearsed was.	*recited*

JOHN EVANG. "Dabo duobus testibus meis et prophetabunt diebus mille, ducentis et sexaginta amicti saccis." These things are in the Book of Apocalypse, chapter 11.*

157ff. The interpretation of the vision here offered is again traditional.

164+Latin "They shall be given into his hand until a time and times and the dividing of times" (Daniel 7.25).

172+Latin "And I will give power unto my two witnesses, and they shall prophesy a thousand two hundred and threescore days, clothed in sackcloth" (Apocalypse [Revelation] 11.3).

I, John, Christ's own darling,   *beloved*
         as I lay in great longing   *languishing*
175   upon my Master's breast sleeping,
         wonders saw I, many one.   *many a one*
         My ghost was ravished, without leasing,
         to Heaven before that Highest King.*
         There saw I many a wondrous thing.
180   One will I tell you anon.   *at once*

         There heard I God greatly commend
         two witnesses which he thought to send   *intended*
         false faiths for to defend   *beliefs; repel*
         that raised were by his foe.
185   He said they should prophesy
         a thousand days, witterly,   *truly*
         two hundred and sixty.
         In sacks clad they should go.   *sackcloth*

         He called them "Chandelours of great light   *candles*
190   burning before God's sight."
         Fire out of their mouths they should flight   *send out*
         their enemies for to destroy.
         Whosoever them harmed, as said he,
         dead behoved him for to be.   *he deserved*
195   To let the reign they had posty
         in time of their prophecy.*

         He said they should have power good
         to turn the water into blood,
         and overcome their enemies that were wood,   *mad*
200   and master them through their might.   *dominate*
         And when they had done their devoir,   *duty*
         a beast should come, of great power,
         from beneath, withouten were.   *the pit; assuredly*
         Against them he should fight.

177–78 "Truly, my spirit was transported to heaven before the Highest King."
Traditionally, the vision which John wrote in Patmos (Apocalypse 1.9–10) was
received when he slept on Jesus's bosom at the Last Supper; see play 15, 80+SD.

195–96 "They had power to hinder the reign (of Antichrist) during the period in
which they prophesied."

205   And slay them also should he
in midst of the Holy City
where Christ was nail-ed on a tree,
for sooth as I you tell.   *the truth*
But after three days and half one,

210   they shall rise, speak and gone,   *go*
and into Heaven be taken anon,   *at once*
in joy evermore to dwell.

EXPOSITOR   Now, lordings, what these things may be,   *sirs*
I pray you harken all to me.

215   As expressly in certainty   *clearly; assuredly*
as I have might and grace,
I shall expound this ilk thing   *same*
which Saint John saw thus sleeping   *while asleep*
through help of Jesu, Heaven-King,

220   anon-right in this place.   *immediately*

These two witness, witterly,   *witnesses; truly*
he said they should come and prophesy,
that one is Enoch, the other Hely—   *Elijah*
shall have great might and main   *power*

225   that when Antichrist comes in hie   *so that; in haste*
God's people for to destroy,
that he deceiveth falsely   *those whom*
they shall convert again.

Many signs they shall show   *display*

230   which the people shall well know,   *recognise*
and in their token truly trow   *signs; trust*
and lieve it steadfastly.   *believe*
And all that turn, lieve you me,   *convert; believe*
Antichrist will slay through his posty;   *power*

235   but verray martyrs they shall be   *true*
and come to Heaven on hie.   *at once*

The beast that John spake of here
is Antichrist, withouten were,   *without any doubt*
which shall have the Devil's power

240   and with these good men meet.
And at the last, witterly.   *truly*
He shall slay Enoch and Hely   *Elijah*
in Jerusalem, as read I,

even in midst of the street.

245	Now, that you shall know and seen	*see*
	what men Enoch and Hely been,	*what kind of; are*
	I will you tell, withouten ween,	*certainly*
	while that I have time.	
	They are two good men, lieve ye me;	*believe*
250	to Paradise through God's posty	*power*
	were ravished both, and there shall be,	*transported*
	ever, till the day do come.	

	The one was taken, for he was good,	
	long before Noah his Flood,	*Noah's flood*
255	and there he lives in flesh and blood,	
	as fully lieven we.	*believe*
	The other was taken, withouten were,	*definitely*
	after that many a hundredth year;	*century*
	and there together they been in fere	*are both*
260	until that time shall be.*	

Fifteen Signs: The fifteen great signs which, according to the opinion of scholars, shall come before the Last Judgement, selected from the ancient books of the Hebrews by a scholar for recital in this play:*

	Now fifteen signs, while I have space,	*time*
	I shall declare, by God's grace,	
	of which Saint Jerome mention mase	*makes*
	to fall before the Day of Doom,	*happen*
265	the which were written on a row	*list*
	he found in book of Hebrew.	*a book in Hebrew*
	Now will I tell in word-es few,	
	a while if you will dwell.	*remain*

The first day, as I written find,

245–60 On the two prophets, see above, play 17, 228+SD-52, where they are found in the Earthly Paradise awaiting their summons.

260+Heading The *Fifteen Signs* before Doomsday was another traditional theme. Their ascription to St. Jerome's researches, stated in the following stanza, is also traditional, but without substance. It is not clear if this heading, which is here translated from the Latin of the play-texts, was intended to be recited or merely a visual indicator in the text to authenticate the passage.

270 (1) the sea shall rise, against kind   *contrary to Nature*
    and as a wall against the wind,
    above all hills on high
    forty cubits, as read we;
    (2) the second day, so low shall be
275   that scarcely a man the sea shall see,
    stand he never so nigh.   *however near he may stand*

    The third day after, as read I,
    great fishes above the sea shall lie,
    yell and roar so hideously
280   that only God shall hear.
    The fourth day next after then,   *that time*
    sea and water all shall bren
    against kind, that men may ken,
    tinder as though it were.*

285   The fifth day, as read we,
    all manner of herbs and also tree   *plants; trees*
    of bloody dew all full shall be,   *blood like dew*
    and many a beast all dased.   *shall be bewildered*
    Fowls shall gather them, as I find,   *birds*
290   to fields. Each one in their kind   *species*
    of meat and drink shall have no mind,   *food; thought*
    but stand all mad and mased.   *bemused*

    The sixth day in the world overall,
    builded things to ground shall fall—
295   church, city, house and wall—
    and men in graves dare.   *lie in fear*
    Layt and fire also, verament,   *lightning; truly*
    from the sun to the firmament
    up and down shall strike and glent,   *flash*
300   and all night so foul fare.   *go on so horribly*

    The seventh day both rock and stone
    shall break asunder and fight as fone.   *enemies*
    The sound thereof shall hear no man,
    but only God Almight.   *almighty*

281–84 "The fourth day next after that, all sea and fresh water shall burn contrary to Nature, so that men may know, just as though it were tinder."

305   The eighth day earthquake shall be,
       that men and beast, lieve ye me,   *beasts; believe*
       to stand or go shall fail posty,   *lack power*
       but fall to ground all right.   *at once*

       The ninth day, as our books sayen,   *say*
310   hills shall fall and wax all plain,   *become level*
       stone turn to sand through God's main;   *might*
       so strait men shall be stad.*
       The tenth day, men that hid be,   *are hidden*
       out of their caves they shall flee—
315   to speak together have no posty,   *power*
       but go as they were mad.   *go about as if*

       The eleventh day from morrow to e'en   *morning; evening*
       all burials in the world open shall been   *graves*
       that dead may rise, withouten ween,   *certainly*
320   above the earth standing.   *and stand*
       The twelfth day stars shall fall in hie   *hastily*
       and fire shoot from them hideously.
       All manner of beasts shall roar and cry
       and neither eat nor drink.

325   The thirteenth day shall die all men
       and rise anon again right then.   *at once; immediately*
       The fourteenth day, all shall bren,   *burn*
       both Earth and eke Heaven.   *also*
       The fifteenth day made shall be
330   new Earth, new Heaven, through God's posty;   *power*
       which Heaven God grant us in to be,
       for his names seven.*

       Now have I told you, in good fay,   *truly*
       the tokens to come before Doomsday.   *signs*
335   God give you grace to do so ay   *always*
       that you then worthy be   *may be*
       to come to the bliss that lasteth ay.   *for ever*

---

312 "With such severe difficulties will men be beset."

332 *his names seven* is a conventional oath, possibly referring originally to the
seven names of God in Rabbinical tradition.

As much as here we and our play
of Antichrist's signs you shall assay,
340   he comes—soon you shall see!*

THE END

338–40 "Inasmuch as you must assess the accuracy of us and of our play of the
signs of Antichrist, he comes—you shall soon see!" The signs of Antichrist are
perhaps distinguished here from the signs of Doomsday in the prophecies of
Zechariah, Daniel and John the Evangelist.

PLAY 23: THE COMING OF ANTICHRIST

Performed by the Dyers

SPEAKING OF THE DAY of Judgement in 2 Thessalonians 2, St. Paul refers to "the son of perdition who opposeth and exalteth himself above all that is called God or that is worshipped; so that he as God sitteth in the temple of God, shewing himself that he is God" (verses 3–4). From these and other hints (e.g., 1 John 2.18–19 and 22; 2 John 7; Apocalypse [Revelation] 11, 13, and 20.7) a full legend of the reign of Antichrist developed which took influential form in *Libellus de Antechristo* by a tenth-century Burgundian monk, Adso of Montier-en-Der. We do not know the immediate source of Chester's play, but most of its details can be found in Adso's narrative and the numerous other works which developed from it.

Chester is unique among the English cycles in having a play of Antichrist. It was probably a late insertion into the cycle (see prefatory note to play 22) and the version described in the Post-Reformation Banns seems to have been rather different from our extant play since it describes Antichrist's Counsellor as expounding "who be Antichrists the world round about."

The Pre-Reformation Banns describe "a wurthy cariage that is a thing of grett costage." The action takes place primarily within the temple in Jerusalem. An agreement of 1531 or 1532 indicates that the performing company, the Dyers, shared a waggon with the Vintners (play 8) and the Goldsmiths (play 10). Plays 8 and 10 are both set in the court of Herod, and parts of that set were probably re-utilised in *Antichrist*. Given the craft of the Dyers, the set presumably included rich hangings, and the play would be costumed with some splendour. The reference to the two prophets as "muffled in mantles" (390) suggests a contrasting drabness. Play 23 is a play about pretence and contains a warning about the deceptive nature of convincing acting, for Antichrist imitates miracles already played. He seems to raise the dead from tombs, to effect his own resurrection, and to send down his spirit upon the kings. The set must therefore include two tomb-slabs, perhaps set close to the waggon-floor, from which "the dead" rise, into which they retreat when their deception is discovered, and which can also serve as entrance to hell for the disposal of the body and soul of the dead Antichrist. Such traps were presumably used in play 10 for the collection of Herod's body. A larger, more elaborate table-tomb, perhaps set in front of an altar, would be Antichrist's burial-place. There seems no necessity here for an upper level representing heaven. It is not clear with what visual effects, if any, the "spirit" is transmitted; red streamers thrown by the attendant devils have been used in modern productions. Antichrist also claims to turn trees upside down—an emblematic reversal of nature—which seems to require an additional feature. The action includes formal ceremonial in the solemn offerings of lamb and goat by the kings and the distribution of lands (land-deeds?) by Antichrist.

The turning-point of the play is the entry of the strange figures of Enoch and Elijah, presumably at ground-level. They engage in a hilariously abusive slanging-match with Antichrist, producing a comic disintegration of the order set up in the first part. Here the theology and sacraments of the contemporary Church prove more powerful than Antichrist's replicated wonders of the past. Though God's followers are martyred, Michael kills Antichrist who is borne down to hell in a parodic reversal of the Ascension. True order is restored with the resurrection and ascent into heaven of the two prophets to liturgical song.

Cast   ANTICHRIST, FIRST KING, SECOND KING, THIRD KING, FOURTH KING, FIRST DEAD, SECOND DEAD, ENOCH, ELIJAH, COUNSELLOR, THE ARCHANGEL MICHAEL, FIRST DEVIL, SECOND DEVIL.

ANTICHRIST	De celso throno poli, pollens clarior sole,
	age vos monstrare descendi, vos judicare.
	Reges et principes sunt subditi sub me viventes.
	Sitis sapientes vos, semper in me credentes
5	et faciam flentes gaudere atque dolentes.
	Sic omnes gentes gaudebunt in me sperantes.
	Descendi praesens rex pius et perlustrator;

"Princeps Aeternus" vocor, "Christus, vester Salvator."*

All ledes in land now be light	*peoples; happy*
10 that will be ruled throughout the right.	*completely by*
Your Saviour now in your sight	
here you may safely see.	*confidently*
Messias, Christ, and most of might,	*Messiah*
that in the Law was you behight,	*promised*
15 all Mankind to joy to dight	*prepare for*
is comen, for I am he.	*come*

Of me was spoken in prophecy	
of Moses, David and Isay.*	*Isaiah*
I am he they call "Messy,"	*Messiah*
20 "Forbuyer of Israel."	*Redeemer*
Those that lieven on me steadfastly,	*believe*
I shall them save from annoy,	*torment*
and joy right as have I	*just as*
with them I think to deal.	*intend to share*

Of me is it said in the thirty-sixth chapter of Ezechiel:
"Tollam vos de gentibus et congregabo vos de universis
terris, et reducam vos in terram vestram."*

25 But one hath ligged him here in land,*	
"Jesu" he hight, I understand.	*is called*
To further falsehood he can fand	*has contrived*
and fared with fantasy.	*proceeded; magic*

1–8 "From the high throne of the heavens, shining brighter than the sun, I have
come down to make you see, to judge you. Living kings and rulers are put down
beneath me. Be wise, believing in me always, and I shall make those who weep
and grieve rejoice. Thus all nations placing hope in me shall rejoice. I have come
down in your sight as a benevolent king and for your scrutiny; I am called
'Eternal Prince, Christ, your Saviour.'" No source for these lines has been found.

17–18 The references are perhaps to Deuteronomy 18.18 (Moses); 2 Kings (AV 2
Samuel) 7.13 and Psalms 5 (David); Isaiah 2 and 40–56 (Isaiah). All, however, also
contain warnings against false prophets, lending irony to the allusions.

24+Latin "For I will take you from among the heathen and gather you out of all
countries, and will bring you into your own land" (Ezechiel 36.24).

25 "But one has misrepresented himself here on earth."

	His wickedness he would not wond	*cease*
30	till he was taken and put in bond	*bondage*
	and slain through virtue of my sond.	*power; messenger*
	This is sooth, sickerly.	*true; assuredly*

	My people of Jews he could twin	*dispersed*
	that their land came they never in.	
35	Then on them now must I min	*have mind*
	and restore them again.	
	To build this temple will I not blin,	*cease*
	as God honoured be therein	
	and endless weal I shall them win,	*joy*
40	all that to me been bain.	*are obedient*

About me is it said in a psalm: "Adorabo ad templum sanctum tuum in timore tuo."*

	One thing me glads, be you bold.	*pleases; sure*
	As Daniel the prophet before me told,*	
	all women in world me love should	
	when I were come in land.	*into the land*
45	This prophecy I shall well hold	*keep*
	which is most liking to young and old.	*pleasing*
	I think to fast many hold	*tightly embrace*
	and their fairness to fand.	*try out*

	Also he told them, lieve you me,	*believe*
50	that I of gift-es should be free,	*generous*
	which prophecy done shall be	*fulfilled*
	when I my realm have wonnen;	*won*
	and that I should grant men posty,	*power*
	rived riches, land and fee—	*abundant; reward*
55	it shall be done, that you shall see,	
	when I am hither comen.	*come*

"Dabit eis potestatem, et multis terram dividet gratuito,"

40+Latin "In thy fear will I worship toward thy holy temple" (Psalms 5.8). But the context (7–8) contrasts the true worshipper and the liar, giving the reference an ironic edge.

42 The reference is partially to Daniel 11.39, cited below, but also to verse 37.

the thirteenth chapter of Daniel.[*]

What say you kings that here be lent?	*dwelling*
Are not my words at your assent?	*agreeable to you*
That I am Christ Omnipotent	
lieve you not this eachone?	*believe; all of you*

60

1ST KING

We lieven, lord, withouten let,	*believe; truly*
that Christ is not comen yet.	*come*
If thou be he, thou shall be set	
in temple as God alone.	

2ND KING
66

If thou be Christ, call-ed "Messy,"	*Messiah*
that from our bale shall us buy,	*torment; redeem*
do before us mastery,	*an act of power*
a sign that we may see.	

3RD KING
70

Then will I lieve that it is so.	*believe*
If thou do wonders or thou go	*before*
so that thou save us of our woe,	*from*
then honoured shalt thou be.	

4TH KING
75

Foul have we lieved many a year	*wrongly; believed*
and of our weening been in were.	*expectation; doubt*
And thou be Christ comen here,	*if; come*
then may thou stint all strife.	*make an end of*

ANTICHRIST
80

That I am Christ, and Christ will be,	
by very sign soon shall you see,	*true*
for dead men through my posty	*power*
shall rise from death to life.	

85

Now will I turn, all through my might,	
trees down, the roots upright—	
that is marvel to your sight—	*a wonder*
and fruit growing upon.	
So shall they grow and multiply	
through my might and my mastery.	*domination*
I put you out of heresy	*remove you from*
to lieve me upon.	*believe*

56+Latin "He shall cause them to rule over many, and shall divide the land for gain" (Daniel 11.39). The text's reference is wrong.

90	And bodies that been dead and slain,	*have been*
	if I may raise them up again,	
	then honour me with might and main.	
	Then shall no man you grieve.	*harm*
	Forsooth, then after will I die	*truly*
	and rise again through my posty.	*power*
95	If I may do this marvellously,	*in wondrous fashion*
	I read you on me lieve.	*advise; believe*

Men buried in grave as you may see,
what mastery is now, hope ye,   *act of power; think*
to raise them up through my posty   *power*
and all through my own accord?   *consent*
Whether I in my godhead be
by verray sign you shall see.   *true*
Rise up, dead men, and honour me,
and know me for your lord.

Then the dead shall rise up again from the grave.

1ST DEAD   Ah, Lord, to thee I ask mercy.   *of you*
106   I was dead, but now live I.
  Now wot I well and witterly   *know; certainly*
  that Christ is hither comen.   *come*

2ND DEAD   Him honour we and all men,   *let us worship*
110   devoutly kneeling on our knen.   *knees*
  Worshipped be thou there—Amen—
  Christ, that our name has nomen.*

ANTICHRIST   That I shall fulfill Holy Writ   *Holy Scripture*
  you shall wot and know well it,   *know*
115   for I am wall of weal and wit*
  and lord of every land.
  And as the prophet Sophony   *Zephaniah*
  speaks of me full witterly   *most truthfully*
  I shall rehearse here readily   *repeat; forthwith*
120   that clerks shall understand: *clerics*

---

112 "Christ, who has taken our name," i.e., assumed human form. The line is
corrupt in all manuscripts.

115 "For I am the well-spring of joy and understanding."

"Expecta me in die resurrectionis meae in futurum quia
judicium ut congregem gentes et colligam regna," Zephaniah 3.*

Now will I die, that you shall see,
and rise again through my posty.   *power*
I will in grave that you put me
and worship me alone.
125   For in this temple a tomb is made;
therein my body shall be laid.
Then will I rise as I have said—
take tent to me eachone!   *heed; all of you*

And after my resurrection
130   then will I sit in great renown   *splendour*
and my Ghost send to you down   *(Holy) Spirit*
in form of fire full soon.   *immediately*

I die, I die! Now am I dead!

1ST KING   Now sith this worthy lord is dead   *since*
135   and his grace is with us led,   *committed to us*
to take his body it is my read   *counsel*
and bury it in a grave.

2ND KING   Forsooth, and so to us he said   *truly*
in a tomb he would be laid.
140   Now go we further, all in a braid;   *forth; an instant*
from disease he may us save.   *distress*

Then they shall go across to Antichrist.

3RD KING   Take we the body of this sweet   *beloved one*
and bury it low under the greet.   *earth*
Now, Lord, comfort us, we thee beseech.
145   and send us of thy grace.   *(some) of*

4TH KING   And if he rise soon through his might
from death to life, as he behight,   *promised*
him will I honour day and night

_____

120+Latin "Therefore wait ye upon me, saith the Lord, until the day that I rise
up to the prey; for my determination is to gather the nations, that I may assemble
the kingdoms" (Zephaniah 3.8).

as God in every place.

*Then they shall withdraw from the grave-mound as far as the
ground.*

1ST KING 151	Now wot I well that he is dead,	*know*
	for now in grave we have him laid.	
	If he rise as he hath said,	
	he is of full great might.	

2ND KING 155	I cannot lieve him upon	*believe*
	but if he rise himself alone	*unless*
	as he hath said to many one,	
	and show him here in sight.	*reveal himself*

3RD KING	Till that my Saviour be risen again,	
	in faith my heart may not be fain	*happy*
160	till I him see with eye.	

4TH KING	I must mourn with all my main	*strength*
	till Christ be risen up again	
	and of that miracle make us fain.	*by; happy*
	Rise up, Lord, that we may see.	

Then Antichrist shall raise his body up, rising from the dead.

ANTICHRIST 166	I rise! Now reverence does to me,	*do*
	God glorified created of degree.	*by rank*
	If I be Christ, now lieve ye	*may be; believe*
	and worch after my wise.	*act after my fashion*

1ST KING 170	Ah, Lord, welcome must thou be.	*may*
	That thou art God now lieve we.	*believe*
	Therefore, go sit up in thy see	*throne*
	and keep our sacrifice.	*accept*

Then they shall go across to Antichrist with a sacrifice.

2ND KING	Forsooth, in seat thou shalt be set	*truly*
	and honoured with lamb and get	*goat*
175	as Moses' Law that lasteth yet,	*still endures*
	as he hath said before.	

174–75 I.e., Leviticus 3.7 (lamb) and 3.12 (goat).

3RD KING	Oh, gracious Lord, go sit down then,	
	and we shall, kneeling on our knen,	*knees*
	worship thee as thy own men	*servants*
180	and work after thy lore.	*according to your teaching*

Then Antichrist shall go up to the throne.

4TH KING	Hither we be comen with good intent	*are come; will*
	to make our sacrifice, Lord excellent,	
	with this lamb that I have here hent,	*taken*
	kneeling thee before.	
185	Thou grant us grace to do and say	
	that it be pleasing to thee ay,	*what may be; always*
	to thy bliss that come we may	
	and never from it be lore.	*lost*

ANTICHRIST	I Lord, I God, I High Justice,	*judge*
190	I Christ that made the dead to rise!	
	Here I receive your sacrifice	
	and bless you, flesh and fell.	*completely*

Then they shall withdraw from Antichrist.

ANTICHRIST	I will now send my Holy Ghost,	
	you kings also to you I tell,	
195	to know me Lord of might-es most	*acknowledge me as*
	of Heaven, Earth, and Hell.	

Then he shall send forth his Spirit, saying: "Dabo vobis cor novum et spiritum novum in medio vestri."

KINGS (*in chorus*)		
	Ah, God! Ah, Lord mickle of might!	*great*
	This Holy Ghost is in me pight.	*fixed*
	Methinks my heart is very light	*it seems; joyful*
200	sith it came into me.	*since*

1ST KING	Lord, we thee honour day and night	
	for thou showest us in sight	
	right as Moses us behight.	*promised*

196+SD "A new heart also will I give you, and a new spirit will I put within you" (Ezechiel 36.26).

        Honoured must thou be.

ANTICHRIST 206	Yet worthy works to your will	*for your delight*
	of prophecy I shall fulfill.	
	As Daniel prophesied you until*	*to you*
	that lands I shall devise,	*assign*
	that prophecy it shall be done	*accomplished*
210	and it you shall see right soon.	*at once*
	Worship me all that ye mon	*may*
	and do after the wise.	*what is wise*

You kings, I shall advance you all,   *promote*
and, because your regions be but small,   *territories*
215   cities, castles shall you befall,   — 2nd Temptation   *come to you*
with towns and towers gay;   *splendid*
and make you lords of lordships fair,*
as well it falls for my power.   *befits*
Yea, look ye do as I you lere   *teach*
220   and harkens what I say.   *pay attention to*

I am verray God of might.   *true*
All things I made through my might—
sun and moon, day and night.
To bliss I may you bring.
225   Therefore, kings noble and gay,   *splendid*
token your people what I say—   *signify to*
that I am Christ, God verray—   *true*
and tell them such tiding.   *news*

My people of Jews were put me from.
230   Therefore great ruth I have them on.   *pity*
Whether they will lieve me upon   *believe*
I will full soon assay.   *find out*
For all that will lieve me upon,   *believe*
worldly wealth shall them fall on   *descend upon*
235   and to my bliss they shall come
and dwell with me for ay.   *for ever*

And the gifts that I behight   *promised*

---

207 Cited above after line 55.

217 "And create you lords of splendid realms."

you shall have, as is good right.   *right and proper*
Hence or I go out of your sight   *before*
240   eachone shall know his dole.   *everyone; portion*

To thee I give Lombardy;
and to thee Denmark and Hungary;
and take thou Patmos and Italy;
and Rome it shall be thine.*

2ND KING   Gramercy, Lord, your gifts today!   *thank you for*
246   Honour we will thee alway,   *always*
           for we were never so rich, in good fay,   *truly*
           nor none of all our kin.   *race*

ANTICHRIST   Therefore be true and steadfast ay,   *always*
250   and truly lieves on my lay,   *believe; law*
             for I will harken on you today,   *listen to*
             steadfast if I you find,

             Then Antichrist shall withdraw, and Enoch and Elijah shall
             come.

ENOCH   Almighty God in majesty,
          that made the Heaven and Earth to be,
255   fire, water, stone, and tree,
          and Man through thy might—   *Mankind*
          the points of thy privity   *attributes; holy mystery*
          any earthly man to see   *(for) any mortal*
          is impossible, as thinks me,   *it seems to me*
260   for any worldly wight.   *mortal person*

          Gracious Lord, that art so good,
          that who so long in flesh and blood
          hath granted life and heavenly food,*
          let never our thoughts be defiled;
265   but give us, Lord, might and main,   *power and strength*

241–44 Though all these lands were centres of struggle and religious controversy
in the sixteenth century, they may well be chosen at random here, merely as
familiar names.

261–63 "Gracious Lord, who art so virtuous, who hast granted life and heavenly
sustenance to whoever exists in flesh and blood."

	or we of this shrew be slain,	*before; wretch*
	to convert thy people again	
	that he hath thus beguiled.	*deceived*
	Sith the world's beginning	*since*
270	I have lived in great liking	*happiness*
	through help of high and Heaven King	
	in Paradise without annoy,	*distress*
	till we heard tokening	*evidence*
	of this thief's coming	
275	that now on Earth is reigning	
	and doth God's folks destroy.	*peoples*
	To Paradise I was taken that tide,	*time*
	this thief his coming to abide,	*await*
	and Hely, my brother, here me beside,	*Elijah*
280	was after sent to me.	
	With this champion we must chide	*dispute*
	that now in world walketh wide,	
	to disprove his pomp and pride	
	and pair all his posty.	*diminish; power*
ELIJAH	Oh Lord that madest all thing	
286	and long has lent us living,	*given us life*
	let never the Devil's power spring	*grow*
	this man hath him within.	*(which)*
	God give you grace, both old and young,	
290	to know deceit in his doing,*	
	that you may come to that liking	*joy*
	of bliss that never shall blin.	*cease*
	I warn you, all men, witterly,	*admonish; truly*
	this is Enoch, I am Hely,	*Elijah*
295	been comen his errors to destroy	*(who) are come*
	that he to you now shows.	
	He calls himself "Christ" and "Messy."	*Messiah*
	He lies forsooth, apertly.	*truly; plainly*
	He is the Devil, you to annoy,	*come to harm you*
300	and for none other him knows.	*recognise*
3RD KING	Ah, men, what speak you of Hely	*Elijah*

---

290 "To recognise the deception in what he is doing."

    and Enoch? They been both in company.   *are;companions*
    Of our blood they been, witterly,   *are;truly*
    and we been of their kind.   *are;kindred*

4TH KING
306
    We readen in Books of our Law   *read*
    that they to Heaven were idraw—   *drawn up into*
    and yet been there is the common saw,
    written as men may find.*

ENOCH
310
    We been those men, forsooth iwiss,   *are;most truly*
    comen to tell you do amiss,   *come to say that*
    and bring your souls to Heaven-bliss
    if it were any boot.   *there were any improvement*

ELIJAH
    This Devil's limb that comen is,   *is come*
    that saith Heaven and Earth is his,
315
    now we be ready, lieve you this,   *believe*
    against him for to moot.   *argue our case*

1ST KING
    If that we here wit mon   *may know*
    by proofs of disputation   *argued demonstration*
    that you have skill and reason,   *power*
320
    with you we will abide.   *remain*

2ND KING
    And if your skills may do him down,   *arguments*
    to die with you we will be boun   *ready*
    in hope of salvation,
    whatever may betide.

ENOCH
326
    To do him down we shall assay   *attempt*
    through might of Jesu, born of a may,   *virgin*
    by right and reason, as you shall say,
    and that you shall well hear.
    And for that cause hither were we sent
330
    by Jesu Christ Omnipotent,
    and that you shall not all be shent.   *destroyed*
    He bought you all full dear.   *redeemed at high cost*

    Be glad, therefore, and make good cheer,   *rejoice*
    and I do read as I you lere,   *counsel;teach*

307–8 "And that they are still there is the general opinion, recorded as men may discover."

335	for we be comen in good manner	*are come; rightly*
	to save you everychone.	*all*
	And dread you not for that false fiend,	
	for you shall see him cast behind	
	or we depart and from him wend,	*before; go*
340	and shame shall light him on.	*disgrace; descend*

And thus Enoch and Elijah shall go across to Antichrist.

ENOCH	Say, thou verray Devil's limb,	*true*
	that sits so grizzly and so grim—	*fierce*
	from him thou came, and shalt to him,	
	for many a soul thou beguiles.	*deceives*
345	Thou hast deceived men many a day	
	and made the people to thy pay,	*manipulated; pleasure*
	and bewitched them into a wrong way	*course of action*
	wickedly with thy wiles.	*cunning tricks*

ANTICHRIST	Ah, false faitours, from me ye flee!	*scoundrels*
350	Am I not most in majesty?	*greatest in kingly power*
	What men dare main them thus to me	*act*
	or make such distance?	*discord*

ELIJAH	Fie on thee, faitour, fie on thee,	*scoundrel*
	the Devil's own nurry!	*foster-child*
355	Through him thou preachest and hast posty	*power*
	a while through sufferance.	*for a time*

ANTICHRIST	Oh you hypocrites that so cryen!	*cry out*
	Losels, lourdens! Loudly you lyen!	*liars; rascals; lie*
	To spill my Law you aspyen.	*destroy; set a trap*
360	That speech is good to spare.	
	You that my true faith defyen	
	and needless my folk divine,	
	from hence hastily!* But you hence hi-en,	*hasten*
	to you comes sorrow and care.	

ENOCH	Thy sorrow and care come on thy head,	
366	for falsely through thy wicked read	*counsel*
	the people is put to pine.	*torment*

361–63 "You who hurl defiance at my true faith and needlessly practise divination against my people, get out of here quickly."

I would thy body were from thy head
twenty mile from it laid,
370   till I it brought again!

ANTICHRIST   Out on thee, roisard, with thy wiles,*
for falsely my people thou beguiles.   *deceive*
I shall thee hastily hong,   *hang*
and that lourden that stands thee by—   *scoundrel*
375   he puts my folk to great annoy   *trouble*
with his false flattering tongue.

But I shall teach you courtesy,
you Saviour to know anon in hie,   *straightaway*
false thieves with your heresy,
380   and if you dare abide.   *if*

ELIJAH   Yes, forsooth, for all thy pride,   *indeed*
here we purpose for to abide   *remain*
through grace of God Almight.   *Almighty*
And all the world that is so wide
385   shall wonder on thee on every side
soon in all men's sight.

ANTICHRIST   Out on you, thieves both two.
Each man may see you be so
all by your array,   *dress*
390   muffled in mantles! None such I know.
I shall make you lout full low   *stoop*
or I depart you all fro,   *before;from*
to know me Lord for ay.   *acknowledge;ever*

ENOCH   We be no thieves, we thee tell,
395   thou false fiend comen from Hell.   *come*
With thee we purpose for to mell, *intend to debate*
my fellow and I in fere,   *together*
to know thy power and thy might
as we these kings have behight,   *promised*
400   and thereto we be ready dight   *prepared*
that all men now may hear.

ANTICHRIST   My might is most, I tell to thee.

---

371 "Damn you, stupid babbler, with your deceitful tricks."

	I died, I rose through my posty.	*power*
	That all these kings saw with their ee,	*eye*
405	and every man and wife.	*woman*
	And miracles and marvels I did also.	*wonders*
	I counsel you, therefore, both two,	
	to worship me and no moe,	*other*
	and let us no more strive.	*contend*

ELIJAH	They were no miracles but marvellous things	*wonderful*
411	that thou showed unto these kings.	
	Into falsehood thou them brings	*wickedness*
	through the Fiend's craft.	*power*
	And as the flower now springs,	*grows up*
415	falleth, fadeth, and hangs,	*wilts*
	so thy joy—now it rings	*flourishes*
	that shall be from thee raft.	*taken away*

ANTICHRIST	Out on thee, thief that sits so still!	
	Why wilt thou not one word speak them till	*to*
420	but let them speak all their will	*all they wish*
	that comen me to repreve?	*come; rebuke*

COUN-	Oh Lord, Master, what shall I say then?	
SELLOR		

ANTICHRIST	I beshrew both thy knen!	*curse; knees*
	Art thou now for to ken?	*do you have to be told*
425	In faith, I shall thee grieve.	*truly; make you weep*
	Of my godhead I made thee wise	*through*
	and set thee ever at mickle price.	*great worth*
	Now I would feel thy good advice	*sample*
	and hear what thou would say.	
430	These lollers, they would fain me grieve	
	and nothing on me they will lieve,*	
	but ever be ready me to repreve	*rebuke*
	and all the people of my lay.	*law*

COUN-	Oh Lord that art so mickle of might,	*great*
SELLOR	methink thou should not chide ne fight;	*argue; nor*

430-31 "These villains, they would happily bring me to grief and they will have no belief in me whatsoever."

436	but curse them, Lord, through thy might.	
	Then shall they fare full ill.	*do badly*
	For those whom thou blesses, they shall well speed;	*prosper*
	and those whom thou cursest, they are	
	but dead.	*as good as dead*
440	This is my counsel and my read,	*advice*
	yonder heretics for to spill.	*destroy*

ANTICHRIST	The same I purposed, lieve thou me.	*believe*
	All things I know through my posty.	*power*
	But yet thy wit I thought to see,	*wisdom*
445	what was thine intent.	*will*
	It shall be done full sickerly;	*most certainly*
	the sentence, given full openly	
	with my mouth, truly,	
	upon them shall be hent.	*delivered*

450	My curse I give you, to amend your meels,	*arguments(?)*
	from your head unto your heels!	
	Walk ye forth in your way.	

ENOCH	Yea, thou shalt never come in caelis,	*into heaven*
	for falsely with thy wiles	*deceitful tricks*
455	the people are put in pine.	*torment*

ANTICHRIST	Out on you, thieves! Why fare ye this?*	
	Whether had you liever have, pain or bliss?	*which; rather*
	I may you save from all amiss.	*trouble*
	I made the day and eke the night	*also*
460	and all things that are on Earth growing—	
	flowers fair that fresh can spring;	*grew up*
	also I made all other thing—	*things*
	the stars that be so bright.	

ELIJAH	Thou liest! Vengeance on thee befall!	*fall*
465	Out on thee, wretch! Wrath thee I shall!*	
	Thou callest thee "King" and "Lord of all"?	
	A fiend is thee within!	

---

456 "Damn you, thieves! Why do you carry on like this?"

465 "Damn you, wretch! I'll give you something to be angry about."

ANTICHRIST	Thou liest falsely, I thee tell.	
	Thou will be damned into Hell.	
470	I made thee, man, of flesh and fell,	*flesh and skin*
	and all that is living.	
	For other gods have ye none.	
	Therefore worship me alone,	
	the which hath made the water and stone,	
475	and all at my liking.	*pleasure*

ENOCH	Forsooth thou liest falsely.	*indeed*
	Thou art a fiend, comen to annoy	*trouble*
	God's people that stand us by.	*beside*
	In Hell I would thou were.	

ELIJAH	Fie on thee, felon, fie on thee, fie!	
481	For all thy witchcraft and sorcery,	
	to moot with thee I am ready,	*dispute*
	that all the people may hear.	

| ANTICHRIST | Out on you, harlots! Whence come ye? | *wretches* |
| 485 | Where have you any other god but me? | |

ENOCH	Yea—Christ, God in Trinity,	
	thou false faitour attaint,	*corrupt scoundrel*
	that sent his Son from Heaven-see	*heavenly throne*
	that for Mankind died on rood-tree,	*the cross*
490	that shall full soon make thee to flee,	
	thou faitour false and faint.	*scoundrel; puny*

| ANTICHRIST | Ribalds, ruled out of ray!* | |
| | What is "the Trinity" for to say? | *does it mean* |

ELIJAH	Three Persons, as thou lieve may,	*believe*
495	in one Godhead in fere—	*together*
	Father and Son, that is no nay,	*no denying*
	and the Holy Ghost stirring ay.	*Spirit; active always*
	That is one God verray;	*true*
	been all three named here.	*are*

| ANTICHRIST | Out on you, thieves! What sayen ye? | *say* |
| 501 | Will you have one God and three? | |

492 "Villains, directed out of your appointed places"; i.e., upstarts.

How dare you so say?
Madmen, madmen! Therefore, lieve on me   *believe*
that am one God—so is not he!
505   Then may you live in joy and lee,   *happiness*
all this land I dare lay.

ENOCH   Nay, tyrant! Understand thou this:
without beginning his Godhead is
and also without ending, iwiss.   *truly*
510   Thus fully lieven we.   *believe*
And thou, that engendered was amiss,   *wrongfully*
hast beginning and now this bliss,
an end shall have—no dread there is—   *no doubt*
full foul, as men shall see.

ANTICHRIST   Wretches! Gulls! You be blent!   *fools; are blind*
516   God's Son I am, from him sent.
How dare you maintain your intent,   *wilfulness*
sith he and I be one?   *since*
Have I not, sith I came him fro,   *since; from*
520   made the dead to speak and go?
And to men I sent my Ghost also   *(Holy) Spirit*
that lieved me upon.   *believed*

ELIJAH   Fie on thee, felon, fie on thee, fie!   *monster*
For through his might and his majesty
525   by sufferance of God Almighty,
the people are blent through thee.   *blinded*
If those men be raised witterly   *certainly*
without the Devil's fantasy,   *magic*
here shall be proved apertly   *(it) be; openly*
530   that all men shall see.

ANTICHRIST   Ah, fools! I read you lieve me upon   *advise; believe*
that miracles have showed to many one,
to the people everychone,   *all*
to put them out of doubt.
535   Therefore I read you hastily,   *advise*
converts to me most mighty.
I shall you save from annoy,   *anguish*
and that I am about.

ENOCH   Now of thy miracles would I see.   *something of*

| ELIJAH
541 | Therefore comen hither be we—
to see what is thy great posty
and some thereof to lear.* | *are come* |

| ANTICHRIST

545 | Soon may you see, if you will abide,
for I will neither fight nor chide.
Of all the world that is so wide
therein is not my peer. | *dispute*

equal |

| ENOCH

550 | Bring forth those men here in our sight
that thou hast raised against the right.
If thou be so mickle of might
to make them eat and drink,
for verray God we will thee know
such a sign if thou wilt show,
and do thee reverence on a row
all at thy liking. | *wrongfully*
great

true; acknowledge

together
entirely at your pleasure |

| ANTICHRIST
556

560 | Wretches damn-ed all be ye!
But nought for that! It falleth me
as gracious God abiding be,
if you will mend your life,*
You dead men, rise through my posty.
Come, eat and drink, that men may see,
and prove me worthy of Deity;
so shall we stint all strife. |

power

Godhead
stop; contention |

| 1ST DEAD | Lord, thy bidding I will do ay
and for to eat I will assay. | *always*
attempt |

| 2ND DEAD
566 | And I also, all that I may,
will do thy bidding here. | *as far as I can* |

| ELIJAH

570 | Have here bread both two.
But I must bless it or it go,
that the Fiend, Mankind's foe,
on it have no power. |
before it is given

may have; over it |

541–42 "To see what your great power amounts to and to learn something about it."

556–58 "But enough of that! It befits me as a gracious God to be tolerant, if you will reform your way of life."

This bread I bless with my hand
in Jesus' name, I understand,
the which is Lord of sea and land
and King of Heaven on high.
575   "In nomine patris" that all hath wrought,
"et Filii Virginis" that dear us bought,
"et Spiritus Sancti" is all my thought,
"one God and Persons three."*

1ST DEAD   Alas! Put that bread out of my sight!
580   To look on it I am not light.   *happy*
That print that is upon it pight,   *mark; set*
it puts me in great fear.

2ND DEAD   To look on it I am not light.   *happy*
That bread to me it is so bright
585   and is my foe both day and night,
and puts me to great dere.   *fear*

ENOCH   Now, you men that have done amiss,
you see well what his power is.
Converts to him, I read iwiss,   *truly advise*
590   that you on rood hath bought.   *cross; redeemed*

3RD KING   Ah, now we know apertly   *clearly*
we have been brought in heresy.   *led into*
With you to death we will forthy,
and never eft turn our thought.*

4TH KING   Now, Enoch and Hely, it is no nay
596   you have tainted the tyrant this same day.*
Blessed be Jesu, born of a may!   *virgin*
On him I lieve upon.   *believe*

575–78 "'In the name of the Father' who has made all things, 'and of the Virgin's
Son' who redeemed us at high cost,' and 'of the Holy Spirit' which informs all
my thought, one God and three Persons." Elijah consecrates the bread with a
Trinitarian formula as a priest consecrates the Host.

593–94 "We will therefore go with you to our deaths and never again alter our
resolve."

595–96 "Now, Enoch and Elijah, there is no denying that you have proved the
tyrant guilty this same day."

1ST KING   Thou faitour fared with fantasy,*
600   with sorcery, witchcraft, and necromancy,
            thou hast us led in heresy.   *into*
            Fie on thy works eachone!   *all*

2ND KING   Jesu, for thy mickle grace,   *great*
            forgive us all our trespass   *sin*
605   and bring us to thy heavenly place,
            as thou art God and Man.
            Now am I wise made through thy might.
            Blessed be thou, Jesu, day and night!
            This grizzly groom graithes him to fight*
610   and slay us here anon.   *at once*

3RD KING   Of our lives let us not retch,   *for; care*
            though we be slain of such a wretch,   *may be*
            for Jesus' sake that may us teach   *show us how*
            our souls to bring to bliss.

4TH KING   That was well said, and so I assent.
616   To die, forsooth, is mine intent   *truly; resolve*
            for Christ's love Omnipotent,
            in cause that is rightwise.   *righteous*

ANTICHRIST Ah, false faitours, turn you now!   *scoundrels*
620   You shall be slain, I make avow;   *vow*
            and those traitors that so turned you,   *converted*
            I shall make them unfain,   *distressed*
            that all other by very sight   *true witness*
            shall know that I am most of might,   *greatest of power*
625   for with this sword now will I fight,
            for all you shall be slain.

            Then Antichrist shall kill Enoch and Elijah and all the con-
            verted kings with the sword, and shall return to his throne—
            at which point Michael with a sword in his right hand, shall
            speak.

MICHAEL   Antichrist, now is comen this day.   *come*

---

599 "You scoundrel hidden by your evil magic."

609 "This ugly thing is arming himself to fight."

	Reign no longer now thou may.	
	He that hath led thee alway,	*always*
630	now him thou must go to.	
	No more men shall be slain by thee.	
	My Lord will dead that thou be.	*desires*
	He that hath given thee this posty	*power*
	thy soul shall underfo.	*receive*

	In sin engendered first thou was.	
635	In sin engendered first thou was. ✓	
	In sin led thy life thou has.	
	In sin an end now thou mase	*makes*
	that marred has many one.	*harmed*
	Thou has ever served Satanas	*Satan*
640	and had his power in every place.	
	Therefore thou gets now no grace.	*obtain*
	With him thou must gone.	*go*

	Three years and half one, witterly,	*truly*
	thou hast had leave to destroy	
645	God's people wickedly	
	through thy foul read.	*evil counsel*
	Now thou shalt know and wit in hie	*understand at once*
	that more is God's majesty	*greater*
	than eke the Devil's and thine thereby,	*also; with it*
650	for now thou shalt be dead.	

Then Michael shall kill Antichrist and as he is killed Antichrist shall cry "Help, help, help, help!"

ANTICHRIST	Help, Satanas and Lucifer!	*Satan*
	Beelzebub, bold bachelor!	*knight*
	Ragnell, Ragnell, thou art my dear!*	*beloved*
	Now fare I wonder evil.	*strangely ill*
655	Alas, alas, where is my power?	
	Alas, my wit is in a were.	*mind; turmoil*
	Now body and soul both in fere	*together*
	and all goeth to the Devil.	

Then Antichrist shall die, and two devils shall come and shall speak as follows:

651–53 Antichrist calls upon the names of a number of devils.

1ST DEVIL	Anon, master, anon, anon!	*at once*
660	From Hell-ground I heard thee groan.	
	I thought not to come myself alone	
	for worship of thine estate.	*honour; position*
	With us to Hell thou shalt gone.	*go*
	For this death we make great moan.	*lamentation*
665	To win more souls into our wone—	*dwelling*
	but now it is too late!*	

2ND DEVIL	With me thou shalt—from me thou come.	*shall go; came*
	Of me shall come thy last doom.	*from; final judgement*
	for thou hast well deserved.	*deserved (it)*
670	And through my might and my posty	*power*
	thou hast lived in dignity	*high estate*
	and many a soul deceived.	

1ST DEVIL	This body was gotten by mine assent	*begotten*
	in clean whoredom, verament.	*pure lechery truly*
675	Of mother womb or that he went,	*mother's; before*
	I was him within	
	and taught him ay with mine intent	*ever; will*
	sin, by which he shall be shent.	*destroyed*
	For he did my commandment,	*because*
680	his soul shall never blin.	*find rest*

2ND DEVIL	Now, fellow, in faith great moan we may make	*lamentation*
	for this lord of estate that stands	*high rank*
	in this stead.	*place*
	Many a fat morsel we had for his sake	
	of souls that should been saved—in Hell be they hid!*	

*Then they shall take hold of his soul, and later his body.**

1ST DEVIL	His soul with sorrow in hand have I hent.	*seized*
686	Yea, penance and pain soon shall he feel!	
	To Lucifer, that lord, it shall be present	*presented*

---

666 The construction here is broken.

683–84 "Through him we had many a fat morsel from souls that should have been saved (but instead) they are hidden in hell!"

684+SD The soul and body are evidently separate components and are moved separately.

	that burn shall as a brand. His sorrow shall	*misery*
	not keel.	*grow cold*

2ND DEVIL	This proctor of prophecy hath procured	*procurator*
	many one	
690	on his laws for to lieve, and lost for his sake	*believe*
	their souls be, in sorrow—and his shall be soon!	
	Such masteries through my might	*great deeds*
	many one do I make!	*contrive*

Then the body of Antichrist is borne away by the devils.

1ST DEVIL	With Lucifer, that lord, long shall he leng;	*dwell*
	in a seat ay with sorrow with him shall he sit.	*ever*

2ND DEVIL	Yea, by the heels in Hell shall he heng	*hang*
696	in a dungeon deep, right in Hell-pit!	

1ST DEVIL	To Hell will I hie without any fail,	*hasten;delay*
	with this present of price thither to bring.	*worth*

2ND DEVIL	Thou take him by the top and I by the tail.	*feet*
700	A sorrowful song, in faith, shall he sing!	

1ST DEVIL	Ah, fellow, a dole look that thou deal	
	to all this fair company hence or thou wend.*	

2ND DEVIL	Yea, sorrow and care ever shall they feel.	
	In Hell shall they dwell at their last end.	

ENOCH	Ah, Lord, that all shall lead	
706	and both deem the quick and dead!	*judge;living*
	That reverence thee, thou on them read	
	and them through right relieve.*	
	I was dead and right here slain,	
710	but through thy might, Lord, and thy main,	*power*

701–2 "Ah, fellow, look that you hand out a portion (of blessing) to all this splendid company (i.e., the audience) before you go hence."

707–8 "You take heed of those who worship you and bring deliverance to them through righteousness"; *read on* does not appear to be recorded in a sense appropriate to this context.

	thou hast me rais-ed up again.	
	Thee will I love and lieve.	*believe in*
ELIJAH	Yea, Lord, blessed most thou be,	*may*
	my flesh glorified now I see.	
715	Wit ne sleight against thee	*cunning not deceit*
	conspired may be by no way.	*planned; no means*
	All that lieven in thee steadfastly	*believe*
	thou helps, Lord, from all annoy,	*out of all trouble*
	for dead I was, and now live I.	
720	Honoured be thou ay.	*for ever*
MICHAEL	Enoch and Hely, come you anon.	*Elijah; at once*
	My Lord will that you with me gone	*desires; go*
	to Heaven-bliss, both blood and bone,	*bodily*
	evermore there to be.	
725	You have been long, for you been wise,	*are*
	dwelling in Earthly Paradise;	
	but to Heaven where himself is	*(God) himself*
	now shall you go with me.	

*Then leading them to Heaven, the Angel shall sing "Gaudete justi in Domino," etc.**

THE END

728+SD "Rejoice in the Lord, O ye righteous, for praise is comely for the up-right" (Psalms 32 [AV 33].1). Of the possible liturgical sources, the Communion of the Mass of Two or More Martyrs has been strongly proposed.

PLAY 24: THE LAST JUDGEMENT

Performed by the Websters

TIME, WHICH BEGAN with the fall of man, comes to an end with the second coming of Christ in glory to judge mankind, a recurring theme throughout the Bible and a frequent subject of art and literature. The most influential passages for the Chester play are in Matthew 24 and 25, which include the manner of coming and the criteria by which men will be judged. Chester, however, distinguishes clearly between the particular judgement upon the soul immediately after death and the general judgement at the end of time. The resurrected dead in this play already know their fates but are come to have those judgements explained. Since only patriarchs, prophets and saints have been received into heaven on their death, the others among the redeemed have spent the time post-mortem in purgatory where their earthly sins have been purged in order that they may enter heaven at the Judgement purified. Christ explains that the criterion for salvation is the performance of acts of charity based upon knowledge of his teachings and his sacrifice, while damnation results from the wilful disregard of such acts.

All the risen dead occupied positions of authority on earth and would be richly costumed according to rank. The groups with greatest national and international power—pope, emperor, king and queen—are equally represented among both the redeemed and the damned. But the damned also include representatives of groups with local social importance—the corrupt lawyer and the unscrupulous merchant *cum* property-speculator—adding more pointed satire to the traditional complaints of abused power.

The play is on a large scale. It requires twenty speaking parts (not doubling God and Jesus), together with two further angels and an unspecified number of prophets and patriarchs, and there is obviously scope for multiplying those numbers as resources allow. The waggon-set must accommodate the three levels of heaven, earth and hell. Some form of lifting device made to look like clouds seems required to lower Christ from heaven. The dead presumably rise out of "graves"—probably two traps set into the floor of the waggon, one for the redeemed and the other for the damned. The traps may also serve as entrances to hell, through which the devils enter and the damned descend. Possibly the lower part of the waggon was decorated as an impressive hell-mouth. It seems unlikely that the redeemed would use the lifting device to ascend to heaven; possibly ladders were lowered to them. The action incorporates some strong aural and visual effects—the trumpet-blasts; the descent of Christ; the emission of blood from the wounds; the triumphal procession of the redeemed to the accompaniment of liturgical song; and the horrific entry of the devils, who obviously have strong visual "appeal." The devils are granted access to legalistic arguments which reinforce God's inability now to offer mercy. Ironically, they can claim a legitimate role within God's overall plan.

The play has the weight of the cycle behind it. Its opening words echo the very first words of God the Creator in the cycle. The recollected promise of Judgement, the instruments of the Passion which are displayed, and the summary and explanation of the Incarnation given by Christ, all look back to earlier plays. The play ends not at the noisy exit of the damned and the closing of heaven, but in a coda outside historical time. The four evangelists from the past enter to speak authoritatively of the future to the contemporary audience. The play comes to rest on the Gospels, to which the whole cycle looks for validation.

Cast   GOD, FIRST ANGEL, SECOND ANGEL, REDEEMED POPE, REDEEMED EMPEROR, REDEEMED KING, REDEEMED QUEEN, DAMNED POPE, DAMNED EMPEROR, DAMNED KING, DAMNED QUEEN, DAMNED JUDGE, DAMNED MERCHANT, JESUS, FIRST DEVIL, SECOND DEVIL, MATTHEW, MARK, LUKE, JOHN.

GOD   Ego sum alpha et omega, primus et novissimus*

Latin before line 1 "I am alpha and omega, the beginning and the end, the first and the last" (Apocalypse [Revelation] 22.13)—the opening words of plays 1 and 2.

	I, God, greatest of degree,	*rank*
	in whom beginning none may be,	
	that I am peerless of posty,	*unequalled in power*
	now apertly shall be proved.	*plainly*
5	In my Godhead are Persons three;*	
	may none in fay from other flee.	*truly; depart*
	Yet sovereign might that is in me	*royal power*
	may justly be moved.	*rightly be activated*

	It is full yore since I behight	*long ago; promised*
10	to make a reckoning of the right.	*tally of righteous*
	Now to that doom I will me dight	*judgement; prepare*
	that dead shall duly dread.	*which the dead; rightly*
	Therefore, my angels fair and bright,	
	look that you wake each worldly wight	*mortal person*
15	that I may see all in my sight	
	that I blood for can bleed.	*for whom; bled*

	Show you my cross apertly here,	*openly*
	crown of thorn, sponge and spear,	
	and nails to them that wanted ne'er	*never*
20	to come to this annoy;	*distressing occasion*
	and what weed for them I wear,	*garment*
	upon my body now I bear.	
	The most stoutest this sight shall stear	*daunt*
	that standeth by street or sty.	*stile*

1ST ANGEL	Lord, that madest through thy might	
26	Heaven and Earth, day and night,	
	without distance we be dight	*unreservedly; ready*
	your bidding for to done.	*to do*
	And for to awake each worldly wight	*mortal person*
30	I shall be ready, and that in height,	*at once*
	that they shall show them in thy sight.	*themselves*
	Thou shalt see, Lord, full soon.	

2ND ANGEL	Take we our beams and fast blow.	*trumpets*
	All Mankind shall them know.	*recognise*
35	Good account that now can show	

---

5 The speaker at this point is evidently the Trinitarian Godhead, as at the
opening of play 1.

                soon it shall be seen.*
                That have done well in their living,   *those who; life*
                they shall have joy without ending.
                That evil have done without mending   *those who; reform*
40   shall ever have sorrow and teen.   *for ever; torment*

Then the angels shall take their trumpets and shall blow, and all the dead shall rise from the graves. Of them, the Redeemed Pope shall speak first.

REDEEMED   Ah, Lord, mercy now ask we,
POPE   that died for us on the rood-tree.   *the cross*
                It is three hundred years and three   **303**
                since I was put in grave.
45   Now through thy might and thy posty   *power*
                thy beams' blast hath rais-ed me   *trumpets'*
                in flesh and blood, as I now see,
                my judgement for to have.

                While that I lived in flesh and blood,
50   thy great Godhead that is so good
                ne knew I never, but ever was wood   *mad*
                worships for to win.   *honours*
                The wits, Lord, thou sent to me   *mental faculties*
                I spent to come to great degree.   *expended; high rank*
55   The highest office under thee
                in Earth thou puttest me in.

                Thou grantedst me, Lord, through thy grace,
                Peter's power and his place.*
                Yet I was blent. Alas, alas!   *blind*
60   I did not thine assent.   *what you desired*
                But my fleshly will that wicked was,
                the which rais-ed now thou has,
                I furthered, Lord, before thy face
                shall take his judgement.*

35–36 "It shall soon be seen who can now present a good book of accounts."

57–58 St. Peter was traditionally the first pope and had the power to loose and bind on earth and in heaven committed to him by Christ, a power recommitted to his successors in papal office.

61–64 "I furthered the wilful desire of my body that was wicked, which you have now raised, [and it] shall receive its judgement before you."

65 When I in Earth was, at my will
this world me blent, both loud and still;[*]
but thy commandment to fulfill
I was full negligent.
But purged it is with pains ill *severe*
70 in Purgatory that sore can grill.[*] *torment*
Yet thy grace I hope to come till *to*
after my great torment.

And yet, Lord, I must dread thee
for my great sin when I thee see,
75 for thou art most in majesty. *greatest; royal estate*
Of mercy now I call. *for*
The pains that I have long in be— *been*
as hard as Hell, save hope of lee— *except for; joy*
again to go never suffer me *to go back to*
80 for ought that may befall. *whatever*

REDEEMED Ah, Lord and Sovereign Saviour,
EMPEROR that living put me to honour *when I lived; high rank*
and made me king and emperor,
highest of kith and kin— *all men*
85 my flesh, that fallen was as the flower, *decayed*
thou has restored in this stour, *time*
and with pains of great langour *distress*
cleansed me of my sin.

In Purgatory my soul hath been
90 a thousand years in woe and teen. *torment*
Now is no sin upon me seen,
for purged I am of pine. *through agony*
Though that I to sin were bain and boun[*]
and coveted riches and renown,
95 yet at the last contrition

65–66 "When I was on Earth, this world completely blinded me at the consent of my own will."

70 *Purgatory*, in Roman Catholic teaching, is the place to which are committed after death those souls which have left earthly life in a state of venial—as opposed to mortal—sin or have not completed temporal penance for remitted sins during earthly life.

93 "Although I was ready and prompt to sin."

has made me one of thine.

As hard pains, I dare well say,
in Purgatory are night and day
as are in Hell, save by one way—   *in one respect*
100   that one shall have an end.   *i.e., Purgatory's pain*

Worshipped be thou, High Justice,   *Great Judge*
that me has made in flesh to rise.   *caused*
Now wot I well, those that have been wise   *know*
shall come into thy weal.   *joy*
105   Grant me, Lord, amongst moe,   *others*
that purg-ed am of sin and woe,   *misery*
on thy right hand that I may go
to that everlasting heal.   *bliss*

REDEEMED   Ah, Lord of lords and King of kings,
KING   and Informer of all things,   *inspiring force*
111   thy power, Lord, spreads and springs,   *flourishes*
            as soothly here is seen.   *truly*
            After bale, boot thou brings,   *suffering; remedy*
            and after teen-tide, tidings   *torment-time; good news*
115   to all that ever thy name mings   *call to mind*
            and buxom to thee been.   *are obedient*

While I was lord of land and lede   *people*
in purple and in rich weed,   *garb*
methought to thee I had no need,   *it seemed to me; of*
120   so wrong the world me wiled.   *wrongly; tricked*
Though thou for me thy blood can shed,   *had shed*
yet in my heart more can I heed   *did I care*
my flesh to further and to feed,   *prosper*
but the soul was ever beguiled.   *deceived*

125   My foul body through sin blent,   *blinded*
that rotten was and all to-rent,   *corrupt; torn*
through thy might, Lord Omnipotent,
raised and whole it is.
My soul that is in bales brent   *torments; burned*
130   to my body thou hast now sent
to take before thee judgement
of that I have done amiss.   *for what; wrong*

But, Lord, though I were sinful ay,   *was; always*

135	contrition yet at my last day	
	and alms-deeds that I did ay	*always*
	hath holpen me from Hell.	*helped*
	But well I wot that ilk way	*know; same*
	that Abraham went, wend I may,	*may go*
140	for I am purg-ed to thy pay,	*satisfaction*
	with thee evermore to dwell.	

REDEEMED	Peerless prince of most posty	*power*
QUEEN	that after langour lendeth lee,	*distress; sends joy*
	and now in body has rais-ed me	
	from fire to rest and ro—	*repose*
145	my flesh, that as flower can flee	*pass away*
	and powder was, through thy pity	*dust*
	together has brought, as I now see,	*you have brought*
	the soul the body to.	

	While I in Earth rich can go,	*in splendour*
150	in soft sendal and silk also,	*fine linen*
	velvet also—that wrought me woe,	*caused misery*
	and all such other weeds!—	*garments*
	all that might excite lechery—	
	pearls and precious perry—	*gems*
155	against thy bidding us-ed I,	
	and other wicked deeds;	

	neither prayed I ne fast,	*nor fasted*
	save alms-deeds, if any passed,	*any (needy) came by*
	and great repentance at the last	
160	has gotten me thy grace,	*gained*
	that saved I hope fully to be	*so that*
	for purg-ed sins that were in me.*	
	Thy last doom may I not flee,	*judgement; avoid*
	to come before thy face.	

165	After Purgatory-pains
	from me thy lordship thou ne lains.
	To warn thy doom me ne gains,
	though I were never so great.*

---

162 "Because the sins that were in me have been purged."

165–68 "After the pains of purgatory, do not hide your protection from me. It

170	Sith I have suffered woe and teen	*since; torment*
	in Purgatory long to been,	*by being for long*
	let never my sin be on me seen,	
	but, Lord, thou it forget!	*please forget*

Then the Damned shall come.

DAMNED	Alas, alas, alas, alas!	
POPE	Now am I worse than ever I was.	
175	My body again the soul has	
	that long has been in Hell.	
	together they be—now is no grace—	*(there) is*
	filed to be before thy face,	*disgraced*
	and after my death here in this place	*(second) death*
180	in pain ever to dwell.	

	Now bootless is to ask mercy,	*it is useless*
	for, living, highest in Earth was I,	
	and, cunning, chosen in clergy;*	
	but covetousness did me care.	*caused me sorrow*
185	Also, silver and simony*	
	made me Pope unworthy.	*unworthy (to be)*
	That burns me now, full witterly,	*most assuredly*
	for of bliss I am full bare.	*quite devoid*

	Alas, why spent I wrong my wit	
190	in covetousness my heart to knit?*	
	Hard and hot now feel I it;	
	Hell holds me right here. ⸸	*even here*
	My body burns every bit.	
	Of sorrow must I never be shut.	*rid*

---

doesn't avail me to reject your judgement, however great I might have been."

182–83 "For, when alive, I was the highest on earth and, being learned, privileged in my spiritual knowledge." The lines are obscure, with some variation among the manuscripts.

185 *Simony* was the practice of buying or selling Church offices or ecclesiastical preferments. The sense here may be either that the pope abused his power or had gained it by such practices.

189–90 "Alas, why did I expend my intellectual talents wrongfully in order to fix my heart upon covetousness?"

195	Me to save from Hell-pit	
	now helpeth no pray-er.	*avails*
	Of all the souls in Christianity	*Christendom*
	that damned were while I had degree	*my high position*
	now give account behoveth me,	*I must*
200	through my laws forlorn.	*utterly lost*
	Also damned now must I be.	
	Account befalls, or else to flee.	*reckoning comes*
	Make me deaf, I conjure thee,	*beseech*
	as I had never been born.	*as if*

DAMNED	Alas, now stirred I am in this stour!*	
EMPEROR	Alas, now fallen is my flower!	*faded; joy*
207	Alas, for sin now cease succour!	*because of; help ends*
	No silver may me save.	
	Alas, that ever I was emperor!	
210	Alas, that I ever had town or tower!	
	Alas, hard buy I my honour!	*position of honour*
	Hell-pains for it I have.	

	Alas, in world why was I ware?	*conscious*
	Alas, that ever mother me bare!	*bore*
215	Alas, there is no gainchare!	*escape*
	Scape I may not this chance.	*escape; misfortune*
	Alas, do evil who is that dare?	
	To threpe no more us ne dare,*	
	for to pain we ordained are	
220	ever, without deliverance.	*for ever*

	Now is manslaughter upon me seen.	
	Now covetousness makes my care keen.	*sorrow sharp*
	Now wrong-working, withouten ween,	*assuredly*
	that I in world have wrought,	*done*
225	now traitorous turns do me teen,*	
	and false dooms all bedene.	*judgements; immediately*

---

205 "Alas, now I am in deep anguish in this hour!"

218 "We no longer dare cause injury."

225 "Now treacherous acts cause me agony."

In gluttony I have in been—
that shall now dear be bought.   *dearly be paid for*

Now know I what I did with wrong
230   and eke my lither living long.
Falsehood to Hell makes me to fong,
in fire ever foul to fare.
Misbegotten money ever I mixed among.
Now is me yielded in Hell yong.*
235   Why were I not dead as is the dung?
For doel I droop and dare.   *sorrow; sink; fear*

DAMNED   Alas, unliking is my lot!   *misery; fate*
KING   My weal is gone, of woe I wot.   *joy; know*
          My sin is seen I was in set.*
240   Of sorrow now may I sing.
To Hell-pain that is so hot
for my misdeeds wend I mot.   *must go*
Alas, that I had been sheep or goat   *if only*
when I was crown-ed king.

245   When I was in my majesty,   *royal position*
sovereign of shire and of city,   *country area*
never did I good. In no degree   *by no means*
through me was any grace.   *mercy*
Of poor had I never pity.
250   Sore ne sick would I never see.   *suffering; nor; regard*
Now have I langour and they have lee.   *sorrow; joy*
Alas, alas, alas!

Wrong ever I wrought with each wight.   *did; person*
For pennies, poor in pain I pight.   *put*
255   Religion I reaved against the right.   *plundered*
That keenly now I know.   *sadly; acknowledge*
Lechery? I held it light.   *of little importance*
In covetousness my heart was clight.   *fixed firm*

229–34 "Now I acknowledge what I did wrongfully, and also my long life of evil.
Lying makes me take the path to hell, to continue in torment in everlasting fire.
I always mixed ill-gotten money (with legitimately acquired money). Now it is
repaid by me going to hell."

239 "The sin I was confirmed in is now visible to all."

One good deed in God his sight *God's*
260   now have I not to show.

DAMNED   Alas, alas, now am I lorn! *lost*
QUEEN   Alas, with teen now am I torn! *agony*
Alas, that I was of woman born,
this bitter bale to bide. *torment; endure*
265   I made my moan both e'en and morn *complaint; evening*
for fear to come Jesu beforn *in front of*
that crown-ed for me was with thorn
and thrust into the side. *pierced*

Alas, that I was woman wrought! *created*
270   Alas, why God made me of nought *did God make*
and with his precious blood me bought *redeemed*
to work against his will?
Of lechery I never rought, *worried about*
but ever to that sin I sought, *looked for*
275   and of that filth in deed and thought
yet had I never my fill.

Fie on pearls! Fie on pride!
Fie on gown! Fie on guide! *possessions*
Fie on hue! Fie on hide! *complexion; skin*
280   These harrow me to Hell. *drag me off*
Against this chance I may not chide. *misfortune; protest*
This bitter bale I must abide. *torment; endure*
Yea, woe and teen I suffer this tide, *agony; time*
no living tongue may tell.

285   I, that so seemly was in sight, *beautiful to see*
where is my blee that is bright? *complexion; fair*
Where is baron, where is knight
for me to allege the law? *mitigate*
Where in world is any wight *person*
290   that for my fairness now will fight, *beauty*
or from this death I am to dight *ordained to*
that dare me hethen draw? *hence*

DAMNED   Alas, of sorrow now is my saw! *speech*
JUDGE   Alas, for Hell I am in awe! *fear*
295   My flesh, as flower that all to-flaw,

now tides a ferly fitt.*
Alas, that ever I learned law,
for suffer I must many a hard thraw;   *moment*
for the Devil will me draw
300   right even into his pit.

Alas! While that I lived in lond,   *on Earth*
wrong to work I would not wond   *shrink from doing*
but falsely causes took in hond   *took on cases*
and much woe did als.   *caused; also*
305   When I sought silver or rich sond   *a rich present*
of baron, burgess, or of bond,   *from; bondman*
his moot to further ever I would fond,   *suit; try*
were it never so false.   *however false it might be*

Now is the Devil ready, I see,
310   his moot to further against me   *suit; prosecute*
'fore the Judge of such posty—   *before; great power*
that me will not avail;   *will not help*
heart and thought both knoweth he.
Though I would lie, no boot will be.   *no avail*
315   Alas, this hard fit to flee   *cruel situation*
ruefully I must fail.   *sadly*

All my life ever I was boun   *ready*
to trouble poor in tower and town,
pair Holy Church's possession   *limit*
320   and sharply them to shend.   *cruelly; destroy*
To reave and rob religion,   *plunder; religious orders*
that was all my devotion!
Therefore me tides damnation   *befalls*
and pain withouten end.   *without*

DAMNED   Alas, alas, now woe is me!
MERCHANT   My foul body, that rotten hath be,
327   and soul together now I see.
All stinketh, full of sin.
Alas! Merchandise maketh me—   *trade*
330   and purchasing of land and fee—   *acquiring; rentals*

295–96 "A terrifying situation now befalls my flesh, like a flower that has
completely fallen to pieces."

in Hell-pain evermore to be,
and bale that never shall blin.   *torment; cease*

Alas! in world fervent was I   *eager*
to purchase lands falsely.   *acquire*
335   (Poor men I did such annoy,   *caused such misery*
made them their lands to sell.)
But when I died, witterly,   *truly*
all that I had, my Enemy
both body and soul damned thereby   *by all I had*
340   ever to the pain of Hell.

Yet might not false purchase suffice,   *acquisition*
but oft I dealed with merchandise,   *dealt; trade*
for there methought winning would rise.
I used it many a year.
345   (Oft I sat upon false assize,   *presided over; court action*
reaving poor with laining miss,)*
Falsely, by God and saints his
a thousand time I sware.   *swore*

Ocker I used wilfully.*   *usury*
350   Won I never so much thereby   *however much*
to Holy Church never tithed I,   *paid my due*
for methought that was lorn.   *wasted*
Why madest thou me, Lord, of nought? Why?
To work in world so wickedly
355   and now burn in the Devil's belly?
Alas, that ever I was born!

When the laments of the dead have ended, Jesus shall come down as if in a cloud, if it can be contrived, because, according to the opinions of scholars, the Son of God shall give judgement in the air close to the Earth. The angels shall stand with the cross, the crown of thorns, the lance, and the other instruments; they shall display them.

---

346 "Robbing the poor with false concealments."

349 *Usury* was the practice of lending out money for interest, usually at an exorbitant rate. The merchant has practised it in wilful defiance of Church teaching.

JESUS   You good and evil that here been lent,   *are present*
     here you come to your judgement,
     if you wist whereto it would appent
360   and in what manner!*
     But all mine, as I have meant—   *my own; intended*
     prophets, patriarchs here present—*
     must know my doom with good intent.   *judgement; properly*
     Therefore I am now here.

365   But you shall hear and see express   *clearly*
     I do to you all righteousness.
     Lovesome deeds more and less   *charitable*
     I will rehearse now here.   *declare*
     Of earth through me made, Man, thou was
370   and put in place of great cleanness,   *purity*
     from which thou was, through wickedness,
     away then waived were.*   *banished*

     When thou had done this trespass,   *committed this sin*
     yet waited I which way was best   *perceived*
375   thee to recover in this case   *restore; plight*
     into my company.   *fellowship*
     How might I do thee more grace
     than that self kind that thou has   *same nature*
     take here, now as in this place
380   appeareth apertly?   *clearly*

     After, died on the rood-tree   *(I) died; cross*
     and my blood shed, as thou may see,
     to prive the Devil of his posty   *deprive; power*
     and win that was away;   *win back; lost*
385   the which blood, beholds ye,
     fresh holden till now I would should be
     for certain points that liked me,

359–60 "If only you knew how it would all turn out, and in what way!"

362 Jesus's words indicate that he is accompanied not only by the angels bearing the instruments of the Passion but also by a company of the saints, evidently those released from Limbo in play 17. The idea is based on such biblical texts as Matthew 19.28 and 1 Corinthians 6.2. c/s- shows i- Art

369–72 The syntactical duplication here of *was/were* seems to be an error but cannot be resolved.

of which I will now say.*
One cause was this, certainly—
390   that to my Father Almighty
at my Ascension offer might I
this blood, praying a boon: *asking a favour*
that he of you should have mercy   *on*
and more gracious be thereby,   *in that act*
395   when you had sinned horribly
not taking vengeance too soon.

Also, I would, withouten were,   *desired assuredly*
this blood should now be show-ed here   *shown*
that the Jews did in this manner
400   might know apertly
how unkindly they them bear.*
Behold on me and you may lere   *learn*
whether I be God in full power
or else Man only.   *human*

405   Also, my blood now show-ed is   *shown*
that good thereby may have bliss   *the good; through it*
that avoided wickedness, iwiss,   *truly*
and ever good works wrought.
And evil also, that did amiss,   *each evil one*
410   must have great sorrow in sight of this
that lost that joy that was his   *who forfeited*
that him on rood-tree bought.   *the cross; was bought*

Yet, for all this great torment
that suffered here while I was lent,
415   the more spared in your intent.
I am not as I feel.*

385–88 "I desired that the same blood, behold, should be kept fresh-flowing till now for certain reasons which pleased me, of which I shall now speak."

399–401 "[The blood] which the Jews produced in this way should now be displayed here, (so that the Jews) might openly acknowledge how unnaturally they conducted themselves."

413–16 "Yet, because of all this great torment that I suffered while I was living here (on earth), I spared you the greater (pain) for your pleasure. I do not appear the way I feel." Jesus seems to say that although he appears in a resurrected

	For my body is all to-rent	torn apart
	with oaths false, always fervent;	in anger
	no limb on me but it is rent	torn
420	from head right to the heel.	

	Now that you shall apertly see—	plainly
	fresh blood bleed, Man, for thee—	
	good to joy and full great lee,	happiness
	the evil to damnation.	
425	Behold now, all men! Look on me	
	and see my blood fresh out flee	flow
	that I bled on rood-tree	the cross
	for your salvation.	

Then he shall send forth blood from out of his side.

	How durst you ever do amiss	
430	when you umthought you of this	*considered*
	that I bled to bring you to bliss	
	and suffered such woe?	*sorrow*
	Me you must not wite, iwiss,	*blame; truly*
	though I do now as right is.	*what is just*
435	Therefore each man reckon his,	*assess himself*
	for rightwiseness must go.	*justice must be done*

[handwritten marginalia: Abelardian Theology]

REDEEMED POPE	Ah, Lord, though I lived in sin,	
	in Purgatory I have been in.	
	Suffer my bale for to blin	*torment; cease*
440	and bring me to this bliss.	

REDEEMED EMPEROR	Yea, Lord, and I have therein be	*been*
	more than three hundred years and three.	
	Now I am clean, forsake not me,	
	although I did amiss.	

REDEEMED KING	Lord, receive me to thy grace	*admit*
	that pain hath suffered in this place.	
447	Although I foul and wicked was,	
	washen it is away.	*washed*

---

form, the act of crucifixion has continued mystically and his agony has continued through history; each man's sin is a further crucifixion.

REDEEMED	And I, Lord, to thee cry and call,	
QUEEN	thine own Christian and thy thrall,	*servant*
451	that of my sins am purg-ed all.	
	Of thy joy I thee pray.*	*for*

JESUS	Come hither to me, my darlings dear,	*dearly beloved*
	that blessed in world always were.	
455	Take my realm, all in fere,	*together*
	that for you ordained is.	
	For while I was on Earth here	
	you gave me meat in good manner;	*food; graciously*
	therefore in Heaven-bliss clear	
460	you shall ever leng, iwiss.	*dwell; truly*

	In great thirst you gave me drink;	
	when I was naked, also clothing;	
	and when me needed harbouring,	*I needed; lodging*
	you harboured me in cold.*	*lodged; harsh weather*
465	And other deeds to my liking	*delight*
	you did on Earth there living.	*when alive*
	Therefore you shall be quit that thing	*rewarded for*
	in Heaven an hundredfold.	

REDEEMED	Lord, on this can I not min:	*recall*
POPE	Earth when I was dwelling in,	
471	thee in mischief or any unwin	*misfortune; misery*
	to show such a will.	*desire*

REDEEMED	No, sickerly! I can have no mind	*recollection*
EMPEROR	that ever to thee I was so kind,	
475	for there I might thee never find,	
	such kindness to fulfill.	*perform*

JESUS	Yes, forsooth, my friends dear,	*truly*

452-53 The Post-Reformation Banns, line 186, suggest that here the *Venite Benedicti*, the Benedictus anthem for the first Monday in Lent, is to be sung, though no indication exists in the play text.

461-64 Jesus bases his judgement upon the acts of mercy set out in Matthew 25, addressing—as he there says—first the saved and then the damned. The acts are: feeding the hungry, giving drink to the thirsty, giving lodging to the stranger, clothing the naked, visiting the sick and visiting the prisoners. Traditionally, a seventh act—burying the dead—was added to this biblical group.

	such as poor and naked were,	
	you clad and fed them both in fere	*at the same time*
480	and harboured them also.	*gave them shelter*
	Such as were also in great danger,	
	in hard prison in Earth here,	
	you visited them in meek manner,	*in humility*
	all men in such woe.	

485	Therefore, as I you ere told,	*before*
	you shall be quit an hundredfold.	*repaid*
	In my bliss, be ye bold,	*sure*
	evermore you shall be.	
	There neither hunger is ne cold	*nor*
490	but all things as yourselves would—	*might desire*
	everlasting joy to young and old	
	that in Earth pleased me.	

495	Therefore, my angels, go you anon	*at once*
	and twin my chosen every one	*separate*
	from them that have been my fone	*foes*
	and bring them unto bliss.	
	On my right hand they shall be set,	
	for so full yore I them behet	*long ago; promised*
	when they did withouten let	*without ceasing*
500	my bidding not amiss.	*properly*

1ST ANGEL	Lord, we shall never blin	*cease*
	till we have brought them bliss within,	
	those souls that been withouten sin,	*are; without*
	full soon, as you shall see.	

2ND ANGEL	And I know them well afine	*completely*
506	which bodies, Lord, that been thine.	*are*
	They shall have joy withouten pine	*without grief*
	that never shall ended be.	

✓ *Then the angels shall go and as they come and go they shall*
sing "Laetamini in Domino," "Salvator mundi, domine."
And all the redeemed shall follow them. Then the devils shall
come, and the first of them shall speak.[*]

508+SD Two hymns are offered here. The first, Psalms 31 (AV 32).11, "Be glad in
the Lord and rejoice," is from the Offertory for the Common of Martyrs. The

1ST DEVIL	Ah, righteous Judge, and most of might,
510	that there art set to deem the right, *judge; righteous*
	mercy thou was, now is gright,*
	to save these men from pine. *torment*
	Do as thou hast yore behight. *promised long ago*
	Those that be sinful in thy sight,
515	to reckon their deeds I am dight *total up; ready*
	to prove these men for mine. *to belong to me*

Judge this pope mine in this place *adjudge*
that worthy is for his trespass— *sin*
and ought to be thine through grace—
520 through sin comen mine. *who has become*
A Christian man I wot he was, *know*
knew good from evil in each case, *every instance*
but my commandment done he has,
and ever forsaken thine.

525 Through mercy he should be thine,
but mine through wickedness and sin;
thine through Passion thou was in,
and mine through temptation.
To me obedient he was ay, *always*
530 and thy commmandment put away. *set aside*
Thou righteous Judge therefore I pray,
deem him to my prison. *condemn*

This emperor also that standeth by,
I hold him mine full witterly, *most assuredly*
535 that held him ever in heresy
and lieved not on thy lore. *believed; teaching*
Therefore I tell thee verament *truly*
mine he is without judgement.*
Thou said when thou on Earth went,
540 that lieved not, damn-ed were. *whoever believed not*

---

second, "Saviour of the world, Lord," is a verse hymn. The presence of devils at the Judgement is attested by 2 Peter 2.4 and other texts.

511 "You were the embodiment of mercy, now mercy is denied."

538 "He is mine without passing any formal sentence."

"Qui non credit, jam judicatus est."* 〽 3.18

	This king and queen would never know	*recognise*
	poor men, them alms to show.	
	Therefore, put them all from you	
	that stand before thy face,	
545	and I shall lead them till a low;	*to a flame*
	there fire shall burn though no man blow.	
	I have them tied upon a row;	
	they shall never pass.	*escape*

2ND DEVIL	Nay, I will spute with him this	*argue*
550	that sitteth as High Justice,	
	and if I see he be rightwise,	*may see; righteous*
	soon I shall assay.	*test (him)*
	And other he shall, forsooth iwiss,	*either; certainly*
	forsake that of him written is	*what*
555	or these men that have done amiss,	
	deem them us today.	*(he) shall adjudge to us*

	These words, God, thou said express,	*openly*
	as Matthew thereof beareth witness:	
	that right as man's deeds was	*just as*
560	yielden he should be.	*rewarded*
	And lest thou forget, good man,	*fine sir*
	I shall min thee upon,	*remind you of it*
	for speak Latin well I can,	
	and that thou shall soon see:	

"Filius hominis venturus est in gloria Patris sui, cum angelis suis; et tunc reddit unicuique secundum opera sua."*

(not trans, but

565	Therefore, righteous if thou be,	
	these men are mine, as mot I thee,	*may I thrive*
	for one good deed here before thee	
	have they not to show.	
	If there be any, say on! Let's see!	

540+Latin "He that believeth not is condemned already" (John 3.18).

564+Latin "For the Son of Man shall come in the glory of his Father, with his angels; and then he shall reward every man according to his works" (Matthew 16.27)—the reference in the preceding lines.

570	If there be none, deem them to me! ⟩	*judge*
	Or else thou art as false as we—	
	all men shall well know.	

1ST DEVIL	Yea, this thou said, verament,	*truly*
	that when thou came to judgement	
575	thy angels from thee should be sent	
	to part the evil from the good	
	and put them into great torment,	
	there reeming, grenning very fervent;*	
	which words to clerks here present	*clerics*
580	I will rehearse, by the rood:	*repeat; by the cross*

"Sic erit in consummatione seculi: exibunt angeli, et separabunt malos de medio justorum, et mittent eos in caminum ignis: ibi erit fletus et stridor dentium."*

	Therefore, deliver me these men henne	*hence*
	and, as broke I my pen,	*may I break my head*
	I shall make them to gren	*gnash their teeth*
	and ruefully to reem.	*miserably; weep*
585	And in as hot a chimney	
	as is ordained for me	
	bathed they all shall be	
	in bitter bale, and bren.	*torment; shall burn*

	This popelard pope here present	*hypocrite*
590	with covetousness was ay fully bent.	*always*
	This emperor also, verament,	*truly*
	to all sin did incline.	
	This king also all righteous men shent,	*destroyed*
	damned them through false judgement	
595	and died so without amendment;	*repentance*
	therefore I hold him mine.	

This queen, while she was living here,

576–78 "To separate the evil from the good and put them into great torment, where (there is) most heartfelt wailing and gnashing of teeth."

580+Latin "So it shall be at the end of the world: the angels shall come forth, and sever the wicked from among the just, And shall cast them into the furnace of fire: there shall be wailing and gnashing of teeth" (Matthew 13.49–50)—the reference in the preceding lines.

	spared never sin, in no manner,	*by no means*
	and all that might, by Mahound so dear,	
600	excite her lechery	
	she used, man's heart to stere,	*stimulate*
	and thereto fully ordained her.	*committed herself*
	Therefore she hath lost her lere,	
	Heaven-bliss, right as did I.*	

JESUS 606	Lo, you men that wicked have been,	
	what Satan sayeth you hearen and seen.	*hear and see*
	Righteous doom may you not fleen,	*justice; escape*
	for grace is put away.	
	When time of grace was enduring,	*operative*
610	to seek it you had no liking.	*desire*
	Therefore must I, for anything	*whatever the case*
	do righteousness today.	*what is right and just*

	And though my sweet mother dear	
	and all the saints that ever were	
615	prayed for you right now here,	
	all it were too late.	*would be entirely*
	No grace may grow through their prayer—	
	then righteousness had no power.	*justice; would have*
	Therefore, go to the fire in fere.	*together*
620	There gains no other grace.	*avails; other form of*

	When I was hungry and thirsty both,	
	and naked was, you would not me clothe;	
	also, sick and in great woe,	*(when I was)*
	you would not visit me;	
625	nor yet in prison to me come,	*to come*
	nor of your meat give me some,	*food; to give*
	nor me to your harbour nome	*lodging; to take*
	never yet in will were ye.	*did you desire*

DAMNED POPE	When was thou naked or harbourless,	*homeless*
	hungry, thirsty, or in sickness;	
631	either in any prison was?	*or*
	We saw thee never a-cold.	*cold*

603–4 "Therefore she has lost her desired goal, heaven's bliss, just as I did"; *lere* seems to be a variant of *lure*, "something that entices," but the form is not otherwise recorded.

DAMNED	Had we thee hungry or thirsty seen,	
EMPEROR	naked, sick, or in prison been,	
635	harbourless or in any teen,	*homeless; distress*
	have harboured thee we would.	*sheltered*

JESUS	Nay! When you saw the least of mine	
	that on Earth suffered pine,	*distress*
	with your riches you would not rine	*bother about*
640	ne fulfill my desire.	*nor*
	And sith you would nothing incline	*in no way*
	for to help my poor line,	*offspring*
	to me your love it was not fine.	*true*
	Therefore, go to the fire!	

1ST DEVIL	Ah, Sir Judge, this goeth aright.	*proceeds properly*
646	By Mahound much of might,	
	you be mine, each wight,	*person*
	ever to live in woe.	
	A doleful death to you is dight,	*miserable; ordained*
650	for such hire I you behight	*recompense; promised*
	when you served me day and night,	
	to be rewarded so.	

	Go we forth to Hell in hie.	*in haste*
	Without end there shall you lie,	
655	for you have lost, right as did I,	
	the bliss that lasteth ever.	
	Judged you be to my belly	*condemned*
	there endless sorrow is, and noy.	*suffering*
	One thing I tell you truly—	
660	delivered been you never.	*may be*

2ND DEVIL	Nay, Master, forget not these thieves two,	
	for, by Mahound, they shall not go!	*Mahommed; escape*
	Their deeds, Lord, among moe,	*amongst many others*
	soon I can them spy.	*detect them*
665	This justice, Lord, was ever thy foe,	
	but falsehood to further he was ever throw.	*eager*
	Therefore deem him to sorrow and woe,	*condemn*
	for he is full well worthy.	

	This merchant also that standeth here,	
670	he is mine, withouten were.	*certainly*
	As oft-times he him forsware	*perjured himself*

	as seeds be in my seck.	*sack*
	And ocker also us-ed he	*usury*
	that my pouch is so heavy,	
675	I swear by Mahound so free,	*so noble*
	it well-nigh breaks my neck.*	

Then the devils shall carry them off, and the four evangelists shall come.

MATTHEW	I, Matthew, of this bear witness,	
	for in my Gospel I wrote express	*plainly*
	this that my Lord of his goodness	
680	hath rehearsed here.	*repeated*
	And by me all were warned before	*in advance*
	to save their souls evermore	*for eternity*
	that now through liking they been lore	
	and damned to fire in fere.*	

MARK	I, Mark, now apertly say	*openly*
686	that warned they were by many a way	*many means*
	their living how they should array,	
	Heaven-bliss to recover;	
	so that excuse them they ne may	
690	that they been worthy, in good fay,	
	to suffer the doom given today	
	and damned to be for ever.*	

LUKE	And I, Luke, on Earth living,	
	my Lord's works in everything	
695	I wrote and taught through my cunning	*knowledge*
	that all men know might.	
	And therefore I say, forsooth iwiss,	*most certainly*
	excusation none there is.	*excuse*

671–76 The Second Devil evidently carries a sack, and also a pouch slung round his neck, in which are allegedly the sins committed by the damned. He protests that he is weighed down by them.

683–84 "Now because of their desires they are lost and condemned together to the fire."

687–92 "How they should order their way of life in order to regain heaven's bliss, so that they cannot excuse themselves—so that they are indeed worthy to suffer the sentence passed today and to be damned for ever."

Against my talking they did amiss.   *word; offended*
700   This doom, it goeth aright.   *judgement; proceeds justly*

JOHN   And I, John the Evangelist,
            bear witness of things that I wist   *know*
            of which they might full well have trist   *in; trusted*
            and not have done amiss.
705   And all that ever my Lord saith here,
            I wrote it in my manner.   *my own way*
            Therefore, excuse you, withouten were,   *truly*
            I may not well, iwiss.   *indeed*

THE END

APPENDIX

The following is not a list of all the instances in which this text differs from the base text of the 1974 Early English Text Society (EETS) edition, which was primarily the version in the Huntington Library manuscript (Hm). Its purpose is to identify some changes that are particularly significant for metre, rhyme, or meaning, and to enable the reader to correlate this edition with the EETS edition where lines have been omitted from or added to the EETS text here. In the list, the line-number is that of the present edition; the EETS reading is given first, and the reading in this edition, with its source, appears after the lemma. The source of the change is indicated by the letters used in the EETS edition to designate the various play-manuscripts, and in the chronological sequence there employed; where the change is editorial in origin, that fact is indicated by the addition of *edit*. Variants from the Post-Reformation Banns are not included here.

Play 1 (1600 [R] as base since Hm lacks this play): 7 parente] parents BH; 8 my essention] mea essentia *edit*; 18] inserted from BH; 20 licencill] licentia B; 60 Angell] Angeli BH, Arkeangelle] Archangeli BH; 69–88] *EETS full lines set each as two lines*; 70 bee] be attending BH; 71 begyninge] benignity H; 107 ever] will ay B; 136+SD] *inserted (translated) from H*; 163+SH Cherubyn] Seraphim AB; 217 wynde] wend ABH; 223+SD] *inserted from H*; 226+SD] *inserted from H*; 246 dungeon] a dungeon BH.

Play 2: Before 1 SD] *inserted from B*; 6 ondly] only ARBH; 8 liever] kever H; 18 water] waters ARBH; 33 yearth] earth that ARBH; 35 frute] fruits ARBH; 104 workes] work ARBH; 107 ryse] rade H; 237 *transposed from after* 240 H; 240 alsoe] als *edit.*; 274 this] these ARBH; 286 thye] thine own ARBH; 288 forbydd] forbade RBH; 290 gave] gave me ARBH; 312+SD] *inserted from H*; 345 I am ilente] am I lent ARB; 404 wyninge] wonning ARB; 447 sonne] some BH; 456 them swe] it find BH; 472 as] as I ARBH; 495 learne yee] learn H; 496+SD] *inserted from H*; 500 would not wee shoulde] ne would *edit.*; 518 sonne] soon ARB; 528 leese] lose RH; 676 of sorrowes may none nowe cease] from sorrow may none me save H.

Play 3: 31 shutte] sit H; 34 rowfed] ronet Hm *restored*; 36 make] mase *edit.*; 46 nor] and ARBH; 63 bowte] without H; 72 fable] fail ARBH; 80 agayne] against ARBH; 88+SD] *moved from 112+SD Hm edit.*; 91 baste] blast ARBH; 131 forgotten] forgetten B; 143 myghtes] my mights AR; 167 of kynde] kind ARBH; 169 dogges] and dogs H; 180 nere] nigh ARBH; 214 yonder] yonder ship ARBH; 222 sonne] sons ARBH; 244+SD] *inserted from H*; 246+SD] *inserted from H*; 260+SD hee] they R; 260+SD] *substituted from H*; 261–307+SD] *inserted from H*; 310 borne] lorn *edit.*

Play 4: 25 worne] wond H; 26 landes] land ARH; 29 have wone] can win H; 39 I] my BH; 48+SD Latin] *om.*R; 48+English Messenger] Knight *edit.*; 80 beeseche] beseek A; 83 God that] God AR; 88+SD *second sentence*] *om. edit.*; 88+SH] *inserted edit.*; 96+SD *first sentence*] *inserted (translated) from H*; 115 the] that the ARB; 123 all] *inserted from H*; 173 soe] to *edit.*, forther] father *edit.*; 193 takys] take this ARB; 204 may] might ARBH; 257 sonne] son dear ARBH; 257+SD] *inserted from B*; 264 upon this] in AR; 265 afrayde] aferd *edit.*; 328+SD] *inserted from AR*; 367 doe your vowe] you bow ARBH; 368 yee] I ARBH; 430 faye] fray ARH; 435] *inserted from H*; 451 highe] het H; 460+SD] Docter] Expositor B; 476+SD Docter] Expositor *edit.*; 490 the same] he save ARB.

Play 5: 90] *replaced from H*; 118 graweth] gnaweth *edit.*; after 124] *40 lines in Hm om. H.*; 165 hoste] hest B; 228 pearle] perry B; 253 wave] have AR; 271 them to God] them *edit.*; 276 thrye] twy *edit.*] 277 the] thou B; 278 thrye] twy *edit.*; 347+SD Doctor] Expositor *edit.*; 376 to] spake to B, now] me ARB; 399 moe] more R; 403 beforen] before AR; 407 borne] bore *edit.*

Play 6: 30 holye one] holy ARBH; 65–72] *transposed from 79–86 Hm edit.*; 98 mylde] meek ARBH; 155 for I] I BH, yt] her AB;; 160+SD] *inserted from H*; after 184+SH] *24 lines in Hm om. edit.*; 187] *combines two lines in Hm edit.*; 191 destret] discret *edit.*, sua] je suis *edit.*; 192 mater] mere *edit.*, viva] vivant B; 195 pryest] priests RBH; 303 in mee] I see ARBH; 340–3] *inserted from ARBH*; 345 non] not ARBH; 383 those] these ARH; 384 store] store now ABH; 394 my] by my AR; 407+SD] *inserted from H*; 468 awaye] the way ARBH; 599 to] that H; 605 wemmostlye] wemlessly *edit.*; 626 postee] power H; 627 baron] barn *edit.*, that] so H; 628] *inserted from H*; 667 maye] mon ARBH; 674 maye] queen *edit.*; 702 within] in AB.

Play 7: 87 bowe to his wife] to his wife bown ARBH; 91 wyll] will I ARBH; 111 to] for to ARBH; 116 greese well] grease ARBH; 125–32] *inserted from H;* 134 put] pull BH, ont] out *edit;* 167 note] mote ARBH, meetinge] miting ARBH; 172 lowd] lote BH; 173–80, 181–87, 188–95, 196–203] *each as one stanza;* 181 beelongen] be needing *edit.*; 183 tarboyste] nettle tarboist *edit.* (cf.H); 184] *inserted from H,* needen] needing *edit.*; 187 cheeffe] choice ARBH; 200–1] *inserted from H;* 204 this lottes] these lotes *edit.*; 231 wages] wage H; 235 any] every ARBH; 275+SD] *inserted from H;* 289+SD] *inserted from H;* 308 thought] though H; 415 sayde] began ARB; 418 hee] ye AB; 451 never] for never ARBH; 457+SD *sentence 2-* 465] *transposed from following 489 edit.*; 485 kinge] kings ARBH; 540 to have never seene] never to see H; 579 baronne] barn ARBH; 639 rocke] rocks ARB; 648 handes] thumbs AR; 657 hee] thou ARBH; 659 his] thy ARBH; 664 all] ever ARBH; 668 goe abowt now] about go *edit.*; 670 no more now] now no moe *edit.*; 676 I] here I ARH; 687 alwayse] once ARB; 687–94] *one stanza.*

Play 8: 22 fayled] failed him ARBH; 33 I] ye ARBH; 37 a] some ARBH; 66 gardes] regardes *edit.*; 88+SD] *transposed from 84+SD HL;* 159 querenues] enquirons nous *edit.*; 164+SD] *inserted from B;* 208+SD] *inserted from ARB;* 238 hard] heard them ARBH; 303+SD] *inserted from B;* 307 godlinge] gedling H; 317 they were livinge] their living was BH; 322 death] birth ARBH; 324+SD] *transposed from 326+SD ARB;* 326 godlinge] gedling H; 365+SD *second sentence*] *inserted from B;* 374 by your leave] beleve ARBH; 413 hoaste] boast AR; 413+SD] *inserted from ARB.*

Play 9: 47] *inserted from H;* 86 rowtinge] rotting ARH; 93 lastlye] lasteth ARBH; 235 without] withouten AR; 250 you] us ARBH; 252 may befall] befall ARBH; 254 land] lands BH; 259 in] is in ARBH.

Play 10: 15 marye] mar BH; 73 on hye] in see ARBH; 92 sore] full sore RBH; 153 lord] my lord *edit.*; 216 bout] without ARH; 275 ther] till ARBH; 297 dogge] bitch ARBH; 298 thy] thou *edit.*; 299 stike] stitch ARBH; 326 abyd] abode BH; 401 right] aright ARBH; *after 416*] *line om. edit.*; 443 Hell there] Hell ARB; 452 grave] grace ARBH; 456 daye] days *edit.*

Play 11: 51 hee that] he B; 111] *inserted from ARB;* 130 bade] bede *edit.*; 137 here to] now to ARB; 152 Christ] my Christ ARB; 213] *inserted edit.*; 214 hath binne us with] with us hath been *edit.*; *after 214*] *line om. edit.*; 215] *inserted edit.*; 216–19 *asc. to MARY*] *asc. to JOSEPH edit.*; 216] *transposed from after 219 edit.*; 220–27] *transposed from after 207 edit.*; 256–83] *transposed from after 299 edit.*; 263 lawe] saw H; 278 not] none *edit.*

Play 12: 47 hongarye he is] hunger he has *edit.*; 76 withouten] without H; 96 unhappingly] unhappily ARBH; 98 discent] deceit ARBH; 100 on] a *edit.*; 113 so high] on height *edit.*; 165 then] them ARB; 190 greatly] only ARBH; 244+SD] *transposed from after 240 H*; 253+SD] *inserted from H*; 258+SD] *inserted from H*; 278 worke] all works H; 284 these thinges] this thing H, were] was ARBH; 296 blenquyshe] blemish ARH.

Play 13: 51] *inserted from BH*; 95 his] is ARBH; 130 come] came ARBH; 136 I] it ARBH; 166 here] there ARBH; 175 ere] that BH, wee] you A; 177 descent] deceit ARBH; 210 I] we ARBH; 230 God] Gods ARBH; 234 I here] here ARBH; 272-75] *inserted from BH*; 276-77] *reversed ARBH*; 276 falseye] foul and falsely ARBH; 283 nor] believe *edit.*; 324 this] this place ARBH; 344 a] his ARBH; 360 Chester] thester H; 362 tidings] tiding H; 373 as] that *edit.*; 398 maye] may be ARBH; 410 calleth] and calleth ARBH; 414 donne] do *edit.*; 433 gowle] a ghoul BH; 438 borne] bore *edit.*; 468 froo] us fro B; 478 knees] kneen *edit.*

Play 14: 75 you] your ARBH; 114 thee] thou thee BH; 120+SD] *inserted from H*; 154 then] nor ARB; 167 daye] days ARBH; 175 this] this world ARB; 220 commen] come H; 242 thinges] thing ARBH; 262 more] moe ARBH; 289 hundeth] hundred *edit.*; 357 comes] came RBH.

Play 15: 13 biddinges] bidding ARBH; 30 thinge] things ARBH; 50 preparde] prepare ARBH, bee] we ARBH; 59 you and I] we B; 64+SD] *inserted from H*; 68 greater] great ARB; 167 to] so to ARBH; 197 Father] Fathers ARBH; 255 with] which ARH; 315 saye] said B; 352 armerye] armere R; 365 hand] hands ARH.

Play 16, Pt.1: 4] *substituted from H*; 10 postie powere] power H; 17-20+SH] *inserted from RBH*; 82 him in] in ARBH; 87 makes] mase *edit.*; 91 nowe nowe] now ARBH; 102-105+SH] *inserted from RBH*; 106 sore stryke] him beshite H; 108 myne] me ARBH; 110-113+SH] *inserted from RBH*; 134 fellowe] fellows ARBH; 136 donne] doom ARBH; 137 that he] thee that ARB; *after 145*] 2 *lines om. H*; 149 miseraye] mis-array BH; 161 steyne] sayen RH; 163 rafte] reft H; 164 blemished] blemish RBH; 180 sent] send AH; 191 scalward] stalwart *edit.*; 219 beleave] by leave *edit.*, on] of ARB; 272 have] so han H; 275 were] were it ARB; 297 should] should truth ARBH; 342+SD] *inserted from H*; 348+SD] *inserted from H*; 355 an oyntment] anointment ARB; 373 have] han *edit.*; 386 behind] be hend BH; 388+SD] *inserted from H*; *after 388+SD*] 16 *lines om. H.*

Play 16, Pt.2: 2 boote he] boots him *edit.*, beker] bicker H; 12 warne] were H; 40+SD] *inserted from H*; 48+SD] *inserted from H*; 52 this waye] thus away B; 54 thy] the BH; 67 stryke] shite H; 75 is] is there H; 79 inclind] incline ARBH; 88+SD, 124+SD, 130+SD, 133+SD, 142+SD] *inserted from H;* 143 synnce] cinques *edit.;* 144 sweene] swem H; 147 synke] cinques *edit.;* 163 wronge] wrung *edit.;* 176+SD] *inserted from H;* 189 beheight] bethought *edit.;* 192+SD, 200+SD, 208+SD] *inserted from H;* 221 mon] men ARH; 237 mon] none ARBH; 240+SD] *inserted from H;* 241 leere] lee BH; 257–72] *inserted from H;* 305 ye] is H; *one line after 360]* as 361–62 H; 361 eloye eloy] eloi eloi eloi eloi H; 362 my God] my God my God H; 374 wend] wand *edit.;* 384 knowe] see *edit.;* 394 bade] bede A; 476 myghtiest] mightes R; 483 clyft] clight *edit.*

Play 17: 8 yere] yore H; 18 come] comen ARH; 19 people] people thou ARBH; 31 to] to my ARB; 83 nyf] nor ARH; 85 nyf] nor R; 111 bolster] bluster *edit.;* 192 wonn] win B; 220+SD] *inserted from H;* 231 come] came ARB; 261 synnys] signs ARH; 314 combes] comb ARB.

Play 18: 3 sum] son *edit.;* 4 ou] qui *edit.,* fuit] fait *edit.;* 5 luces] luce *edit.,* lucite] lucide *edit.;* 8 estreite] elit *edit.; one line after 13]* as 14–15 *edit.;* 20 he] they *edit.;* 23 great] piteous BH; 68 hard] hardy BH; 95 wend] wand *edit.;* 99 drawes] draw H; 100 lawes] law H; 101 awes] awe H; 106 tatch] tack *edit.;* 107 him dare] he dare BH; 127 trewe Jewe] Roman true *edit.;* 184 the] there ARBH; 202+SH-210] *transposed from after 218 H;* 225 us] as ARBH; 226] *substituted from H;* 252 beforn tomorn] *inserted from H;* 253 think no scorn] *inserted from H;* 265 swoone] swow *edit.;* 282 the] thy *edit.;* 326 ys] is all ARBH; 433+SD-End] *inserted from RH with H as base;* 499 know] known *edit.;* 504+SD *second sentence] inserted from R;* 526 mere] more R.

Play 19: 2 my owne] mourn *edit.;* 6 both] half dead H; 21 that] that he ARBH; 30 any] my ARBH; 69] *inserted from H;* 95 better] bitter *edit.;* 112 lord] lore BH; 160 thrall] throw AR; 184 tree] rood *edit.;* 213 synnes] sin H.

Play 20: 71 Samarye] Samaria ARBH; 76 fullye] fullought *edit.,* save] saved ABH; 102 fullfilled] followed RBH; 104+Latin (d) propinquator] propugnator H; 120 were] was H; 133 I shedd] shall H; 134 and] I H; 151 fleshe] fresh ARBH.

Play 21: 41 Mattheus] Matthias ARBH; 56+SD Mattheum] Matthias ARB *(translated);* 60+SH Mattheus] Matthias ARBH; 84 steede] steigh *edit.;* 92+SH Mathias] Matthew ARBH *(translated);* 122 store] stour ARH; 127 length] leech H, or] our *edit.;* 129 hee] ye B, seaven monethes] seven *edit.;* 143 ye] yea *edit.;* 144+SH Mathias] Matthew ARB *(translated);* 152+SH Lyttle God] God the Son A; 158+SD Deus] God the Father *edit.;* 158+SH] *inserted from H (translated);* 160 here] I hear *edit.;* 183 send] sent RB;

190+SH] *inserted edit.*; 233 gadd] glad ARBH; 238+SH Angelus] First Angel ARH; 246+SH The Second] Second *edit.*; 252 ever] over ARBH; 269 doe] die ARBH; 286+SH Mathias] Matthew ARBH (*translated*); 288 while] while that *edit.*; 298+SH Mattheus] Matthias ARBH; 299 steegh] stight H; 301 drest] dight AR; 302 the love of God] God *edit.*; 326 fayre bodye] body *edit.*; 342+SH Mathias] Matthew ARBH (*translated*); 354+SH Mattheus] Matthias RBH.

Play 22: 8 flesh] flesh or fell ARH; 71 feete to] fit may ARBH; 80 learn] lear *edit.*; 111 as] are H; 136 fortredde] fortrod B; 191 feight] flight *edit.*; 282 burne] bren ARH; 318 shall be open] open shall been ARBH; 336 them] then H.

Play 23: 185 grant] grant us P; 217 lordshipp] lordships BHP; 250 lawe] lay P; 300+SH] Primus] Third P; 344 deceaves] beguiles *edit*; 412] *inserted from H*; 416 raygnes] rings *edit.*; 419] *inserted from H*; 452 the xx devylles waye] your way P; 513 and] an AR; 541 doe what] to see P; 609 greetes] graithes P; 610 flea] slay ARBHP; 639–42] *transposed from after 650 P*; 643–6] *inserted from ARBHP*; 684 have bine] been A; 692+SD] *inserted from H where it follows 684*; 708 releaved] relieve *edit.*

Play 24: 51 mee] ne ARBH; 57 grantest] grantedst H; 104 welth] weal *edit.*; 108 health] heal *edit.*; 115 names] name ARBH; 150 sandalles] sendal H; 153–6] *transposed from after 164 H*; 160 to thy] thy *edit.*; 183 closen] chosen ARH; 189 also] alas BH, spend] spent R; 276 that] my ARH; 302 wrought] wrong AERBH; 304 elles] als H; 319 church] churchs ARH; 386 fleshe] fresh ARBH, tell] till BH; 419 lent] rent AR; 427 *and* 431 bleede] bled BH; 498 beheight] behet *edit.*; 548 passe that place] pass *edit.*; 576 put] part BH; 578 reemynge and] reeming ARBH; 580 by the rood] *inserted from BH*; 581 men] men henne ARBH; 582 panne] pen H; 583 grynne] gren *edit.*; 603 lure] lere *edit.*; 692 ever] for ever RBH; 700 donne] doom RBH.